WEDDING THE WOLF

A WOLF SHIFTER PARANORMAL ROMANCE

STEFFANIE HOLMES

BACCHANALIA HOUSE

1

WILLOW

*B*ianca's hands grabbed my face, trapping me in place as her lips clamped over mine. My whole body froze in shock as her tongue slid against my teeth.

It figures that I haven't even lost my virginity, and my first amorous experience in Crookshollow is having my mouth defiled by a drunk bisexual tattoo artist.

I scanned the crowded ballroom, frantically searching for some object I might use to pry Bianca off me. But all I saw was a sea of glittering faces: Bianca's crazy artist friends didn't seem to realise my peril; instead, they threw the metal horns in the air and cheered her on.

Bianca swirled her tongue around my mouth like a washing machine. Her breath stank of absinthe and bubblegum-flavoured lipstick. Finally, I managed to jolt my shocked body into action. I tried to wriggle away, but for such a tiny girl she had an iron grip on my face. Instead, I grabbed her shoulders and shoved her backwards, but all that did was make her lips tighten their seal around mine.

I can't breathe. This is how I'm going to die – drowning in a wall of absinthe-scented saliva.

"Bianca?"

A voice – sharp and deep and dripping with hurt – cut through the hooting and pounding music of the party. Bianca's eyes grew wide. She tore herself from me, staggering back.

Thank you, kind stranger. I whirled around to face my saviour, and met the eyes of Robbie, Bianca's groom. Technically, he was her fake-groom, although from the way he was staring at her, I don't think he remembers that theirs was only a marriage of convenience.

Shit. This is quickly turning into the most chaotic wedding I've ever managed.

I'd only met Robbie Maclean a few times over the last couple of weeks, when Bianca roped him in for the wedding prep. She'd told me the whole story about their fake-marriage – her grandmother had left her a Victorian mansion, but only if she was married to a man. Robbie volunteered so Bianca could keep the house and turn it into an artist's retreat – although she didn't seem to realise that Robbie was madly in love with her.

She also didn't tell me Robbie was a werewolf, but I'd figured that out for myself.

It was the same story every time I met someone of his kind, which thankfully had only been a few times in my life since The Incident. His heady smell scratched against the back of my nose, and the stump of my right leg started to ache, as if it remembered what the last werewolf I'd met face-to-teeth had done. The smell was usually my clue that it was time to run away, but Robbie was also a client, and given the circumstances, that would give the wrong impression.

I never thought I'd be glad to see a werewolf, but in the three years I'd been a wedding planner, I'd never expected to be accosted by a horny bisexual bride either, so I'd take what I could get.

"Please don't eat me." I raised my hands. "I didn't have any part in this."

Robbie gaped at Bianca and I, hurt marring his handsome features. His whole face crumpled, and I sensed something stirring inside him. The heady smell grew stronger.

No.

I froze, realising what was about to happen but powerless to stop it. My leg itched with a burst of phantom pain.

Not here. I can't deal with this.

The whole world slowed. I willed my limbs to move, to turn and run, to save myself. But I remained frozen in place. The memories tore at my mind; teeth flashing, dark, evil eyes blazing, and searing, wrenching pain in my leg. I stood suspended between my past trauma and the very present danger.

Before my eyes, Robbie's face contorted, his nose extending into a long muzzle. Grey fur pushed through his skin, sprouting from his forehead and cheeks and covering his whole face. He toppled forward, his clothes tearing away from his body as his bones cracked and rearranged themselves, his muscles reattaching and forming new limbs. A stench rose around him as he embraced his inner beast.

Behind me, someone screamed. The air rushed from my lungs.

Robbie's hands – now paws – hit the polished floor of the ballroom, and he stared up at Bianca with those same hurt eyes. Only he wasn't Robbie anymore. Instead of the handsome, quiet man I'd come to admire, there now stood a terrifying wolf, his lips pulled back to reveal rows of jagged teeth.

My head spun as the smell rose all around me. Red welts burned in my eyes. *This is it. This is where the werewolves finish the job.*

Robbie tossed his head back and howled, the sound sending a wave of terror through my limbs. The fear took over. Teeth filled my vision. Sharp pain rocketed through my leg. No, not pain, the memory of pain. The memories of nerves and muscles that no longer existed.

"Robbie, no!" Bianca's face broke, her façade collapsing as she realised how much she'd hurt him. I remained frozen, expecting Robbie to leap forward and sink his teeth into Bianca's alabaster skin, or to take another chunk out of me. Instead, he gave a low, sad growl, then turned tail and raced toward the entrance hall. Terrified guests leapt out of the way as Robbie stalked past. Bianca raced after him, pushing through the panicking crowd, her jet-blue train flapping behind her.

All around me, people scrambled for cover, crying and screeching as they fought to get out of the werewolf's way. The band dropped their instruments and fled the ballroom. I noticed Elinor Baxter – Bianca's tattoo apprentice and maid of honour and my next potential client – running after her friend, her red gothic gown streaming behind her.

The ballroom emptied quicker than a public swimming pool after someone mentioned they saw a poo floating by the kiddie end. Within moments, I was the only one left, frozen in place like some broken Greek statue. I still couldn't move. In my head, those teeth loomed over me, drawing closer, the sharp edges scraping against my skin, ready to sink into my flesh and tear away another part of me—

"Why are you here?" A deep voice interrupted me. A thick Scottish accent rolled over the words, drawing me back to the empty room.

At least, it had been empty only a moment ago. Now, a tall man stood in front of me, his head tilted to the side as he ran a hand over his short, dark hair. The heady wolf scent poured from him in waves. *Werewolf. Danger.*

I wanted to run, but he was the most beautiful man I'd ever seen. Cold grey eyes bore into mine, holding me entranced. Heat spread over my skin as I took in the rest of him. A square, strong jaw ran parallel to a pair of broad, muscular shoulders. He wore a Scottish kilt and sporran, the tartan of a red-and-green design – different from the groom's, so they weren't related. He looked like the sort of highlander who regularly tossed fair maidens over his shoulders and stole them away to his castle where he'd teach them to swing claymores and then repeatedly ravish their bodies.

No way could a guy that hot be real. I must be dreaming him. That would explain why a sizzle of weird energy danced over my skin. *The fear has finally driven me crazy.*

I blinked, certain he'd have disappeared. But no, the Scottish hottie was still there, staring at me with those steel eyes, like he was concerned about me or something.

"Why are you here?" he asked again.

"I—I—I'm the wedding planner," I managed to choke out. That weird energy hummed under my skin, even dancing along my right leg, over the edge of my stump.

"That's not what I mean. Everyone in this room just saw a man change into a wolf." The Scot jabbed a finger back toward the hallway, where the guests were crowded – all shouting and screeching at the top of their lungs like a flock of frightened seagulls. "They're out there in a panic. All except you."

I managed to lift my shoulders into a tiny shrug. "Maybe I'm just not easily frightened."

The gorgeous Scot shook his head, a wide grin spreading across his face. Dammit, that was the kind of smile that sunk ships. "You're frightened all right, but nae for the same reason."

I bit my lip, a habit I'd picked up in high school that I couldn't seem to shake. *Why is a guy like this even talking to me? Why can't I get my legs to work?*

He continued. "You didnae leap out of the way and grab for

your camera phone. You're nae running after the bride like her other friends. You froze. I came out here to unfreeze you."

The Scot reached out for me, and that hand coming toward me snapped me out of my frozen state. *Werewolf. Danger.* I glared at him, and yanked my body away. "Don't come any closer."

"Can I get you a drink? You look like you could use one."

"I don't drink."

"I just wannae help you—"

"Don't." I stepped back again, the panic rising up in my stomach as I leaned weight on my right limb.

The Scot held up his hands. "Okay, okay, I'm not gonnae touch you, I promise. I dinnae want to scare you. I just want to find out why you didnae run away. And also, because that kiss between you and Bianca is gonnae haunt my dreams."

A flush burned my cheeks. I lowered my head, tearing my gaze away from him. My whole face stung from embarrassment. He'd seen Bianca kiss me. *He must think ... oh, crap ...*

"I didn't—"

"Aye. I've been thinking about coming over to talk to you," he continued. "But now I ken you're nae interested in men. You saved me embarrassing myself, so I thank you for that. Although, I am insanely jealous of Bianca right now."

The Scot's words burned into my mind. He wanted to talk to me, *to kiss* me ... That didn't compute. *He must be joking. Probably Bianca or Elinor put him up to it. No way would a guy like this notice me in a party filled with exotic and sexually adventurous artists. It's just not possible.*

It didn't matter. Even if he *had* been interested, which he wasn't, I'd never have been able to talk back, let alone manage anything else. I couldn't maintain eye contact with someone that gorgeous—

What am I even thinking? He's a werewolf. As in, big scary teeth, sharp claws, lack of basic human morality. Inhuman urges to maim and kill. I came to Crookshollow specifically to get away from everything werewolf, and yet I seemed to have walked right into the thick of it.

As hot as he was, if this Scot or any of his friends knew who I really was, they wouldn't hesitate to tear my throat out.

The Scot waved his hand in front of me. "Hello in there? Are you all right? Do you need me to get you a pint—"

"I know you're one of them," I blurted out.

That caused a reaction. The Scot's grey eyes flashed with something like curiosity. He recovered quickly, and that grin was back. "One of what?"

As soon as the words were out of my mouth, I wished I could take them back. *I'm a fool. Why did I say that? He may be hot, but if I make him angry, I know what those claws and teeth can do—*

"A werewolf." I whispered the word, desperate for him to deny it, to find some reason that I was wrong about him. *Please let me be wrong about him.*

The Scot's gaze faltered. "Now, there's a curious thing. How did you ken that?"

He took a step toward me, his hands raised. I whimpered, shuffling back. I knew I should be terrified, but those eyes kept me transfixed. *Please, don't hurt me.*

"Stay away from me. I'm armed and dangerous." I thought back to the silver stake I'd stolen from my mother before I left London, lying at the bottom of the suitcase back at my new flat. I wished like hell I'd decided to bring it tonight.

"You packing a Kalashnikov under that corset?" The Scot grinned. "I'd kind of like to see that."

My face must have been glowing from the heat that flared in my cheeks. My mother's voice pounded in my ears. *Run away! If you meet a werewolf, you get away as fast as you can.* But I couldn't move. His eyes pinned me in place, and the strange energy surging through my veins made me want to inch closer, not further away.

I don't understand. What's going on with my body? Why do I feel so ... desperate for him?

I wanted to ask the Scot, but he spoke first. "You're new in town, aren't you? Bianca and Elinor mentioned you came from London."

"I am, but I'll be leaving soon for some place less infested with your kind. I'm not losing another leg."

"What are you talking about?"

I reached down to the hem of my dress, and lifted it up to my thigh. The Scot's eyes narrowed as he took in the carbon fibre prosthetic that replaced my lower right leg, starting just beneath my knee.

My whole body trembled. *I can't believe I'm doing this.*

The whole reason I'd fled London in the first place was to start over with a clean slate, in a tiny backwards village where no one knew about my leg or how it had happened. Never, *ever* in my whole life had I shown a person who wasn't my mum or my family doctor or my first boyfriend the prosthetic. It didn't matter, because they'd all seen it anyway – on my mother's crazy website or in the tabloids. The story of my leg and how I'd lost it reached every person in my life, often before I even met them. Every person I spoke to regarded me with that pitiful look that told me they knew my secret, my hidden shame.

I wasn't whole.

And here I was, after finally winning my freedom and anonymity, standing in the middle of a crazy wedding showing some Scottish *werewolf* the amputation that changed my life forever.

As the Scot stared at my prosthetic, realisation dawning on his face, hope seized my stomach, clenching the muscles tight. Hope for what, I did not know. Hope that he wouldn't guess my true identity. Hope that he wouldn't give me that same pathetic, pitying look that everyone in London used around me.

Neither thing happened. He didn't bare his teeth and take another chunk out of me. His mouth didn't droop. His eyes didn't flick away. They remained locked on mine, and the look on his face almost resembled ... respect.

"I'm sorry," he said. For the first time, the words didn't sound like hollow curiosity – the result of a sick desire to get me to talk about *The Incident* without outwardly asking me.

Instead, a flash of pain crossed his face. His eyes darkened, the cold light inside them flickering out like a torch.

"Don't be. It's not your fault." I dropped the corner of my dress and straightened up. "I'd just like to keep the other foot, if it's not too much trouble."

The light in his grey eyes flickered back again, blazing like a fire. "I'll nae hurt you. I dinnae ken who did that to you, or why. But if I ever caught them, I would make them pay."

The venom in his voice threw me. "Why do you care? You don't even know me."

"I dinnae have to. That's a disgusting thing for anyone to do, especially one of my kind." Those steel eyes bore into mine. "Especially to such a beautiful woman."

A beautiful woman. I wanted to fold my arms and laugh off that comment, the way Bianca did whenever a man fell over her with obvious flattery. But I wasn't Bianca, and I could already feel the flush creeping up my neck and spreading across my cheeks and neck. No one had ever called me *beautiful* before. It wasn't a word that could possibly belong to my broken body.

The heat in my veins flared against my skin. "I ... you ... don't say things like that."

"Why not?"

"It ... I ... just don't do it."

"You're a very odd woman." The Scot studied my face in a way that made me feel utterly naked. "I cannae figure you out."

"Look, you don't need to figure me out or worry about me. I'm not going to reveal your secret. I know more than anyone how important it is that you wolves stay hidden, although Robbie's little display might take a bit of explaining. I just want to forget this whole night ever happened. I promise I'll leave town as soon as I can and you can get back to whatever it is you and your friend Robbie here are trying to do in Crookshollow. So you can just go back to the party now and—"

"Do you want to get out of here?" His eyes danced over my body, before focusing on mine once more. My stomach fluttered.

"You mean, leave the party? With you? Why?"

The Scot shrugged. "Parties are hard work when you dinnae really ken anybody. I thought ... maybe you and I could go for a walk and ken each other."

He's smiling at me. He looks hungry for more than just flesh. Why is it lighting my whole body up like a Christmas tree?

I opened my mouth to say no. I was in charge of this party. I had to go into damage control mode, get the thing back on track somehow. I couldn't be outside, alone, with a werewolf—

"Yeah, sure."

Um, what? Hello mouth, it's me, your brain. Asking what the hell do you think you're doing?

I'd gone crazy. Those grey eyes had destroyed all rational thought. It was as if some magnetic force drew me to the Scot, my whole body begging to close the distance between us.

"Aye, you've made a poor wolf very happy." He held out a hand, and I took it. As soon as our skin touched, a jolt of electricity shot through my arm, surging in my chest. His fingers tightened around mine, and the electrical charge circled through my body. My heart skipped in my chest. Even if I wanted to, there was no way I'd be able to pull my hand away now.

I didn't want to, not one bit.

I let the Scot lead me out into the garden. A cool breeze brushed against my bare shoulders. The wolf removed the cropped jacket he wore, and laid it over my shoulders. Underneath, he wore a crisp white shirt and waistcoat that accentuated his broad shoulders. The edges of tattoos peeked from his cuffs and collar. The kilt slung low across his narrow hips. Around his neck, a small coin hung from a leather chain.

My fingers itched to run down his body, to unbutton his shirt and discover the hard muscle beneath. Where was this coming from? I never thought about men like this unless I was alone in my room with my Rabbit and a Benedict Cumberbatch DVD.

I have to stop thinking like this. Even if he wasn't a wolf, which he is, he knows about my leg, which means he couldn't possibly want me. Look at his face, how satisfied he looks. He doesn't feel the weird churned energy the way I do.

Does he?

A set of steep wooden steps led down into the back garden, which backed right down to the edge of the forest. I moved down them sideways, which was easier on my prosthetic. At the bottom, the Scot adjusted his grip, knitting his fingers into mine. The warmth of his hand sent another shot of heat from my fingers straight to my chest.

"I don't think I introduced myself," he said, as we strolled down one of the cobbled garden paths. Strings of solar fairy lights bordered the flower beds, casting a warm glow over us as we walked away from the house. "My name is Irvine, from the Baird pack of Aberdeen."

"Willow." I managed to choke out. The name still sounded odd on my tongue, but after a month in Crookshollow I was getting used to it. "Willow Summers, formerly of London."

"It is a pleasure, Willow."

How long ... how long since I'd held hands with another person ... since I'd felt the excitement and anticipation of an unspoken promise, of the possibility of a kiss. I knew exactly how long – four years, seven months, twenty-one days, since Curtis broke up with me.

Not that I was counting.

Irvine led me across the garden, navigating through the maze of beds as if he knew exactly where he was going. He moved slightly ahead of me, keeping a slow pace that was easy for me to match. At the edge of the garden, he walked down a final set of steps with me, until we stood right on the edge of the forest.

Down here, the noise from the party faded into a steady hum. The rolling lawn and garden beds gave way to gnarled roots and pools of purple primroses. The waxing moon – only a few days away from full – shone down on us, casting Irvine's strong features in a cool blue glow. I knew I should be terrified of standing with a werewolf so far from the safety of the crowd, but with Irvine's fingers tingling against my skin, I felt about as far from terrified as it was possible to feel.

I was *exhilarated.*

Irvine turned to me. "You are a dream," he said, those grey eyes wide with wonder and desire.

Before I could react, his lips found mine, hard and urgent. A shudder of delight coursed through my body as he parted my lips and his tongue claimed my mouth.

I tried to pull away, terrified of what he'd discover if we went further. But then I remembered ... I'd already shown him my prosthetic. And he was still kissing me. He still wanted me.

God, it felt *so* good to be wanted.

Especially by this man, with his tight muscles and deep eyes and husky Scottish brogue.

Overcome by the draw of Irvine's body, I rose to return the kiss. Our lips seared against each other, drawing the heat around us. His hands seemed to be everywhere – touching my cheeks, tangled in my hair, cupping my neck, caressing my hips …

I'm kissing a werewolf.

My mother's voice burned in my ears, echoing the warning she gave me every time I asked about my father. *You cannot trust a werewolf, Carol. That animal nature may seem attractive, but it will only lead to heartache when he loses control, like the animal he is.*

Irvine's hands slid over my body, and Mum's voice faded away. All that existed was Irvine, his touch searing my skin, his tongue dancing with mine, his hard chest pressed against mine. His body heat radiated through his clothes. I longed to strip away the layers between us and collapse into him.

All around us, the air crackled with energy – a heat that burned against my skin and drew out every touch, every sensation to its absolute height.

I closed my eyes, sinking deeper into the kiss, losing myself in the heady wolf scent … and in my mind, Curtis' face appeared, his mouth set in a firm line, his eyes wide with shock and disgust.

That's disgusting, Curtis' voice burned against my skull. *I can't fuck you. I'm never going to get hard staring at a stump.*

No. I tried to shove the image away, but it was too late. The words pounded in my ears, pushing out all the fire that Irvine had stirred up within me. I wrenched away, stumbling back as my prosthetic limb slid over the uneven ground. I grabbed onto a tree trunk to steady myself, and tried to shuffle my foot back to steady ground.

Irvine reached for me, but I dodged his hands and slipped back, collapsing against another tree as my prosthetic foot hit a gnarled root. My hands and knees burned as they scraped against the bark, and my leg screamed in pain as my stump sheared inside the socket.

"I can't do this," I gasped, turning away so Irvine wouldn't see the tears brimming in my eyes as I tried to stand up.

"Willow," he growled, his voice rough with desire. He reached out for me again, his hand circling my waist.

No. Don't touch me. Don't make me believe that things could be different.

I tore myself from Irvine once more, leaned hard on my left foot, and managed to propel myself to my feet. I fled back across the garden as fast as my prosthetic would take me.

2

IRVINE

I stared after the retreating woman, every muscle in my body screaming at me to follow her. But I ken that look on her face – it was a look that said she needed to escape. I ken that feeling well.

I just wish like hell she didn't want to escape *me.*

My body burned with desire for her. It was more than just lust, although there was plenty of that. And no wonder – Willow Summers was fucking *gorgeous*. It was more than the fact that she ken what I was, because I still hadn't quite got to the bottom of how that could be. It was way more than the fact I wanted to find out who'd taken her leg so I could rip their throat out.

A surge of burning energy rolled through my veins, and I knew exactly what that meant. Every werewolf did. It was the biological connection tying me to my fated mate.

Willow was the one I'd been waiting for, the partner I would love and protect for the rest of my life. And everything I ken about her so far told me I was one lucky guy.

Finding one's fated mate was pretty rare. In my own pack, the Bairds, there were only five mated pairs, and only two were what we called *fated* – possessing that unique connection that meant they were perfectly in sync. Weirdly, the Lowe pack whom I was supporting in Crookshollow contained six fated pairs. That was almost unheard of – but then, everything about the Lowe pack was unconventional.

I rubbed my arm, where the heat still surged in my veins. Willow's intoxicating scent swirled around me. Not even the sickly scent of the primrose bushes on the edge of the forest could extinguish it. *My fated mate, right here in Crookshollow.*

Now that I ken she existed, I had to figure out what, if anything, I was going to do about it.

The timing could *not* have been worse. Of course I had to find my mate *now,* right on the cusp of the most important task I would ever complete in my entire life. The whole reason I'd come down to Crookshollow and aligned with Caleb Lowe's unorthodox pack was because we were planning to reveal the existence of shifters to the world. My whole life I've fought against the idea that our kind had to live in the shadows, without options or opportunities, all because of some misguided ancient belief that we couldn't openly coexist with humans. It was an earth-shattering, worldview imploding course we'd undertaken together, one I believed in with every hair on my wolfish body, and I couldn't afford any distractions.

Even if they were earth-shatteringly beautiful brunettes who bit their lip and hid a world of hurt behind their dark eyes.

I sucked in a deep breath, drawing in the scent and taste of her. My cock stirred against my leg, telling me just what *he* thought about Willow's sudden appearance in my life.

Down boy. I exhaled, pushing out Willow's taste, expelling her. *Time to get serious. Even if Willow Summers wanted me, which she clearly doesn't, I can't be with her and do my duty. Fated mate or not, the plan is more important.*

Besides, I should be more on guard. I was too distracted by her pretty face to even ask her how she ken I was a werewolf. That just doesn't make any sense, unless there's more she's not telling me. Is it a coincidence she's turned up now, right when Caleb's reputation is starting to grow? Maybe not. She could be dangerous.

Oh, she's dangerous all right. I licked my lips, relishing the lingering taste of her.

Time to stop dreaming and get back to that party. I've got bigger things to worry about than one human, even if she is the most interesting person I've met since I arrived.

I took one last, lingering look at the path down which Willow had fled. Half of me wished she was waiting there, the moonlight dancing off her silky brown hair, biting her lip in that way that made her utterly irresistible. But she wasn't. Of course not. If I'd been through what she had, I'd never get involved with a werewolf, either – fated mates or not.

Willow Summers, if only things could have been different, I would've given you everything your heart desired.

WHEN I RE-ENTERED PRIMROSE HOUSE, Caleb ran up to meet me, his usually jovial features set hard. Caleb Lowe was the alpha male of the Lowe pack, and my ally, and he didn't need to speak to tell me he was spitting tacks over Robbie's accidental shift.

Caleb and I had actually grown up near each other in the forests near Aberdeen, in rival wolf packs. Caleb's stepfather, Douglas Maclean, ran A-class drugs through the city and across most of Scotland. My father – Jonas Baird, alpha of our pack – was his biggest rival, until the day he was shot by a gamekeeper while taking a shortcut to deliver a shipment. After I took over as alpha of our pack, I got out of the drug trade, but that meant conceding a lot of power to the Macleans. Caleb and I had come up against each other in turf wars between our packs, but it was always clear to me that neither he nor his stepbrother Robbie really wanted to commit the crimes Douglas forced them into. They were trapped by circumstance, just like me.

When I heard that Caleb had left his stepfather to return to Crookshollow to take back his birth father's ancestral lands, I ken that he would become a worthy alpha. At the same time, his mother came to me with the story of the Benedict Ring, an ancient Lowe-family artefact that contained unmentionable power. She wanted the same thing I did – freedom for all shifters. She convinced Caleb and I to form an alliance and find the ring, so that we could use its power to free all shifters.

Even though we'd spent most of our lives as rivals, Caleb and I made a good team. We were both tired of living in the shadows, of being forced into the sidelines of society, of having shifter crimes go unpunished and shifter victims ignored under the banner of secrecy. We wanted freedom for our people, and I ken as soon as I saw his face that Caleb believed Robbie had just blown our chance.

"I'm going to *kill* him," Caleb growled, his usual jovial features twisted into a nasty scowl. He balled his hands into fists at his sides. "This is the single stupidest thing he's ever done, which is saying a lot. He's cost us *everything*."

"It *was* idiotic," I agreed. "But I think there might have been mitigating circumstances." I doubted the image of Bianca and Willow kissing would leave Robbie any time soon. It was definitely permanently burned into my memory, but for entirely different reasons.

As I recalled the image of Willow's lips pressed against Bianca's, my cock stirred to life. *No. Don't think of Willow now. You have to forget about her. Caleb's right. We have a huge problem on our hands.*

"I don't care how upset he was. This could destroy everything, and we don't even have the ring yet."

At the mention of the Benedict Ring, Caleb's scowl deepened. He'd entrusted the hunt for the ring to Robbie, and I knew he was regretting that decision. After several weeks of research, we were no closer to having the ring, which meant all our plans were currently stalled until we had it in our possession.

While I agreed with Caleb that we needed the ring sooner rather than later, I also needed to diffuse him before we had a second agitated wolf shifting tonight.

"You Lowes, so dramatic." I picked up an open bottle of champagne from the sideboard and took a swig. The sickly sweet alcohol did little to calm the fire rushing through my veins. "We can fix this. We just need to control the story—" I glanced up, just as a man in a tiger costume rushed by, waving his smartphone at a friend of his who wore a capelet covered in black feathers. An idea leapt into my head. "It's easy. We need to make everyone believe this was some kind of performance art. If anyone's gonnae buy that, it's this crowd."

Caleb clapped me on the shoulder, his face lighting up with excitement. "That's perfect. It's exactly how Ryan got away with fighting Isengrim in the middle of his exhibition opening. I knew there's a reason I let you hang out with us."

I grinned. "I thought it was my rugged good looks."

"I'll get the pack to spread the word that it was just a publicity stunt." Caleb leaned against the heavy banister, some of the tension in his face dissipating. "Of course, I can't find Robbie or Bianca anywhere. We'll need them to confirm this if we're going to pull this off."

"Maybe they're making up," I said, raising an eyebrow.

Caleb shook his head. "I don't even want to know. For Robbie's sake, I hope not. I warned him this fake-marriage was a bad idea, and you know how much I hate being right all the time. By the way, where did you go off to? I saw you run outside. I could've done with this revelation of yours twenty minutes ago."

Had it only been twenty minutes since Robbie changed? I rubbed my arm, where the heat from my connection with Willow still burned against my skin. It was what your fated mate did to you – burned you inside and out. I already felt as though I'd known Willow for days, for weeks ... that kiss alone seemed to last for hours. Or maybe that was just my own wistful thinking. "I went after Willow. You ken, the wedding planner? She was a bit freaked out."

"What did you say to her?"

I paused. I should tell Caleb that Willow ken about the existence of werewolves, and that she was my fated mate. But he was already so agitated, it would just give him one more thing to worry about. And besides, I didn't want to go telling Willow's secrets. I couldn't tell Caleb what had happened without mentioning her prosthetic leg, and that was not my story to tell. Instead, I shrugged. "I told her it was a publicity stunt, to promote Bianca's art house. That's where I got the idea."

"She bought it?"

"Oh, yeah." I thought of Willow biting her lip. "She bought it hard."

"Good. Let's find the others. We need to get this sorted."

I followed Caleb back inside the ballroom. This time, I saw it in a completely new light. When I'd first entered the room at the beginning of the night and seen the skull decorations everywhere and scantily-clad aerialists hanging from silk ribbons secured to the chandeliers, I'd thought it was classic Bianca. Now, I realised Willow's hand was everywhere – she'd taken Bianca's crazy ideas and pulled the whole thing together in no time at all. The creativity and organisation required to pull an event on this scale off ... my mate really *was* something special.

Stop thinking about her. You're getting distracted. This is exactly *why you cannot have her, even if she wanted you.*

I trailed behind Caleb as he approached each group of

huddled guests and informed them in his affable manner that what they'd just seen was another of Bianca's stunts. I marvelled as one by one, the guests all bought the story. They laughed and slapped each other's backs and held up their phones so we could see the pictures and videos they'd caught.

Caleb grinned and shook their hands and admired their social media posts. He could spin a good tale when he needed to. The last time I'd had to cover up a shifter sighting, it had been much less amicable.

At the thought of it, a sharp pain twisted in my gut. The edges of my vision blurred, and the familiar darkness started to settle over my heart.

No, not now. You can't afford to think about it now. There's nothing you can do to change what happened. You need to focus on what you're doing in the here and now to change the future.

But it was no good. I was so unnerved and horny from meeting Willow that I couldn't guard my own mind. The memory crept back and pressed against my skull. I shoved it back, but I couldn't completely rid myself of the rage it induced.

I managed to drive the blackness away, but my chest tightened, forcing out the heat of Willow's bond. The party raged on, with every last drunken guest easily convinced they'd just seen an impressive performance art piece. Eric's band started playing again, blasting out a raging guitar-and-violin riff, and people gathered around the stage, gyrating to the pounding music. Not one of them had any idea of the secret world of shifters that lived amongst them, suffering and dying so they could party on in ignorance.

Enjoy it now, you lucky bastards, because it's all about to change.

The walls leaned in, the dark wood suddenly oppressive, like a cage crashing down around me. Laughing faces leered at me. Sticky alcohol splashed my clothes. The rage drew up my inner wolf, who clawed against my skin, desperate for freedom. I realised I was only moments away from losing control and repeating Robbie's performance.

Gritting my teeth as I forced the wolf back down, I backed out of the ballroom and pushed my way to the front door. Willow's face flashed before my eyes, and once again I faced that terrified look she'd given me just before she'd fled.

I know what you are, she'd said. Perhaps she truly did. Perhaps she was the only one who did.

I raced down the front steps and darted into the trees. My wolf took over as soon as I crashed through the hedge and into the woods, my bones cracking and grey fur poking through my skin. I pitched forward, my knees hitting the hard dirt. My fingers dug into the earth, transforming into paws with long, curved claws.

Claws that would never be clean. Claws that had drawn the blood of an innocent man.

When Willow had looked at me in the trees, she saw the monster. She was reminded of the creature that took her leg. She didn't realise that he had nothing on me.

I threw back my head, soaking in the cold glow of the waxing moon, and howled.

You made the right choice, Willow. You should run as far as you can from me. I am exactly the monster you fear.

3

WILLOW

*B*bbbbbrrrrrrrzzzzzzzz.
Bbbbbrrrrrrrrrrrrrrrrrrrrrrrrrrrrrzzzzzzzz.

A frantic buzzing dragged me from sleep. *Is there a bee loose in my flat?* I lifted my head, squinting into the bright light streaming through the window beside the bed, hunting for the offending insect.

Since Bianca had moved into The Prim, she'd talked me into subletting her flat above the tattoo parlour. She left me her enormous bed, a leather sofa her cat had clawed to shreds, and some creepy skull artwork she'd drawn directly onto the walls. The space was tiny, draughty, reeked of cat piss and pot smoke, and the noise from the shops below could be pretty annoying, but it was *mine* and I adored it, bees and all.

It was the first time I'd ever been truly and completely on my own. Mum hadn't even let me live in student housing when I was at university. I thought I might be able to convince her to let me flat with friends in my second year, but I didn't make any friends and then Curtis happened, so she got her way and I dropped out. But here, in this dingy flat, I was finally my own woman.

All it took was a daring escape and a new hair colour and an assumed name. That's totally normal, right?

I rubbed my eyes and flailed at the window. *Where's that damn bee?*

It took me a few moments to realise the sound was coming from my mobile phone, and only because it was vibrating so hard it tipped off the packing box I was using as a bedside table and clattered on the floor.

I grabbed the phone and raised it to my ear. "Hello?" I mumbled into the mouthpiece. My mouth tasted like soap.

"Darling Carol, I'm so glad to hear your voice!"

Shit. Speak of the devil.

"You won't believe how frantic I've been." My mother's voice was breathless with panic. My stomach tightened. I *could* believe it. When Mum worked herself up, she was wired for days. *Dammit, why hadn't I checked who was calling before I answered?*

"Hi, Mum." I poured every ounce of fake happiness I could summon up into my greeting, which considering I was currently pre-coffee, wasn't much. "I'm about to head into a client meeting, so—"

"There's been another attack! It was at a wedding in this little Loamshire village. A werewolf appeared in the middle of the reception and terrified the guests. They're saying it was some sort of a publicity stunt but of course we know the truth. I'm talking to the *Daily Post* today about it. *Tell me you're not there.*"

"No, I was at a wedding last night, but there weren't any werewolves." I hated lying to her, but what could I say? *Yes, Mum, I was at that wedding. That werewolf shifted right in front of me because I was snogging his wife, and then I told another hot Scottish werewolf I knew what he was and I walked with him alone into the forest and he kissed me and it was the most amazing thing ever.*

The memory of Irvine's lips burning against mine flashed in

my mind. His cold eyes drew me in, raw and primal, promising
something I'd spent years trying to pretend I didn't want.

Did I dream it all?

I rubbed my lips, where a faint taste of Irvine still lingered.
The blue corset and cocktail dress I'd worn for the party hung
over a chair in the corner of the room. No, it wasn't a dream. I
really had been kissed. I, the newly re-invented Willow
Summers, a 23-year-old virgin amputee who couldn't even string
a sentence together around a guy, had been kissed by the hottest
werewolf at the hottest party in town. And then, like an idiot, I'd
run away.

No, not like an idiot. Like a woman who'd spent her whole life
believing that werewolves were evil. Given the circumstances, it's a
wonder I didn't run sooner.

Why didn't I?

Mum was screeching into my ear. I took the phone away and
checked the time. 6:49 a.m. It wasn't even seven in the morning
on a *Sunday*. I cursed myself again for not thinking to turn my
phone off.

Damn that Irvine. I'd tossed and turned for hours after I'd got
back last night, his scent lingering on my lips and that weird
tingling fire still coursing through my body. That damn kiss had
distracted me from the whole reason I'd been upset – Robbie's
shift. A werewolf revealing himself in public like that didn't
happen very often, and I would know, because Mum had docu-
mented and commented upon every single real werewolf sighting, and quite a few that weren't real at all. If Irvine and his pack
hadn't been able to cover it up with the performance art story,
the world of werewolves might've been revealed for real.

Just the thought of werewolves being out in the open made
my whole body shake, and a shiver of phantom pain shoot down
my non-existent leg. If that happened, every ounce of indepen-

dence I'd managed to claw away for myself would be gone forever.

I'd been so busy replaying the kiss over and over in my mind last night that I'd forgotten that Helen Winters would jump on this story like a wolf in the sheep pen. There were journalists and bloggers and photographers all over that party. Of course she would have seen the news about Robbie's shift as soon as it hit the web. I was just lucky she hadn't noticed me lurking in any of the photographs.

"—we're going to be issuing a statement to the *Daily Post* this afternoon. You must come back to London for it. We need you to be here for the photographer."

My chest tightened. "I've told you a hundred times, Mum, I'm not doing any more interviews or photoshoots or appearances. I'm done. I don't want to be involved with your crusade any longer."

"But Carol, this is *war*. Our work is vital to the survival of the human race. We're revealing the truth about the werewolf evil lurking in the shadows. The truth is more important than your ridiculous teenage rebellion."

I gritted my teeth. I wanted to scream at her that my "ridiculous teenage rebellion" had come about because she'd spent my entire life forcing me to appear in every kooky periodical or conspiracy theory TV show with my stump on full display while she told the story over and over of how my own father had bitten my leg off. Or because the kids at school and university, and my clients, had found those articles, and they'd made my life such a living hell that I'd finally decided to change my name and run away somewhere where no one knew about crazy Helen Winters and her pathetic crippled daughter.

I balled up the bedspread into my fists. Yelling never did any good. Mum yelled much louder than I did. Instead, I sighed. "I'm not coming back. You're on your own this time, Mum."

I could have avoided this whole thing if I'd been in my right mind. But that kiss addled my head. Damn werewolves, even when you try to escape them, they're just waiting there to fuck up your life.

"After everything I've done for you, looking after you on my own when your father left, trying to get you the justice you deserve, giving you a cause to believe in, this is how you repay me—"

"I *really* have to go now, Mum."

"Fine," she huffed. "I really do wish you'd tell me where you are, Carol. I'm going to give myself a heart attack every time I watch the news."

"Just don't watch the news, Mum. It's not hard."

"How can I not watch when those *creatures* are still out there, running free without remorse or consequences? How many more people are they going to hurt before the government stands up and takes action? I have to make sure that my legacy is to protect innocent children from their heinous violence, but I can't do it alone. You should have stayed here, Carol. I *need* you. The computer is doing that blinking thing again."

I sighed. Despite the fact that she was completely computer illiterate, my mother ran a website called *Werewolf Watch*, where she exposed werewolf activity around the world, as well as a dozen other wacky conspiracy theories she believed in. Most people considered it a harmless nutty fake news site, but she did have her fair share of devoted fans. At various times in our life werewolves had taken offence to something she published and threatened us. In addition to my jobs as her maid, personal shopper, and werewolf-violence poster-child, I was also her IT support desk and webmaster – all jobs I'd happily given up when I'd left London and changed my name.

"I wrote the instructions down for you. They're on the legal pad in the left-hand drawer."

"Come home, Carol, *please.* You don't have to prove anything to anyone. You had a perfectly wonderful career here in London. I don't understand why you gave it all up to—"

I gave it up because I was a 23-year-old virgin amputee who still lived with her mother. I gave it up because clients were finding your crazy videos online and were hiring me out of curiosity instead of because I'm a brilliant wedding planner. I gave it up because if I looked into the eyes of one more person and saw that horrible, soul-crushing pity for the poor defenceless cripple girl, I was going to go on a murderous rampage. No, Mum, you're wrong. I have everything to prove to everyone. "Oh, Mum, I've got to go, I'm in the car and a cop is behind me. You don't want me to get a ticket, do you?"

"You're driving a car? Oh, Carol, that's so dangerous. You've never even had a lesson. What if your foot slips and—"

"Bye!" I clicked the phone off and tossed it on the bed. Fire raged in my veins, but it wasn't the residual lust for Irvine. This time, it was anger.

I thought parents were supposed to want their kids to grow up, become independent, get out in the world. But nooooo. I got the mother who wants to coddle me for the rest of my life, and force me to dance like a monkey for her own anti-werewolf campaign. I never got to fall down, make my own mistakes, have friends, go to parties, get drunk, drive a car, fall in love. Hell, I never even got to have sex.

Maybe it's time to take care of that.

As soon as the thought entered my head, my whole body started to shake. Curtis' face flashed in front of my eyes. Again, I watched that wild blond hair I'd always loved flop over his face as he bent over the bed to kiss me. Again, his hands stroked my skin as he removed my clothing. Once more, his carefree smile dropped into a frown, and his eyes looked away as he fought the urge to throw up.

Tears spilled down my cheeks as his words pounded against my skull. *You're disgusting ... disgusting ...*

I stared down at the stump below my knee that was all that

was left of my right lower leg. I wasn't whole. I didn't look like a woman in a magazine. I was a misshapen monster. How would I ever find a guy who'd find me attractive enough to sleep with me, who'd look at my body and see something desirable, instead of an aberration—

Irvine. He called me a beautiful woman. He said that after I'd shown him my leg.

With trembling hands, I lifted the edge of my t-shirt, revealing my abdomen. The rose tattoo I'd had done only a month ago stood out against my pale skin. Elinor had designed it for me based on my own idea – a blooming red rose, symbolising my new beginning. Three droplets of blood dripped from one of its thorns – the blood that had been spilled when I lost my leg, and for all the pain that had bled my life away ever since. They were the thorns that stuck in my soul.

I dropped the shirt, wringing my hands together. They still trembled.

You have to stop thinking about him, because it's not going to happen. That kiss was a freak occurrence. Shove it to the back of your mind and try to forget about it. You have a new life to get on with.

4

IRVINE

*I*rvine Baird, you've found yourself a mate.

Rolf Wulfric regarded me from across the clearing, his canine smile revealing a row of sharp white teeth. The air between us crackled with tension. We were meeting to discuss the terms of our alliance, and in true Wulfric fashion, Rolf insisted on us both being in our wolf forms. I stepped into the clearing and sat down on my haunches, straightening my back and greeting Rolf as an equal.

His statement didn't surprise me. Wolves had a sharp sense of smell, and even though the kiss happened two days ago, Willow's scent still lingered on my skin. If Rolf's nose was particularly keen, he might even be able to sense the connection between Willow and I, the connection that still sizzled in my veins.

If Caleb had noticed it, he hadn't mentioned anything, but he was so absorbed in preparations for "the big reveal" that I doubt he even noticed if he was wearing pants. The only reason he remembered to eat was because his fiancée, Rosa, brought him food twice a day.

His distraction was a good thing. I still hadn't told Caleb

about how Willow ken I was a shifter. It was my duty to give him this information, but I held it back. I didn't ken why.

No, that was a lie. I kept Willow's secret because her touch still burned in my veins. The memory of her body tight against mine. Her lips wet and hungry. Her dark eyes fierce with desire.

I wanted more of her. Even though she ran away, I hoped there was a chance for us ... but there wouldn't be if Caleb started hounding her. She was clearly terrified of shifters already.

Which was why I didn't want Rolf to make a big deal about her smell.

It is complicated, I growled at him through the call – the psychic connection that allowed us to talk with each other inside our heads. *And I'd appreciate if you kept this news to yourself.*

Anything for an old friend. But don't come crying to me if your pack figures it out on their own. You're not exactly being discreet. You reek of her, whoever she is. He sniffed again. *She might even be your fated mate.*

Urgh. I really didn't need *that* coming out. *Enough about my love life. We need to move to business. Let's nail this thing out.*

Rolf pawed the ground in front of him. *I never thought I'd be doing business with Irvine Baird again.* Rolf was here in Crook-shollow to nail out an alliance with the Lowe pack. Caleb had asked me to deal with it since Rolf and I had a longstanding relationship. Before I'd gotten out of the business, our two packs had controlled much of the drug trade flowing between England and Germany. Now, the few members of the Baird pack who could work had jobs in forestry – we weren't as rich and powerful as we'd once been, but at least we were no longer responsible for putting more drugs on the streets.

Things are changing, I replied. *This is just the beginning. When we go public with this, things will nae be the same again.*

You're telling me. If we decide to publicly stand with you, we're going to have to clean up our act, or the minute this breaks, they'll just toss us all in das Gefängnis.

Are your alphas prepared to do that? I asked. The Wulfric pack was enormous – hundreds of shifters spread across Germany and Eastern Europe. They had an extremely sophisticated hierarchy system – with the entire pack split into smaller bands, each ruled as an independent entity by an alpha who claimed a seat on a pack council. It was this council who decided major issues and dispensed justice within the pack. The Wulfrics were evidence that shifter society could benefit from structure and laws and regulations, and it was one of the key reasons Caleb was so keen to have them on board. Unfortunately, since the Wulfrics had earned their vast fortune through largely illegal means, they would need to make some serious changes or they'd become a target for human opposition.

Rolf grinned, showing a row of sharp teeth. *The Council have all sorts of plans. With shifters in the limelight, there's more money to be had by legitimate means. The rich will pay a pretty penny to employ our wolves as bodyguards, and that's just the beginning.*

Despite myself, I felt a grin tugging at the corners of my own mouth. This was almost too easy. If we had the Wulfrics behind us, other influential packs would soon follow. This thing could actually happen. I could actually keep my promise.

So we have an accord?

Not quite yet.

Damn, I ken it was too easy.

We're behind you, and we're prepared to back you with as many wolves as you need when you make your assault on your Parliament. Rolf's eyes glinted. *I must admit, I am excited at the prospect of storming the House of Lords.*

Trust a German to get excited about storming the fortress.

But? I pushed him.

But the alphas want to make sure our interests are represented. If we scratch behind your ears, you have to scratch ours.

What exactly did you have in mind?

It is simple. If we help you, you in turn will help us negotiate with the German government. And possibly the European Union. We can't have you getting distracted with what's going on here in England. You need to commit the wolf power to our cause, or we won't commit to yours.

Caleb and I had predicted this. As the respective alphas of our packs, it was exactly the demand we both would have made. I gave Rolf our prepared answer. *Provided our power is secure in England, we will commit a force of two hundred shifters from across the Lowe pack and their allies, including the Bairds.*

We didn't actually *have* two hundred allies yet, but Rolf didn't need to know that. Besides, if we had the Wulfrics on board, I ken at least two other packs that would sign on.

That's good, but it's not enough. We want to use the ring.

Shite. I hadn't expected that. The Benedict Ring, which we also didn't have yet, possessed untold power. We ken very little about it except that it had been used for hundreds of years to persuade governments and people in power to alter the course of history. Until we found it, we wouldn't understand what it could do, or how it could help us. I didn't ken if we should be handing out the ring for everyone to wield, especially not a pack that was several times our size.

And by that, Rolf added, *I mean the real ring, not that fake one Caleb's been flashing around.*

Double shite. Caleb wore a fake copy of the ring around his neck, and he'd spread the word that we had the ancient power behind us. Caleb's mother and I were the only people outside Caleb's pack who ken it wasn't real.

How did you—

Easy. I followed Robbie to the library the first day I got here. He was looking up old records, and I figured out what he was looking for. I thought to myself, now why would the Lowes still be looking for the ring if they already had it in their possession? Rolf gave me a smug look, kenning he'd pulled out a trump card. If we backed out of the deal, he could tell any of the other packs the ring was fake, and the whole thing would be over.

I cannae agree to let you use the ring. I dinnae have that authority. I'd have to speak to Caleb.

You do that. Our agreement is contingent upon being able to wield the ring. And I want a title.

Aye?

A title, he repeated. *You know, some kind of official government thing. I'd like to be a Lord. Or a Duke. The Duke of Wulfric has a nice ring to it.*

I dinnae ken if you can be a Lord without actually being English.

Rules are made to be broken, Baird. Rolf bared his teeth even wider.

I barked. Rolf was crazy, but he'd make an excellent ally. We touched our paws to each other, sealing our terms.

Once I get Caleb's answer, it will take us a few days to iron out the agreement, I responded. *Will you remain in Crookshollow?*

I'm planning to stay indefinitely, Rolf replied. *My pack wants me to remain here to ensure our needs are represented. I'll be working directly with you on all matters concerning the big reveal. Since Caleb has said I'll be staying at The Prim, I'll begin by helping that moronic halfwit you have in charge of locating the Benedict Ring.*

Dinnae speak about Robbie like that, I growled.

Rolf continued as though he hadn't heard me. *Did you see the latest news? That crazy* Werewolf Watch *lady is doing another article on the* Daily Post *about Robbie's idiotic stunt at the wedding.* Rolf shook his head. *That guy is a complete fool. He nearly destroyed our chance to do this thing right.*

I tried not to think of anything loud enough for Rolf to hear.

Secretly, I agreed with him. Robbie didn't seem to be the ideal choice for the task of locating the ring. Both he and his brothers had a similar upbringing to me, which meant he wouldn't have had much, if any, schooling.

But Caleb had given Robbie the job. The Lowes were my allies and I couldn't badmouth another alpha's choices, especially not in front of such a vital ally. That wasn't the way to create a new world for all shifters. Some things were more important than what I thought of some of Caleb's decisions.

Besides, the lady who ran the *Werewolf Watch* site was nuts. No one took her seriously, even if she did stumble upon the truth on occasion.

Rolf grinned again. *Fine, don't engage. Your silence confirms your agreement. Robbie is an idiot. I don't know how he ended up mated to that firebomb, Bianca.*

Wow, Rolf had got that wrong. *They're nae mated. Their marriage is fake. Some old relative of Bianca's died and left her The Prim on the condition she married a man, and Robbie volunteered.*

Open your eyes, Baird. For a fake marriage, they sure did take their wedding night seriously. You're not the only one around here getting your piece of tail.

Interesting. Rolf seemed to be saying that Bianca and Robbie were together. Good. Robbie had wanted Bianca for so long, and it was hard to watch your mate shag her way through Crookshollow, oblivious to your connection.

I ken a little of what that felt like.

Shit, there went my mind, straight back to the night of the wedding. Willow's lips pressed against mine, dark curls spilling over her shoulders. Her hands clutching the back of my head, her eyes begging for more—

Nice. Rolf's voice thundered through my ears, destroying the image. *She's damn fine.*

Stay out of my head, I growled.

Make me, Baird.

Rolf and I parted ways, agreeing to meet the following night after I'd discussed his terms with Caleb. He headed back toward his car, and I circled back through the forest toward my cabin, a whirlwind of thoughts churning in my head.

Overrunning the House of Lords. Backing up the Wulfrics in the German government. Petitioning the EU. Press conferences. Campaigning for shifter rights ... the gravity of what we were attempting weighed heavily on me. For the past five years, I'd been caught up in the idea of a better future for shifters. But now that it was actually upon us, I hadn't given much thought to what it would take to build that future. We were so close, but there was so much work left to do, and only a few of us had the vision to see this through.

The fact that the Wulfrics were willing to give up their entire operation to make this happen showed me how vital our goal was – not just for me, not just because of my own selfish reasons, but for every shifter. Every one of us had a story like mine; a reason why going public about our existence would bring us new opportunities, and save the lives of countless shifters and humans.

As my paws padded against the soft earth, my father's face flashed in front of my eyes – his fur matted with blood, one paw dangling in the air. His eyes, usually narrowed with malice, were wide and glassy as he stared unseeing at the cold moon.

The vision changed, and now it wasn't my father, but Willow who stared up at me with those cold, glassy eyes. Her body lay in the dirt, twisted at a horrible angle. A deep slash from an animal's claw marred her beautiful face.

As long as shifters live in secret, I am putting Willow in danger.

Something she said at the wedding came back to me. *"I'm not going to reveal your secret. I know more than anyone how important it is that you wolves stay hidden."* I didn't understand why she thought that. Surely she'd want the world to ken the injustice that had been done to her?

But I didn't ken, because I didn't ken Willow. She was still a mystery. A delicious, beautiful, wonderful mystery.

Now that I'd found Willow, I wanted nothing more than to drop everything and go to her. I wanted to spend a week in bed with her, learning every inch of her gorgeous body. I wanted to ken her mind, to hold her heart, to ravish her body until she begged for more.

But if I did that, I'd be giving up on what we were doing here. I'd be turning my back on my pack, on Caleb and his pack, on every shifter across the world who'd been forced to become the monster. We were so close, but I had to give everything I had if we were going to make this happen.

But I couldn't. Not when my mind was on those sweet lips and that gorgeous ass.

Here I was, talking shite about Robbie being a liability, when I was the biggest liability of all.

Even today, when I was with Rolf, my mind wasn't on the game. I'd slipped so bad that he'd seen Willow in my mind. What if he wasn't an ally? What if he was one of the shifters opposing the reveal? My distraction would not only jeopardise the entire operation, it would put Willow in danger.

I can't afford any distractions. The shifters have *to be more important.*

It was the right thing to do.

Now I just had to get Willow Summers out of my head.

5

WILLOW

"—*I*f you won't tell me where you are, I'm going to hire a private investigator," Mum said triumphantly into my ear. "I saw one on a TV show last night. She'd triangulate your location from your mobile phone, and then drag you back to me by your hair."

I cradled my mobile in the crook of my shoulder as I rolled the liner and sock onto my limb, then slid it into the socket. "What show was this?"

"It's called *Jessica Jones*. She is a very vulgar young woman, but she gets the job done."

"Jessica Jones? You mean, the comic superhero?" I rubbed lotion around my knee at the top of the liner, then rolled the sleeve attached to the socket up over the liner to create a good seal. The vacuum held my prosthesis in place and stopped the socket rotating or shearing against my residual limb. "Did she also lift a car over her head?"

"She did. I was impressed with her upper body strength."

I resisted the urge to burst out laughing. "That's fine, Mum. You call your buddy Jessica and see if she can find me." I hung up the phone, and tossed it onto the bed. I wondered if I'd have to throw it away, in case she really did find some non-fictional PI to track me down.

I rolled a pair of merino socks over both feet, and stretched them out in front of me. I almost couldn't tell that one wasn't real.

I wiggled the toes on my left foot. My right foot remained as still and dead as a rock. I sighed, and slipped on a pair of wide-legged cotton trousers. It was hot outside, but I didn't own anything that was hemmed above my ankles. No way was I going to risk anyone noticing my prosthesis.

I stood up, and gave my hips a little shimmy. Bianca left behind a full-length mirror at the end of the bed (knowing her, I could imagine the significance of its placement), and I stood in front of it, smoothing down the matching blazer over the front of my trousers. My brown curls spilled over my shoulders. I smiled at myself as I fastened the blazer's single button. I looked so *different*.

This suit had come from one of my secret shopping trips in London, just before I left. The pale green would've looked all wrong with my blonde hair, but now that I was a brunette, it deepened the colour of my eyes and made my skin appear to glow. The lapels were cut low, plunging down my front and drawing attention to the tiny peek of cleavage I dared to reveal. I'd never worn anything like it before, but it felt like a powerful symbol, a rite of passage. Underneath, I was sporting my first ever black bra and my brand-new tattoo.

So this is independence.

I like it.

I imagined Irvine standing behind me, his huge frame towering over me as he reached down, sliding his hands along my collarbone before slipping under my bra. An ache welled inside me. I rubbed the side of my neck, as though the heat of his lips really did burn my skin. What would it be like to stand here while he undressed me, watching my layers of clothing fall away, seeing his hands as they explored every part of me—

No.

I shook my head, and suddenly, the woman in the mirror no longer appeared as the warrior princess, ready to conquer the Crookshollow wedding scene. She was Carol Winters again, the broken girl, the poor, pathetic cripple, in a ridiculous suit.

Irvine would never want a broken girl.

I blinked, forcing back the tears that prickled at the corners of my eyes. *Who cares if no one wants me? Sex isn't that great, anyway. It's perfectly possible to live a fulfilling life without sex. And even if I were to have sex, at some point in the distant future, it's not going to be with a werewolf, even a devilishly sexy one.*

I checked my mobile phone. *Yikes.* I had only seven minutes to make my way across town for my client meeting. Not only was Irvine distracting me 24/7, but he was making me late for appointments.

I checked my hair one last time, grabbed my client folder and organiser, locked up the apartment, and hobbled down the stairs. One thing I did *not* love about my new apartment was the fact that it was above *Resurrection Ink*, which meant slogging up and down a narrow flight of stairs. Stairs and prosthetics didn't mix well.

I raced around back to the shop's parking lot, where Bianca allowed me to park my car. Just seeing the little blue Fiat made my heart soar. I'd never owned a car before. Mum never even allowed me to learn to drive. I took a month of lessons in secret, learning how to parallel park and operate my accessible lever while Mum was at her weekly tarot reading. I purchased the Fiat the day I got my full license, threw a suitcase full of new clothes and my organiser in the backseat, and drove it out of London that very afternoon.

Ever since I arrived, I've been driving around Crookshollow

and the surrounding Loamshire county so much that I was practically ready for Bathurst. Which was a good thing, since I had exactly five-and-a-half minutes to make it across town.

I gunned the engine, stuck the Fiat in reverse, and yanked the lever on the steering column to lay on the juice. Because I only had limited sensation from the foot of my prosthesis through to my leg, I'd had a special lever fitted to the car that allowed me to control the accelerator and brake with my hands. I backed out of the space, flipped into drive, and yanked the wheel around. The car bounced over the curb and out onto Honeysuckle Road.

I didn't need directions to find the place. Even though I'd only been in Crookshollow for a few weeks, I relied on Raynard Hall as an important landmark. The enormous manor towered over Holly Avenue, and was the home of reclusive artist Ryan Raynard and his fiancée Alex Kline.

Elinor and Bianca were friends with Ryan and Alex, and they must've said something nice about me, because Alex had called a couple of weeks ago, wanting me to plan her upcoming wedding. The couple would be my first celebrity clients in Loamshire, which was not something I'd expected to happen when I'd chosen the tiny village by jabbing my finger blindly at a map. Back in London, I regularly organised secret weddings for movie stars and raucous engagement parties for Top 40 musicians. I'd even done a royal wedding once.

That should've been the shining moment of my career, but the whole event was tainted by the fact that the royal in question – who was a bit of a "black sheep" – chose me because I was Helen Winters' daughter. The bride couldn't even remember my name; she kept calling me "peg-leg." She forced me to wear a knee-length dress to the event so all her friends could see my prosthesis. I cried all the way through the reception, and that was when I'd vowed to myself that I had to leave London.

Luckily, Alex seemed not to know anything about me beyond what her friends had told her, and she'd never once called me peg-leg or even glanced down at my foot during the one meeting we'd had at a local cafe called *Bewitching Bites*. Alex was also friends with the couple who owned it – a quiet Chinese lady named Belinda and her raven-haired partner Cole – and they'd made some amazing food for Bianca's party, so I knew they were a good choice for the catering. Alex's vision of her dream wedding day was very different from Bianca's, and with 400 high-profile guests coming from all corners of the world, this wedding had to be absolutely majestic.

Majestic I could handle.

Since that meeting, I'd been so busy with Bianca's crazy party and Elinor's elegant gothic affair, not to mention the recent distraction of Irvine, I hadn't had much chance to think about the scale of what Alex was asking me to do. As Raynard Hall's wrought iron gates swung open to admit me, it all came flooding at me. I *had* to pull this off. This was Willow Summers' chance to make a name for herself, completely devoid of my mother's notoriety, with an entirely new customer base in the art world who didn't know me from trash TV and tabloid newspapers.

No pressure or anything.

Oak trees bent over the drive as I rolled toward the house, and I had the unsettling feeling I was driving into a gothic horror film. I was also late. Only by seven minutes, but still, that would not do wonders for my reputation. The tires squealed as I shoved the lever forward to brake, avoiding the edge of the stone steps by mere inches.

The bald butler standing at the open door regarded me with a disapproving expression. *Don't blame me, Jeeves. I've only had my license for a month. I'm still getting used to driving.*

"Carol—I mean, Willow Summers," I huffed as I hobbled up

the stairs, carrying my sample folder under my arm. "I'm here to see Alex."

He nodded, and beckoned for me to follow him inside. I didn't have time to pause and admire the ornate entrance hall nor the stodgy dark hallways with the walls covered in gilt portraits of grumpy-looking people. Just keeping up with the butler as he wound his way through the labyrinthine halls took serious effort. For an old guy, he was surprisingly fast. *How does he remember where everyone is?*

The butler dropped me into an elegant drawing room, decorated in shades of cream and furnished in a modern Scandinavian style. The room stood in stark contrast to the dark furniture and dusty portraits in the hall. Alex sat on the couch, wearing a cream-coloured dress accentuating her long, bare legs. Both the dress and her legs were splattered with paint. She rose to greet me with a kiss on each cheek.

"I'm so sorry I'm late," I puffed as I sank into the chair opposite her. A stab of jealousy hit me in the chest as I regarded her bouncing blonde hair and perfect figure, complete with two working and very shapely legs. Alex had everything – the burgeoning career in the art world, the beautiful figure, the perfect husband, the insane mansion. And soon, thanks to me, the perfect wedding. If she wasn't so nice, I'd probably hate her.

Alex reached over and poured me some tea. "It's fine. I didn't even notice. Here, you must be thirsty after trying to keep up with Simon."

"Thanks. I love this room," I said, taking the cup from her. I glanced around the room and took in the thoughtful details. Along one wall, floor-to-ceiling bookshelves housed colourful art books and bright ceramics. Floor-to-ceiling windows lined the other wall. Free of the heavy drapes that usually accompanied a house like this, they gave a full view of the wild back garden and allowed light to stream through the room. A stack of bean bags were stacked in a corner. Paintings of galavanting foxes hung over the fireplace. Even though the room was enormous, it seemed cosy and intimate.

"Thanks." Alex beamed, although the smile didn't quite reach her eyes. "I decorated it myself. Ryan and I are slowly redoing all the rooms in Raynard Hall, trying to drag it kicking and screaming into the 21st century."

"Well, you're doing a remarkable job. I see you haven't quite got to the hallway yet."

Alex rolled her eyes. "This house must have twelve miles of hallway. Quite frankly, taking on that job terrifies me. Here, Simon's made some scones." Alex gestured to the plate beside us. I picked up a scone covered in jam and clotted cream, noting a delicate ring of gold around the saucer's rim. Alex's fingers gripped her teacup so tight, the tension ran all the way up her arm.

Something's wrong. I studied her eyes, noting a mix of nerves and ... something else. Sadness? What did Alex Kline possibly have to be sad about?

No, I definitely wasn't imagining it. I knew someone trying to put a brave face on when I saw it, mostly because it's something I did most days of my life.

What do I do? Should I ask her if she's okay?

No. Alex was a client, not a friend. Whatever was bothering her was none of my business. If she wanted to pretend she was fine, then I'd do her the decency of going along with it.

I bit into my scone as delicately as I could, trying not to get cream on my face. Alex crossed one elegant leg over the other, and continued to stare at the teacup clutched in her hand without drinking. "What do you have to show me?"

"Er ... right, yes." I set down my saucer and rolled out the vision board on the coffee table. My face flushed as I started to talk about the ideas, so I kept my eyes focused on the bright colours and photographs so Alex wouldn't see. "I've taken all the elements you discussed and created an overall theme for the day. I'm thinking a lot of natural tones and textures, creating a kind of whimsical forest grotto. We'll set up the marquee right at the back of the grounds, on the edge of the forest. We'll use potted plants and miniature trees to extend the forest around the marquee, creating this idea that the guests are entering an enchanted garden. There'll be strings of Chinese lanterns, and I have this supplier in London who does chandeliers that project shapes like tree branches. The ceremony will be outdoors, under an arch made of fallen logs, like this—" I tapped the photograph I'd cut from a magazine, and glanced up to check Alex's reaction.

She whipped her head away, but not before I noticed the fat tears rolling down her cheeks. *Shit. Okay, something's really wrong.* Clients sometimes hated my ideas, but they usually just yelled at me instead of crying about it.

I opened my mouth to say something, but Alex beat me to it.

"That all looks lovely," she croaked, her usually musical voice hoarse. "What are the next steps?"

"Um ..." *Okay, so we're ignoring the tears. Gotcha.* "... yes, so I'll need to order all this stuff, which means I'll need to charge you for the deposits ..." My stomach churned. *I shouldn't say anything. She clearly just wants me to pretend everything is normal.*

"Yes, that's fine." Her voice shook.

"And ... um, I'll arrange a meeting for you with the couture designer we discussed at the last meeting. Her studio is in Crooks Crossing, and I think she'll be perfect—" Alex's hand shook violently, and droplets of tea stained her dress. "Alex ... um, I'm sorry, but are you ... are you okay?"

"I'm fine," Alex sniffed, wiping furiously at her eyes with the back of her hand. "I just had some bad news, is all."

"Do you want me to come back later?"

"No, no, I'm sorry. Just give me a moment." She slid the cup onto the table and gripped the edge of her chair as if it were the only thing holding her upright. A river of tears spilled down her cheeks. Thinking quickly, I grabbed my purse and dug out the packet of tissues I kept in there. I handed it to Alex. She tore out one of the tissues and dabbed at her eyes.

"This is ridiculous," she sniffed. "I'm planning my wedding. I should be so happy."

"What's wrong? Are you nervous about marrying Ryan?" I'd had a couple of brides who weren't sure they were making the right decision. They usually sorted themselves out before the big day, and they had some of the happiest marriages, at least according to the tabloids. I mentally dragged up the speech I usually gave to nervous brides, and prepared to launch into it, when Alex laughed – a sweet tinkling sound, like water flowing down a stream.

"No, no." She wiped her eyes again. "Ryan is amazing. I'm so happy to have him in my life. I'm really so lucky. It's just that we decided we were going to have a baby before we got married. We've been trying for the last 18 months, but so far ... nothing. We've been to the fancy doctors and I'm taking these giant horse pills and we've been following the calendar and I *really* thought this time, you know ... but I got my period today. Again."

Oh jeez. Alex broke down again, burying her face in her hands. I've had sobbing brides before, but usually it was because their manicurist split a nail or the caterer couldn't make a vegan lemon meringue pie. Something panged in my gut. I knew what it felt like to desperately want something and know you'd probably never have it. I felt guilty for envying her, and my heart ached for her.

"It's okay," I said, then instantly regretted it. I had no idea what I should say. "Some people have to wait a long time. Maybe it will be next month?"

"I had such a good feeling about this month." She grabbed her tea and gulped at it as if it was a pitcher of wine. "What's wrong with me?"

"Nothing. You're young. You have so much time. I'm sure it will happen. I'm sorry, I'm probably making things worse."

Alex sniffed. "No, you're not. I'm sorry for unloading this on you. You just came to talk about colour samples, and I'm a big mess."

"It's fine, really."

"This isn't like me. I'm usually so ... go with the flow. I know that sometimes it takes a while, and there are ... other factors that might be having an impact. Maybe Ryan and I aren't as compatible as I thought."

"Don't say that," I cooed. I moved across to sit beside her on the sofa, and placed my arm around her shoulders. It felt odd to be treating a client like this, and my stomach flipped with nerves that I might be overstepping a line, but if I'd been in Alex's position, I'd want someone to comfort me.

Not that I'd ever be in Alex's position. No one would ever want to have a baby with someone as broken as me.

"I just want a baby *so badly*," she sniffed, grabbing another tissue. "I can see what the rest of our lives look like, and I just want to make it happen. I've bought all these little baby clothes and now they're just sitting in a box mocking me. All this waiting makes me feel as though I'm standing still. The others are all pregnant – Anna and Rosa and Belinda – and I bet it will be bloody *Bianca* next. If they can have babies, then why not me? *Where's my baby?*"

"Hey, hey, hey ... " My own hands shook as I rubbed Alex's shoulder, not knowing what else I could do. My heart ached for her. "Plenty of couples have gone through what you're going through. My aunt tried for three years with four different guys to get pregnant, she wanted a baby so bad. There are so many things you can try – not the four-guys thing, unless Ryan is into that – you've got plenty of options left. And you're so young, I'm sure you'll get your baby."

"Thanks, Willow." Alex screwed up the tissue into a tiny ball. "I'm so sorry to dump all this on you."

I shrugged. "It's all part of the service."

"Honestly, the only thing that's keeping me together is this wedding. I just need something to focus on that doesn't remind me that I'm a failure as a mate."

Mate. At the word, a jolt of shock ran through me. It was such an odd choice of words. It was almost … animalistic.

The kind of word a werewolf might use.

Her using that word made me wonder if Ryan was a shifter. He was friends with Irvine and Robbie, so it made sense. But that wasn't possible. I'd met Ryan at our coffee meeting, and I was 100% certain he wasn't a werewolf. He didn't have that smell of wolf about him.

You're just reading too much into it because you have werewolves on the brain. Alex is a perfectly normal person, and she's not marrying a werewolf. You're fine. You can do this.

But as I walked Alex through some of the other details about her wedding and she flipped through books of colour samples, a nagging sensation crept into my head. *What if I'm wrong?* I didn't know why I could smell werewolves, but maybe it didn't work all the time. Maybe there were really hundreds more of them hiding all around me, and I didn't even know.

And even if that wasn't true, there was definitely something weird going on in Crookshollow. Apart from my father, who I was too young to remember, I'd only ever smelt five werewolves in my entire life – three I passed randomly in the street on separate occasions, one who came to our house to yell at my mother (we hid in the utility cupboard until he went away), and one in the audience of my college graduation. I'd only been in Crookshollow a month, and already I'd watched Bianca fake-marry a werewolf. Add Irvine and his friend Caleb to the mix and that was three wolves just in this one tiny village. It couldn't be a coincidence. Why were there so many shifters in Crookshollow, and why did they all seem to know each other?

A sliver of fear crept through my stomach. Why would so many shifters appear around me as soon as I left the safety of my mother's house?

I touched my hair. What if they'd seen through my disguise? What if they'd figured out I was Helen Winters' daughter, and they were closing in on me in order to get to her?

Had I just walked into a trap?

6

IRVINE

"—*A*nd apart from that fact that he hasn't turned up any decent leads on the ring, he's now being openly rude to Rolf. I'm starting to seriously doubt if he was a good choice for this mission."

I nodded, even though I hadn't heard a word Caleb just said. He didn't seem to notice, stopping just long enough to take a slurp from his milkshake before he launched into another rant about Robbie. It would be a comical image if I didn't already feel like shit.

After a morning of conference calls with alphas from prominent US bear and wolf packs, we stopped at *Bewitching Bites* for lunch. Caleb was pleased with the progress we'd made this morning, but I wasn't so cheery, mainly due to the fact that I'd hardly heard a word that had been said.

So far, my plan to get Willow Summers out of my head hadn't exactly worked. In fact, it was a massive fucking failure.

Willow's soft, dreamy voice floated around me, crowding out all the other, less Willowless conversation. Her dark curls bounced in and out of my view. And she was—

—walking into the bakery.

I blinked. No, I wasn't imagining it. That was Willow Summers, walking up to the counter, dragging her right leg with a slight limp. She wore a tailored suit that clung in all the right places, and the neckline plunged deep, revealing the hint of cleavage that made my breath hitch. Her eyes scanned the rows of treats on display. She didn't seem to have seen us.

"—if I didn't know better, I'd swear it was like he can't even read or something—" Caleb was still droning in, as if the hottest girl in the universe hadn't just walked in.

I stood up, grabbing my coffee cup. "I need another coffee," I said.

"But you haven't finished that one—"

I leaned against the counter, placing myself between Willow and her view of the cakes. "Willow Summers, as I live and breathe."

Willow jumped. "H-h-hi, Irvine," she stammered. Her eyes darted toward the door, and she gripped a thick organiser against her chest, sadly obscuring her glorious cleavage.

"I didnae think this place could get any sweeter, but you proved me wrong." Behind me, Caleb snorted at my ridiculous line, but from the way Willow's cheeks were burning red, I ken I'd hit the mark. "What brings you here?"

Willow bit her lip. "I-I have a meeting with Belinda. We're going over m-m-menus for a wedding."

"Sounds delicious. If you want my recommendation, try the Heaven and Hell cake." I pointed to the multi-layered cake decorated with whisky ganache and chocolate curls that took pride of place in the cabinet. "It's innocent on the outside, but wicked bad on the inside. Reminds me of someone I ken."

"Um ... sure." Willow barely glanced at the cake. Her dark eyes fell on mine. I lost myself in them. The connection crackled between us, and it took every ounce of self control I had not to slide her up on the counter and tear open that sexy jacket.

I leaned in closer and lowered my voice. "The thing about Heaven and Hell cake is that sometimes, the first taste isnae enough. You need another taste, and another."

Willow swallowed.

The foot of space between us shrunk away to nothing. The way she was looking at me was even more intimate than the kiss we'd shared. That look said *I'm scared, but I want you.*

I'm scared too, Willow Summers.

Caleb's arm draped over my shoulder, and he leaned in, shoving his face between us. "Irvine, won't you introduce me to your friend."

Shite. The last thing I wanted was Caleb scrutinising our connection. "Sure thing. Willow, this is my friend Caleb. We're just having coffee. Caleb, this is Willow Summers. She recently moved to Crookshollow from London."

"My pleasure, Willow." Caleb held out his hand, shooting her one of his brilliant smiles. Even though I ken he was insanely devoted to his fiancée, Rosa, I had to fight off the urge to deck him.

"We've already met," Willow said, shooting me a nervous glance. She didn't take Caleb's hand, and after a few awkward moments, he retracted his hand.

"We have? I can't say I remember you."

How can anyone forget someone that gorgeous?

"It was at Bianca's wedding. Elinor introduced us. I was the wedding planner."

"That's right. I remember now. Elinor and Bianca have been singing your praises. We're all friends, and there are probably quite a few couples who could use your services." Caleb grinned, clapping me on the shoulder.

"Oh, that's ... that's great." Willow forced a smile. I glared at Caleb. Couldn't he see she was uncomfortable?

"In fact," Caleb continued, giving me a sly wink. "We're all heading to the pub tonight, to celebrate an important merger Irvine and I negotiated. You should join us."

Actually, that wasn't a bad idea. A chance for Willow to get to know more people in Crookshollow, and see that shifters weren't all bad, even if some of them did want to do bad things to her body.

And maybe a chance for me to see her in another cleavage-baring outfit.

"I-I-I have something tonight," Willow stammered out. "But thank you for the invitation." Her eyes met mine and she bit her lip. Damn. It was hard to focus when she did that.

"You should come. Elinor will be there," I said. "And Alex. Bianca, too."

"Not Bianca," Caleb said. "But it'll be a fun group."

Now it was my turn to arch an eyebrow at him. Not Bianca? Was Caleb really that pissed at Robbie that he wouldn't invite either of them out with us?

Apparently, he was, because he gave a curt nod, then turned his attention back to Willow. "I'll see you there, Willow. Irvine, meet you back at Raynard Hall when you're done here."

Caleb gave us both a final wink, and shoved his way out the door. Inwardly, I cringed, knowing I'd have to explain how I ken Willow later. But it was hard to dwell on my problems when I was alone with the most beautiful woman in the world, and she was biting her lip in that way that drove me crazy.

"Well, will you come tonight?" I wanted to kiss that worried look right off her face. "I'd really like to see you again."

"I ..." She shook her head. "I don't think it's a good idea."

"Why on earth would you think that?"

"Because what happened the other night was a mistake." Willow's eyes darted to the door again.

"If that's true, it's the most glorious mistake I've ever made.

And judging by the way your tongue wrapped around mine, you agreed at the time. So what changed?"

She looked like a deer caught in headlights. "We can't talk about this *here*."

I swept an arm around the bakery. The line had snaked around us, and the tables were all full. Everyone was either talking and laughing or staring at their phones. "No one's listening."

She leaned forward, rewarding me with another tantalising glimpse of her cleavage. Her cheeks flushed an even darker pink. "After what Robbie did, it's already dangerous enough—"

"Forget about that for a moment. We sorted it. I want to ken why it is you're so determined to ignore the attraction between us." I reached out and grazed her hand with the tips of my fingers. The energy leapt between our skin, igniting my whole body. Willow's eyes widened, but she didn't pull away.

"Because I'm human, and you're ... what you are."

"It's nae unnatural, us being together. Werewolves and humans have been mating since the beginning of time. It's how our species continues." I stoked her finger, and a small sigh escaped her lips. "Not all shifters are evil."

"I beg to differ."

"That wasnae what you were saying when my hands were all over your body."

Willow's breath hitched, and her dark eyes widened further. "That's not ... I'm not usually ..."

"All I'm asking is that you give me a chance to show you that good things can happen when shifters and humans co-mingle. Come to the pub with us tonight. I promise it will be worth your while."

I traced my finger over the back of her hand. She shuddered, her eyes fluttering closed as the connection sparked between us.

"I'll ... I'll think about it." I could tell from the way the flush spread all the way down her neck, she wouldn't be able to stay away. She held up her organiser, obscuring half her face. "I have to work."

"Of course. In that outfit, you wonnae have any trouble knocking 'em dead."

The spark in Willow's eyes told me that compliment had hit home. "Goodbye," she whispered, and hurried around the counter, where Belinda was waiting for her.

I ken she'd come tonight.

If I had anything to say about it, she'd come more than once.

I'd seen that look in her eyes. For all her fear, she wanted it just as much as I did.

She felt the connection, which meant I'd just dug an even bigger trap for myself.

Willow Summers, you're under my skin. Maybe, if I can show you that not all shifters will hurt you, there might be a chance for us yet.

7

WILLOW

I can't go.

There are a million reasons why it's a bad idea. I can list them. I'll be walking into a pub filled with werewolves. I don't drink. I can't run fast enough to escape them if something goes wrong. They may all act friendly, but they'll just turn on me, like all the other friends I've tried to make before. I'll risk someone standing on my foot, or tripping over my shin, and discovering the truth.

I was standing in front of the mirror again, wearing a pair of tailored black jeans that flared at the bottom, and a red-draped top that left one shoulder bare. It was the tenth outfit I'd tried on, and not a single one looked right. Nothing I owned said what I wanted it to say.

What *did* I want it to say?

Irvine, take me now.

Stick your tongue down my throat.

Lick me all over.

Fuck me hard against the wall.

I don't want to be a virgin anymore.

I rubbed my hand where Irvine had grazed it earlier. My skin still tingled from his touch. My lips ached for the warmth of his mouth on mine. Further south, there was another ache, one that had never before been satisfied.

That look in Irvine's eyes at the bakery today flashed in my mind. The look that said he saw right through me. He knew everything I desired, and he'd happily give it to me, if only I was brave enough to ask.

He's a werewolf. Take that ridiculous outfit off, climb into bed, and put on an episode of Midsomer Murders.

I knew that was the smart thing to do, which was exactly why I threaded on a pair of dangling amethyst drop earrings, smoothed my hair down one last time, and glanced around for my purse.

I never claimed to be smart.

I spied my purse sitting on the windowsill. I hobbled over the pile of discarded clothes on the floor and grabbed it. I ran my fingers over the quilted leather – a new purchase, not my usual style, but it seemed perfect for Willow Summers.

I stared out the window, marvelling at how much my life had changed. I had my own windows, where I could gaze down on my tiny kingdom of independence. The window in my kitchen/living area pointed over the intersection, but this window looked out over the parking lot behind the shop and the forest beyond. Bianca's tattoo parlour and my flat were part of a tiny cluster of shops on the corner of Blossom and Honeysuckle. Honeysuckle Road was your typical street of terraced houses that met up with the high street in a couple of blocks. I'd be walking down there in a few minutes, if I decided to go to the pub, which I totally shouldn't do.

In the other direction, Blossom Road was lined with sprawling Victorian and Edwardian mansions. Elinor and Eric lived right at the end of that street, in the impressive Marshell House at number 22. I'd never visited there, but I'd walked past a couple of times – it was pretty infamous in the village. Behind all the houses, the trees of Crookshollow Forest loomed large and foreboding – a giant dark shadow obscuring the horizon.

I shimmied my hips, enjoying the way my draped top moved with my body. I'd been invited to my first ever "drinks". Carol Winters may have been a hopeless amputee loser, but Willow Summers was kicking arse and taking names.

My phone buzzed. Mum's face popped up on the screen, no doubt calling to try and figure out where I was again. For a moment, my finger hesitated over the START CALL button. Even though she was a nut job, she'd always looked after me. It would be so easy to tell her that I was surrounded by shifters. I could go back, stay locked up in her house and eat her questionable food and never have to deal with the outside world and all the cruel things it contained—

No.

I tossed the still-buzzing phone across the room. It hit the wall and bounced onto a pile of wedding magazines.

To hell with it. If I was truly going to be free of Mum, then it's time I figured out things for myself. She'd tried to shelter me from the real world my whole life, and I never got to do stuff like go to the pub with friends. Alex and Elinor were so nice, and Belinda at the bakery said she'd be there, too. So there would be plenty of non-werewolves, and ... maybe Irvine was right, and I should give werewolves a chance. I should give him a chance—

What was that?

I leaned my face against the window pane and squinted at the tree line, trying to see deep in the shadows. At the far corner of the parking lot, where Bianca stored the recycling bins, something moved through a shaft of moonlight. For a moment, I picked up the figure of a man dressed all in black, and then it was gone again.

The fear clenched at my stomach. Someone *was* out there watching me.

It's just some guy out for a ramble. It could be a hunter heading into the forest, or some drunk stumbling home. Just because I can see a person dressed in black doesn't mean they're watching me.

But what if they are? My chest tightened. *What if Caleb has realised who I am and has sent someone to spy on me? What if Mum really did hire a private investigator, and he's tracked me down, or it's my father, back to finish the job?*

Screw this.

I grabbed my purse and phone, ripped my coat off the back of my chair and raced for the door. Damn this to hell. I was going to go out and have fun and forget about men skulking in the shadows and lose myself in Irvine's eyes.

As I passed the kitchen, I drew out a long carving knife from the block and hugged it against the lining of my coat. Just in case. That should cover me from the door to the car, because even though I was braving the pub, there no way in hell I'd walk two blocks by myself now. I checked the contents of my purse – keys, mobile phone, pepper spray, loose coins, spare lipstick, condom ... just seeing it there made my cheeks flush with heat, but I didn't remove it

I locked the door behind me, and descended the steps into the narrow corridor that led to the tattoo shop. Outside, I dared one last glance at the tree line, but I couldn't see that shadow man, so I raced around back to my car.

I'd just managed to get the door open when a voice shouted behind me. Heart pounding, I dived into the driver's seat, and slammed the door behind me. The knife bumped against my chest.

"Hey, miss!"

I jammed my key into the ignition and the Fiat puttered to life. I backed out of my spot just as a black-clothed man ran jerkily across the parking lot and leapt in front of the car.

"Argh!" I slammed the car into drive and jerked my lever

forward. The wheel arch squeaked as it juddered across the curb. I yanked the wheel around and skidded across the footpath, coming out on the other side of the man and racing toward the village high street. My taillights caught his features – a young guy, mid-twenties, with broad shoulders, buzzed hair and an expression that was cold and hard and twisted with rage. He raced after me.

"You! Hey you!" he yelled as he waved his arms. "Stop! I need to talk to you. It's a matter of life and death!"

8

IRVINE

"*I*t needs to be a public reveal." Caleb slammed his pint down on the table. "Some event where millions of people are watching worldwide. There needs to be enough eyewitnesses that the evidence can't be argued with."

"Like a football game?" Luke suggested. Beside him, his wife Anna sipped her ginger ale and checked her mobile phone again. It was one of her first nights out since the birth of their son, Colin, so she was nervous about leaving him with Ryan's mother Clara. Clara was kind of a surrogate grandmother to the pack, and she was thrilled to be on babysitting duties. Even though Clara was sharp as a tack, Anna seemed to think something could go wrong at any moment.

Speaking of wrong, I glanced toward the door again. No Willow. *Where is she?*

I thought for sure she'd be here.

"Something smaller, I think." Cole – the pack's resident raven shifter – tossed his waist-length black hair over his shoulder. "I'd hate to cause a panic and have so many people in danger of trampling each other."

"Agreed. What I want to know is, how do you think this

'reveal' will go?" Caleb's fiancée, Rosa, asked, tucking a strand of her frizzy black hair behind her ear. It bounced right back out again. "Aren't you worried security at an event like that will just pull out their guns and shoot you all down?"

"It absolutely cannot be seen as any kind of attack," Caleb said. "That's how the media will portray it anyway, so we need to make absolute sure we give them as little fodder as possible. Ideally, it would be an event where we had control over the security, which means major sporting events are out, unless anyone has any contacts."

"Agreed, but with the Wulfrics and Irvine's pack on our side, we could probably manage a small security crew." Luke shovelled a handful of chips into his mouth. "We set up our own security firm and win the contract for whatever event we decide to do. I think the Wulfrics have already got uniforms and a website and everything."

I remembered what Rolf had said about the Wulfrics plans to become high-priced bodyguards and security as their "legitimate" business.

Caleb was nodding. "I think, a three-pronged approach. We start with a smaller event with a crowd we can control, but one that's trending on social media or whatever it is … where thousands of people are watching online. We want this to go viral. Then, as soon as the news starts to hit the media about the reveal, we need as many shifters as possible to march on Westminster. We'll camp outside until we get a voice. The occupation needs to be strictly non-violent, but we'll need to demand our rights loud and clear. The whole world needs to be aware that there's no going back from this."

"And the third group?" Luke pushed him, knowing he was heading off on a tangent.

"The third group needs to make sure the word gets out among the shifter community and encourage others to rise up and join us. The more supporters – human or shifter – we can get to occupy, the better, but it all needs to be done without violence. If we start hurting people, they're going to round us up and shoot us all—"

I tried to pay attention to all of the talk around me, but my mind kept flitting back to Willow. Why wasn't she here? It wasn't just that I wanted to see her, or that I was dreaming of being inside her, it was that she'd fit so perfectly in our little group. I imagined her nestled against my arm, sitting around the table, nursing a G&T while she laughed at Caleb's stupid jokes and contributed her own ideas to the effort.

Willow doesn't drink, remember?

I amended my vision to replace the G&T in her hand with a ginger ale, like Anna's, and that made me imagine the Willow in my vision as being pregnant, her beautiful stomach swelling with a new life.

I'd have a baby with you, Willow Summers. I'd have a whole brood of them, and they'd all have your gorgeous smile—

" ... earth to Irvine." Caleb waved his hand in front of my face. "Are you awake in there?"

Yikes. I jerked upright. "Aye, I'm here."

"Good. No, look lively, because we've a new addition."

He nodded toward the door, where Willow stood awkwardly, her gorgeous lips set in a thin line and her dark curls spilling over her shoulders. Even though it was a cool night, she wore trousers, and a black top that left one shapely shoulder naked. Her hands clutched a tiny leather purse like it was the only thing holding her upright. My breath caught at the sight of her. *My mate.*

Already, the connection drew me to her, shrinking the huge room so that the only people who existed were her and me. Her eyes swept the room, and when they fell on mine, her whole body shuddered. But it wasn't desire in her eyes, it was terror.

Instantly, I ken something was very wrong. Willow stood rigid, her whole body frozen in place. Her eyes begged me to come to her, to catch her before her terror overwhelmed her. Was her fear of werewolves that intense? But then, why had she been able to have a conversation with Caleb and I at the bakery, let alone thrust her tongue into my mouth at the wedding?

No, this is something else.

I pushed my chair out, ready to pull her to me, but Elinor beat me to it.

"Oh look, Willow's here!" Elinor raced to the door. She took Willow's hand and pulled her over to our group. Trust the girls to make Willow feel welcome. "You have to come join us. We're celebrating. I'll introduce you to everyone." Elinor went around the table. When she got to me, I gave her a wave and a secret wink, as if we'd never met before. Willow's face turned scarlet. Caleb gave me an odd look.

"Nice to meet you all. I ... I'll come sit down in a moment." Willow smiled at Elinor, but her eyes locked meaningfully with mine. "I just need to go to the bathroom."

"No problem. I'll get you something to drink. Non-alcoholic, right? Lemon, Lime and Bitters?"

Willow nodded. With one last lingering glance at me, she headed off toward the bathrooms.

I counted backward from thirty, then excused myself and followed her. Both men's and women's bathrooms at the *Tir Na Nog* were down a narrow hallway accessed by a single swinging door. If I'd read Willow correctly, we would have at least a few private moments to talk.

As soon as I pushed open the door, I saw her waiting at the end of the hall, leaning against the wall and gripping her elbows so hard, she was leaving welts on her own skin. I took her hands in mine, and found them shaking.

"What happened?"

"I don't know ... maybe nothing, but I am so freaked out right now."

"Why? Because of all the werewolves in the room?"

She shook her head. "No. I mean, partly. There was this guy outside the flat when I left, and he kind of chased after me."

"That bastard," I growled.

Willow nodded. "I was just inside getting some things together to go out, and through the window, I saw a shadow in the trees – a very human-shaped shadow. It was only a moment, and I thought I'd imagined it, but then when I went out to the car, he rushed at me. He tried to block me from leaving and he was yelling at me!" She shuddered. "I managed to get in the car and lose him, and then I came straight here ... I ... didn't know else to do."

I wrapped my arms around her and drew her close. Her body trembled against me, and she buried her face in my shoulder. My whole body lit up from her touch. The warmth of her breath against the side of my neck drove me crazy.

Willow stiffened, and pulled back. She stared at her shoes. "I shouldn't have done that."

"Why not?"

"Because ..." She switched and started staring at the ceiling instead. "Because I'm so confused. I know I should be afraid of you, but I'm just not. And when we're together, there's this *feeling* ... like I don't want to let you go. It's weird."

The bond. I ken I should explain about fated mates, but her face was so stricken, I couldn't bring myself to give her any more cause for fear. *She came here, where she ken all the Lowe pack would be, and that is a huge step. Monumental.*

Willow shrugged. "It's fine. It's not a big deal. He was probably just drunk. We should go out there and socialise."

"Come home with me."

Her eyes widened. "What?"

"If there's some guy hanging out at your place, you cannae go back there. I think you should come home with me tonight. Did you see his face? Should I take you to the police?"

Willow shook her head. "Yeah, I saw him, but it doesn't matter. It's probably nothing—"

"You dinnae ken that." I squeezed her hand. "If you're scared, then it's a big deal. You shouldn't have to be afraid at your own flat. Come home with me. I've got a cabin out in the forest. No creepy stalkers for miles around. I'll protect you, I promise."

"You don't even know me. Why would you offer that?"

I searched for the words. "Because you've dealt with enough. You deserve not to be scared. Now, come on." I yanked her toward the door.

Willow shook her head, more vehemently this time. "No, I don't want to leave. It took a lot of guts for me to be here tonight. I'm not leaving just because of this."

"So what do you want to do?"

"I want to have a drink with you and your friends." Willow set her mouth in a determined line. "I want to chat and laugh like a normal person."

I dared a grin as I ran my finger over her knuckle. "And what about after? Where will you be sleeping tonight?"

Her cheeks reddened, and she bit her lip. Damn, but she was driving me crazy already. "I ... I have to think about it."

I linked my fingers in hers, and pulled her toward the door. "While you think, let me provide you with a list of my most winning attributes. Get ready to take notes, because it's a long list."

WILLOW SAT NEXT to me at our big table. Apart from a boring conversation with Elinor and Alex about wedding dresses, we pretty much ignored everyone else. I supplied Willow with an endless stream of Lemon, Lime and Bitters, and she provided me with endless radiant smiles and adorable breathy laughter.

We found so much to talk about. I hadn't felt this instantly comfortable around someone since my father was alive. We loved the same films, books, and TV shows. I told her stories about living in Aberdeen, and she did an impression of her crotchety history professor from university. Every word out of her mouth made me fall deeper for her.

After the first half hour, the tension in Willow's shoulders fell away. She smiled and drank and talked and teased, and only stuttered a little when one of the others asked her a direct question. Her brown eyes sparkled with so much joy. Caleb said something ridiculous, and Willow tilted her head back and laughed with her whole body, and I had to dig my fingers into my thighs to resist the urge to pull her against me and assault her mouth with mine.

Who would've thought that just sitting at the pub would bring someone so much joy? Willow Summers was a total mystery – a mystery I wanted to unravel.

Time passed too quickly, and before I ken it, the others had left, and Willow and I were the only two at the table. After I plonked down another drink in front of her, Willow reached across and squeezed my hand. "I haven't had this much fun in years."

"Even surrounded by all these monsters?"

She nodded. "Everyone's nice. I am glad I trusted you."

"You should always be able to trust me, Willow Summers."

She looked thoughtful. "I barely know you."

"Aye. That's why we're having drinks. It's how we get to ken each other. Well," I raised my pint to my lips, "I can think of some other ways."

Willow's cheeks reddened, and she stared down at her lap. Her fingers tightened against mine. "Um ..."

She bit her lip.

My cock strained against my jeans. I'd been hard since my third drink, but now I was practically throbbing. Every touch between us was driving me crazy. The connection sizzled around us, the tension in the air so thick, everyone in the room must've sensed it.

But now our friends were gone, which meant I could ask the question that had been nagging at me since the wedding. "Willow, how did you ken I was a werewolf?"

"I ... I guessed. You're friends with Robbie and he's a werewolf, so it just makes sense. Werewolves and humans don't tend to mingle."

"You didnae guess. You should've never ken Robbie was a wolf, either. Go on, you might as well tell me."

"Um ..." Her eyes darted around the room. "You can't tell the others."

"I promise." I placed my hand over my heart.

"You're going to think it's weird ..."

"I'm a werewolf. I think I can handle it."

"Right ... yes ... well, um, I can smell you. Not that you stink or anything," she said quickly. "You have this woody, heady scent ... all werewolves do. When I smell it, I know someone's a werewolf."

"Can you smell non-werewolf shifters, or only wolves?"

Willow's head snapped up, her eyes wide. "There are non-wolf shifters?"

"Of course. Foxes, lions, tigers, even some domestic cats. In America and Russia, there are a lot of bear shifters. I even met a squirrel shifter once. They're not tied to the moon like we are, but some species have their own unique conditions." I thought of Cole, who was a Bran – a raven-shifter whose species primarily served as slaves and messengers to human masters. Luckily, Cole had been freed thanks to his woman, Belinda, and members of the Lowe pack.

"What do you mean, tied to the moon?"

"All shifters can control when we transform into animals. When we're in our animal form, we're still *us* inside. We can still think and remember and make decisions as a human. But during the full moon, we werewolves transform whether we want to or not. It's a different kind of shift – we lose our base layer of human reasoning. We're dangerous to be around, so we usually head into the forest. It means that in a few days' time, you're going to have to do without my charms while I'm out communing with nature."

She smiled. "I think I can manage. I've got my Rabbit."

At the thought of her playing with a vibrator, my cock hardened. "Willow Summers, if that's you flirting, I warn that you could do some serious damage to a man."

She bit her lip, and that adorable flush reddened her cheeks once more. "So ... um, what does it feel like? Being a wolf during the full moon, I mean. You said it was different."

"Aye. The whole world narrows, and all deeper concerns fade away. Everything becomes instinctual – we operate out of animal desires to find food, dominate our territory, and protect our mates."

"Mates?" Her tone was sharp.

"Most shapeshifter genes pass through the male line. We find our partners – called mates – among humans. Like Robbie and Bianca, well, sort of."

"And Alex and Ryan?" Willow's face flashed with recognition. "She said that word at our meeting the other day, but I've never smelt the wolf scent on him."

"Good guess. He's a vulpine – that's a fox shifter."

"Oh. I never knew there were ... special names."

"Now you do. Dinnae go spreading it around."

"Don't worry, I won't say anything." She made a zipping motion across her lips. "I'm good at keeping secrets."

That makes two of us, I thought, but didn't say. Instead I gestured to her empty glass. "Another Lemon, Lime and Bitters?"

Willow shook her head. "That's probably enough sugar for me tonight. I'll stick with water, thanks."

"Aye, a real party girl."

She tossed her hair over her shoulder, a flirtatious smile playing across her lips. "I am tonight."

My lips tingled at the idea of kissing her long, elegant neck. My cock stirred as I thought of what I wanted to do to her. But I still had questions, and she was clearly feeling like talking. "So you really cannae smell non-werewolf shifters?"

"I don't know. I don't see many shifters in their animal forms, just as humans." She looked away again. "You're looking at me like I'm a freak."

"You're nae even remotely a freak. It's odd, is all. I've nae heard of a human being able to discern this werewolf 'scent' before."

She shrugged. "My father was a werewolf, so maybe I inherited some kind of gene from him that's extra sensitive to these things."

"Your father was a werewolf?"

"Yeah. He was the one who ..." Willow flicked her wrist toward her legs.

Realisation dawned on me. "Shite. Your father was the one who attacked you?" Rage boiled inside me. The idea that someone who was supposed to protect Willow would be the one to do that to her ...

"It's fine." Willow pulled a strand of hair in front of her face. She didn't look fine, but I wasn't about to argue with her. "I was very young, so I don't really remember him, or the attack. I don't even really remember having a leg."

"Is he still alive?" *Did someone tear his throat out for doing that to you?* If a wolf in my pack had done that to his own daughter, he'd be lucky to escape with his manhood intact.

"I don't know. He ran away, didn't he? My mother went to the police but all they did was search the neighbourhood for some rabid dog."

"What about his pack?" Most wolf packs had some kind of crude justice system of code of honour to prevent these kinds of things happening.

"I don't think he had one."

"But every werewolf lives in a pack. Your mother must've been pursued by other wolves looking for a mate—"

Willow made a weird snorting noise. "No werewolf would dare go after my mother, trust me. Look, I was only three when it happened, and I haven't seen my father since and I really, *really* don't want to talk about it."

"Is that why you dinnae want anyone to know about your leg?"

"I just ... I'm not ready for that. You understand, right? Some things just need to stay secret. It's like you, with ... what you are. You had to adapt to living in the human world, and keep your identity a secret, because to be public with it would bring you no end of trouble. Which is good, because if shifters were in the open, I'd have to go somewhere far away. So I get it. I don't want people to know about that," she jabbed her thumb at her leg again, "because it's brought me nothing but trouble."

Shite. Okay, this just got more complicated. Willow had no idea that I was working with the Lowes to reveal the existence of shifters. I wanted desperately to explain everything that was going on, but the stricken look on her face told me this was not something she wanted to hear.

It's probably also not a good time to mention the whole fated mates thing. Perhaps it was better to keep that to myself for now. Time to move back to a safer and much less complicated topic of conversation: flirting.

"Um ... yeah, sure." I shrugged, as if it was no big deal. "A secret it is."

She bit her lip. "Thanks, Irvine."

I leaned in close to her, my breath just dancing over her ear. "Do you ken how fucking crazy you make me when you bite your lip like that?"

Willow's breath caught, and she bit her lip harder. She didn't move away. I ken she wouldn't flirt back, not yet, so I went for the direct approach.

"Let me take you home, Willow Summers. I'll ravish your body until you forget all about stalkers and werewolves and secrets."

"I—"

I stroked her hand. "What say ye?"

Willow slid her hand out of mine, and clutched it in her lap. Her body tensed. "You should know something," she whispered. "You're wasting your time on me. I don't have a lot of experience with guys."

"You are many things, Willow Summers, but you are nae a waste of time."

She shook her head, staring down at her hands. Her face was red. "No, I don't think you understand. I mean that I have *no* experience with guys. With ... sex."

I growled low in my throat. *A virgin.* Willow seemed to think it was a bad thing. Little did she ken the thought drove me even more wild for her. To be the first person inside her, to be the first to touch her the way she deserved to be touched, the first to make her come, the first name she screamed in ecstasy ...

"Do you want to change that?" I whispered, flicking my tongue on the edge of her earlobe. She shuddered.

"I don't know." She glanced up at me then, and I saw the battle in her eyes – her emotions torn between her fear and her desire. "I need to think, but it's so ... you're so ..."

"The offer is still open. Come back to my place."

"I don't know if I'm ready."

"That's fine. If you're not ready, then you're not ready."

"You wouldn't ..."

"Dinnae even ask that question. I'd never force you to do anything that made you uncomfortable. I make no secret that I want you, Willow Summers. I want to taste every inch of you. I want to feel your hips tighten around me as you come on my face. But I winnae lay a finger on you until you're ready, until you're begging for it. Anything else is unacceptable. But I still think you should come home with me."

"But—"

"That guy who followed you could still be waiting for you. He kens where you live, and the security on Bianca's building is shite. Come back with me and I'll keep you safe. We dinnae even have to share a bed." I kissed her earlobe again, loving the way her lips parted as she gasped.

"Irvine—" she moaned.

I kissed a trail down her neck, savouring the sweetness of her skin. My cock ached with need of her. I had a distinct feeling that even if she said yes, I was going to end up with blue balls, but I wanted her to feel safe. I wanted her to trust me.

Willow gulped, wringing her hands together. "Yes," she whispered. "Let's go."

9

WILLOW

I can't believe I'm doing this.

I was still trembling as Irvine led me on the moonlit path through the forest to his cabin, but not from the cool night air. I can't believe I'd told him that. I kept waiting for him to laugh at me. *A 23-year-old virgin. It's pretty damn laughable.*

Instead, he seemed to find my virginity attractive. What he'd said to me ... *I want to taste every inch of you. I want to feel your hips tighten around me as you come on my face ...* I replayed them over and over in my mind as I walked. My whole body was rigid with tension, and an ache rose inside of me that cried out to be sated by him. Irvine's fingers in mine burned against my skin.

"Here we are." Irvine gestured to a clearing ahead of us, where a small wooden cabin sat nestled amongst the trees. It was gorgeous, made of rough, round logs, with a gabled roof and wide porch running around two sides. Irvine steadied me while I climbed the steps, then he let me inside.

The cabin was small, containing only a small kitchen to the left of the door, with one long bench against the wall and a small table in front. Behind that was a bed covered with navy sheets and a fur blanket. A tall stack of books stood on a small wooden stool beside the bed. In the far corner, a single overstuffed chair sat in front of a pot-belly stove, with a basket of wood all cut up next to it.

It was comfortable and cosy, but rugged and masculine – perfect for Irvine.

Irvine gestured to the bed. "You can have the bed. Do you want a drink?"

"Tea," I said automatically, my mind reeling.

He wasn't kidding. He really wasn't going to try anything. A wave of disappointment surged through me. It was odd, almost as if I wanted him to push me, to take the intensity of the decision away from me. *This is totally nuts.*

I was totally nuts, not least of all because I was alone, in the middle of the forest, with a werewolf. Mum's voice echoed in my ears. *Run away. Run as fast as you can.*

But I didn't want to run. I trusted Irvine. I saw only genuine concern for me in his eyes. That, and hunger. But it wasn't hunger for fresh meat, it was hunger for my body. And it mirrored my hunger for his.

Carol Winters might've run crying back to Mummy, but Willow Summers knew what she wanted.

Irvine puttered in the kitchen, filling the kettle and setting out cups and tea bags. Instead of setting the kettle on his hotplate, he knelt down in front of the stove and built a fire. In a few moments, he had a blaze going, and he shut the door, placing the kettle on top.

I sat down on the edge of the bed, painfully aware that this was where Irvine slept. His naked body had been between these sheets. He might have even taken other woman back to this cabin, woman with perfect bodies and two functioning legs who knew how ...

I want to feel your hips tighten around me as you come on my face.

I squeezed my legs together, trying to force down the ache inside me. But it only flared worse than ever.

Irvine handed me a hot mug of tea, and I wrapped my fingers around it, grateful to have something to focus on other than the way his broad shoulders pulled against the fabric of his t-shirt, or how his intricate tattoos wound around his forearms. I imagined what it would feel like to have that body pressed against mine, skin to skin.

I gulped down my tea, unable to take my eyes off him. The words were on the tip of my tongue, but I held back. As much as I wanted him, I wasn't ready. And the guy tonight, running after me and yelling like that, was still fresh in my mind.

"You finished your tea?" Irvine asked, his voice gruff. I nodded. He leaned over and took my cup from his hands, and before I realised what was happening, his lips were on mine. This kiss fired up my whole body, sending a shiver of electricity that fed the ache growing inside me.

He kissed me harder, his lips and tongue a force of nature. I drowned in that kiss, sinking deeper.

"You said you wouldn't—" I moaned against his lips.

Irvine pulled away, and gave me the faintest smile. "And I'll abide by my word. But that doesnae mean I cannae make a convincing argument for myself."

I looked away, biting my lip. "I can't. I want to so bad, you have no idea—"

"Oh, but I think I do," he growled. He stroked my cheek with his hand, the action lighting a thousand candles under my skin.

"—but not tonight. There's so much ..." My tongue caught on the words. What could I say? *My mum taught me that your kind are evil and monstrous. I'm just starting to see that things might not be so black and white. I need some time to wrap my head around it.*

But that wasn't true. Not really. *No one has ever wanted me. The only person who's even seen me naked told me I was disgusting. I'm just getting to know you. I'm just starting to like you. To see your face curl up with loathing like that … I can't deal with it.*

I'm broken. I'm deformed. And you … you're the most beautiful man I've ever seen. As soon as you realise that, this is all over, and I don't want it to be over.

I wanted to savour the ache, the desire in his eyes, just a little longer.

I met his gaze, my lips begging for his touch. "Can't we—"

The look Irvine gave me was wracked with need. "Willow Summers, do you have any idea what you do to me? If I taste those sweet lips again, I'm gonnae blow. And as much as I need that right now, I want to save it until I can come inside you."

His words sent a shiver through me that nearly made me change my mind. "I'm sorry."

Irvine tipped my chin up, assaulting me with an intense gaze. "Donnae ever apologise for being your gorgeous self. But you'll be forgiving me if I pop outside to the bathroom for a moment to get things in order."

I nodded. "The bathroom is outside?"

"Aye. You have to walk around the back of the cabin, and there's no light. But Dinnae worry, I'll hold your hand if you're scared."

"I think I can manage."

Irvine drew back, a sigh escaping his lips. He reached into a drawer under the bed and handed me a t-shirt. "You can sleep in this," he said. "I'll be right back, and then you can use the bathroom."

I glanced at the chair beside the fire. "Are you really going to sleep there? It doesn't look very comfortable."

Irvine shook his head. "I'm gonnae be outside."

"Outside? It's freezing out there!"

"I wonnae feel it through my fur."

I gulped. He was going to *shift*, right here in front of me. "I'm not sure I'm ready for that, either," I said.

"Willow Summers, I swore that I'd protect you, and protect you I shall. I can do that much better if I can stand guard out there, with my wolf senses ready to catch the scent of any would-be stalker. Besides, you showed me your secret, the hidden side of you that no one else sees. It's only fair that I give you the same courtesy."

I found myself nodding, even as a heavy ball of fear rose in my throat. Irvine kissed the top of my head. "I'll do it outside," he said, his eyes boring into mine. "On the porch. You can see me through the window over the bed. You donnae have to look, but I'll be there, Willow Summers. I'll protect you."

Before I could say another word, he backed away, and disappeared outside. I heard a door creak open as he went to the bathroom. The lump of fear rose through my throat, but I gulped it down. I leaned over and pulled off my shoes and socks, then slid off my trousers and finally released my prosthetic leg, rolling the sleeve and liner off the limb.

With shaking hands, I pulled the one-shouldered top over my head, unclipped my bra, and dragged on Irvine's t-shirt. I breathed in the heady scent of him that clung to the fabric, and lay back against the sheets, trying to quiet my swirling mind.

Irvine was outside, beating himself off and transforming into a werewolf, so he could stand guard over me.

The door creaked again. Was Irvine back from the bathroom? Was he human, or wolf? I couldn't look, even though my fingers itched to grasp the windowsill and pull myself up. The curiosity ate away at me as Irvine's scent invaded my nostrils.

If I looked, it would make everything real.

I'd remember that he was a werewolf. That he was a monster.

It would all be over.

He called me beautiful.

I wasn't ready. I wasn't ready to lose the first person who'd made me feel like I was okay, like I wasn't broken. Even if he was supposed to be my enemy.

10

IRVINE

I hope you ken what you're doing, Irvine Baird.

I snorted, trying to quiet my thoughts. But they refused to be tamed. Everything I'd done tonight was a bad idea – I'd flirted with Willow, I'd got her to open up, at least a little, I'd introduced her to the pack, and they would quickly sense the connection between us. And, worst of all, I'd brought her here, the most delicious temptation, her gorgeous body and wide eyes begging me to give up my destiny for her.

I'd tried the last few days to get her out of my head, but it wasn't going to happen. And after what she'd told me about that guy outside her flat, I couldn't turn my back on her.

I peered in the window, a warmth spreading through my veins as I watched her sleeping body curled up in my bed. I'd expected her to toss and turn, sick with the ken that I was outside in my wolf form. Instead, she fell asleep within minutes, her hair falling over her face as a thin line of drool snaked from her lips to the pillow.

Willow was just beginning to trust me, and to believe that shifters were not all evil. And here I was, the very monster she should fear most of all.

If Willow found out the truth, she'd never speak to me again. And while the thought of that tore at my heart, I ken that I would survive the guilt and the loneliness. I'd survived it for the last five years. But I wouldn't be able to live with what it would do to her.

She cannot ever ken.

I ken we were doomed from the start, but I didn't care. I would protect her with my life, and that started with this stalker. Who was he? Why was he after Willow? I peered back through the window at her sleeping figure, trying to puzzle it out. I believed her when she said she didn't recognise the guy, which meant it wasn't an ex-boyfriend, or one of her grooms with an axe to grind. Unless someone had hired a guy to keep his identity secret. But then, surely a professional would be better at spying and stalking. This guy seemed pretty amateur. He didn't seem to care if she saw his face. He wanted to talk to her, deliver a message, perhaps?

If it wasn't one of those things, then what could it be? It could've been a harmless drunk, but I doubted it. They were rich houses up around Blossom Road – not the sort of area where drunks were staggering around in the early evening. No, I reckoned it had to do with why Willow left London. She didn't speak about it, and evaded every question I had about her mother. I had a creeping sensation she was deliberately hiding something from me.

I glanced up at the sky, noticing how large the waxing moon had grown. The full moon was only days away. When it came, I'd have to leave Willow, but how could I do that when I ken she might be in danger? I needed to get to the bottom of this, and fast.

Come out, come out, wherever you are, creepy stalker dude. My teeth and claws want to have a little conversation with you.

I STAYED OUTSIDE ALL NIGHT, my ears and nose pricked for someone stirring in the trees. The crazy stalker didn't show.

I spent a lot of time staring at Willow through the window. She looked so serene when she slept, her face smushed against the pillow.

My mobile phone started ringing. *Shit.* I didn't want Willow to pick it up. I forced my change, and dashed inside and grabbed it, just as Willow's phone also started to buzz angrily. She groaned as she rolled over and reached for it. Her eyes widened as she saw me running at her completely naked.

I didn't have time to savour her expression. I snatched up my phone and pressed it to my ear.

"Irvine, it's Caleb."

"Mmmmgh ... Caleb ... what's up?" I rubbed my eyes. My body ached for sleep. I fumbled along the bench for the kettle. *Coffee, need coffee.*

Behind me, Willow sat up and answered her phone. "Elinor, hey. What's going on?"

"Irvine, listen, we have a massive problem." Caleb sounded desperate. "Someone broke into *Resurrection Ink* last night and trashed the entire place. It looks like it might've been a wolf. You need to get over here *right* now."

11

WILLOW

"*W*illow, I'm so sorry to wake you." Elinor sounded frantic. "I banged on your door, but there was no answer and I couldn't see your car. So did you go home after the pub last night? You didn't hear anything?"

"No ... I wasn't home. Hear what?" My heart pattered against my chest.

"Someone trashed *Resurrection Ink*. The front window's smashed and all our equipment is completely ruined. The police are saying it's some kind of wild animal."

Shit.

My throat went completely dry. Phantom pain shot through my leg. The stalker. The guy dressed in black who'd chased me outside my flat ... he must've done it.

A shifter broke into the tattoo shop. That was no coincidence. Had it hit my place, too?

What if I'd been home last night? What would've happened to me? My whole body trembled.

When I didn't say anything, Elinor continued. "I wanted to see if your place was hit too, and also if you saw or heard anything unusual last night."

Only a crazy stalker trying to attack me as I went to my car. Only Irvine's words that lit my body on fire.

In the corner of the room, Irvine fumbled with the coffee canister while he listened to Caleb. Judging by the way his eyes burned into mine, he'd just received the same news.

This was crazy. If the stalker was actually committing property damage, that was only one step away from hurting an innocent person. But if I said anything, they'd want to dig into my past, to try and figure out why this guy was after *me*. I couldn't deal with that, not when Willow Summers was just starting to enjoy her new life.

A vision of bared teeth and pain flashed in front of my eyes. This was about saving lives. Maybe I could find a way to speak the truth without alerting them that I might be the cause.

"Um, I actually didn't go home last night. I stayed with a ... a friend."

"Oh, I *see*." Elinor lowered her voice. "Irvine?"

"No! Just a friend. You wouldn't know her." I took a deep breath, then said. "But I did see something. I've noticed what I think was someone in the bushes behind the shop last night. A man dressed in black. He ran at me when I went to my car to head to the pub. He didn't say anything, but he looked pretty unhinged. I thought it was just some drunk guy."

Irvine raised an eyebrow at me, clearly wondering why I'd decided to tell such a half-truth. I waved a hand at him. *Not now.*

"Did you see what he looked like?"

I'd never forget those wild eyes or the venom in his voice. "Yeah, he had really short hair and a black hoodie. He was young, but muscular, like he worked outdoors. He looked angry, or upset. When he ran at me he was screaming incoherently ... Maybe he was on drugs or something?"

"Maybe." Elinor's voice was heavy. "Anything else?"

"No, but it was pretty dark when I left to meet you guys."

"Okay. I'm here at the shop now so when you get the chance, come over and we'll take a look at your flat. The police are here, and they're going to need your statement. They might get you to sit down with a sketch artist. And Caleb will probably want to talk to you, too."

Great. Just what I need, to be interrogated by a wolf. I was just about to say that, when I remembered I wasn't supposed to know about werewolves or that Caleb was the alpha of their pack. "Um ... why does Caleb need to talk to me? I hardly know him. Is he with the police?"'

"He sort of ..." Elinor paused. I think she realised she'd said something she shouldn't. "... looks after things around here. If this guy is after you or Bianca, he'll be able to help protect you."

"How? Is he the mafia?" Irvine gave me an amused look as he handed me a hot cup of tea.

"No, Willow. He's not the mafia. I promise I'll explain someday. Just not today."

"How's Bianca holding up?"

Elinor paused. "Not good, but she'll be fine. Just come as soon as you can."

"Okay, I'll—"

But Elinor had already hung up. I dropped my phone. My mind blurred. *The stalker isn't just a stalker. He attacked the shop. He's a werewolf. He's coming after me.*

Strong arms wrapped around my chest. "Willow Summers, you listen to me," Irvine's deep voice boomed in my ear. "Everything is going to be just fine. He's not gonnae get anywhere near you. We'll make sure of that."

A sob escaped my throat. "I only just escaped. I had my first taste of freedom and it was amazing. And now I'm trapped again."

"I dinnae ken. What did you escape from?"

I buried my face in his shoulder, my body shuddering as I let out all the tension that had worked its way through my bones. The phantom pain subsided as all of my fear bled out in vicious tears.

"Isn't it enough that I have to live without a leg? Isn't it enough that I've been paraded around like a circus freak to further a cause I'm not even sure I believe in anymore? Why is this person after me? Am I that disgusting? Am I that wrong ..." I broke down again.

"Willow, you're not disgusting, and I'll hurt the person who said that to you."

"Curtis, my ex-boyfriend."

Irvine's face darkened. "Then he's a dead man. But that's for another day. If there's something you've nae told me ... I cannae keep you safe if I dinnae ken what's going on."

"I—" I opened my mouth to tell him everything, about my mother and *Werewolf Watch* and why I wanted to start over, but all that came out were more strangled sobs.

"Ssssh, sssshh, not now." Irvine stroked my hair. "We'll get this guy, Willow Summers. That is my promise to you. Everything's gonnae be fine."

I couldn't even turn into the parking lot behind the shop because of the broken glass on the footpath. Instead, I found a park down the road. Elinor stood beside the shop window with a police officer, but came running over as I pulled up.

"This is what the bastard did," she said, grabbing my hand and dragging me to the window, so I could get a good look at the damage inside.

"I'm so sorry." I came into *Resurrection Ink* the first week I arrived in Crookshollow. I'd read online that it was a female-friendly clinic that wasn't full of intimidating bikers. It had seemed pretty intimidating to me, with the skull paintings on the walls and the black tiles across the floor. But Bianca and Elinor had put me at ease, and it wasn't long before the terrifying surroundings had actually seemed snug and homely.

Elinor looked like she was trying to hold back tears, but her expression was stern, businesslike. "It's not your fault. Come on, let's go see if he hit your place, too."

I made Elinor go up the stairs first, so she wouldn't see my limp. I shoved my key in the lock and opened the door to my flat, my stomach clenched tight at the thought of what I might see. But the sight that greeted me as I swung the door open was the same as the one I'd left last night – the secondhand couch covered with bridal magazines and folders, the kitchen covered in unwashed coffee cups, the sheets on Bianca's old bed rumpled and unmade.

I let out a breath I didn't realise I'd been holding. "He hasn't been in here."

"That's a good sign, at least," Elinor said, placing her hand on my shoulder as we walked back downstairs. "Come have a closer look in the shop. I want to know if anything jogs your memory."

"You seem very calm."

Elinor gave me a thin smile. "I'm not calm on the inside, trust me. But I know what has to be done. I was a lawyer in London before I moved here to start my apprenticeship with Bianca. I guess it's hard for me to let go of that analytical process."

A lawyer to a tattoo artist? "That's a bit of a career shift. What made you move here and change your future so drastically?"

This time, Elinor's smile was genuine. "Love, of course. The only worthwhile reason to do anything. After you."

She held open the door and I stepped over the police tape in the door of the shop.

It looked like a hurricane had torn through the place, flinging the heavy massage tables against the walls and snapping the legs off the chairs. The artwork had been torn from the walls and smashed across the tiles. Broken needles and pots of ink splattered every surface. The blood-red velvet on the chaise-lounge under the window was in ribbons, almost as if …

… *as if it had been clawed to shreds.*

I sniffed the air, but apart from the smell of the inks, there was no heady wolf scent beyond the faint smell of Robbie, who must visit frequently since Bianca owned the shop. I frowned. That didn't make sense. If a werewolf did this, then why didn't the place reek of him?

I thought back to last night. I hadn't smelt the wolf scent when the guy ran at me, either. That could've been because I was too far away, or too scared, but now I wasn't so sure.

But if a wolf didn't do this, then who did?

What kind of creature is loose in Crookshollow? And why is he after me?

My phone buzzed. In a daze, I lifted it to my ear. "Irvine, I'll—"

"Irvine, who is Irvine?" Mum's voice screeched down the phone. "Willow, I need to know where you are, *right now*. There's been a serious uptick of werewolf activity in the news. I just heard about this tattoo parlour in Loamshire that was attacked by some kind of animal. They're getting bolder! I need you here to help me film another video. We need to get the word out and stop them before any more innocent people get hurt."

"Mum, I'm fine. I've never set foot in a tattoo parlour before, and I'm nowhere near Loamshire, but I'm not telling you where I am." The lie stabbed me in the gut, but it was necessary.

"Carol Winters, I am your mother and I demand you answer

me. If you don't tell me where you are *right now*, I'm going to have to take matters into my own hands—"

I hung up the phone, my hands shaking. How had she heard about this attack so quickly? Why did she sound *so* panicked? Mum was usually pretty crazy about shifters, but her paranoia seemed to have got worse since I left. Was this just because she didn't know what to do with herself without me, or was it because she knew someone was chasing me?

The threat in her words was implicit. Had Mum *already* hired someone to come after me, to bring me back to London? Had she given that person unlimited reign to terrify me so that I'd break and go back to her?

It was a terrible thought, but as I thought back over Mum's behaviour, I became more and more convinced that was what was happening. If she thought it was the right thing to do, she wouldn't hesitate to do it, even if it meant hurting me.

That was why Mum was calling to check up on me, so she could see if she'd got me. Now that she knew she had failed, she'd have to pull out the big guns.

"Willow?" Elinor waved her hand in front of my face. "You okay? You've gone all white."

I tried to speak, but the words caught in my throat. My heartbeat pounded in my ears.

Shards of glass crunched under my feet as I moved in to peer out the window.

Elinor came up behind me. "Did you stand on some glass? You're limping."

"It's fine, don't worry." I shoved my hands in my pockets so Elinor wouldn't notice them shaking. A familiar car pulled into the parking space behind mine.

"Hey, there's Irvine—" Elinor started, but I was already out the door.

Irvine waved as I walked across the street. He'd wanted to

drive me straight to the shop, but I didn't want Elinor to know we'd been together, so I made him wait ten minutes before following me.

His face fell in surprise as I crashed into him, burying myself in his leather jacket. I knew that Elinor would be able to see us, thus destroying my ruse, but in that moment, I didn't care. I needed Irvine. I needed his brave stoicism.

"Willow," he whispered as he patted my hair. "What's wrong, my lass?"

"My mother," I whispered. My whole body shook.

"What about your mother?"

"She won't give up. She'll send everything she has after me until she's convinced me she's right. She'll never let me be free. I was just starting to build a life here and now she's trying to take it away by faking a shifter attack."

"Willow, you're rambling. Are you saying your mother did this? If she wants to hurt you, why go after *Resurrection Ink?*"

I gripped my elbows with my hands, trying to control the shaking in my body. "Because she wants to hurt you guys. She wants you to turn me aside so I'll go home again. If I don't leave Crookshollow and go back to her, this is only the beginning of your troubles."

12

IRVINE

I tapped my foot impatiently while Willow finished giving her statement to the police officer. Elinor stood beside me, shooting me knowing glances that I tried to ignore. Willow didn't want Elinor to think we were together, which was ridiculous because Elinor could read the heat between us like a book. But if it made Willow feel better, I'd keep up the charade.

Caleb arrived just as Willow was finishing up. "Tell me everything you told them," he said to her.

As Willow repeated what she'd told the police about seeing the guy, I thought back through what she'd said about her mother. She was so certain her mother was behind the stalker, but that didn't make any sense. Some kind of shifter had clearly done the damage to the shop, and from what Willow had alluded to, her mother wasn't likely to be in league with shifters. I wondered if her father could possibly be behind it. What other reason would a shifter have to be after her?

"You shouldn't stay at your flat," Caleb told Willow. "I don't want to risk this guy coming back. We can put you in a guest room at Raynard Hall. Alex and Ryan would be happy to have you."

"That's okay," Willow said, a brief glance in my direction. "I have a friend I'm staying with. I'll be fine."

"Do you want me to drive you there? You must be pretty shaken up."

"Irvine's already offered a ride."

"Has he just?" Caleb couldn't hide the smile in his voice.

"Aye. I'll take her there now." I interjected. Caleb looked like he was ready to argue, but I mouthed *later*. He nodded, and we said our goodbyes. I walked Willow over to where I'd parked. The full truth about our relationship would come out at some point, but it didn't have to be today.

Willow slipped into my car, her hands clenched tight in her lap. Instead of driving her back to the cabin, I stopped by the market and picked up some salami, crackers, grapes, and fancy cheese. I nearly grabbed a bottle of champagne before I remember that Willow didn't drink.

"Where are we going?" Willow asked as I dropped the shopping bags at her feet and headed out of Crookshollow into the fields, the opposite direction of my cabin.

"If I told you, it'll spoil the fun," I said, as I turned the car down a narrow country road.

After ten minutes, I found the place I was looking for. I pulled into a parking area, pleased to see it was deserted. Teenagers often came up here to smoke weed, scare each other and make out. I opened Willow's door and held out my hand. "Grab the bags. The ground's a little uneven, but I'll help you."

"Why are we at a cemetery?" Willow asked as she hobbled along beside me past the charred English Heritage sign that described the history of the area.

"This isn't just any cemetery," I said, as I led her down a gentle hill to a newly installed bench. It faced across the crooked graves and overlooked the rolling countryside. The forest stretched along the edge, extending for miles as it snaked down the valley and back around the village. In the field across the way, fluffy sheep munched on vivid green grass. "Do you notice anything odd about it?"

Willow unwrapped the salami and managed to saw off a slice with the plastic knife I'd brought. She added a wedge of brie to her cracker and popped the whole thing in her mouth. She chewed in silence for a few moments before saying, "The stones. The ones that aren't broken are bent outward, and there are scorch marks all over the ground. It's as if there was an explosion here."

"Aye, there was. This is the Witches Cemetery. I'm sure you heard the stories about Crookshollow burning more witches than any other place in England. Well, they buried those poor souls here, on unconsecrated ground."

"What does that have to do with the explosion?"

"A couple of years ago, an evil werewolf came to Crookshollow. He had amassed a pack of rogue shifters – foxes and stags and birds and all kinds of animals. He brought them here to conduct a sadistic ritual to bring these witches back to live – a sick kind of half-life, called *barghast*. He planned to use these spirits to overthrow the current government, place his pack in charge, and basically enslave humanity."

Willow gasped. "What happened?"

"Ryan and Alex stopped him. They caused the spell to malfunction, killing the whole rogue pack and burning the cemetery in the process."

"What's a rogue?"

"They're shifters without a pack, usually because they've been cast out for breaking the rules, or they're mutts and too dangerous to be part of a normal pack."

"Mutts?"

"Shifters who are genetically deformed. Many of them have trouble keeping control of their shift or their animal instincts.

They're usually cast out because they're a liability to a pack." I peeled off a grape and held it up. "Open up."

Willow opened her mouth and I placed the grape on her tongue, my finger brushing her cheek. She chewed and swallowed. "Why did you bring me to see this?"

"Because I wanted you to see that there are good shifters in the world, ones that place the safety of humans above even their own lives. Ryan wants shifters to be free, but not if it meant Isengrim was in control. He ken that our place is nae to control and dominate humans, but to be part of their society, abiding by the same laws and morals that govern you."

"Is this ... what you want, too? For shifters to be free?" Willow asked in a small voice.

I wasn't going to deny it. "Yes. But it is nae as simple as wanting. There's so much work to be done. If shifters suddenly revealed themselves, humans would be scared. And fear quickly turns to violence. There are packs who would fight for control and power. There are packs who would oppose the reveal, and who would rather die than co-exist with humans. There's so much work to do to ensure any attempt wouldnae blow up in our faces. The last thing anyone wants is an all-out human/shifter war, or for one race to enslave the other."

"That's why you have to remain secret," she said, her voice firm. "There's too much that could go wrong. Living in the shadows is better than suffering in the light."

"There is so much that could go right, too. You could have justice. Your father could be trialled and convicted for his crime. Don't you want—"

Willow shook her head. "I can't live in a world where shifters are free. I'm sorry, Irvine. I just can't support it."

"But why not? What about your father—"

"I don't want to talk about it." She looked away. "Please don't ask me again."

Great. So that hadn't worked. I decided to change the subject. "Fine. Tell me why you came to Crookshollow. Why are you so sure your mother is behind the attack on the shop?"

She didn't turn around. "I can't, Irvine. I can't."

"Willow, you ken that I need this information if I'm to keep you safe. Especially now that someone attacked the shop. The pack will be asking questions, and they'll need answers."

She sighed. "Yeah, I ken ... I mean, I *know*. Okay ..." She sucked in a deep breath. "I came to get away from my mother. I think that's why this guy is here. He's some kind of private investigator she's hired to track me down and drag me back."

"Why would she do that?"

Willow sighed again. Clearly, having to talk about herself was making her uncomfortable. Good. It was driving me crazy trying to figure her out while pretending the bond didn't exist. I needed something more from her.

"She'd do that because she's legitimately, bona-fide nutty. After my accident, Mum went a bit bonkers. I think she blames herself for what happened to me, so she's tried to make up for it by being extra-protective. She never let me go anywhere that wasn't school or home. She wouldn't let me stay over the night at other girls' houses, or join after-school activities. I got into Cambridge, but she wouldn't let me go because it meant I'd have to leave home. Instead, I fought her for years to let me do an arts degree at University College of London, but after ... after my first boyfriend, the famous Curtis, dumped me, she pulled me out."

"Why did she pull you out because of that?"

She looked away. "I didn't handle it very well. I never had a boyfriend before or since him. I was so happy that someone wanted to be with me that I threw my whole person into the relationship. I let him take over my life. I spent every minute with him or thinking about him. I even changed my major to be in all his classes. I was ready to go all the way with him, but the first time he saw my leg, he ..." She choked. "He called me disgusting. He said no one could ever find me attractive without a leg."

"He's disgusting," I growled.

"No, Irvine, he's right."

"He's nae right. You've got me in a permanent state of arousal, Willow Summers. You're a total catch, a smokin' hot lass, and don't let anyone tell you otherwise. Pricks like him just want you to feel bad about yourself, because it gives him power over you. If I met him, I'd cut his prick off, so he'd nae be hard again."

Willow looked up at me then, and her tiny smile tugged at something in my chest. I pulled her tight against me, thinking how lonely her life must have been. I wanted to take her pain and tear it to pieces, to hurt all those who hurt her, starting with her parents and ending with this bastard Curtis. I gripped her body fiercely, wanting to hold her until she had no memory that wasn't our bodies touching.

"Finish your story about your ma," I said softly.

"Mum got it in her head that she could save others from a similar fate, so she made me tell the story of my father's attack, over and over again. Not the werewolf part," Willow said quickly, her face clouding over. "But the part about him being a brute. We've been in every tabloid newspaper and shock reporter and daytime radio show that would have us. Everywhere I went, people recognised me from Mum's stories. It got to the point where London celebrities were hiring me just so they could say they booked the 'peg-leg wedding planner'."

Rage burned in my veins for what she'd endured at her mother's hand. I understood now her fear of others knowing about her leg, even about the two of us. "That's why you wanted everything to be secret."

"I've been living with secrets for so long, it's a big deal to me." Willow stared at the sky. "I ran away, Irvine. I taught myself to drive in secret. I had to have lessons to learn how to use the lever in my car, and I snuck out while my mum was at her weekly tarot reading. The day I got my license I packed up my things, emptied my bank account, and left London behind me. She had to come home and find me gone, and a note telling her that I needed to find my own way. I must've hurt her so much. You don't know what she's capable of. She's behind this, I'm sure of it."

"Why did you have to leave? Why couldn't you just tell her how you felt?"

"I just ... didn't want to be the freak anymore." Willow's eyes focused on a spot on the other side of the cemetery. I expected her to cry, but her eyes were dry. "I wanted to pretend to be a whole person, a normal person with a proper life. I should have known that was a foolish dream."

"Aye, it is, but only because you're nae normal. You're extraordinary, like a star going supernova, a meteor shower burning up the sky. You, Willow Summers, need to stop calling yourself a freak, or a broken person, because to me—" I paused. If I said what I was thinking, I could never take it back.

"What?" Willow whispered. "Irvine, what?"

I kissed her. I threw all the fire and rage inside me into the kiss, pouring myself into her. Willow rose up to meet me, devouring my lips with hers. Her hands knitted around my neck, tracing the muscles of my shoulders.

The energy sizzled around us, drawing us together. The outside world ceased to exist. All that was real was the fact that Willow Summers was in my arms, and her lips were pressed to mine, and her tongue was warm and adventurous, and all was right with the world ...

... until I tasted salt on her lips, and noticed the thin trail of her tears down her cheeks.

I pulled back. "What's wrong?" I wiped the tears from her cheek. "Did I hurt you?"

"No, I ..." Willow wiped at her face. "It's nothing."

"I'm doing my best work here." I stuck out my lip. "You're making me feel inadequate."

That got me a thin smile. "I'm sorry."

"Dinnae apologise. Do you want to tell me what's wrong?"

Willow shook her head. She sat back, breaking the bond between us. She adjusted that sexy black top, her face and neck flushed with heat, breathing hard. "I have to get back," she said. "I have a client meeting."

"You gonnae be okay on your own?"

She nodded. "Thank you, for showing me this. I didn't mean to—"

"I said, dinnae apologise."

This time, I was awarded with a genuine smile that made my chest tighten. "Thank you for everything, Irvine."

"For you, Willow Summers, there is nothing I wouldnae do. Come on." I stood up, and offered her my hand. "Let's get you back to that client."

13

WILLOW

I hadn't lied to Irvine – I really did have to meet with a marquee hire company in Crooks Worthy. But it was just as well. Being there with him, hearing about what Ryan and Alex had done, about the mutts, and all those things he said about me ... so much of what I'd known about shifters was wrong. I felt all twisted up inside, and that wasn't good when Irvine was staring at me with that hungry look in his eyes.

I could tell he was disappointed. We drove back without a word, and he kept his eyes on the road – no sneaking glances at me the way he had on the way out here. I'd only picked up on it because I'd been checking him out even worse.

Irvine dropped me off at my flat. "You sure you're going to be okay?"

"I'll be fine. There are heaps of people around. The guy wouldn't dare try anything in broad daylight." Irvine's eyes drooped, and for the first time, I noticed they looked a little bloodshot. "Please, go and get some sleep. You deserve it."

"Will you stay with me again tonight?" he asked.

"I don't know," I said, honestly. "I need to think. I'll call you this evening and we'll discuss it."

He winked. "That gives me a few hours to plan my methods of persuasion."

"No. It gives you a few hours to *sleep*. Please, Irvine. You're no good to me if you haven't slept in two days."

Odd how after only a few days of knowing him, I understood exactly what would convince him. He had a protective nature, and he wouldn't do anything for himself, but if another person needed him, he'd step up without hesitation.

Irvine ran his finger along my cheek. My whole body lit up. Damn, how did his touch have such power over me?

"Take care of yourself, Willow Summers," he murmured. "You're too special to lose."

His grey eyes bore into me, as if he saw straight into my soul. I almost didn't leave him, but a car honked behind me, startling me from the trance.

"Bye." I pulled away and raced across the street, before I changed my mind. I had to climb over the police tape to reach the stairs to my apartment. My stomach twisted with fear, but when I unlocked the door, the apartment was still untouched.

I had a quick shower, sitting on the stool I used in the stall to keep my balance while I soaped myself down. As my hands trailed over my body, I imagined what it would be like to see Irvine's hands there instead. The ache inside me pulsed with renewed urgency, and it was all I could do not to turn the shower head between my legs and sate it however I could.

Instead, I turned the shower on the coldest setting and washed the soap off as quickly as I could.

I changed into a new, more professional outfit, grabbed my purse, went back downstairs (doing my best to ignore the police officers who were scrabbling around in the shop), and climbed into my car. I drove to Crooks Worthy with Irvine on the brain.

It wasn't until I was halfway to Crooks Worthy that I realised

I'd forgotten my organiser. Damn, Irvine Baird was messing with my head in a *big* way.

The marquee company took me on a tour of their factory and hiring centre. I walked through the warehouse in a haze, not hearing a single word they said about capacity or lighting options or mock cathedral windows. Around every corner, Irvine stared at me with those vivid grey eyes. The warmth of his lips still lingered against mine. My body still ached for everything he could give me.

As I drove back to Crookshollow after the meeting, my mind whirred with possibilities. Even when I was miles away from her, with a completely new name, my mother was still running my life. Despite my own good feelings about them, her voice in my head told me I couldn't trust Irvine and his friends. And Irvine ... he was supposed to be a monster, but when I looked into his eyes, all I saw was someone who looked right back.

He was the first person who really saw *me* – not the peg-legged wedding planner or the daughter of the crazy werewolf lady – but he reached right through into my heart.

And he *wanted* me. He'd seen my leg, and still he wanted me. I'd never thought I'd get the chance to be with someone ... but Irvine was offering that.

Carol Winters would've run a mile from the werewolf who called her beautiful, but I wasn't Carol Winters any longer. I could be whoever I wanted to be. I could ask for what I wanted, and bugger it all to hell, but what I wanted was him.

I cruised down the main street of Crookshollow. Instead of turning off onto Honeysuckle Road to return to my flat, I yanked the wheel hard around, and parked in front of the Family Planning Clinic.

My hands gripped the wheel so tightly, my knuckles turned white. My heart clenched with terror. Despite this, a shaky smile played across my lips.

I, Willow Summers, was going to lose my virginity. And I knew just the wolf for the job.

14

IRVINE

*B*ANG BANG.

My eyes flew open, my whole body instantly on alert. A lifetime of watching over my shoulder for the Macleans had hardened my instincts.

Someone's banging on the door.

No one apart from the other pack members ken I was living in one of the rented artist's cabins in Crookshollow Forest. Only Caleb came to visit me, and he wouldn't knock since I'd given him a key. I bolted upright, my wolf clawing against my skin, ready to leap into action in case my visitor had violent intent.

I grabbed the wrought-iron poker from the ash bucket beside the stove. Brandishing it at my side, I approached the door.

It could be Willow's stalker, here to finish me off before I can get to him.

My body tensed. I slipped across the room and flattened myself against the kitchen wall. The window over the bench looked out onto the cabin's tiny porch. I'd pulled the shutter down before going to bed, but a tiny tear on the edge gave me a clear view of who was standing out there.

It was Willow Summers.

I dropped the poker on the table, grabbed a pair of jeans off the floor and tugged them on over my rising cock. I debated putting on a shirt, but then decided against it. In two strides, I'd crossed the tiny cabin and flung open the door.

Willow leapt back as the door flew open, grabbing at the porch railing to steady herself. She wore a crisp white shirt, perfectly tailored to fit tight across her tiny breasts, and a pair of wide-legged suit pants. Her brown hair tumbled loose over her shoulders, and she bit down on her lower lip as she studied me.

What's she doing here? We weren't supposed to meet until later tonight.

"Willow Summers, this *is* a surprise," I said as I stared down at her. Willow glanced up, her huge brown eyes locking with mine. The electric charge sizzled between us, and it took all my self-control not to sweep her in my arms. "Did something happen? Did the stalker come back?"

"No," she whispered, breathing hard. She dropped her gaze, staring at my bare chest and avoiding my eyes. "Can I come in?"

"Sure." I stepped aside and held the door open. Willow shuffled inside with that slight limp of hers, still looking at her feet. I kicked aside some clothes and pulled out a chair for her at the rickety table under the other window. "You want some tea or coffee?"

"Y—y—yes. Tea, please." Willow was still whispering. She didn't take the chair, but hung back beside the door, shifting her weight from foot to foot. She was nervous. I wondered why. She hadn't seemed this timid last night.

I went to the kitchen and put the kettle on, and wiped out two mugs. While I fished around for tea bags, I waited for Willow to start talking, but she didn't. Finally, I set down two steaming cups of tea on the table, and sank into one of the chairs. I raised my cup to my lips. "So, Willow Summers, I thought I wouldnae have the pleasure of your company until later this evening. Is there something I can do for ye?"

"Yes, actually." Willow grabbed her elbow with one hand, her fingers digging into her own skin. Finally, she looked up. Her eyes flicked over my body, hovering on my naked chest before settling on my face. Those deep brown pools swirled with emotions, but I couldn't read what she was thinking.

"Well, go on. What is it you're after?"

She bit her lip. "I ... I'm ready."

"For?"

"For you to take my virginity."

15

WILLOW

I can't believe I'm doing this.

As soon as I'd said the words, I wished I could take them back. A violent heat rushed to my cheeks, and I knew I must be as red as a tomato. I itched to turn around and run away, but that weird magnetic energy between us urged me to stay.

"Willow Summers, you do ken how to surprise a man." Irvine's eyes burned into me. In the daylight, he looked even sexier, although that might have something to do with that fact he was only wearing a tight pair of jeans that left nothing to the imagination. His torso was even more muscular than I'd imagined, and every inch was covered in those intricate tattoos. A huge crest on his shoulder showed a crouching wolf, teeth bared, and the latin epithet AMOR VINCIT OMNIA. A thin line of dark hair led from Irvine's belly button down to the waist of his jeans, and my eyes couldn't help but flick over the bulge of his crotch. A surge of heat mingled with the fear inside me.

No turning back now, Willow. You're here. You're doing this thing ... with a werewolf.

Unless he doesn't want to. Maybe he's changed his mind. He's gonna tell me I'm an idiot and he finds me disgusting and he would never even be able to get hard—

"Willow …" There was a note of sadness in Irvine's voice.

This is it. This is where he rejects me.

I closed my eyes, not wanting to see Irvine's face crumple with disgust like Curtis' had. "Please, before you say anything, just … hear me out. I know I said I wasn't ready, but I've changed my mind. I came to Crookshollow to experience freedom, and it's time I truly embraced what that means. I'm not good at asking for what I want, and I know I'm … not like other girls. I'm not beautiful. I'm broken." My throat caught on the word. *Please don't let me start crying in front of him.* "But I'm tired of feeling as though I'm missing something. So if you can stomach being with me and if you promise that you won't turn into a wolf in front of me … then I … um, want to be with you."

I dared a peek at Irvine. He stared at me with those daring eyes, silent as stone.

My face flared even hotter. "Um … so … right. I went and got the injection today, and an STI test, so we don't even have to worry about protection, provided you're clean … so, if you're worried about—"

"I'm clean." Irvine's deep voice boomed inside my head. "And I'm not worried about that. I'm worried about you thinking I cannae … *stomach* being with you?"

"You can't have forgotten that I'm missing a leg."

"I ken," he said. "I also remember I told you that you were beautiful."

I hunted Irvine's face for any sign that he was lying, or leading me on to be cruel. A boy had done that to me in high school – Raymond Keen. He'd told me all sorts of nice things – I had pretty hair, he loved my eyes, he thought it was cool that I was the smartest in the class. All the while, he and his friends were laughing about me behind my back. Raymond kissed me at a party – my first and only kiss until Curtis – but while I was swooning over him, he was taking a selfie with his phone of him touching my leg, which he sent to everyone at my school.

But Irvine's eyes were warm, and they burned with an intensity I'd never seen before. My stomach flipped. He looked ... *hungry*. And the same hunger was rumbling inside me.

"So ..." I tore my gaze away from his, staring down at my feet. Piles of crumpled clothing hid the rough-cut floorboards of Irvine's cabin. "Will you do this for me?"

A hand caught my shoulder, turning me back around. Strong fingers held my chin, lifting my face up. "Willow, look at me," Irvine said.

I turned. Irvine's face was inches from mine. I could see the shadow of stubble on his chin, the sharp angle of his nose. The silver coin still hung around his neck. That hungry look in his eyes burned into me, making an ache spread through my stomach.

"You're a very fascinating woman." Irvine's gaze burned into mine. His lips were so close to mine that I could feel the heat of his breath. "I find you utterly ... enchanting. And I'm nae going to deny that I would very much like to tear all your clothes off and fuck you up against a wall right now."

I gulped. His words rolled over me, that rich, thick Scottish accent shooting an arc of desire down my spine. The ache in my stomach throbbed with need.

"But ..." Irvine's expression looked pained. "I cannae have a relationship right now. There's something very important I have to do here in Crookshollow, and I cannae have any distractions, as welcome a distraction as you would be."

"I'm not asking for anything serious," I said. "I don't think I can handle that right now, either. So this can just be a casual thing."

Willow Summers can do casual. She's a totally casual kind of girl.

Carol Winters, however, is ready to throw up on her shoes.

"Aye, just a casual thing." Irvine reached up with his hand, and his thumb stroked my chin. That touch was the first we'd had since the kiss this morning, and it was like a jolt of electricity shooting through my body, drawing out the full force of the ache within me. "You're okay with that?"

"I'm definitely okay with that." I gulped as his finger traced across my lips. My whole body lit up, desperate for his hands to be on my skin, for all the things that he could show me. My stomach throbbed with a hunger that matched that in his eyes. "If you … if you promise that you won't shift. Not in front of me."

"Aye, I can promise you that. But I have one more question." The corner of Irvine's mouth turning up into a wolfish grin. "You ken what I am, so why me?"

"I—I—I don't know. Because you're the first person who's wanted to."

"I dinnae believe that."

Because you're the first person who's ever seen me. But I couldn't say that. I pressed my trembling hands against my thighs. "I'm a bit—"

"Terrified?"

I nodded.

In a moment, Irvine closed the gap between us, his naked chest pressed against mine. He wrapped one arm around me, his palm pressed against my back. My skin burned where he touched me, slivers of molten energy dancing across my body.

His lips hovered so close to mine, his breath caressed me. Every pore on his face stood out in high relief. My body froze, a perfect storm of tension and terror and pure, diabolical lust.

"Your first time should be special, Willow Summers," Irvine whispered, his words rumbling through my core, "I promise I'll going to make sure you remember it *forever.*"

"I … er …"

Irvine's lips covered mine, and the stammering nonsense I was about to spit out fled my head. Nothing existed except that kiss – the warmth of his lips pressed against mine, hard and urgent as he teased my mouth open and slipped his tongue inside. The heat of his mouth drew me in, so I melted against him, drowning in his raw energy and primal scent.

Irvine's hands snaked across my back, tracing the line of my bra through the thin linen shirt I'd worn. The ache in my stomach spread down between my legs.

Kissing Curtis had been *hot,* but it wasn't anything like *this.*

Irvine's hands moved over my body, his fingers snaking along the hem of my shirt. Electricity jolted through me as his skin brushed mine. I raised my hands around his neck, drawing us closer still. My fingers traced the thick muscles of his neck and shoulders, wanting to commit every inch of him to memory. I touched the leather throng that hung around his neck. His heady wolf scent drifted over me, but instead of being frightening, it intoxicated me. My head swam with the sensations of him.

So far, so good. What happens next?

I tried to recall my favourite sex scenes from movies, so I'd know what to do. My hands swept across Irvine's chest, drawing the lines of his tattoos and the edges of his tight muscles. God, he felt so good. Who knew a man could feel that good? I traced the waist of his jeans. My fingers trembled as I unbuttoned his fly.

"Whoa there, lassie." Irvine grinned, grabbing my wrists and pulling my hands away. "While I admire your enthusiasm, you dinnae have to go *quite* so fast. We've got all the time in the world."

"Don't you have important shifter things to do?" I gasped. Irvine laid a trail of kisses along my neck, sending a shiver of delight through my body.

"When a beautiful woman is in your bed, nothing else is important," he growled, cupping my cheek and tipping my face up. His lips assaulted mine again, and I drank in the ecstasy of his attention.

Irvine walked me backward until my skin grazed the side of his bed. His strong hands gripped my hips, and he half lifted, half pushed me back onto the bed, laying me down on my back.

The bed was softer than it looked, and Irvine's wolfish scent danced over the blankets. A flutter of fear circled my stomach as I lay back, knowing what was coming soon, but then Irvine crawled up beside me and his lips found mine again. The fear disappeared as I sank into the kiss.

Irvine's leg pressed up against mine, and something hard dug into my thigh. It took me a few moments to realise it was his penis. He was hard as a rock. For me. He was hard *for me*.

My heart skipped a beat. *I can't believe this is happening. I can't believe he's real.*

Irvine trailed kisses down my neck, pulling aside the collar of my shirt to snake his tongue along my collarbone. Every touch of his lips set my skin on fire. We were going to burn up together like comets entering the atmosphere.

He reached up with his fingers, and grasped the top button of my shirt. His eyes met mine, and he lifted his lips from my skin. "You sure about this?"

I nodded.

"And today's the big day? You dinnae want to wait—"

I shook my head.

Irvine grinned, his whole face lighting up. "Good."

His fingers grazed my bare skin as one by one he undid my buttons. Nerves fluttered in my stomach. He folded back my shirt, and tugged it free. As Irvine stared down at me, I thanked myself that I'd thought to change into my nicest black bra and panties before I came over. He gave me that wild grin of his again, and my nerves surged.

He's looking at me. He sees me.

Nothing in his eyes said he was disgusted or scared of me. All I saw was that cold intensity. Irvine laid his lips on my sternum, his eyes locked on mine as he laid a gentle kiss upon my skin. He reached behind me. Almost without thinking, I lifted my torso. Irvine's fingers grazed my skin as he pulled off my bra.

I sucked in my breath. This was the first time since Curtis that someone had seen my breasts. My stump tingled, and my stomach danced. That wild grin stretched further across Irvine's face, and my heart flipped.

"You like what you see?" The words came out much sassier than I felt.

"I do indeed. Nice ink." He traced a finger over the bleeding rose. "I recognise Elinor's work."

"Yeah. I had it done a few weeks agooooooooohhh ..." My words turned into a moan as Irvine bent down and took my nipple in his mouth.

Oh, it was exquisite. Irvine's tongue drew across my nipple, sending shivers through my body. He started slow and delicate, then dragged his teeth across my sensitive skin. A sharp pain flared up, but it only intensified the ache inside me. Irvine's eyes remained locked on mine, and his hands roamed across my body as he licked and sucked until the ache inside me grew into a raging inferno.

He moved to the other nipple, giving it the same attention. While he licked, his fingers danced over my chest, lingering over the fly of my trousers. The first button popped open. Another flicker of nerves made me gasp, and Irvine removed his hand, continuing his attentions.

A few moments later it was back again, and the next button

popped off. I sucked in a breath, and a flare of phantom pain shot through my leg.

Don't panic. People have sex every single day. It's a perfectly normal, totally not-scary thing, and most people don't even get to do it with a hot guy like Irvine. You managed to get this far, so don't chicken out now.

I tried to fight through the fear as Irvine got all the buttons undone, flipping the corners of my trousers. I reached down with trembling hands to push them off my hips, but Irvine grabbed my wrist again.

"But I have to remove my—"

"Goddammit, woman, you are impossible. I'm trying to be the gentleman here. Let me unwrap you like a Christmas present and savour every part of you before we get down to business, aye?"

"No, I mean, my prosthesis—"

Irvine leaned back, tearing his warm presence from me. "Oh, shite. I'm sorry."

"No, no, don't be ... I just ... I don't want ..." I reached down, tugging up the hem of my trousers, revealing the ankle pivot of my prosthesis sticking out of the top of my shoe.

"Is it uncomfortable?" Irvine looked on as I rolled up the rest of my trouser leg, revealing the vacuum seal that attached the socket to my stump. "I should have asked."

"No ... I mean, yes, it is uncomfortable sometimes. Not right now ... I just thought—" *I just thought we should get it out of the way now, so you could change your mind once you see my stump and I could get out of here with at least some of my dignity intact.*

"If you're trying to scare me off, it's nae gonnae work." Irvine took my hand from my leg and brought it to his lips. His fingers grazed my knuckles, and an arc of fire shot down my arm. He placed my hand between his legs, right against his hardness. A deep flush crept across my cheeks.

"You feel that?" he growled. "That is how I feel looking at you. Your leg is nae going to change that. Now, will you relax and let me work my magic? You don't have to rush to the finish line. There's so much I still want to do to your body, if you'll let me."

"I—I—"

"Lie back, lassie." He placed his fingers on my stomach, right against the stem of the rose, and pushed me gently back against the bed. "Relax. I got this."

"Okay, but I ..."

I couldn't think of any other words. Irvine hooked his fingers under the edges of my panties, and pulled them and the seat of my trousers over my hips. My stomach tied in a knot as Irvine bent down, and lightly kissed the top of my mound. The touch lit every cell in my body.

Irvine's tongue slid along my length, parting me and searching out deep places I never knew existed. He danced across me, playing me like a fiddle, and boy did my whole body dance.

I lay back against the pillow, letting the waves of pleasure wash over me, relishing the energy coursing through me. I didn't exist. I was no longer a person, only a puddle of firing synapses and aching need.

Irvine's tongue searched deeper, pounding against me. The ache inside me exploded, breaking me apart in a great super-nova of light and heat. Something like pain that wasn't pain at all tore me open, and out spilled every fear and doubt. All that was left was pure, untamed joy.

Maybe I cried out, maybe I clawed the sheets, maybe I spoke in tongues, but I didn't know because I'd left my body behind. I sailed across the galaxy, carried on stardust, riding the wake of pleasure out to the edges of the universe.

When I surfaced, and the room came into focus, Irvine's face peered down at me, his steel eyes catching the moonlight. "So ye liked that, then?" he grinned.

I nodded, unable to speak.

Irvine kissed me. "Plenty more where that came from."

"Mmmmmm." I couldn't wait.

Irvine reached down and rolled my trousers off my legs. Now, I was completely naked, with my prosthesis on full display. With the stardust still in my veins, I barely cared, until Irvine said, "At this point, I'm a bit out of my league."

My leg. The last taboo. The last piece of my armour that had to be cast aside if I was going to rid myself of my virginity.

"Here, let me." I leaned forward and reached for the top of the socket. Irvine watched in interest as I pulled the sock away from the silicone sleeve I wore around my stump. My hands only trembled a little. I felt as though I was standing outside my body, looking over my own shoulder, detached from the action. I broke the vacuum seal, and the leg popped free. I dropped it over the end of the bed, rolled off the sleeve, and tossed that after it.

My stump rested on the bed between us. Just below my right knee, my leg narrowed to a rounded tip of skin and nerves – the place where my leg had been surgically removed after the were-wolf bite had gone septic. I'd been three years old when it happened, and I barely remembered the attack or the surgery – just flashes of teeth and fur and pain, and worried doctors and Mum sobbing and looking down at it in the hospital in horror and begging them to put my foot back.

I studied Irvine's face as he studied the stump. The nerve endings tingled with anticipation. His face shifted, but not with disgust. I could tell he'd never seen an amputation before, not up close like this. "Does it hurt?" he asked, his hands hovering above my leg. "Will I hurt you if I touch you?"

I shook my head. "There are some nerve endings close to the

skin, so it's very sensitive, and sometimes it hurts if I hit it or jolt it, but you don't have to touch it. I know it's creepy."

"Nothing about you is 'creepy.' I want this to be amazing for you, Willow." He looked up, and his eyes burned into mine, deep grey pools where I drowned in his kindness and his desire. "You must tell me if it's good for you."

"I will."

Irvine bent down, and kissed my stump, his lips light on my skin. The nerves collected around his lips, dancing and jolting with delight. He walked his fingers up the inside of my thigh, brushing over my most sensitive skin.

He lay his body over top of me, lowering himself slowly down, letting the warmth of his skin envelop mine. His lips found mine, tender and searching. While he kissed me, Irvine's hands stroked my folds, drawing out the ache once more. The threads of fire that drew me to him wrapped around us, cocooning me in protective heat.

Irvine's hard cock against my leg drove the ache deeper. I pushed my hips wider, and his tip rubbed against me. A flutter of fear danced in my stomach, but it was quickly captured by Irvine's searching lips. He grabbed my hand, resting it by my shoulder and knitting his fingers in mine. He slid inside me. Only a little.

"You okay?"

I nodded.

He pushed in a little deeper. I expected pain, but all I felt was the pressing urgency of the ache, begging him to give me everything.

"How about now?"

"Just get in there, wolf." I grinned. "I can take it."

Grinning back at me, Irvine pushed himself all the way inside me in one solid stroke. I cried out as a sharp pain coursed through me, but in moments, the ache inside me had taken away the pain. His length felt glorious, like it was perfectly sculpted for me. Irvine held still, allowing me a few precious moments to savour the fullness of him. Our lips met, and I devoured him.

Irvine moved against me, slowly at first, squeezing my hand as he thrust right up inside me. He drew himself back, his whole body moving against mine. His fingers squeezed mine. With my free hand, I drew circles over his back and stroked his ass, enjoying the way his muscles tensed and relaxed as we moved together.

My body lit up as the stardust in my veins stirred to life. Every muscle and sinew shimmered with newly awoken feeling. Irvine moved faster, grunting as he thrust deep inside me. I lifted my thighs to meet him, relishing every thrust.

As Irvine rose up to thrust again, his foot brushed my stump, sending a shock through the nerves that still remained there. I expected it to jolt me from the moment, but instead, it drew me deeper into the sensations. I ground my hips against Irvine, begging for more, deeper, faster, harder.

The ache inside me spread out from my stomach, racing down my arms, exploding as it reached my core. I came again, the waves crashing through my body as Irvine drove himself deeper still.

My nails dug into Irvine's back. In response, his mouth claimed mine, the strength of his kiss forcing my head back. I drank in every sensation – his scent deepening, his cock stiffening inside me, his own fingers digging into my skin.

With a groan, Irvine came too, his whole body stiffening as he drove himself deep. He collapsed against me, his body shuddering as his own pleasure rolled through him. His warm skin grew hot against mine. I wrapped my arms around him, clinging to him like he would float away at any moment if I didn't.

"Willow Summers," he murmured against my lips. "I cannae feel my legs."

I laughed, giddy with the high of my orgasm. Irvine rolled off me, wrapping me in his arms and pressing me back against his chest. His breath brushed against my ear.

One thing was for sure. My mother was wrong. Sleeping with a werewolf wasn't a deadly mistake. It was the most glorious thing I'd ever done.

I want more.

16

IRVINE

*W*illow fell asleep against my shoulder. I watched her chest rise and fall, marvelling that such a simple, biological motion could be so beautiful. At the end of my bed, the prosthetic limb leaned against the kitchen cabinet.

Well, that was unexpected.

Willow Summers, the mate I thought I'd never be able to have, was right here in my bed, her supple body pressed against mine. She was so timid, and yet to come here and ask what she asked of me ... there was a fire in her belly yet. I wanted to see more of that fire.

To think, no man nor woman had ever before wanted her ... except for Bianca, of course, not that it counted. Bianca wanted everyone and everything when she was drunk. Before I met Willow Summers, I hadnae thought there were any virgins left in Jolly Old England.

She's not a virgin anymore.

Willow snorted, and leaned deeper into my shoulder, sending a spasm of pain through my already throbbing muscles. As lovely as it was to have her warm body against mine, it was hell on the shoulder after a while. With a bit of wriggling, I managed to slide my arm out from beneath her, and rolled off the bed without waking her up. I glanced out the window – the sun was high in the sky, sending golden shafts of light down through the very tops of the ancient trees.

We'd fucked at least three more times last night, before finally collapsing against each other, too exhausted to even talk about what had happened between us. Not surprisingly, my stomach rumbled. It must be well past lunchtime. I went to the kitchen to cook us something to eat.

When I had a pot of spaghetti bolognese on the stove, I sat down at the table, my eyes wandering over Willow's body. Her skinny frame stretched across the bed. Her hair hung in dark waves over her shoulders, falling over her tiny, perfect breasts. Her stump was hidden beneath the edge of the sheet. I ken the sheet hadn't been there when we'd gone to sleep. I suspected she'd woken up at some point and pulled it over herself. Even after everything that had passed between us, she didn't want me to see her leg.

The prosthesis stood at the end of the bed, where she had dropped it. Curiosity piqued at me. I picked it up and turned it over in my hands. Strange, how light it was. I tapped the pylon. Carbon fibre, of course. Fascinating how the vacuum seal kept the socket worked, and how the—

"Hey, don't touch that."

I whipped my head up, guilt surging through my body. Willow sat upright in bed, glaring at me with narrowed eyes. I set the prosthesis down.

"If you want to know something about my leg, just ask me." She turned away, hunting on the floor for her bra and shirt. She started to pull them on.

"I didnae mean to offend."

She still wouldn't look at me. "I know. I just ... this is all very new to me. You might find out something that will make you detest me."

"That's nae going to happen." I held out a plate as a peace offering. "I made you lunch, if you're hungry."

Finally, Willow looked up. I was relieved to see there were no tears in her eyes, but the expression on her face was pensive. "You want me to stay for lunch?"

"Aye, of course." I ladled out some pasta and bolognese for myself, and sat down on at the small table under the window. "Why wouldn't I?"

"I didn't know food was part of the deal with one-night-stands ... or three-in-a-night-stands."

"Aye, this may come as a shock, but there's a whole range of degrees between 'in a committed relationship' and 'fucking and fleeing.' Sometimes they can include food, or other crazy stuff like talking and going on dates in public."

"Really?"

"Aye, yes." I took a big bite of pasta. I'd added some jalapeños, so it had a real kick. As I ate, I studied Willow. Her left foot peeked out of the side of the bed, her toes small and the arch of her foot impossibly delicate. She still kept her stump hidden under the blankets. Her hair fell over her face as she ate, and she didn't bother to tuck it behind her ears. I realised she kept it long and thick precisely so she could hide behind it.

I still ken next to nothing about Willow, except that she was a wedding planner, she'd come to Crookshollow from London, her amputation had been caused by her father, who was a were-wolf, she'd been a virgin, and she was intoxicatingly, devastatingly beautiful. I desperately wanted to tell her that she was my mate, and that the attraction she felt that had compelled her to my door had to do with the fact that we were destined to be together. But I had a feeling that wouldn't go down well.

Even now, the bond sizzled between us. My body ached to

hold her again. Willow must've felt it too. She darted glances at me in between bites of scran. Neither of us spoke for a time. I didn't trust my tongue to speak without breaking the fragile connection we had made.

Willow set down her spoon. She bit her lip again. "Can we … " she started. Through her hair, I could make out a flush across her cheeks. "No, it's dumb."

"Do you always second-guess everything you say?"

She looked away, fixing her gaze on the wall behind the bed. "Pretty much."

"You dinnae have to do that around me. Go on. Spit it out."

Willow kept staring at the wall. Even the back of her neck had turned red. "Can we do this again …"

"You liked my scran that much, aye?"

The flush on her neck deepened. "I just … I know we're still casual, but I … would like more bolognese."

"Willow—"

"I'm sorry. I knew it, I knew I was hopeless." Her voice cracked.

I crossed the room and sat down beside Willow, grabbing her under her chin and turning her head around. Tears streamed down her face.

I didn't ask her why she was crying. I suspected I knew the answer. It was the same reason someone as gorgeous and fun and interesting as her was still a virgin at 23. She was terrified of rejection. She thought no one could ever want her just because she didn't have a leg.

If I ever met that bastard ex of hers, I'd tear his throat out. Her father's, too.

Well, I sure as hell wasn't going to be the reason she cried. There was no way Willow was getting any rejection from me.

"You present an interesting proposal, Willow Summers. Let me get this straight. What you're saying is that you'd like to sleep together some more, whenever either of us want to, but you dinnae want to have a relationship? And you're somehow worried I'd think this was a shite idea?"

She nodded, looking miserable.

"There's only one appropriate response when a beautiful woman makes this proposal, and that is, 'Yaaahoo!'"

Willow smiled, her whole face lighting up. I loved seeing her smile almost as much as I loved her biting her lip or screwing her face up in ecstasy. And it looked as if I'd get to experience all those things a lot more from now on.

"You can't shift around me, *ever,* or it's over."

"Aye. I agree. So, we have an accord." I put out my hand, and Willow shook it firmly.

"You're on, Irvine Baird." She wiped her eyes with the back of her sleeve.

"When do you want to do this again?"

"Um ... as soon as possible?" Her eyes widened.

"You're in charge here. If you want to have another go, just say so. It's nae a question."

"Then, yes, I'd like to do this again tonight."

I kissed her, drawing the scent of her deep inside me, wanting to commit every part of her to memory. "Alas, but I'll be outae commission for a few days. The full moon is upon us, and I made a promise to a beautiful woman that she wouldnae see me shift."

Her face fell slightly, but she didn't shrink away. "Then as soon as you shift back. You know how to find me."

"As *soon* as I'm back, aye? The very *second*? From novice to enthusiast in a single night, Willow Summers, you do amaze me."

Willow's tongue wound around mine, exploring my mouth. She sank against me, deepening the kiss, but then pulled back, as though something had startled her. "Are you going to tell any of your friends about me … and us?" she asked.

"I hadnae intended to. Why, do you want me to tell them we're having wild casual sex out of wedlock?"

"No!" she yelled, then clamped her hand over her mouth.

Something prickled against the back of my throat. "Is something the matter?"

She shook her head. "I didn't mean to insult your friends. I like them a lot. I just … I'd like to get to know them a bit more before I spill more of my secrets, especially if my mother's spy is skulking around. I'd like to tell them myself, if that's okay?"

I nodded. "Of course. I only hope that when you *do* tell Elinor and Alex, you make sure to give them the most *explicit* details. I'm tired of hearing about Ryan's enormous cock or Eric's dextrous musician fingers. It's time they discovered they're missing out on the love of a true Scotsman."

Willow smiled as she leaned in to kiss me again. "I promise to leave nothing out."

"Are you sure you're gonnae be okay? That stalker of yours might still be hanging around your flat."

Willow shook her head. "No, I'll be fine. It's weird, but he doesn't scare me so much any more." She gave me a thin smile, and I felt a burst of pride in her. She grabbed her prosthesis from the end of the bed. Her face reddened as she rolled on the sleeve over her liner, sealed the vacuum and swung herself off the bed, rocking unsteadily as she tugged on her jeans. I noticed that she didn't ask me not to look.

"Until we meet again." Willow leaned over as I held the door open, and her lips grazed my cheek. The gentle touch burned against my skin.

"Aye, Willow Summers, until then." I loved the taste of her name on my lips. I leaned against the cabin door, watching

Willow disappear into the forest. In the daylight, the slight limp caused by her prosthesis was even more obvious.

As soon as she disappeared from view, I shut the door behind me and sank into my chair. The heat of our connection still surged in my veins, battling with my wolf, who was already desperate to be free. I rubbed the stubble on my chin.

I ken this was a bad idea. I should have told her to stay away from me. She's already been hurt enough.

Willow had no idea she was my fated mate, and that her destiny was to be part of the world that had already taken so much from her. She didn't know that very soon werewolves and other shifters were going to be visible in the world. And I ken from our visit to the cemetery yesterday that she definitely wasn't open to the idea.

I sighed. If I told Willow about the pack's plan, not only would I be betraying Caleb's trust, but I'd ensure she never came within a foot of me ever again. I'd lose my one chance at being with her. But if I didn't tell her, I'd be deliberately keeping it from her just so we could keep going on with our affair. Both options were shite.

She's going to find out anyway, I reminded myself.

But there's no telling how long it will take Robbie to find the ring. It could be months. By then, I might have convinced her to feel differently about werewolves. After all, she came to the pub with the others, and she was here in my cabin, shagging my brains out instead of running in terror, so given time she could come around to it.

The longer you hide it, the worse it will be when she finds out.

My head throbbed. I rubbed my temples as conflicting thoughts swirled around my brain. *Willow Summers, what in God's name am I going to do about you?*

17

WILLOW

There's so much I still want to do to your body, if you'll let me.

Irvine's words from the previous night replayed over and over as I waited on the porch of Marshell House. Warm sunlight poured down upon me, as if the weather itself had realised a miracle had taken place last night.

I, Willow Summers, was no longer a virgin.

At the thought of it, I grinned wider. I couldn't seem to wipe that grin off my face. Every time I pictured his hands on my body, his broad shoulders hovering over me, the feeling of his cock buried deep inside me ...

Even though I'd had a full day to process the event on my own, while Irvine wandered around the forest as a wolf, the thrill still hadn't worn off. I wanted to skip around the front lawn. I wanted to shout to the whole world to rejoice in this miracle. Instead, I shifted the box of wedding magazines and my planning folder into my other hand and rung the ancient bell again.

"Coming!" Elinor cried from deep in the house. A moment later, she threw the door open.

As usual, her beauty stopped me short. Elinor had one of those stunning heart-shaped faces, and enormous brown eyes framed by dark-rimmed glasses. Her body was all luscious curves accentuated by tailored clothing. Elinor would be marrying rock violinist Eric Marshell in a massive wedding in the back garden of Marshell House. Eric's band would be performing for two hundred guests, including close friends and family and a whole swathe of important record executives. Unlike Bianca's crazy art bash faux-wedding, Elinor and Eric's was going to be pure gothic romantic, complete with a six-tier cake finished with blood-red roses and a banner saying, "Til death do us part."

Their wedding wasn't for several months yet – they needed to plan it for when Eric wasn't away touring – but we needed to get a start on it now if I wanted the marquee booked and the other preparations made. I was pretty excited about the project, which we'd started discussing at the pub the other night, especially since I thought Elinor and I might be ... maybe ... possibly ... becoming friends, but it did mean yet another connection to Caleb's pack and whatever they were planning.

Don't think about it. It's none of your business. As far as Elinor knows, you are completely oblivious to shifters, and the existence of Irvine's cock. You're just Willow Summers, wedding planner and totally normal, not-sleeping-with-a-werewolf, two-legged lass ... I mean, girl.

Elinor threw her arms around me. "It's great to see you, in a much less dramatic setting. Come on in."

I followed Elinor through the house, noting the drab Victorian wallpaper and dark-wood furnishings that dominated the home her fiancé had inherited. She was starting to put her own touches everywhere, recovering the chairs with sumptuous velvet and replacing the stuffy frowning portraits with modern art. I recognised her own hand on a large painting beside the coatrack, of a girl in a diaphanous gown swimming in a pool under the moonlight, with a wolf watching from the shore beyond. I started to comment on it, then changed my mind, in case it started a discussion about wolves that I didn't want to have.

Elinor boiled the kettle and invited me out into the conservatory on the back of the house, overlooking the expansive lawn where her wedding marquee would be set up. Various fruit and deciduous trees were scattered around the perimeter of the lawn, and in the far corner of the garden, a small stone mausoleum provided a suitably gothic backdrop. I buttoned my coat against the crisp breeze, and Elinor handed me a blanket to place over my legs as she settled herself in the chair opposite me.

"I love sitting out here in the evenings," she said, pouring the tea and opening a *Bewitching Bites* bakery box to reveal a selection of cheesecakes and lemon tarts. "It feels so peaceful, especially after all the noise of the shop."

"Any news about *Resurrection Ink*?"

"The insurance company are giving me the runaround, of course. And the police are completely baffled, but at least no one was there when it happened." She studied my face as she sipped her tea. "You seem a little ... distracted today. Even worse than yesterday."

"No, I ..." I always got so tongue-tied around Elinor. She was so elegant and beautiful. Her and Bianca and all of their friends – they were like the cool kids back at my high school. The girls I so desperately wanted to be.

"Did you see anything else?"

I shook my head.

"Don't make me guess here, Willow." Elinor set down her tea. "It's Irvine, isn't it?"

My face flared with heat, giving me away. Elinor grinned. "I *knew* it. You guys are shagging. It's so obvious."

The heat spread down my neck. I stared at the cup in my hands, unable to meet Elinor's eyes. "I shouldn't talk about it."

"No way. You're not getting away with that nonsense. Tell me everything. How is he in the sack? I always imagined he's intense, Mr Grumpy-Scottish-Git."

I nodded, aware that my face must've been as red as a beet-root. *So much for keeping it secret.* "He was pretty spectacular."

"Spectacular, aye?" Elinor pushed the box toward me. "That deserves a second cheesecake. How did you even meet him? I can't believe you didn't say anything to me earlier."

"I met him at Bianca's wedding," I mumbled. "And we wanted to keep it secret. That is, Irvine did. He thought it would reflect badly on his dedication to Caleb's pack. So if you could—"

"Well, that was a silly idea, seeing as you two couldn't keep your hands off each other the other day at the shop."

"That's not true." At the thought of Irvine's naked body pressed against mine, the heat in my skin flared into red hot torture.

"Come on, Willow. The two of you tried to pretend you arrived at separate times, and that you'd stayed the night with some nameless girlfriend, but you were wearing the same clothes you had on at the pub. I may have been distracted, but I can still see what's right in front of me."

My whole body burned. Elinor laughed and hit my knee. I jumped in fright. If her hand had been an inch further down, she would have felt my prosthesis.

"You don't have to jump out of your skin. I'll keep my mouth shut, but don't be surprised if everyone else hasn't already figured it out." Elinor smiled. She must've thought my jump was about her figuring out that Irvine and I had been together. "I think it's awesome. No offence, but you look like you could do with a bit of fun."

"Yeah." My face flushed even darker. "I could."

"I wish I could have a little fun." Elinor slumped down on the sofa. "Eric's spending the week at the studio in London, working on the band's new album, and it's been nothing but drama ever since the shop got trashed. Honestly, I've barely had a chance to go through the samples you sent over. Bianca and Robbie broke up."

"What?" Irvine hadn't mentioned that. As far as I knew, they were suddenly madly in love.

"Well, I guess they didn't break up, since technically they weren't actually together. But it looks like Robbie was the one who trashed our shop. He's been jealous of this other guy, Rolf, who's been staying at The Prim, and he tried to pin the crime on him. But Eric saw Robbie hanging around the shop when he came home last night. Caleb thinks the guy you saw was Robbie, as well. He was going to come talk to you when he had a chance but he's uuh, tied up at the moment."

You mean he's roaming the forest with Irvine.

Elinor leaned forward. "Do you think it could have been Robbie you saw?"

"Maybe … I don't know …" The guy had similar build, and the same buzzed haircut as Robbie. But even in the dark, surely I would have recognised Robbie's face?

"So anyway, Bianca tossed him out, but now she's in a total state. And as well as dealing with the insurance company, I'm cleaning her snot and tears out of my favourite clothes and holding her head over the toilet while she throws up all the whisky she's drank."

"Sounds rough. Do you want me to leave? I can come back another time."

"No way. I need the distraction—hang on a sec. I'd better get this." Elinor's phone buzzed across the table. She grabbed it and lifted it to her ear.

"Hey Ryan, what's up? ... *What?*" she cried, her voice rising several octaves. "When did this happen? ... Which hospital? ... Thanks. I'll get there as soon as I can." She flung down the phone and grabbed for her purse. "I have to go. Bianca's in the hospital. There was some kind of attack."

"Attack?" *A werewolf attack?* My stomach tightened, and a jab of phantom pain arced through my foot.

Elinor pressed her lips together. "Ryan didn't say much, just that she's unconscious and that I should get—oh, shit! Eric has our car in London. I'll have to grab a taxi." She grabbed her phone again. "Shit, shit, what's the taxi number?"

"I didn't even know there *was* a taxi in Crookshollow."

"It's slow and terrible." Elinor frantically jabbed at her phone. "Why is the wifi not working?" Her eyes flashed, and her usually perfect hair had fallen in disarray.

"Don't worry about that," I said. "I'll give you a ride."

My heart pounded against my chest. If I let Elinor into my car, she'd see my lever. She'd know I wasn't normal. But looking at her panicked face, I couldn't let her sit here and wait for the taxi when her best friend was in the hospital.

"You would?" Elinor's brown eyes grew even wider.

"Yeah, sure." I shrugged, like it was no big deal, even though my chest was tight with fear. "Let's go."

ELINOR CLAMBERED into the Fiat's passenger seat. Taking a deep breath, I turned the ignition and pushed the lever forward to ease down the drive. Elinor didn't even glance my way. She stared at her blank phone screen, speaking a steady monotone of reassurances to herself.

"She has to be okay. She's Bianca. She's so tough. She saved my life once, you know? Some drug dealers broke into the house, and she hit one over the head with a cricket bat."

"Wow, that's pretty crazy," I said, pulling out of Marshell House's long drive and onto the street. A few moments later, we sped past *Resurrection Ink*. Elinor let out a strangled sob as the damaged window came into view. My chest tightened again.

Elinor said that Robbie had been responsible for the attack, which meant that it hadn't been my stalker. But I was so sure I hadn't recognised that man that had come running toward me. I thought back to the last time I'd seen Robbie, just before he'd transformed into a wolf at his fake-wedding. He'd called out Bianca's name in his deep Scottish accent. The guy I'd seen also had a Scottish accent, but his was lighter, younger. Maybe I was so scared, I couldn't trust what I'd seen and heard.

Or maybe ... maybe he was just some drunk asking for change, and it was just a coincidence that he happened to be near the shop and I happened to walk out. Maybe I was so afraid that Mum would find me that I read more into it than I should?

And now Bianca had been attacked ... we didn't know anything yet, but I was willing to bet that a wolf was responsible. Was it Robbie? I had smelt his scent at the shop. Irvine had said none of the wolves in his pack were dangerous, but was he wrong? Had someone lost control? What the hell was this group up to, and how had *I* ended up in the middle of it?

Phantom pain soared up my leg, and I had to grip the wheel harder to stop my hands shaking. My mother's voice drummed inside my head. *Never trust a werewolf. They may talk as smooth as any guy, but they can't control their monstrous urges. You and I both know how it soon ends in blood.*

No. I can trust Irvine. I know I can.

The hospital was in Crooks Crossing. While I drove out into the countryside, Elinor frantically texted on her phone, probably informing all the other members of the pack about what happened. *Maybe we'd get all the way to the hospital without her even noticing—*

"What's that lever for?"

I gulped. So much for her not noticing my accelerating lever.

"Um ..." I whispered, my voice catching. "It's an accessible adaptation for the pedals. You push it forward to accelerate, and pull back to brake."

"Why do you need it?" Elinor had leaned in closer to inspect the lever.

Quick, I need a clever story to explain it.

My heart pounded in my chest. I heard myself say, "I'm an amputee."

What clever story could possibly account for having a weird lever in my car?

"You are? How did I not know this?"

I shrugged. Heat flared on my face. I focused on the road, trying to stop my hands from shaking as they gripped the wheel. *This isn't what I wanted. I didn't want anyone to know. All I wanted was the chance to be normal.*

"Willow, I'm so sorry." Elinor's voice was sweet. It was such a dumb thing to say. All the reporters Mum stuck me in front of said the same thing. All the letters of support for *Werewolf Watch* poured waves of sympathy at me that made my throat close with rage.

But her tone was so genuine, my protests dried on my lips. "It's not your fault." It was my standard answer.

"How did it happen, do you mind if I ask? Was it a birth defect?"

There's no use hiding anymore, might as well get the whole story out in the open. If Elinor and I are going to be maybe hopefully friends, it might be good that she knows. Better to find out now if I have to stop seeing her ... "My father attacked me. He caused so much damage, I lost my right leg below the knee."

"Shit. That's horrible. I hope the bastard is in jail."

"He was never caught." My knuckles were turning white.

"Shit," Elinor said again. An uncomfortable silence hung between us. I hoped like hell Elinor wouldn't start with the other typical platitudes – *I don't know what I'd do if I had a missing leg, I think you're just so brave ...*

Thankfully, the hospital loomed ahead, dragging us back into the present. I pulled into the hospital parking lot. Elinor scrambled out of the car before I'd even come to a complete stop.

After a tense conversation with the ward nurse, we managed to find the right room. Bianca lay in a hospital bed, her eyes staring straight ahead into nothing. Needles and drips stuck out of her, and machines beeped. Scratches and cuts marked her beautiful porcelain skin, and bandages around her thigh and shoulders showered the severity of her injuries.

Bianca was always so full of life. To see such a strong woman lying completely helpless chilled me right to my bones. If a wolf could bring down Bianca, what chance did I have?

I glanced up at the window, and leapt back in fright. Pressed against the glass was a wolf's face, its eyes drooped and its mouth turned down, almost as if it was sad.

"Willow, are you all right?" Elinor grabbed my arm, bracing me as I steadied myself.

"A wolf ..." I gasped. "There's a wolf in the window."

"It's just the trees making strange shapes," Elinor said, although her eyes flashed with panic. "There aren't any wolves left in England, and certainly not on the hospital grounds. Look, I can't see a wolf there, can you?"

I followed her gaze back to the window, where the wolf's face had disappeared.

Elinor hustled me out of the room mighty fast. Ryan and Alex stood in the corner of the waiting room, their arms around each other. Ryan stroked Alex's hair while she sobbed into her shoulder. A pang of envy hit me as I watched them. How nice it must be to have someone you could count on when things got tough. Irvine said he would protect me, but that would only last as long as our fling did, which I didn't anticipate being a long time. A guy that hot and nice and *that* good with his hands and tongue must go through women like I went through Cadbury chocolate blocks.

"What happened?" Elinor asked, striding over to them.

She was mauled by an animal, is what happened. Hanging around shifters all the time is a bad bad idea.

"I haven't got all the details yet, what with Robbie being upset and Bianca being in a coma and all." Ryan ran a hand through his dark hair. "That reporter, Serenity, who was staying at The Prim, stabbed her multiple times. I think she was intending to—" He glanced at me, then gave a little cough. "Anyway, Robbie was supposed to have left town on Caleb's orders, but he showed up at Luke's place a few hours ago. He'd figured out Bianca was in trouble. He got there just in time to stop Serenity from killing her, but she's in pretty bad shape."

My head swam. Nothing he'd said made any sense. Irvine had said that only males could be werewolves, which meant that this Serenity was just an ordinary human psychopath. But that was so insane. Why would she stab Bianca? What did this have to do with my stalker or … or anything that had been going on?

"What about the shop?" I asked Ryan. "Do you think this has anything to do with the break-in?"

Ryan nodded. "I'd say they're related. It looks like this Serenity wanted to kill Bianca, so it makes sense that she would also want to hurt her business. I'm willing to bet she staged the attack and made us think Robbie did it to deliberately drive Bianca and Robbie apart."

I sat down as a phantom pain shot up my leg. This was just too much to take in. If the attack on the shop was all about Bianca, and this Serenity girl was responsible, then that meant my mother wasn't involved in it at all.

But then who was that guy? Had I just been worried about nothing?

18

IRVINE

hy are you trying to keep it a secret? Caleb's eyes burned into mine.

We were standing on opposite ends of the garden at Marshell House, on guard duty for Willow and Elinor, who were settled inside for the night. Even though we now ken who had trashed the shop and she was in police custody, I gathered Willow wasn't keen on staying at her flat. Ryan and Alex had offered for her to stay up at the Hall, but Willow clearly felt more comfortable around Elinor, who was at least human and not *quite* as filthy rich.

Caleb was taking the opportunity to berate me about my relationship with Willow. Now that we'd slept together, the bond was pulsing from my body like a beacon. He couldn't help but see it, and as I suspected, he was *pissed* that I hadn't told him about it earlier. Where I saw my fated mate come to me at last, all he saw was a distraction that could stop me from dedicating myself to the mission.

I didn't blame him, but that didn't mean I didn't also want to claw his eyes out. The only thing stopping me was our alliance, and the fact he was the alpha of the local pack and I was alone. For once, my instincts made the sensible decision.

Irvine, Caleb growled inside my head. He was waiting for an answer.

She asked me to, I said. *Her father was a shifter. He attacked her, and because of that, the doctors had to remove her leg.*

I hated spilling Willow's secret like that, but I didn't have a choice. Caleb was in charge. If he asked me a question, I couldn't lie to him. My wolf wouldn't allow it.

She look like she's got all her limbs to me.

Watch carefully. She limps a little on her right leg. It's because she wears a prosthesis. Don't say anything to her, because she doesn't want people to ken. After she lost her leg, her mother kept her practically a prisoner. She came here so she could have a normal life. She doesn't want anything to do with shifters. She won't even let me shift in front of her.

But she wanted you?

Only my body, I growled. I'd meant it as a joke, but I was surprised at the venom in my words.

So she knows who we are, then? Caleb pawed at the dirt. *Dammit, Irvine, you shouldn't have told her. We can't have just anyone knowing about us, especially not people who are anti-shifters—*

I didn't. She has this weird ability to smell werewolves. She already ken we were shifters.

Caleb growled again. *That's something I really should have known.*

I hung my head and lay down in the dirt, an appropriate gesture of submission.

It seems odd, though. She could have simply kept secret the fact she knew we were shifters. She didn't have to keep your whole relationship secret.

My old man always told me that trying to understand a woman was like trying to count the grains of sand on a beach.

Caleb snorted. *Ain't that the truth. At least, this explains why you've been so absent of late. But you should have come to me as soon as you discovered your connection and her ability. We can't have anything fucking up the reveal, especially when we still don't have the ring.*

I ken. I handled it all wrong. I was just trying to be sensitive to Willow—

Sensitive isn't your strong suit, Irvine. Try sensible. You could put her in danger, especially with the world about to turn in our direction. Did I tell you that Robbie found the location of the ring?

I blanched. If Robbie found the ring, that meant my time was up. I'd have to tell Willow the truth about what we were planning to do. *I hadnae heard that. Why don't we have it yet?* I tried to keep my thoughts even, so Caleb wouldn't see my distress.

It's buried in the grave of a maid who used to live in Bianca's house. It might take some time to locate her grave, as it's pretty old, but as soon as we do the Benedict Ring will be ours, and we can put the whole plan into action.

Great. That's great. I ken I should be ecstatic. This was what I'd worked for ever since my father's death. But all I could think about was what it would do to Willow when she found out what we were going to do.

I ken I still had time. It could be weeks or months before they found that grave. In the meantime, I'd have to step up my efforts to show Willow that shifters being free would be a good thing.

The only question was, how?

19

WILLOW

I was organising stacks of tablecloth samples for Alex when the door to my apartment crashed open. I spun around in terror, expecting to see the black-clad man who'd rushed at me the night the shop was destroyed.

Instead, Irvine stalked across the room and pulled me into his arms. My heart thundered in my chest as his heady scent invaded my nostrils. All my longing from the last few days rushed at me at once, and my head spun. I had to steady myself against Irvine to keep my balance.

"You're back—" I started to say, but my words were muffled by his mouth on mine.

The kiss took my breath away. Irvine cupped my face in his hands, and the heat of his lips drove me wild with want. The ache inside me flared to life.

"Ah, Willow Summers, I have missed you," he murmured against my lips as he walked me backward toward the edge of the bed.

All the pent-up frustration of missing him hit my body with full force. The room swirled. His hands seemed to be every-where at once – cupping the back of my head, wrapping around my neck, stroking my thighs, clasping the curve of my back. Irvine pushed me back, so I was lying across the samples. Bright-coloured tablecloths cascaded off the bed.

"Stop," I giggled, as his lips traced lines across my neck. "We can't do this on top of Alex's samples."

"Why not?" Irvine looked up, grinning wickedly. "Newly-weds spend half their time christening various things. It seems only fair that the wedding planner gets to christen the tablecloths."

My protests dissolved as Irvine popped the buttons on my shirt and slid it and my bra off my shoulders. He took my nipple into his mouth, his tongue swirling around the sensitive tip. A moan escaped my lips.

Irvine crawled up on top of the samples with me, and I pulled him against me, clinging to him as he assaulted my nipples with his tongue. He kissed down my stomach as his fingers popped the buttons on my fly.

"I want to be inside you so bad," he moaned against my lips.

"Please," I moaned back as I tugged at his pants.

This wasn't like our first night together, when he was gentle. This was pure, animal lust. We tore at each other's clothing, desperate to be skin against skin. Irvine leaned back on the bed, the corner of a package of napkin holders jabbing into the side of his head.

He shuffled me on top of him. I reached over and in a few quick movements had popped off my prosthesis. Irvine's hands grabbed my hips and guided me down on top of him. I sighed with joy as his length filled me completely.

Irvine bucked his hips up to meet me. I ground myself against him, grabbing his shoulders for support as I didn't have the leverage of my other leg. More tablecloths slid over the edge.

"Oooh." Irvine grinned. "Someone's been studying up."

The flush in my cheeks returned. I didn't want to tell him I'd been reading up on sex positions on the internet. I'd also learned more about human depravity than I'd ever expected. *That's the last time I type "sex with an amputee" with the safe search off.*

Irvine grabbed my neck, drawing me against him. He thrust deeper as we moved together, our bodies wrapped in the electrifying warmth of our connection. I lost myself in the sensation of him, in his skin slick against mine, in the way we fitted together like two puzzle pieces who'd finally found their mates.

Harder, I screamed inside my head as he thrust inside me. *Go deeper. I want everything you've got.*

The ache inside me grew and grew, spreading through my whole body. When it reached my head, it exploded in a wave of heat and lust and blinding light, and I lost myself in it, in him.

Inside me, Irvine stiffened. His teeth scraped the edge of my neck. I cried out and he cried out. His body shuddered. We collapsed together against the fabric samples, the lust driven out, at least for the moment.

My body buzzed with wild energy. I turned my head and met Irvine's eyes. All the waiting, all the thinking I'd done while he was gone ... this was even better than I'd anticipated.

"Thank you," I whispered.

"The pleasure is all mine, Willow Summers." Irvine grinned, stroking my cheek with his finger.

I think I can die happy right now.

Irvine lifted himself up on his elbows, those grey eyes sparkling as he leaned over me and planted a kiss on my lips. "Sorry I didnae get here sooner. Caleb made me go to the hospital first. Bianca's awake. She's going to make a full recovery."

"That's so great. I'll go see her today, too."

"Willow, I wannae ask you something."

"Mmmmm, I can't answer questions now."

"If you could change one thing about your life, what would it be?"

"Urgh, I *especially* can't answer deep, existential questions right now."

A serious look passed over his face. "Go on, humour a Scotsman."

"I'd give myself a leg, of course."

"Would you really? All the things in the whole world, and the one thing you'd change is the thing you've already learned to live with?"

I shrugged. "My life would have been very different if I had a leg. Kids wouldn't have been so mean to me. My life wouldn't have been so sheltered. I might've had some friends, even a few boyfriends—"

Curtis would never have rejected me, and I would never have come to Crookshollow, and I would never have met Irvine—

Irvine gave me a look that implied he knew what I was thinking. "Is that really what you want?"

"I always thought so, but actually ..." My heart raced against my chest. "I think you're right. Maybe, I would like to go back to university and finish my degree. I like being a wedding planner, but I really did enjoy studying, too."

"What about your dad?"

"What about him?"

"What if he wasn't hiding anymore?"

"You mean, what if the guy who maimed me just stuck around and I had to face him every day? I would've run away much sooner. He hurt me, and got away with it because he's a werewolf. I don't want anything to do with him."

"But what if he could be tried for his crime? Thrown in jail and—"

"The only way he'd be tried was if shapeshifters had some kind of secret court, which isn't likely, or if werewolves were public knowledge, and if that happened I wouldn't be around to see it."

"Why not?"

I looked away. *Because if shifters were public knowledge, the first thing the government and the press would do is seek out my mother, the only known "authority" on werewolves. And that would mean they'd come after me. I'd never be free again. Willow Summers would have to die, and I'd go back to being 'peg-leg' to the whole world.* But I couldn't tell Irvine that, as much as I wanted to. "I don't want you to bring my father up again."

Irvine's face fell. I snapped my hand over my mouth. I hated myself for lying. "I'm so sorry, that was so rude, and you were just trying to be nice."

"Dinnae ever apologise to me for telling me what you want." Irvine stroked my hair. The sad expression on his face changed to a mischievous grin. "In fact, I think you should practice on me."

"Excuse me?"

"I'm already your experiment bloke, aye? From now on, you need to tell me what you want, every step of the way. I'm your servant, but if you dinnae tell me, I willnae do it." He looked smug.

"That doesn't seem fair." The idea of it sent a shudder through me. I could tell by the twinkle in his eyes that he wanted me to say things like *please eat me out*, or *put your cock inside me*. My cheeks burned just thinking the words.

"Trust me, Willow Summers, you're gonnae love it."

IRVINE

J carried Willow on my back as I stumbled up the path to the cabin. I cursed myself for my idiocy. I'd been so distracted watching Willow and trying to stop her from over-hearing a conversation about the Benedict Ring and the plan, that I hadn't watched what Caleb put in front of me at the pub. I'd drank far too much.

It will be fine, just get her to the cabin.

We'd been at *Tir Na Nog* with the rest of the pack, cele-brating Bianca's release from hospital and Robbie's exoneration and his discovery of the hiding place of the ring. Despite her apprehension about the pack knowing about us, Willow sat beside me and held my hand and let me buy her Lemon, Lime and Bitters.

It warmed me to see her having such a great time, laughing with the girls and talking about their wedding plans. Hope surged within me. *She doesn't want to talk about her father yet, but she'll come around. If I can just convince her that she could have justice, then she'll see how much she will benefit from shifters being public, and then we can be together for real.*

I set a giggling Willow down on the porch and tugged my keys from my pocket. Fitting them into the lock proved a more difficult task. Willow tsked as she grabbed the keys from me and opened the door.

"In you go, you intoxicated beast." Willow grinned as I collapsed on top of the bed. She bent down and started to undo my boot laces. Her eyes darted over my body, sparkling with desire. She bit her lip, and my cock pressed hard against my jeans.

Willow and I, alone again in my cabin, the buzz of alcohol heightening the strength of our connection. My hands ached to tug off her shirt and explore her body, and I could tell by the way she leaned closer and her hands lingered on the skin of my ankles that she wanted the same, but we'd made an agreement. If she wanted me, she'd have to tell me.

I decided to tease her a little. I sat up and pulled my shirt over my head. Her eyes widened as she drank me in. I did a big fake yawn. "I'm really beat. I think I'll turn in now."

She looked away, but not before I caught the disappointment on her face. "Oh, okay. Goodnight, I guess."

"That is, unless you have anything you'd like to tell me."

She shook her head. "No, I'm ..." Her cheeks flared with heat.

"We had an accord," I said, sliding across the bed away from her. "If you want to do anything, you are going to have to spell it out."

"Please, don't make me do that." Willow's whole face flushed with heat. She bit her bottom lip and my cock pressed even harder against my jeans.

"You cannae get out of it. You want to nae be scared anymore? Then you have to take matters into your own hands." I gestured down at my jeans, where my cock was starting to throb painfully against my fly. "Look at me. I want you, Willow

Summers. I want you so bad I can taste it. Now, what do you want me to do to you?"

Willow bit her lip again, screwing up her eyes. A heated silence descended, and the tension crackled between us. After an age, she whispered. "I want you to fuck me."

"Excuse me?" I cupped a hand around my ear. "I cannae quite hear you, lass."

Willow screwed her face up tighter. Her skin turned red all the way down her neck. "I said, I want you to fuck me. I want you to lick me all over and then shove your cock inside me! I want you to be a beast!"

"Why Willow Summers, I thought you'd never ask." I grabbed her arm and dragged her on top of me. We fell against each other, my lips crashing into hers.

She pawed at my skin, her nails digging into my neck. She straddled me and ground herself against me, driving me near wild with desire. This wasn't the Willow who'd been so timid about sex. This Willow was wild, desperate, aching to drive out her fears and insecurities with my cock. And I was only too happy to oblige.

I tugged her shirt off, and she slipped her own bra over her head, forcing her tiny, perfect breasts into my hands. The nipples were already hard as I rolled them in my fingers, causing her to cry out with pleasure.

I reached for her fly, but she shoved me back against the bed, and did it herself. It was some feat of gymnastics how she tugged off her trousers and prosthesis while kneeling over me, but I couldn't stop to contemplate the physics of it because her beautiful body leaned over me and she gripped my zipper, tugging it open and dragging my jeans down over my thighs. "I want to know what you taste like," she whispered against my lips.

"Willow Summers, you are a delight." She bent over me, and

took me into her mouth. Her wet tongue slid down my length. I moaned as she wrapped her hand around me, and started to stroke me, slowly at first, alternating with her hands and her mouth, then faster. I gripped the sheets as I watched my cock slide in and out of her mouth. Her eyes locked on mine, driving me closer to the edge.

"Willow ... sweet Willow ... you must stop ... "

She laughed against me, and stroked me faster.

I gripped her shoulders and hoisted her off me, dragging her back on top of me. "You are a wicked lass," I scolded her, sucking in a deep breath and trying to calm myself before I cut our evening short.

"But I was enjoying that," she murmured.

"I think you'll enjoy this a whole lot more." I fitted her hips over mine, and thrust up inside her.

Oh, sweet exquisite beauty! Her warmth enveloped me, and I lost myself in her. The bond surrounded us, swirling around us but also pulsing through my veins, joining us as one. I wanted nothing more than to drown in the sweetness of her body for the rest of my days.

We bucked against each other like animals. The wolf inside me bayed with his own pleasure as Willow tossed her head back, howling like an animal in heat. Her nails dug into my shoulders, and her whole body tightened around me as an orgasm ripped through her. The bond drew us tighter, wrapping our bodies so close together that I no longer knew where flesh and bone began. All that existed was her bright eyes and her ferocious kiss and her sweet, yielding warmth ...

A rumbling rose within me, starting from my stomach, where the wolf scratched against my skin, and extending out through my whole body, claiming every limb and extremity. Willow's neck brushed against my chin, and the sweet scent of her skin overwhelmed me. *My mate.*

I needed her. I needed to claim her.

I bit down, the rush of the connection surging to my mind. Willow moaned and clutched at me, and I dropped her neck as I realised what I'd done, but I was too far gone. I let out a howl of my own as I lost control, and a powerful surge of hot energy coursed through me, shaking me to my core. I surfaced, struggling to catch my breath as sweat poured down my face.

"Willow Summers," I puffed, as her lips found mine again. "You are something else."

We melted together, our bodies no longer capable of movement. As the heat of our lovemaking subsided, the strength of our bond, now tenfold because of what I'd done, surged between us.

If Willow noticed a change, she didn't say anything. Instead, she fell asleep within minutes, her hair falling over her face as a thin line of drool snaked from her lips to my pec. I remained awake, my gaze moving between the ceiling and the dark welt I'd made on her neck, feeling more and more guilty.

I'd lost control. I'd let the alcohol and the magic of being with her overtake me, and I'd given her the bite. I'd claimed her, without her permission, without even telling her what it meant.

It was unforgivable.

Willow was just beginning to trust me, and to believe that shifters were not all evil. And here I was, proving once again that I really was the monster she feared.

I vowed that I would speak to Clara as soon as I could. She must have a spell that would enable me to break the bond. Willow wouldn't even have to know.

In the meantime, the least I could do was make sure she was safe. And that meant safe from me. While Willow slept, I slid out of bed and moved onto the porch, where I transformed into my wolf form. As my senses heightened to the intense sensations of the forest, I walked around the cabin, trying to calm the horrible churning in my gut.

I peered through the window at her sleeping figure. Again, I was struck with just how intensely I felt about her. I wanted to give her everything I had, and for us to be together forever, but I had a sneaking suspicion I'd just ruined everything.

I STAYED OUTSIDE ALL NIGHT, punishing myself for the horrible thing I'd done.

I spent a lot of time staring at Willow through the window. She looked so serene when she slept, her face smushed against the pillow. It was hard to believe she was so wild last night. In the full glow of the moon, I could just make out the dark bruise of my claiming bite on her neck.

You're a horrible person. You just proved that you are the monster that she feared.

She stirred and sat up. "Irvine?" she called. "Where are you?"

I gulped. There was no way I could keep this secret any longer. I needed to tell her the truth.

Time to face the music.

I transformed back into my human form, pulled on my jeans, and trudged back inside. Willow opened her arms from me, but I slumped down into the chair by the stove. I couldn't bear to look at her. "We need to talk."

"What's wrong? Did you see something?" Fear crept into Willow's voice.

"No, it's not that. How much do you ken about werewolf mating? What has your mother told you about your birth?"

"Not this again. I don't want to talk about them—"

"I ken, I'm sorry. But this is really important. I've done something terrible, and I need to explain it."

Willow sighed. "Not a lot. All she said was that werewolves are men, and they prey on innocent women with certain genes to give them their children. She said my father tricked her into loving him and then threatened to hurt her if she left him. But it was when he attacked me that she finally got the courage to stand up to him, and he ran away with his tail between his legs like the coward he is."

"Then your father is even more despicable than I thought, for taking what is a beautiful thing and turning into an act of violence and horror." *And I'm worse. I'm so much worse.*

"So none of that is true?"

"Aye, it's true enough that there are no female werewolves. The gene is passed down through the male chromosome. If we wish to have children to continue our line, we must find a woman who carries that gene. We're biologically wired to recognise a compatible female. But more than that, there are certain pairings that are more desirable, more perfectly matched – we call those pairings the fated mates. Has your mum ever mentioned that?"

Willow shook her head.

"It's a core part of shifter lore. Almost every species of shapeshifter has this connection to their fated mate. When those two people meet – *if* they ever meet – the connection manifests as a magnetic energy pulling them together."

I let that sit for a moment, and dared a glance at her. Willow's eyes went wide, and she scrambled up, darting as far away from me as she could get in the tiny space. Not exactly the reaction I was hoping for.

"Wait, you're not saying that the weird energy when we touch ... that I ... that we ..." Her eyes were wide with terror.

My heart hammered against my chest. "Willow Summers, you and I are fated mates."

Willow's whole face crumpled. "I can't ... Irvine. I can't be a fated mate. I just can't. You know what I've been through already because of what my father did. It's one thing having this casual thing, but—"

"How casual has this been, really?" Desperation filled me as I saw Willow slipping away. "I see the way you look at me, how you want to be close, even when you push me away. When you were scared, whose arms did you fall into? Is that just casual?"

"I was scared! I wasn't thinking! I've been scared ever since Bianca's wedding, and after everything I told you, I can't believe you'd throw that back in my face." Her eyes hardened, and a chill settled over my heart. "Is this what you wanted to tell me?"

"Yes, and ... there's more." I sucked in a breath. "I'm so sorry. I lost control. Last night, I marked you."

"Marked?"

"That bite on your neck ... it isnae just a hickey. It marks you as my mate. Other shifters can sense the strength of our bond and ken not to come near you. It's a symbol of commitment in our world, and I never ever should have given it to you without your permission."

Willow didn't say anything. I continued, the words rushing out before I could think. "I dinnae ken what came over me. I wasn't in control of myself. Our connection was so intense, and I wanted to be closer to you, and your skin smelt so good and I just ... I slipped. It's unforgivable."

Nothing. My heart jackknifed against my chest. I felt as though I were being torn in two. *I've lost her. I've lost her the way I lost everything else – through my own monstrous nature.*

A lump rose in my throat, and I struggled to get the next words out. "I'm going to see Clara today, and she'll have a spell or something that will strip the mark from you. I'll undo it so it never happened, and then I promise I'll stay away from you. I won't ever speak to you again. I've broken your trust. I cannae ask to have it back. You deserve so much better than me."

"I don't want that," Willow said, her voice barely louder than a whisper.

I whipped my head up. Her eyes met mine, and I saw something there that I didn't expect to see.

I saw an ache for acceptance, for companionship that matched my own.

I saw *love*.

"You dinnae—"

Willow rubbed the side of her neck. "Irvine, I've only known you a few days, but my whole life has changed because of you. Everything that you've done for me has been out of kindness, and I can see now that you genuinely regret this thing. I'm a little freaked out by it, that's true, especially considering what it means, but I'd rather deal with that by your side than alone."

I shook my head. "I dinnae deserve this."

She laughed, a beautiful sound that lifted my heart. "Maybe not, but I think ... I think I do."

"You deserve everything in the world that is wonderful and good, Willow Summers."

"Well then ..." She grinned, and rubbed her neck again. "This mark, is it a domination thing?"

I shook my head. "I would nae seek to dominate you, Willow Summers. If anything, it's you who dominates my heart. In the shifter world, giving the mark is a bit like giving a beautiful gift, or an—" I stopped just short of saying *engagement ring*.

Willow gave a faint smile, as though she'd guessed what I had been about to say. "Then I accept your gift, Irvine."

"You mean it?"

"I'm learning that part of being out in the world means accepting everything." Willow held out her arms again. "Because of you, I've started to accept who *I* am. It's only fair that I accept you as you are."

"You really mean it?"

She nodded. "Now get over here and make love to me, *mate.*"

"Your wish is my command." I tore across the room and crashed into the bed beside her, my lips finding hers and kissing her with renewed intensity. The world faded away – all that existed was me and my mate and the connection that bound us.

21

WILLOW

"You just want the roots touched up?" the hairdresser asked me, as she ran her fingers through my freshly shampooed hair. Her name was Nellie, but I wasn't going to remember that after I left this salon, because I wasn't going to come back.

"Yes please, and try to match the colour as close as possible."

"Sure thing, sugar."

I took a magazine from the pile beside the chair and flicked through it, not registering a single word. My stomach tightened with guilt as Nellie divided my hair into sections and started to brush the dye onto my roots.

I'd been back to a salon every two weeks since I'd arrived in Crookshollow, to get my blonde roots re-dyed. I needed to keep up my disguise, which meant travelling several miles to visit different salons just in case someone in Crookshollow happened to recognise me.

Today's salon was in Crooks Worthy. I'd managed to fit the appointment in between a couple of meetings with suppliers for Alex's wedding. I was supposed to be focused on sourcing the perfect lighting for the reception, as well as getting the sound system organised. Instead, I was here, reading centuries-old issues of *Cleo* magazine and getting my disguise updated.

The pack have been so kind to me, welcoming me to their world and treating me like a true friend. And I'm deceiving them all. Alex and Elinor and Bianca and Caleb and Irvine ... sweet, gorgeous Irvine ...

The guilt flooded me as Irvine's face flashed in my mind. I saw the way he looked at me when I accepted the mark, his eyes dancing with joy. I felt his lips against mine, kissing away my problems. I heard his voice, reminding me that he would protect me, at any cost.

Even when he gave me that mark, he was honourable. He had the strength to come forward and admit that he'd done wrong. He was prepared to walk away, to undo what he'd done. Apart from that one slip, he always put me first. Always.

And I still haven't told him who I really am.

He says my name all the time, like it's a mantra, like it's a magical spell that cures all his pain. What would he do if he discovered that name doesn't even belong to me?

The stupid thing was, I *loved* being Willow Summers. I felt more like myself when I was her than I'd ever felt as Carol.

But the fact that I was sitting in this chair, blotting over the regrowing blonde in my roots, proved that it was a lie. Willow wasn't real. I'd constructed her as a wall to hide behind. And in doing so, I'd trapped myself in my own lie.

What am I going to do?

22

IRVINE

ONE MONTH LATER

I handed Willow a cup of tea as soon as she walked through the cabin door. Her whole face lit up, telling me that the tea was very much needed. Seeing how happy she was to see me filled me with the kind of joy that only seemed possible on hair commercials.

The joy was tinged with an edge of sadness. Even though we'd been seeing each other nearly every day for the past month, and even though she'd accepted the mark and was even calling me her mate, I wasn't any closer to getting Willow to believe that shifters should be able to be free in the world. I'd tried twice more to get her to open up about why she couldn't live in a world where shifters were free, but she refused to talk.

I was also pissing off Caleb. Over the last few weeks he'd made all sorts of plans and forged new relationships with shifter packs across the world. And I'd been there for none of it. The guilt of my lack of involvement had crept up on me slowly, but every time I saw Willow, all other thoughts fled me head. It didn't help that she didn't ken and wouldn't agree with what we were doing.

Even though Willow brought me endless joy, the mission

and my lack of attention to it weighed on me more and more. I ken we were fast approaching the time when we would have to act. And I'd have to choose – Willow, or the shifters.

I didn't ken which I'd choose.

"This Raynard wedding is *insane*," Willow said as she kicked off her shoes and came to peer over my shoulder. A strand of her wavy brown hair fell against my skin, sending a jolt of energy across my flesh. "There's so much to organise, and the date's coming up fast. I'm lucky I have a few vendors down in London who owe me favours, because pulling this thing off is going to be *tight*. What smells so delicious?" She peered over my shoulder as I stirred the sauce.

"Passata. It's an Italian meatball dish."

"I see cheese." Willow lifted the lid on the bubbling sauce. Her hands snaked along my arms, over my shoulder. The force of our connection tugged at me, and it was everything I could do to keep a hold of my spatula and not throw her against the wall and take her there and then. "I'm sold. Can I help with anything?"

"You can sit over there and look beautiful."

She plonked herself down in the edge of the bed. "I'll give it my best shot. Irvine?"

"That's my name." I stirred another handful of grated parmesan into the roux.

"I'm not wearing any underwear."

That did it. I dropped the spatula, crossed the room in two strides, and wrapped Willow in my arms. Our lips smashed together, and her tongue thrust itself into my mouth.

You're weak, Irvine. My father's voice thumped against my ears. *You're neglecting your own pack for this woman who doesn't truly accept what you are. Your weakness will cost you everything you've worked for.*

Stay out of this, old man, I shouted at myself. *She needs me. The shifters have Caleb. He's doing a better job than I could ever do.*

Yet one more thing for me to feel guilty about.

I pressed my lips to Willow's, hoping to drive out my guilt with the warmth of her desire. Willow rose up to meet me, her kiss as aggressive as mine, her tongue forcing itself deep inside my mouth.

As long as my secrets stayed secret, and I kept her safe from any possible threat, then maybe … *her lips are like heaven* … maybe I could hold on to what we had, just for a bit longer … *so soft, so succulent …*

"The passata will burn," Willow whispered against my lips.

"I don't care," I growled. I flicked open the buttons on her shirt, tugging it off her shoulders to reveal the milky softness of her skin. My cock throbbed against my thigh as I yanked her shirt fully away tossed it across the room. Her breasts bounced free. I kissed her ferociously, running my hands over every inch of her, wanting to commit every gorgeous curve of her body to memory.

I hoped Willow liked it hard and fast, because I wasn't going to be able to control myself around her this time.

From the way she was kissing me back, making soft mewling sounds as she clawed at my shoulders, she liked it just fine. We staggered backward until we hit the edge of the bed. Willow leaned back into the covers as I crawled on top of her. We tore at each others clothes, tossing aside the fabric that separated us.

"Hold on," Willow breathed. She reached down and yanked off her prosthesis, dropping it to the floor with a loud bang. I tried to push her shoulders back, but she grabbed my cock, stroking me hard, her fingers hot.

"Careful, Willow Summers," I growled against her ear, enjoying the way she shivered with delight. "You might end up with a handful of wolf juice if you keep that up."

"Mmmm, I think I'll take my chances." She grinned as her grip on my cock tightened.

I moaned as she pumped me harder, her hand sliding over my entire length. With her other hand, she ran her fingers over my balls, scratching the area between my scrotum and asshole and sending a flush of heat through my body.

Oh sweet Jesus Mary and Joseph did she learn that trick from an internet search too? I'm not gonnae last, I'm gonnae ...

I grabbed her wrist, stopping her mid-stroke. *Is this really the same Willow, who was so timid and afraid just last month?* "Sex is making you sassy, Willow Summers."

She grinned. "Maybe I've got ten years worth of scenes from trashy romance novels burning a hole in my head that I want to live out."

"I ken how to wipe that smirk off your face." I shoved Willow back and buried my head between her legs. She moaned as I thrust my tongue against her clit. Her hand dropped from my cock and she tossed her head back, letting out an even louder moan. I loved hearing her lose control like that, and give into her desire.

I attacked her clit with my tongue, pounding it again and again, lapping up the sweet taste of her. Her fingers dug into my shoulder as she drew closer to release.

Willow's thighs clamped around my head, and her body shuddered as her first orgasm tore through her. I planned for it to be her first of many. I didn't even let her finish before I lifted her left leg onto my shoulder, and thrust myself inside her.

Willow arched her back, her eyes wide as I filled her deep. Her walls tightened around me, surrounding my entire length in her delicious warmth. I rode her hard, watching every contortion of her face, every sigh and moan and clench. Her fingers clawed at my arms as I pounded her with all the heat and passion I possessed. Even with her leg resting on my shoulder, she dragged me down and thrust her tongue in my mouth.

Her right leg snaked behind me, and without her other foot in the way, I had even more space for manoeuvring. My body rocked against hers as we moved in perfect unison, rising up to meet each other with each thrust.

My whole body tightened as heat flooded my veins. I howled as I came, the force of my orgasm tearing through me like an earthquake. Willow shuddered against the bed, crying and mewling as her own pleasure enveloped her. Utterly spent, I collapsed beside Willow, withdrawing from her and dragging her into my arms.

A burning smell from the kitchen alerted my nostrils. *Damn.* I dragged myself upright. *I'll have to redo the sauce now—*

Outside the window, a branch snapped.

"What the hell was that?" I whipped around so fast, I dragged the blankets with my foot, tossing Willow off the bed. She yelped as she hit the floor.

"What was that for—" she started, but I held my finger to my lips. I stared into the trees, focusing my gaze on the area directly opposite the window. The moon had just begun to rise, casting eerie shadows through the trees and making it nearly impossible to discern shapes. But I'd seen it. I ken I had.

"Irvine, what is it?" Willow asked from behind me. I didn't take my eyes from the trees, waiting for the landscape to reveal itself to me. I pushed open the window a crack, and a gust of cool air hit my chest. Yes, there it was – a faint scent on the breeze. Human, and not someone I recognised.

So what? That could be any one of the other cabin residents, out for a ramble in the moonlight.

I kept searching the trees. Finally, the tall shape – dressed in green fatigues and nearly invisible amongst the thick foliage – came into focus. A man. He would've been invisible to anyone who didn't have the heightened senses of a werewolf. But he wasn't invisible to me.

"Irvine, please." Willow sounded terrified. She clambered up beside me and thrust her head into the square of the window. "What's wrong?"

As soon as her head appeared, the man disappeared into the bush. Every nerve in my body stood on end. He'd been watching us. That wasn't another resident. That was a deliberate stake-out.

"What's wrong is there's someone out there watching us," I said.

23

WILLOW

There's someone out there watching us.

The stalker put an end to the sexy mood inside Irvine's cabin. "Do you think he's still out there?" I asked, hugging my arms to my chest. A clammy cold shook my whole body, as though my skin crawled with cold, dripping mud. *How much had he seen? Was he taking photographs?*

"I cannae smell him anymore." Irvine pulled his head back in the window. He slid off the bed, and moved to the kitchen, where he started assembling ingredients on the bench to make another pot of sauce. The tension in his shoulders was the only clue that he was even thinking about what happened.

"Why is he here? Did you see his face? Is it something to do with the project you're working on?" I imagined Irvine working as a spy for MI6, and an enemy agent had come to track him down. Werewolves would make great spies. They could squeeze into tight spaces and bring down assailants with a claws and teeth instead of bullets ...

My leg throbbed with phantom pain. *No. I don't want to think about claws and teeth right now.*

"I dinnae ken." Irvine whisked a handful of flour into a

bubbling pot of butter. "It's unlikely. The scent is a man, not a shifter."

"It could be some pervert, trying to get footage of me and you doing ... stuff. That's a thing, you know. Amputee smut. I recently discovered that the internet's full of it." *It's just my luck that just when I start having sex, I end up on some kinky website. Talk about out of the frying pan, into the fire.*

Irvine dumped a handful of parmesan into the sauce, then tipped the drained pasta into the cheesy mixture. "It could be," he said, as he poured a layer of cheesy pasta into the bottom of an oven dish.

Or it could be someone trying to get to my mother. They'll go to her with photographs of her beloved daughter, the star of all her anti-werewolf campaigns, fornicating with the very beast she was trying to destroy. They'll threaten to release the photos to the press unless she agrees to ...

What? Unless she agrees to what? I couldn't think of what someone would want my mother to do. I opened my mouth to mention it to Irvine, but then remembered that I hadn't told him who my mother was. And I never would.

When I left Irvine, I'd call Mum and ask her if anything was going on first, see if I had anything to worry about.

God, I hope it's not about Mum. I hope it's just some garden-variety pervert. Never in my life would I have expected to hope that a pervert was outside the window, but it would honestly be the best of all possible outcomes.

"You seem remarkably calm about this whole thing," I said to Irvine. A bubble of panic rose through my chest, turning my whole body to ice. I grabbed my shirt with shaking hands and pulled it on, wrapping the blanket around my shoulders so any other smut photographers wouldn't be able to see a single inch of skin.

"There's nae much point getting in a tizz until we ken what's going on." Irvine added a layer of meatballs in a thick tomato sauce, then topped it with the rest of the pasta. He then grated a thick layer of parmesan over top, and shoved the dish into the tiny convection oven on the bench to melt the cheese. He grabbed a bowl of salad from the fridge and set that on the table. "After we eat this delicious meal I've prepared and you've calmed down a bit, I'll call Caleb and Ryan. You can go stay at Raynard Hall with Alex while we investigate outside. This intruder, whoever he is, will have left a scent trail. We may be able to hunt him out and—"

I shook my head. "No."

"What?"

"No, that's not happening." *No way are we getting the rest of the pack involved when this night be related to my mother. If there's any risk at all that it can be traced back to her—*

"Why not?" Irvine dropped into the chair opposite mine, regarding me with those steel grey eyes.

Good question. "You know what Caleb's like. He'll dive into uber protective mode to save the pack, and it could just be some pervy hiker or one of the other cabin occupants. I don't want to jump to conclusions before we know more."

"Willow, this could be really important. I cannae just keep it secret from the pack."

"Not forever, just for the moment." *Just until I can figure out if this has anything to do with me and my old life. If it does, then ... I guess I'll have to come clean, or run away.*

Just the thought of that choice turned my stomach.

Irvine sighed, then jabbed his finger toward my plate. "Hurry up and get that down you. We need to head out."

I took a big bite. It was delicious, but I didn't feel much like eating. "Why are we going outside?"

Irvine's fingers tightened around mine. "If you want this to be a secret, Willow Summers, you're gonnae have to help me investigate."

A shiver ran through my body at the thought of going out there. "Can't you just go by yourself?"

"Until we know who that guy is and what he wants, I'm nae letting you out of my sight. I wonnae let anything happen to you."

"You mean, you're going to sit at the end of my bed every night to make sure the bogeyman doesn't jump out and say boo?"

"Aye, you've got it." Irvine nodded, chewing the last bite of his dinner.

"I'm not sure what I think about this."

"Think, 'I'll be seeing a lot more of Irvine,' because that's what's happening until we get to the bottom of this."

"You mean, 'a lot more' than the every waking hour and many of the sleeping ones we spend together now?"

"Aye." He tapped the table impatiently. "Now, finish up, pop your leg on and let's go."

I chewed another mouthful of pasta, and pointed at my ballet flats stacked beside the door. "Those things barely survive on the path to the parking lot. I can't go clumping around the forest in them, especially not with ..." I pointed at my prosthetic. "I'm no good at sneaking. There's a reason private detectives are never amputees."

"Nonsense. I bet you'd make a great private detective."

"Irvine, this is serious!"

"I am being serious. You can do anything you want to do. You should stop telling yourself otherwise. And stop stalling, lassie. I'm nae leaving your side, but I need to see where that man was hiding. That means you're coming with me."

Irvine waited impatiently while I scarfed some more food down and re-attached my leg. He handed me a pair of his boots. They were enormous, but at least they had good traction.

I followed Irvine outside. On the steps, he bent down on one knee. "Climb on," he said, he gesturing to his back. I bit back a protest. I didn't want him to carry me around like a cripple. I could walk just fine. But ... it would be easier. And I kind of wanted to be close to him again.

I climbed on Irvine's back. He hoisted me up, wrapping his powerful arms around my thighs. My feet in his heavy boots dangled free. I gripped him around the neck and pressed my head against his, relishing the smell of him. Irvine stood upright, and dashed toward the forest.

Even though the ground was uneven and I must've been ungainly luggage, Irvine raced forward with incredible speed. We crashed through the trees, moving so fast I couldn't see what was going on in front of us. Instead, I glanced back at the cabin, where only a faint light glowed. Fear stabbed at my chest. It would be so easy to become lost in this forest. Branches scraped my face and arms, and I buried my face in Irvine's shoulders to protect myself from the worst of it.

Irvine pushed on, his strides confident, his gait surprisingly smooth. Beneath me, his muscles rippled, and a layer of sweat slicked down his neck. He didn't slow.

After several minutes, Irvine drew to a stop. He knelt down so I could slide off, and held out his hand to steady me on the uneven ground. I glanced around, waiting for my eyes to adjust to the darkness.

We'd come a small clearing, the trees bending away, providing a small hole in the canopy through which the cold moon shone through. Irvine sniffed the air, then pointed to a spot at the edge of the clearing. I noticed some of the undergrowth had been trampled flat.

"This is where he was hiding," Irvine said. "From the looks

of this, he was watching for a while. Can you have a look in the grass for any other clues? I'm going to sniff around a bit."

"Sure, but remember – I'm no private detective." I sat down on the soft ground, stretching out my leg beside me as I hunted around in the leaves. My fingers scraped against something cold and hard. I grabbed the object and raised it to my eyes, squinting in the cold moonlight as I rubbed away the dirt.

It was a small medallion, one side depicting a majestic stag, and the other side showing three small lines of latin text. A tiny hole had been drilled in the top, through which a thin leather cord was threaded. It looked a little like the coin Irvine wore around his neck.

The stalker must have dropped this. But what does it mean?

24

IRVINE

*W*illow showed me the medallion. "Could it be some sort of pack insignia?" she asked, pointing to the Baird and Lowe crests tattooed on my bicep.

"Maybe." I studied the stag. I doubted it had anything to do with a shifter pack, but anything was possible. Those who shifted into stags tended to be loners – I'd never heard of them organising into a pack before. Two stags couldn't usually stand to share the same territory, let alone work together to manage the complex social hierarchy of a pack. But, then again, a mixed pack like the Lowes was hardly normal, and it had happened.

And it still didn't explain why the man bore no scent of a shifter. There were spells and charms that could disguise a shifter's scent, but they involved a very advanced magic that only a few people would have access to. Our peeper could be a human in the employ of a stag – sometimes packs worked with humans who knew their secrets to run errands or perform other tasks they couldn't – but if that was true, it still didn't explain why he was following *us*. Why were they watching us? Why not watch Caleb? I was an ally, sure, but not nearly as powerful as

Rolf, and I didn't make any decisions. Willow was even less involved than I was.

The more I thought about it, the more I believed this had nothing to do with shifters and the plan and everything to do with Willow and the reason she left London. And I think she ken it, too, which was why she didn't want Caleb involved.

It could be her mother, as we'd originally thought, but if Willow's Ma wanted to find her, then why hadn't she shown up here already? Why was she still calling Willow every few days to beg her to come home?

An ex-lover scorned ... no, that didn't make sense, not given what I ken about Curtis. But what then ...

Willow wasn't telling the whole truth about her past, of that I was certain.

You're one to talk, or did you forget that you haven't told her about what you're planning for shifters, or that you're capable of the very monstrous things that she's so terrified of?

Shaking away the unsettling thoughts, I glanced up at Willow, studying her face of any sign of recognition as her fingers traced the stag on the medallion. She looked as stumped as I felt.

"Is there anything else here?" Willow asked, tucking the medallion into her shirt pocket.

"Just his scent." I ran my fingers over the bent grass and broken branches, thick with the man's distinct scent. There was no clue at all in the odour, apart from the fact the guy laid on thick with the aftershave. If I transformed into my wolf, I'd be able to pick up much more subtle clues with my superior sense, but I'd promised Willow that I wouldn't shift. "I'd like to follow it a little further."

A sliver of fear flickered across her face, but she nodded.

I helped Willow back onto my shoulders. As soon as her

arms were wrapped tight around my neck, I took off, following the scent as it weaved through the trees. It emerged a few miles later on the edge of the gravel road leading deeper into the forest. Tire tracks in the soft earth at the edge of the road showed me how our stalker had arrived. We looked around where the car had been parked, but found no other clues.

"Well, we cannae do anything else tonight," I said, dusting dirt off my jeans. I knelt down and patted my back. "Up ye go."

"Drop me back at the parking lot," Willow said, as she clambered onto my shoulders, her warmth burning through my skin. "I'll head back to my flat and—"

I shook my head. "You'll nae be going back to your place alone."

"Excuse me?"

"This guy is human, which makes me think he's after you, not me. He could be that same guy who was hanging around your flat the night Resurrection got trashed."

Willow's face paled. "You mean ... he was a stalker, after all?"

"Could be. Whoever he is, he could be staking out your place, waiting to get you alone. You need to come back to the cabin. You're staying the night."

A panicked look broke out on Willow's face. "But ... I have things to do."

I folded my arms. "We can do them together. I promised you that I wouldnae let you out of my sight."

"But—" Willow seemed ready to protest. Her mouth moved, but no words came out. *I ken it. There's some secret she's not telling me. Even if she doesn't ken who this guy is, she at least has an idea now of where to find out.*

"No arguments." I stood up, throwing Willow back onto my shoulders. She yelped in protest as I started off toward the forest.

"Irvine, wait! Put me down! Why can't we stay at my place?"

"You live in the village. If someone attacks you, I cannae shift into my wolf form with so many people around. We need to be in the forest."

"You promised you wouldn't shift into your wolf form in front of me. This wasn't part of the bargain—ow!" Willow jerked as a branch scraped across her back. "I said, put me down this instant."

"Careful. I dinnae want to drop you." Willow stopped squirming after that, and I managed to get her back to the cabin without any more protests. I expected her to try to leave as soon as I put her down, but all she did was slump against the bed and remove her prosthesis, a grave expression marring her beautiful face. I think she'd realised that I was right.

I made a fire in the tiny potbelly stove and and moved the two chairs in front of it. Willow curled up in one with a blanket around her shoulders, her stump propped up on the stool I used beside the bed. I grabbed a block of dark chocolate from the fridge and made a pot of bubbling hot chocolate on top of the stove, adding a little chilli for a real kick.

The discovery of our peeper had killed the sexual tension, but the connection still thrummed between us. I pulled my chair closer, and as I handed Willow a mug of hot chocolate, my hand brushed hers and the now familiar jolt of electricity shot up my arm. The moonlight through the window framed her dark hair in a halo of cold light, and the firelight flickered across her face,

My mate. My beautiful, brave, clever, shy mate. What are you hiding? What secrets lurk in your past?

Willow was the first to break the silence. "Hey, Irvine."

"Aye?"

"Why are you here?" Willow sipped her chocolate.

I shrugged. "Why are any of us here? That seems an awfully

deep question to surprise a man with after he's just given you a chocolatey treat."

Willow laughed, the sound like a rushing stream. "No, I mean, why are you in Crookshollow with Caleb and his crew? You must have a pack somewhere else."

"Aye, my pack, the Bairds, is back in Aberdeen. I've placed a wolf I trust as the new alpha there. What I'm doing here with Caleb is something that's going to make life better for all shifters. It's something I've believed in for many years, but Caleb is the only one who will be able to make it happen. It's important to me that we achieve what we set out to do, see it through to the end."

"And what is that?"

I studied Willow's face, searching for a sign that she might be receptive to our mission. I glanced over at her stump resting on the stool, and the force of her loss crashed against my desire to be truthful. The urge to tell her dried my tongue in my throat. *You can't do it. She will never understand, never accept that it would be better for everyone if shifters were known. And can you blame her after her own father took her leg from her?*

"I cannae tell you, I'm sorry."

"Fair enough." Willow rearranged the blanket, pulling it further back from her stump and exposing her bare skin to the fire. I fixated again on her limb, on how the skin had knitted itself together over the amputation, a single long scar the only sign that something traumatic had happened to her. The body healed the damage of the past.

I pictured Willow as a little girl, her brown curls tied up in pigtails with white ribbons. Her bright eyes sparkling as she played some kind of game. I tried to imagine the kind of monster that could see this girl and want to hurt her in such a way, but it just seemed impossible.

Surely thinking like a monster would come naturally to you.

"Oh." Willow's face flashed with heat. She hurriedly replaced the blanket over her leg.

"Why'd you do that? You were getting hot."

"You don't want to look at it."

"I didnae say that. I see it all the time."

"That's different. In the heat of the moment, you can forget about it. But no one wants to look at a broken person. It's fine." She blinked. "I'm used to it."

"You shouldnae have to be used to it, because there's nae a ring of truth to it. You're nae broken, like some toy on the shelf for repair. You dinnae need to be fixed, Willow Summers. And if there's one thing I hope you get out of this arrangement of ours, it's the ken that you're beautiful not in spite of this leg, but because of it. Because it's a part of you, and therefore is beautiful."

Willow glanced away, but not before I saw a tear roll down her cheek. "This is really good hot chocolate," she said, finally, keeping her face turned away as she raised the mug to her lips. "I love the chilli."

Right, so we were done talking about her, then. "Aye. My father used to make it like this all the time. He spent quite a bit of time in South America—"

"On business?"

I guess overseeing the illegal import of cocaine is considered business. "In a manner of speaking. Anyway," I raised my own mug to my lips, "he had a huge sweet tooth, and he couldnae hardly go a day without chocolate, which meant we spent many a night cooking mugs of this over our campfire."

"Where is your father now?"

I paused before taking another sip. My hand went to my throat, closing around the coin he'd given me as a good luck charm. *Careful. Don't say anything to give away the truth.* "He's dead."

"I'm so sorry." Willow still faced the wall, but she snaked her hand over to my lap and squeezed my thigh. "What happened? I mean, if you don't mind me asking."

"I found his body in part of the forest owned by the local manor. It was the full moon, and he was in his wolf form. From the looks of things, he'd killed a baby deer – one of the manor's herd. I found its carcass beside him. The gamekeeper must've seen him. He had put a bullet right through his neck."

That part at least was true. The memory of staring down into Pa's eyes as they glassed over threatened to surface again, but I pushed it down. It wouldn't do to get caught up in the past with Willow here.

Willow whipped her head around, her dark eyes burning into mine. "A gamekeeper shot a *wolf*? How did that not end up in the news?"

Shit. I was an idiot. "We talked him out of it. He's keeping our secret."

The lie tasted bitter on my tongue. I set down my hot chocolate. I no longer had the stomach for it.

Later, after the fire had wound down, we crawled into bed, our bodies twisted around each other. With one less limb to tangle together, we fit against each other in the tiny bed perfectly. Willow curled into my armpit, and a few minutes later, she was fast asleep.

My eyes remained open, trained on the window. A hundred thoughts whirled through my head. Who was the mysterious man who was watching us? Was it the same guy from outside the shop, or was it just a coincidence? Why was he after Willow, and was he just content to watch her or did he have something more sinister in mind? How would I keep Willow safe if she discovered the truth about what I have done, and what I was planning on doing? Because of our agreement, she was starting to open up and realise that shifters could be more than violent monsters.

Yet here she was, in bed with the greatest monster of them all.

25

WILLOW

*D*appled sunlight streamed across my face, and a delicious smell of cooked eggs wafted under my nose. I rolled over, expecting to feel my threadbare charity shop sheets under my fingers, and see my open suitcase of work-appropriate clothing in the corner of Bianca's old flat.

But no, I wasn't in my own bed. Once again, I was in Irvine's cabin. And there he was in the kitchen, frying eggs and sausages in his electric frying pan. He wore only a pair of blue jeans, and my heart thudded in my chest as I admired the sculpted curve of his shoulders and the colourful tattoos entwining his muscles. His face broke into a grin when he noticed I was awake, and my whole body tingled.

In a flash, the events of last night rushed back to me. The man outside, watching us, and the strange medallion he left behind. Fear clutched at me as I remembered that I'd have to figure out a way to call my mum while Irvine was out of earshot, and it would have to be soon, because I was due to meet Alex and I couldn't exactly talk to Mum with her around, either.

If Irvine or the pack finds out the truth about Mum and me, then all this is over.

Irvine held a heaped plate of food in front of me. "You slept well. I dinnae think an earthquake could've woken you."

"I had a comfortable pillow," I said, as I accepted the plate. Just the sight of all that food, lovingly cooked for me by my mate, whom I had deceived, turned my stomach.

Irvine winced as he rolled his shoulder. "Don't I ken it. What do you have on today?"

"I have a meeting with Alex. We're going wedding dress shopping." I fixed him with what I hoped was a withering stare. "And I don't want to hear any 'I've sworn to protect you' nonsense. You can't come with us. This is strictly girls only."

Irvine made a face, indicating exactly what he thought of that. "I dinnae want to leave you alone today."

"I'll be fine. This guy won't do anything in public, and besides, Simon will be driving us. I'll get him to stay close to us and keep an eye out for anything unusual. No stalker will escape that butler's eagle eyes."

"I need to speak with Caleb and the rest of the pack about our stalker." Irvine must've noticed my face, because he held up a hand. "Dinnae concern yourself. I'm nae telling them anything about us, but I need to find out more about that medallion and definitively rule out if this is related to our current mission. But I could ask Ryan to go with you, as well. I'd feel better if I ken there was a shifter with you—"

"No way. You're so clueless. We're going *wedding dress shopping*. Ryan can't see Alex in her dress before the wedding. That's not how things work. Please don't worry. We're going to the salons and for lunch at *Bewitching Bites* – we'll be out in public the whole time. He's not going to try anything."

Irvine's face remained stony. "Fine, but I *am* giving you additional protection."

"I said no! I can't wander around town with a werewolf on my tail."

"Dinnae worry, I ken about discretion." Irvine took my empty plate and rinsed it. "You won't even ken this guy's there. Come on, grab your leg, you dinnae want to be late."

Great. When am I going to get a chance to call Mum with both Alex and some werewolf watching me? But I couldn't exactly say that to Irvine.

Irvine wanted to drive me back into the village in his car, but I pointed out that I'd need my car for getting around. "I can't exactly drive your car," I pointed out. Grudgingly, Irvine climbed into the passenger seat of my tiny Fiat. Even with the seat pushed all the way back, his long legs pressed tight against the dashboard.

"You need a bigger car," he grumbled as I pulled out onto the gravel road, and his head bumped against the roof.

"You need a smaller body," I shot back.

I drove over to Raynard Hall, and let Irvine out at the beginning of the street, so no one at the house could see us together. He waved at me as I drove off.

As I stopped to wait for the gates to swing open, I watched him in the rearview mirror, scanning the houses on both sides of the street, searching for any sign of the guy. My heart thudded. *He doesn't have to keep this secret, but he is. He respects what I ask of him, like a mate should.*

At the thought of the word *mate*, my heart beat faster. I shook my head, trying to rid myself of the ridiculous juvenile thoughts. *Don't get attached. When he finds out who you really are, he won't want to stick around. This whole fantasy will be over, so enjoy it while it lasts.*

Finally, the gates created open wide enough for me to drive through. Alex was waiting on the steps when I pulled up. She looked gorgeous in a long, flowing maxi dress printed with bright birds of paradise, her makeup perfect and not a hair out of place. A genuine smile broke out across her face as she ran toward my car. Before I could stop her, she'd slid into the passenger seat.

"Hey, we're not taking this car—" My voice rose with panic, and I tried to position my body to hide the lever from Alex's view.

She waved a hand. "Oh, I'm sick of being stuck in a car with stuffy old Simon. Come on, let's make this a girl's day out. I'm ready to do some serious damage to my credit card." Alex tossed her purse on the floor, and reached down to adjust the seat. "Yikes. Someone *enormous* has been in this seat. It's like sitting in a crater. Who's the lucky guy, then?"

A hot flush flared across my cheeks, and my fingers gripped the wheel tight. "No one. There's no guy."

"Come on, Willow." Alex shimmied around in the seat. "I'm no fool. This is not normal. The seat even feels a little warm, as though someone was *just* here. It was Irvine, wasn't it? Go on, you can tell me."

My cheeks burned harder. "No, it's just some guy. You wouldn't know him."

"Some guy named Irvine?" Alex beamed.

"Please, I nearly had an accident coming over here, I'd really prefer it if Simon drove us."

I expected Alex to protest, but instead she made a pouty face. "Fine. Come on, then."

Grateful to have escaped any questions about my car, I happily slumped into the backseat of Alex's Alfa Romeo. Irvine trudged past heading up to the house while I was waiting for Alex to find Simon. He gave me a wink, but didn't come over, which I appreciated.

With Simon finally behind the wheel, we drove out of Crookshollow to our first stop – an upmarket bridal salon in the larger nearby town of Crooks Crossing. We parked up and Simon opened his newspaper. I trailed behind Alex as she skipped toward the door, trying to hide my stiff gait from her notice. Just as Alex grabbed for the door handle, a black shape dropped from the sky in front of us. I screamed and jerked back. The shape swooped right in front of the window and settled on top of the rubbish bin.

To my surprise and horror, I realised it was an enormous raven. I shuffled further away, not wanting it to peck me and give me a disease. But grinning, Alex simply reached down and patted the bird's head. "You nearly gave me a heart attack, you stupid git."

"Don't touch it! Birds can communicate disease." I gave Alex a gentle shove toward the door.

Alex looked like she was going to say something, but she must've realised I had a point. She stood up, gave the bird a little wave, and muttered something under her breath that sounded something like, "Hi, Cole."

Cole? That was the same name as Belinda's fiancé, the black-haired man from *Bewitching Bites*. With a start, I realised what was going on. This wasn't an ordinary bird. It was a shifter. Cole was a shifter. So this is what Irvine meant by watching us. He'd sent a raven to spy on me. A raven I'd drank with at the pub.

I sucked in a breath, willing my heart rate to return to normal. *I can handle this. At least if Cole is here, it means Alex and I should be safe if the stalker decides to show up.*

Just thinking about that guy in the bushes last night made my chest tighten in fear. I needed to call Mum, but I couldn't do it in front of Irvine or Alex and alert them to who she was. I decided to send her a text while Alex was in the dressing room.

I took a wide berth around the bird as I entered the shop. When I turned and looked back out the window, the bird was still sitting on the rubbish bin. It met my eyes with its two yellow orbs, and winked. The bloody raven *winked* at me.

I tried to push back the fear and focus on the task ahead of me – finding Alex her fairytale wedding dress. It certainly looked like we'd come to the right place. Racks of dresses lined the walls of the shop, their enormous ruffled and gathered skirts spilling out into the narrow aisle. I felt the familiar rush of joy at being in a bridal salon.

This was my favourite part of the job, helping the bride find her outfit. Academically, I knew a wedding dress didn't possess any magical abilities, but when a bride put on their dress, they *transformed* before my eyes. Suddenly, they weren't just Alice the accountant or Caitlin the B-level celebrity or Lady Henrietta the snobby woman with the obnoxious purse dog, but someone special and magical and blessed – a *bride*. A woman who was loved. A woman who had romance in her life, and was going to have her happily ever after.

I pushed through the racks, running my hands over the soft, silky fabrics and delicate beading, keeping my eyes peeled for something that would suit Alex. A large woman wearing a swirling dress covered in garish daisies bustled toward us. I wondered what the raven would make of her enormous hat covered in tiny stuffed birds.

"Ah, so there's my next appointment. Forgive me ladies, I was out the back tending to the alterations and I didn't hear the bell. Now, which one of you is the bride-to-be?" she gushed. Alex raised her hand shyly, and was greeted with a hug so intense, I swear I heard her ribcage crack.

"Oh, it's so delightful to meet you! I am Marsha Babcock, and if you have any other dress appointments today, you can go on and cancel them now, because your perfect dress is right here in this room. Now," she yanked Alex's arms out to the sides and twirled her around in front of three mirrors, "tell me about this wedding of yours."

Alex glanced at me and mouthed the word *help*.

"The theme is 'an enchanted forest'," I said. "Alex and

her fiancé are both artists who deal with nature and fantastical themes, so we're incorporating that into the theme. Guests will walk through an avenue of ancient oaks, decorated with glittering lanterns. They'll be seated in a half circle around an arch made of branches and herbs and flowers. We want everything to feel natural and organic and flowing, and—"

"So the dress wants to be floaty, majestic, lithe, like a fairy queen ..." Marsha cooed. Alex moved to inspect a rack of dresses. Marsha threw herself in front of it, her arms splayed wide and an expression of horror on her face.

"No! These dresses are not for you! What if that man of yours saw you in one of those, he'll think he was marrying the little matchstick girl instead of his radiant bride."

"They look perfectly lovely to me—" Alex tried to reach around her, but Marsha grabbed her wrist.

"For a woman of your stature, they are *filth*. Now, what is your fine gentleman's name?"

"Ryan. Ryan Raynard—"

Marsha screeched, and threw her arms around Alex, who stared over my shoulder with an expression that clearly screamed *help!* I shrugged. I had no idea what this mad lady was doing but I didn't think I'd be able to get Alex out of there any time soon.

"Argh, so you are the fair woman who has stolen my Ryan's heart? Why, if I'd had known you were planning the wedding at last, I would've come up to that big house with all the dresses and saved you the hassle."

"You ... know Ryan?" Alex looked shocked. I was a bit surprised myself.

Marsha chuckled. "But of course. His mother Clara and I are close friends. We're in the same coven. She's always gushing about her clever sons and their beautiful partners. Why, I can't believe she didn't think to make an appointment for you herself."

"Because that's *my* job." I didn't like the insinuation that I was superfluous. "Excuse me, what do you mean by a 'coven'?"

"Why, it's a group of witches who get together to perform magic and enjoy the occasional Irish coffee, of course." Marsha tore hangers off the racks and piled up a stack of heavy gowns in my arms. "These gowns are my own designs. You won't find them in some high street chain, but only the best will do for you, my dear."

"Excuse me, but did you say *witches*? Don't tell me you think you're a—" I snapped my mouth shut as Alex shot me a warning look.

"Don't tell me you're an unbeliever, dear." Marsha patted my shoulder as she laid a chiffon gown on top of the pile. "Not after I can smell a wolf all over—"

"These are beautiful," Alex practically yelled, grabbing a dress from my arms and holding it up to herself in the mirror. I guessed she was trying to avoid Marsha revealing the truth about her husband to me. Irvine had kept his word. She had no idea I knew anything. "I'll start trying them on."

"Of course, dear." Marsha patted my shoulder again. "Go hang those up for her. I'll hunt out some veils."

Marsha disappeared between the racks of white, but not before I had a chance to wonder at what she'd been about to say. Did Marsha really believe she was a *witch*? And was she trying to tell me that she could smell or sense Irvine in some way? That couldn't be possible.

Except ... of course it was possible. I'd had an intimate relationship with a werewolf for the last month. Believing that witches exist isn't exactly a huge leap.

I could smell werewolves. I'd always thought it was because they somehow reminded me of my father, and the trauma gave me a particular sensitivity to it. But if she could smell them too ... even clinging to my clothing ... then that meant that I wasn't the only person who could.

I wondered what Mum would make of that news.

Mum ... *shit*. I'd been so distracted that I'd nearly forgotten to check on her. With Alex occupied in the dressing room, I sent off a quick text asking her if she was okay and if there was anything unusual going on. I told her not to call me but to text her reply. Alex still hadn't emerged with her first dress, so I started to wander around the shop.

Under the window, I found another rack of Marsha's dresses. These weren't quite as intricate or flashy as the ones she'd chosen for Alex, but they were all the more beautiful for their simplicity. I flipped through the rack, each gown catching my attention more than the last. The woman may have been a bit nutty, but she had serious talent. I shifted aside a gorgeous ivory gown with a dropped waist and a beaded bodice and ...

Omigod. Look at that.

26

WILLOW

*I*t wasn't just any dress. It was *the* dress.

It was hidden right at the back of the rack, stuffed in between a Grecian-style gown and an enormous floofy petticoat. I drew it out and held it up to the light, my breath catching in my throat as I admired the glittering beading catching the light.

The gown was a simple design in soft ivory satin – a sweetheart neckline with scalloped detail around the bust, off-theshoulder cuffs edged with a line of pearls, and a plunging waist accentuated with lines of gold floral beading and more pearls. The fishtail skirt swung across my knees, shots of gold thread catching the light.

It was the most beautiful thing I'd ever seen.

Throughout my career as a wedding planner, a stab of envy always hit me whenever I caught the smile of love on a bride's face, or saw her sob as she tried on her wedding dress the morning of the wedding, or watched her and her beloved kiss at the altar. Over and over I told myself that marriage was just an archaic societal construct and plenty of people lived full and happy lives without ever having a partner, and I was able to bury that little sliver of jealousy deep down, almost so deep I could pretend it wasn't there at all.

But holding that dress in my arms, my whole body ached with a need I'd denied for so long. Tears sprung to my eyes as I breathed in the sweet smell of the beautiful fabric. I ran a finger over the exquisite gold threads, feeling the smoothness of the pearls.

To wear something like this, to pull it over your head and pull tight the neat corset lacing, to feel it shimmer and shift against your skin, to take your first steps in the matching embroidered pumps and to know that after your short walk down the aisle, your prince will be waiting there to kiss you and make you his forever—

"Do you like that one, dearie?"

I jerked so hard I nearly dropped the dress. "Oh, no." I tried to shove the gown back into the rack, but Marsha grabbed it from me and held it up against my body. I backed away, shaking my head. "No, no. I'm not getting married. I don't even have a guy. I'm just the wedding planner. I was just thinking of it for Alex."

"Nonsense. If you're any kind of wedding planner you'd know this cut is all wrong for her. And besides, a pretty thing like you, without a suitor? Poppytosh. You're probably beating the men off with a stick."

I tried to push the gown away. "I'm really not—"

Marsha shoved the gown back into my hands and pushed me into a changing room. "Go on, try it on."

"But—"

"No buts, young lady. You spend more than enough time running around after brides. You might as well relish any chance to be one for a few minutes."

And that's how I found myself standing in a changing room, holding the world's most perfect dress and staring at my terrified reflection. *This is nuts, I'm the wedding planner. I'm not here to try on dresses.*

Still, it *was* an awfully pretty dress. I held it up beside me, noticing how the ivory accentuated the lines of my cheekbones and made my usually pale skin glow. A tiny smile forced its way across my lips.

"Go on, Willow," Alex cried from outside. "I'm the bride, and what I say goes, and I want to see you in that dress!"

Fine. I wasn't going to win this. Sighing, I unbuttoned my shirt, and tugged off my bra. Next, I unbuttoned my trousers, and slid them over my thighs.

When I stepped out of them, the hem caught on the ankle of my prosthesis. I bent down to tug it off, and as my fingers slid over the carbon fibre, the stab of envy returned, twisting in my stomach like a knife.

It's all fine playing dress-up, but don't go thinking this could happen to you for real. Marriage, a family, kids ... that's for people who aren't broken.

I grabbed the fabric, balling my trousers tight. I hurled them at the mirror with all my might. They hit the glass and slid down into a pile. Now I was staring at my body, naked except for a black pair of panties and my prosthesis. Tears sprung in my eyes. Curtis was right, what a disgusting creature I was, not a whole human like Alex. I had no idea what Irvine even saw when he called me beautiful.

"Willow, we are growing impatient!" Marsha bellowed.

Furiously, I wiped the tears away. I was going to have to go out there and pretend I was just a girl trying on a dress, and not let them see this was tearing me up inside. I unlaced the corset and leaned against the wall for support as I stepped into it, careful not to trip while I supported myself on my prosthesis. I straightened up, letting the dress fall around me. It clung to my body, skimming my hips and nipping in just above my knees before flaring out in a wide fishtail skirt. I spun in a slow circle, and the gown flared out, the glittering golden threads shimmering like jets of fire.

Careful to avoid looking in the mirror, I tightened the corset as best I could, smoothed down the front of the bustier and made sure my prosthesis was completely hidden by the long hem. Taking a deep breath, I slid the curtain aside and stepped out in front of the mirrors.

The reflection that greeted me stopped my breath. *Is that me? It can't be me. It's a trick mirror.*

But it was no trick. I looked like a real bride. I looked like a picture in a magazine, joyful and mysterious, a princess waiting for her magic carriage and glass slippers to arrive. I imagined walking up the aisle with soft violin music wafting around me, and my mother handing me off to Irvine ...

Hang on a second, where had *that* come from?

Irvine was lovely and all, and the way I felt around him certainly made me giddy, but he wasn't husband material. Not even close. For one thing, he was a werewolf. For another, we weren't even together. We had that whole *mates* thing, but it was just a biological thing, it didn't mean we were *together* together. We were just ... friends-with-benefits together.

And yet here I was standing in front of a mirror in the world's most perfect wedding dress, and all I could think about was *him*.

"Willow, you look amazing," Alex breathed. She took my hands in hers, and stared approvingly down my whole body. "That dress is perfect for you."

I shook my head. "You're the one who looks amazing."

She did at that. The Grecian-style dress hugged her body in all the right places, the flowing chiffon moving as she did. Marsha had swept her hair back and pinned in a floor-length veil of similar gauzy fabric. With the inevitable breezes that would blow through the trees at her outdoor ceremony, it would create dramatic shapes that would make for beautiful photographs.

She was a dazzling bride. I was a poor imposter in a dress I'd never have the right to wear.

"I think we've found the ones," Alex beamed. "These are the perfect dresses."

"*You've* found the one," I said, dropping her hands and slinking back into the dressing room, where I was already tugging at the corset straps. "You're going to be a beautiful bride."

ALEX BOUGHT THE DRESS, and the shoes to match. Of course she did, it *was* perfect. After much fussing, Marsha put my dress – no, not *my* dress, obviously, I mean, the dress I'd tried on – back on the shelf and made sure I knew exactly where it was, just "in case you come back for it."

I left the shop with that knife of jealousy twisting in my gut. As we passed through the door, the raven croaked defiantly at us, and lifted a wing in greeting, as if to inquire what had taken so long.

I checked my phone. No text from Mum.

There was a jewellery shop nearby that my sources said had great stuff, but Alex insisted we return to Crookshollow. "I know exactly where we need to go," she said. Of course she knew some secret place where cool, rich artists shopped.

But no, she made Simon drop us right on the high street of Crookshollow. It was the middle of the day, so the street was packed with tourists ducking in and out of the crystal shops and tarot readers who lined the street. Crookshollow liked to bill itself as the most haunted village in England, because of the witches burned here hundreds of years ago and were buried at that tiny cemetery Irvine took me to. Supposedly their spirits still hung around the place. I'd thought the whole thing was silly when I'd first arrived, but judging by the sheer number of shapeshifters and now witches in the area, I was starting to believe the claims had some validity.

I got out of the car carefully, making sure my gait wouldn't appear odd. Alex rushed ahead of me. In her excited state, she'd probably never notice my limp.

"Come on, Willow." Alex waved at me from halfway down the street. "You're going to love this."

Alex walked right into one of the strange crystal shops that lined the streets of Crookshollow. I couldn't believe Alex was going to ruin her perfect dress with some cheap gothic junk. When I finally made it inside, Alex stood at the counter, pawing through boxes of crystals, while the stout old woman behind the counter placed her choices in neat rows on a leather mat.

Alex's face lit up when she saw me. "Willow, meet Clara, Ryan's mother and our wedding officiant. Clara, this is Willow. She just moved to Crookshollow from London, and she helped me find the perfect dress at Marsha's store today."

The old woman looked me up and down, Ryan's kind brown eyes giving me the once over. She must've decided I was worth her time, for she shuffled forward, clasping the black shawl around her shoulders with gnarled fingers. Black hair streaked down her back, startling against her wizened features. I gulped when I remembered that Marsha had said she was a witch. Clara Raynard definitely had an air of authority about her. I bet she was the head witch.

Finally, Clara took one of my hands and squeezed it. "Welcome to our village," she said, and her eyes crinkled at the corners. If she *was* a real witch, then I had a feeling she was definitely on the side of good, which made me feel slightly better.

"Thank you, it's nice to meet you."

"And you. Alex was telling me you met my friend Marsha. I'm sorry it didn't occur to me to introduce Alex to her sooner, but I'm glad you found her."

"That's my job." I grinned. "Her dresses are beautiful."

"Of course they are, and enchanted with magic to bless the union. In twenty-four years of running her store, not a single one of Marsha's brides has ever had a divorce."

"No?" I found that a little hard to believe.

"Not a one. Oh, she's had a few brides who've cancelled their weddings after buying their dress, certain that they had made a terrible mistake. But not a single divorce. When you wear one of her dresses, the magic helps you to clear your mind and focus on the one you love, the one you're destined to marry. And it helps to keep the oath you swear to each other foremost in the couple's mind." Clara must've seen something in my face, because she patted my arm. "I'm scaring you, dear. Please, don't you mind an old woman like me. Come and see what Alex has found."

"See these?" Alex held up two crystals. They'd been cut as long, thin points. They were quite beautiful – their dappled surface a brilliant deep blue. "They're Lapis Lazuli. This stone was sacred to the ancient Egyptians. They believed wearing the stone allowed them to commune directly with the gods."

That's ... kind of weird. "They're very pretty, but I thought we were looking for jewellery."

"We are." Alex beamed. "I'm going to wind these points on threads of silver and make them into a tiara."

Suddenly, I understood. "The black crown Bianca wore at her wedding, you made that."

Alex nodded. "I thought I'd do a trial piece first, before I made my own jewellery. Mine won't be quite as dramatic as

Bianca's, but I think I can get something really cool. What do you think?"

I think you're amazing and beautiful and talented and you have both legs and a perfect husband. The stab of jealousy twisted in my gut. Angry at myself for feeling that way about a client and friend who was genuinely wonderful, I plastered a smile on my face.

"I think you'll look absolutely radiant."

AFTER BUYING up several stones from Clara, and a stop *at Bewitching Bite*s to taste a selection of amazing cakes to decide on the flavour for hers, Alex and I ended up back at Raynard Hall. We were hanging Alex's dress at the back of her enormous closet, when Simon called up that the Ryan wanted to see her. Alex practically bounded down the stairs, and I trailed after her, not wanting to witness an intimate moment between them in my current state.

As I descended the stairs into the grand hall, Irvine and Ryan emerged from an adjacent hallway, followed by Caleb and another man. The wolf scent was thick between them, so I guessed the other guy was a werewolf as well. Alex leapt into Ryan's arms, and he spun her around and kissed her long and deep.

I averted my eyes, catching Irvine's gaze. He gave me a wink, and suddenly my body was filled with a different kind of ache. I may not ever have love like *tha*t, but at least I wouldn't die a virgin.

Ryan set Alex down and wiped a strand of hair from her face, gazing at her adoringly. "I hope you had a successful shopping day, and spent every last cent we earned from that last show."

"I don't think I could do that if I tried, but it was so cool. Willow's a genius. She found this amazing dress shop, run by this absolutely crazy lady named Marsha Babcock who is friends with your mum."

"Ah, I know Marsha well." Ryan grinned. "I can't believe I'd forgotten she makes dresses."

"That's exactly what Marsha and your mum said. But it's fine, because Willow found her and I found the perfect dress. Everything is falling into place." Alex beamed. "So what have you guys been discussing?"

"It's not nearly as happy as your news," Ryan said, his mouth set in a thin line. "Irvine noticed someone watching his cabin last night."

"Is that so?" I asked. Irvine was avoiding my eyes.

"Do you think it has to do with the ring—I mean, with your business deal?" Alex asked.

"We don't know yet," Caleb said. "But it makes we wonder if someone is not watching us. I'm reminded of that guy you saw outside your flat when Serenity trashed the shop?" His dark eyes penetrated mine. I nodded, looking away as a flush crept up my neck.

"Yeah, they could be related," Alex said. "Did you get a good look at the guy?"

Irvine shook his head. "It was too dark and he was hidden in the trees. I managed to follow his trail, and he left this behind." He fished the medallion out of his pocket and handed it to her. "I can't make head nor tails of it."

Alex held the medallion up to the light, and studied the stag. "Weird. It looks like it was made in one of those coin-stamp machines in tourist attractions."

"Huh?"

"You know ... you go to Warwick Castle on a school trip, and you stick a pound into the machine, and it stamps the coin with a picture of the castle and now you can't use the coin anymore but you have a pretty castle on it." She turned the coin over. "I must've collected a dozen of them from different tourist spots over the years. Look, you can see where the original coin has been squashed down, there." She pointed to the rim of the medallion. I squinted at it, and could just make out the edge of a pound coin.

"Oh, I don't think I've ever seen one before." Mum didn't even let me stay over at other girl's houses, let alone go on field trips. She didn't think the school would take proper care of my leg.

"Hmmm." Elinor pressed the coin back into Irvine's hand. "Make sure you show that to Anna. She's good at research and symbols and stuff. She might be able to trace where this machine is."

"Good idea." Caleb grabbed the medallion and stuffed it into my pocket. "I'm glad everyone's able to be so helpful. It would be really annoying if a person knew something about this but didn't speak up." He said the last bit looking directly at me.

"Um ... yeah. That would suck." Alex looked confused.

I was saved by the buzz of my phone in my pocket. "I have to get this, sorry." I grabbed my phone and raced outside, checking that no one followed me.

"Hi, Mum," I breathed, hobbling sideways down the steps and racing to my car as fast as I could. I couldn't risk any of them hearing this conversation. "I was worried when you didn't answer my text."

"I was at the pictures. There was a new teen werewolf film out today and I needed to write a review for the site. They're so strict with the mobile phones these days, so I had to turn it off. I called as soon as the film finished. I'm worried. Carol, what's going on? Did you see a werewolf?"

I slid into the driver's side, and slammed the door behind

me. I opened my mouth, but the words stuck in my throat. If I told her the real truth, she'd find a way to get to me and drag me back to London. She was only leaving me in peace because she thought I was safe. I hated lying to her, but if I wanted answers without giving up my freedom I'd need to be careful. "No, where I am seems to be werewolf free, so far. But I had this weird dream last night that something was wrong, that someone was after you, and they were trying to use me to get to you. That's not true, is it? Is something going on there you're not telling me?"

As lies went, it was a particularly clever one. Mum believed that dreams could predict the future or connect people to each other. She also believed that being bit by my father had given me other special abilities, although I'd never experienced anything that could be called paranormal apart from the ability to smell werewolves. If she thought I'd seen something, she'd tell me.

Mum paused for a fraction of a second before launching into a mighty tirade. "Oh, Carol, I didn't want to worry you, but I'm so afraid. The werewolves have sent a bounty hunter after me because of the *expose* I wrote about the werewolf who revealed himself at that tattooist's wedding. They're threatening to find you and use you to make me do their bidding. And if you're having premonitions in your sleep, it means your powers are finally coming in, and you'll need to come back and learn to commune with the spirits from my friend Serena—"

Anger rose within me as I realised what she was doing. "Mum, you're lying to me."

"I am not!" The fierce indignation in her voice gave her away.

"You are. You just made all of that up so I'd come back to London. That's low, Mum."

"Well, I'm sorry, but when a daughter runs away and doesn't even give me a way to find her, drastic measures must be taken.

What happened if werewolves attacked me and I needed you for a blood transfusion but I couldn't find you—"

"Then just commune with me in my dreams. Bye, Mum." I hang up while she was still chastising me and tossed the phone on the seat. My blood boiled with anger, but at least I knew now that she wasn't in trouble. At least, not that she knew of.

I turned back to the house, just as Irvine lowered his head in front of my window. I jumped, banging my head on the roof of the car.

"Ow, jeez." I rubbed my head.

Irvine tapped on the window. "Willow, open the door."

I did. He slid in beside me, his arms falling around my shoulders in that easy way that reminded me of Alex and Ryan hugging in the hall. And that made me think of the wedding dress I tried on, and that make my chest tighten.

"You ken I had to say something," he said, stroking my hair.

"Caleb knows," I said, burying my head into his shoulder.

"Probably he ken you were with me last night. He's nae a fool. But he doesn't ken that you ken we're shifters. Although I think we should tell them."

"I don't want to."

"I ken." He continued to stroke my hair. "But it will help me keep you safe. You ken the full moon is coming soon."

I nodded.

"I'm not gonnae leave you alone. I'll watch you the whole time. But I need help, and that means I need everyone to have as much information as possible. Do you ken?"

I nodded, my chest tightening. "I ken."

"So I can tell them?"

I nodded, squeezing his shoulders. *I hope this is the right decision.*

"Do you want to tell them?"

I shook my head vigorously, sinking into Irvine's embrace. I peered behind him, across the expansive front lawn of Raynard Hall. I'd parked near the end of the west wing, where the edge of Crookshollow Forest crept right up near the edge of the house. I stared at the edge of the trees, thinking that in only a couple of days Irvine would be living in there, running around with a tail and sharp teeth ...

What's that?

I gasped, my whole body stiffening. A shape moved behind one of the raised beds and darted back toward the forest. A man, dressed in black pants and an army shirt. There was a pair of hunting binoculars around his neck. As he ran, he glanced back over his shoulder, and I got a good glimpse of his face.

It's him.

Irvine shook my shoulders. "What is it, Willow? What do you see?"

"That was him," I whispered. "It was the same guy I saw in front of my flat. He was hiding in the garden watching us."

27

IRVINE

*T*hink back on everything she's said to you, every seemingly innocent conversation. Caleb's voice landed in my head. *Has she said* anything *that might give us a clue who might be after her?*

I was sitting some distance from his position, my eyes trained on Marshell House, where Willow and Elinor were enjoying a wine by the fire. Hanging out with the girls so much had changed Willow's mind about drinking, and she now loved a glass of wine if she was around people she trusted.

It was two days since Willow had seen the guy heading into the forest around Raynard Hall. I didn't hesitate in getting the whole pack together to tell them the full story about Willow – at least, the full story as I ken it. I'd wanted to do it before she changed her mind.

Everyone accepted her story with grace and empathy. That is, everybody except Caleb. He didn't like being deceived, especially when it put the plan in danger. Especially when Willow was still holding something back.

Because of my part in hiding the truth about Willow, I was

also in the doghouse with her. I ken I'd lost much of Caleb's trust, and I hated that, but it couldn't be helped.

Now the full moon had come, and we were running shifts to watch Willow and try to catch the guy. A search around Raynard Hall confirmed that he was definitely the same human who'd been watching my cabin, but that didn't give us any clue as to who he was or what he wanted with Willow. I'd given the medallion to Luke's wife Anna, but so far she hadn't discovered anything.

I cannae think of a thing. She didnae recognise him, so he's not her ex-boyfriend, and it's unlikely he's an ex-client of hers. She keeps all her old client files at her mother's house back in London, so we'd have to go there to get them. At first, Willow believed her mother hired a guy to track her down, but now she doesnae believe that, and I dinnae believe it, either. If he wanted to track her down, he would've grabbed her when she was alone the other night. Instead, he just seems to want to talk to her.

You know her the best out of all of us. What's your opinion?

I think it has to do with why she doesn't want shifters to be public, but she wonnae tell me why. Do you have any ideas?

Yes, Caleb said. *I think her father's behind it.*

That didn't make any sense. *She hasnae seen her Pa since she was a wee lass. Why would have come back now?*

A human attacked by a werewolf could be a powerful political tool. Being in possession of that human would be evidence enough that shifters and humans shouldn't mix. This would be especially important if you're a member of one of the packs that want to keep us hidden. Say, if you were responsible for a heinous crime.

My mind reeled. Holy shit. Caleb was right. WIllow's father could hire a human just a readily as any of us to keep an eye on her, learn her routines, and watch for an opportunity to strike.

I shuddered at the thought of what the evil wolf might do to my Willow if he caught her. Willow had just started to make a life for herself. There was no way in hell I'd let her father take that away from her. Not again.

I scanned the treeline, searching again for unfamiliar wolves or faces in the foliage. Nothing.

I wonnae let him hurt her again, I snarled. *I wonnae let her become a pawn in shifter politics.*

You may not have a choice, Caleb growled back at me. *Your duty is supposed to be to this alliance and our mission. I know how amazing it feels to find your fated mate, but I brought you in here because I thought this cause was more important than anything. Lately, you've barely lifted a finger to help us. You need to be careful not to neglect your own kind when they need you most, especially when your mate isn't being entirely truthful with you.*

Caleb didn't have much more time to berate me further, because Luke showed up to relieve me of my shift. I planned to head into the forest for a short nap before coming back to relieve Caleb in a few hours.

I trotted into the forest, my wolfish senses dulling the thoughts about Willow's stalker and the ugly words Caleb had spoken. Hunger surged in my stomach. A rabbit crossed in front of me, and I grabbed it and snapped its neck. As I chewed on the fresh meat, another scent wafted across my nose.

The stalker. He was here.

I dropped the rabbit and raised my nose to the air, sniffing to get the direction. The scent clung to a low hanging branch, only fifty yards from where I stood. I bounded into the trees, rage coursing through my veins as I traced the path of the man who'd brought nothing but trouble.

The scent grew stronger as I moved deeper into the trees. He'd been here not long ago. Perhaps he'd seen us patrolling the house and decided not to come any closer. *Smart boy.* I bared my teeth, wishing he were in front of me so I could take a chunk out of him.

Four hundred metres later, and I realised I might get my wish. I was heading downhill, toward a shallow stream that wound its way through the forest behind Raynard Hall. The scent grew so strong my tongue was hanging out. Every muscle in my body tensed, ready to pounce. I saw something move along the bank of the stream ... an upright shape that could only be a man.

I rocked back on my hind legs, and shoved off from the ground. I burst from the trees directly in front of his path, my teeth bared, my claws digging into the earth as I landed on the rocks right behind him. The stalker swung around, bringing his arms up. A rifle was pressed against his shoulder, the barrel pointed right at my chest.

"Come any closer and you're a dead wolf," he growled.

I pulled up short, my paws skidding on the wet earth. More than the gun that threatened me, my attack was halted by the sound of that voice and the familiar lips that spoke it.

Oh, shite.

I ken that face.

It all fell into place. I ken where the medallion had come from. I ken why the stalker was here. He wasn't after Willow. He was after me.

I deserved that bullet.

28

IRVINE

*T*he gamekeeper's son. After all this time, he'd come for me. I didn't blame him. In his position, I'd have come for me, too.

In the single, agonising moment that the gun's barrel pointed at me, all of the pieces fell into place. The boy had watched us from a distance, so he could figure out my weaknesses and find a way to get me alone. That medallion he wore ... I ken now that the stag printed on the coin was the logo for the Stoneleigh Castle hunting lodge. I remembered it now, painted on a sign beside the high iron gates.

If he wanted revenge on me, then capturing and hurting Willow would be a fine way to do it.

"You killed my father," growled the boy, his hands on the gun steady. There was no fear in his voice, only a cold, hard rage. "I watched you tear his throat out right in front of me. It's taken me five years to track you down, but finally, I've got you exactly where I want you."

Aye, that you do, lad.

I lowered myself onto my stomach, showing my submission. The boy lowered the barrel after me, so it continued to point directly at my face. I ken I should be shaking with fear or rage; I should be tearing him to pieces for daring to threaten me. But even my wolfish instincts gave way to the duty I felt toward this boy. All I had for him was a cold acceptance. This was right. It was proper. It was what I deserved.

"What does a murdering werewolf get for his crimes?" The boy continued, his voice dripping with hatred. "He gets a life. He gets a home and friends and a woman who loves him. How is that fair? My Ma left us after you killed Pa. My family is destroyed, because of you. I should take her from you, make you live with the pain of losing someone. An eye for an eye. But I'm not a murderer, like you. I was only going to warn her about you, about what you are. But she's not going to listen. It's better this way, if I rid the world of your evil, then she'll be able to move on."

I lowered my head. I couldn't argue with him. He was right. I was a murderer.

"Well?" the boy snarled, shaking the gun, his whole body rigid. "Don't you have anything to say for yourself? Don't you want to beg for your life like the flea-riddled mongrel dog you are?"

I met his eyes, and tried to convey my acceptance of his justice. I'd done a horrible thing, and because I was a wolf, I'd got away with it. The boy had sought the only justice he could get ... the justice of revenge. An eye for an eye. A life for a life.

My life, for the life I'd taken.

The vision came at me, as clear as that winter night five years ago. Pa took me with him to meet one of his agents with a delivery. The Maclean pack had raided several of our drops over the last month, and Pa wanted to reach the meeting point as soon as possible, before the Macleans got wind of his plans. So we were taking a shortcut through the area of forest owned by Stoneleigh Castle Lodge.

To cover the ground quickly, we were in our wolf forms. Usually we wouldn't risk being seen on the lodge's land, where trigger-happy hunters lurked behind every tree. But Pa thought on such a miserable night, with the ground knee-deep in snow and a frigid cold wind blowing straight into our bones, no one would be out. Except there was.

We stayed deep in the trees, avoiding the herds of deer that were the main attraction for hunters. I dawdled behind, weighed down by the heavy bag of drugs piled into the sling fitted to my back. Pa howled, calling to me to hurry up. He was worried we'd be late for the drop. His howl must've drawn the attention of the gamekeeper, who came running down the slope of the next hill, just as my pa reached the top of the ridge.

To this day, I don't know why the gamekeeper was out in that weather. As I saw the gamekeeper coming down the slope of the hill, I noticed he had a fox-trap in one hand. A rifle rested on his shoulder and a red-face teen trailed after him, wrapped up in several layers of thermal clothing and at least seven scarves. In a single, terrifying moment, the gamekeeper dropped the trap, grabbed his rifle, and let off a shot.

Pa went down, his nose landing in the snow. My heart leapt into my throat, and I bounded toward him, desperate to reach him. As I watched, a pink cloud spread out in the snow around him, and he forced his shift, so that by the time the gamekeeper and his son reached them, all they saw was a naked man dying in the snow.

The gamekeeper was yelling at the son. He kicked my father's corpse, yelling about spells and witches. He ken he'd seen a wolf, but now he was staring down at the body of a man.

I shrugged the drugs off and took off running as fast as I could in the thick snow, climbing up the ridge at a snail's pace. Every part of my body was numb, but not from the cold. My pa was dead, and I ken what I had to do.

We'd run this drill a hundred times. *Protect the pack at all costs.* The gamekeeper had seen Pa transform. He ken our secret.

I reached the top of the ridge and leapt into the air, hitting the gamekeeper square in the stomach.

He toppled back into the snow. The rifle flew from his hands as he cowered beneath me. His hands shook as he tried to protect his face. My veins buzzed with hot, violent rage.

His eyes were wide with fear but I didn't see it. All I saw was the man who'd killed my father. All I saw was my duty.

I sank my teeth into the gamekeeper's neck and tore out his throat.

"Dad, no!" the boy cried, leaping toward us.

As soon as the acrid taste of the gamekeeper's blood hit my tongue, a wave of shame rolled over me. I spat out the chunk of flesh, and forced my shift, until I was kneeling naked over the thrashing gamekeeper. His hands frantically clawed at his throat, as though he might somehow be able to push all the blood back inside. His mouth hung open, blood bubbling between his lips.

His son wrapped his arms around his father's neck, trying to pull him to his feet. This only made his blood flow faster, staining the son's scarves crimson. The son looked up and saw me, and he clasped his father's head to his chest. "Please ..." he begged. "Please help us."

The fire of my rage still burned within me, and I dug my feet into the snow, knowing it was only moments before I attacked the son, too. "Go!" I screamed at him. "He's dead, and you'll be too if you don't get out of here! If you say a word of this to anyone, I'll be back to finish you."

The boy didn't hesitate. He whirled around and raced into the trees.

And now, that same boy stared back at me, his face hard with hate. Hate that I deserved, for murdering his father while he watched.

I'm the monster.

The boy switched off the safety.

My whole body itched to leap at him and knock that gun right out of his hands. My blood boiled in my veins, incensed that he dared to threaten me. But through the drive of my instinct, I managed to hold myself steady. I stared down my death with what little sense of honour I had left.

Blood pounded in my ears. In slow motion, I watched the boy's finger squeeze the trigger.

Willow, I'm so sorry. I love you. I wish things were different, but this is what I deserve—

Just as the gun went off, a shape leapt out of the trees and crashed into the boy. The bullet whizzed past my face and embedded itself into a tree behind me. Caleb pinned the boy's shoulders to the rock, his teeth bared, his ears flattened.

I tore myself from my trance and darted forward. *Don't hurt him,* I cried at Caleb through the call.

He's trying to kill you, Caleb growled, his teeth scraping the boy's throat.

It's his right. It's the only way there'll be justice.

Caleb's shoulders sagged, and he dropped the boy and sat back on his haunches. The boy trembled as he reached for his rifle, but Caleb knocked it across the rocks with a paw.

What's going on here, Irvine? he growled inside my head. *Why didn't you fight back? This is the guy who's been stalking Willow. He was going to shoot you.*

He wasn't stalking Willow. He was stalking me, because I murdered his father—

The kid lunged for the gun. Luke leapt from behind Caleb, landing between the boy and the weapon. He knocked the boy down, grabbed his collar and dragged him further up the bank. *Who's this punk?*

Let him go, Luke, I pleaded. *He's terrified.*

Luke looked from me to Caleb, who gave a nod. Luke dropped the guy's collar, and he crumpled against the rocks. He cupped his hands over his head and glanced up at me, his eyes wide and his face white with fear.

With his paw, Caleb shoved his rifle off the rocks. It landed in the river with a *plop*.

What are we doing here, Irvine? Caleb asked.

We're letting him go.

Caleb nodded, and stepped back. Luke and I followed suit, backing toward the forest to give the boy the signal that he was free to go. The boy stared between us, and his face crumpled with relief as he realised what we were doing. He shot me one final hateful stare, and scampered into the forest, leaving me to face Caleb and Luke.

My two allies stared at me, their teeth bared, their eyes narrowed with concern.

Right, Caleb's voice, stern and strong, fell into my head. *I guess we know who he was after, now.*

29

WILLOW

While the wolves took their full moon shift in the forest, Elinor and I hunkered down in Marshell House, watching out the windows for my stalker. Before he left, Irvine told everyone in the pack that I'd been attacked by a were-wolf as a child, and that the attack had cost me my leg and also given me this weird ability to sense werewolves. I wasn't there when he did it, because I couldn't handle their pitying stares when they realised that Willow Summers was a broken person.

Strangely, it hadn't been as bad as I expected. It was actually a relief to have my knowledge of them out in the open. They were good people, and I hated deceiving them. I expected them to cast me out of their social circle when they found out, but instead, they'd embraced me like one of their own pack.

And that made me feel even worse. Because they only knew half the truth. And the other half ... it would hurt them all, especially Irvine.

Irvine hadn't left my side in the last few days, and perhaps because of that, we hadn't seen the stalker again. He was hiding in the woods behind Marshell House, taking shifts with Robbie,

Caleb, Luke, and Rolf, and I caught fleeting glimpses of them patrolling the gardens. Just seeing them out there made my stomach sink with dread.

They were worried my stalker might be trying to sabotage whatever they're planning. If only they knew about the true devil in their midst.

I missed Irvine. I missed his touch and his sexy Scottish accent and the way he couldn't say "couldn't" properly. I missed sitting by the stove in his cabin. I missed the comfort of being near him. He was the first person who knew that I was broken, and who treated me like ... a normal person. In fact, he treated me like a goddess.

This fated mates thing still made me nervous, but he'd proven time and time again that he would put my safety and my feelings before even his own. The way I thought about him ... I wasn't sure what we had could be described as "casual" anymore – at least not to me.

As the hours and days went on, my desire to see him only intensified. But I had to wait until the full moon waned.

Waiting sucks.

Okay, it didn't completely suck. Elinor and I ate a lot of take-aways, drank several bottles of wine (I can't believe I'd been avoiding wine for so long – it tasted so sweet and delicious, and I trusted that Elinor wouldn't take advantage of me), and talked until the early hours. We had more in common than I ever realised. She too had fled London to follow her heart in Crook-shollow. She too had overbearing parents who'd practically disowned her when she gave up her law career to become a tattoo artist. We both loved extra-spicy food and *Midsomer Murders*.

On the third day, I was cooking eggs for brunch, while Elinor thumbed through the local paper. "Hey look," she said, pointing to the moon diagram above the astrology section. "The full moon is over. It looks like your man will be back today."

I nodded. I had the moon's phases memorised. I'd been awake since 4 a.m., waiting for Irvine to knock on the door or clamber up to my window. He'd done neither of those things, and my stomach was in knots.

At 5 a.m. this morning, I'd caved and sent Irvine a text, telling him that I missed him and suggested some naughty things we might do together when we were alone. I hoped he'd see it as soon as he shifted back and come racing over here, but so far, nothing.

Elinor must've seen something in my face, because she dropped the paper and ran around the counter to embrace me. "Don't worry. He'll come back for you. He probably just hasn't come out of his shift yet. He's out there protecting you, isn't he? Trust me, guys like Irvine get off on being the strong silent protectors."

"Yeah." I twisted a tea towel in my hands. "I just wish he were here now, so I could say all the things I wanted to say. How do you stand having Eric away so much?"

"Hey, when your fiancé used to be a ghost, you kind of trust the universe is going to look after you—hang on a sec." Elinor's phone started buzzing. She picked it up from the counter.

Elinor had explained to me the extraordinary story of how she and Eric had met, when she'd come to Marshell House as a probate lawyer to settle his dead mother's affairs and discovered his ghost haunting the house. After solving Eric's mysterious murder and battling some drug dealers who were trying to kill her, Elinor, Bianca and Clara had managed to bring Eric back from the dead. If I didn't already have all the evidence I'd ever needed that werewolves existed, I'd never have believed it.

"Caleb, welcome back to the land of the unfurry ... omigod,

no way, that's awesome! " Elinor slumped into a stool, her face radiant with happiness. "I knew Robbie would come through for us ... Of course I want to be there. A little grave robbing is right up my alley ... okay, I'll be over as soon as I can."

Elinor flipped her phone shut and did a merry little dance right there in the kitchen. "He found it! He found it."

"You seem awfully happy for a phone conversation that just contained the word 'grave robbing,'" I said, grinning. "Who found what?"

"Robbie found the Benedict Ring, of course. We're going to go dig it up today. You're welcome to come along, but I figure you and your man will be otherwise occupied." Elinor winked.

"I'm sorry, the what?"

"Geez, you and Irvine really don't do much talking, do you? The Benedict Ring is only the whole reason he's here in Crookshollow. It's an ancient ring infused with powerful magic that's been entrusted to Caleb's family for centuries. It was lost around a hundred years ago. And now Robbie's figured out exactly where it is."

"Which is?"

"In the grave of a maid, Hattie, who used to live in the attic room at Bianca's house. Apparently Hattie was having an affair with Bianca's young ancestor, Silvia, and when an accident killed Hattie, Silvia buried the ring with her as a symbol of their love. We knew that a few months ago, but we had to find the grave, which wasn't easy because it's so old. A lot of graves get moved or destroyed. But he found it! This is awesome. Don't you think it's awesome?"

"Forgive me, but I don't think grave digging is quite as exciting as you do."

Elinor wrinkled her nose. "Yeah, that part's not so great, but it's necessary. The ring is an integral part of Caleb and Irvine's plan."

The plan. The secret project that Irvine and I had danced around the edges of. He didn't want to tell me, and I didn't want to know. But that was before I knew about this ring. *What could a shifter pack possibly be planning that required the use of an ancient, magical ring?* A niggling feeling at the back of my mind urged me to ask the question I swore I'd never ask.

"About this plan." I tried to keep my voice casual, as if I discussed such things every day. "What is it in a nutshell? Irvine was always a bit terse when it came to explaining what they're doing."

"You mean you don't know?" Elinor's eyes gleamed with pride. "They're working to lift the veil of secrecy that surrounds shifters. Soon, humans and shifters will exist side by side, on an equal footing."

What?

Elinor continued. "None of our friends will have to live in secret or fear any longer. Caleb needs the ring's power to help unite the shifter packs across the world and make it easier for humans to accept them into society."

The room span. Sickness welled up in my stomach, and red welts danced in front of my ears. A shot of searing phantom pain jolted through my leg. *They're using this ring to reveal the existence of shifters.*

If that happened, Willow Summers would be no more. The press would hunt me down and drag my story up for everyone to devour. Only this time, it wouldn't just be a tiny article on the fourth page of some shitty tabloid. I'd be splashed across the front page of every major daily in the world. My mum's videos would go viral. I'd be 'peg-leg' again.

Irvine knew about this. He knew all along. He let me believe he was looking out for me ... and all this time ...

My stomach turned. Bile rose in my throat. I rushed from the room, cupping my hands over my mouth in an attempt to stop myself from throwing up.

Shifters will be free. They'll be out in public. And all the freedom I've worked so hard to find for myself will come crashing down.

30

WILLOW

J stayed behind at Marshell House while Elinor went to help dig up the evil ring. I was pleased she was happy, but there was no way I was going to celebrate this so-called "victory". If I had to face seeing Irvine or any of the shifters there, I couldn't be held responsible for my actions.

They're going to use this dark, unholy ancient magic to brainwash humans into accepting them. It's horrific. How could I ever have thought Irvine was a good guy? How could I have ever thought he might have been my ... mate?

My phone beeped. It was Irvine, replying to my text. *I'm back, baby. I got your text, and I missed you, too. Meet me at the cabin and I'll show you just how much.*

His words sickened me. All this time, he'd known this was happening, and he'd just kept piling lies on top of lies. He'd even tried to get me used to the idea with all his questions. He knew how I felt, but it didn't matter to him.

I flung the phone against the wall, and it clattered to the floor in pieces. There was no way in hell Irvine Baird was ever touching me again.

My leg throbbed with phantom pain, and shivers of horror

wrenched at my body. I shuffled around the house, too agitated to sit down, too distracted to read or work. I hobbled up the stairs (seriously, why did the Victorians love stairs so much? Give me a sprawling American one-storey McMansion any day) and lay down on the bed in the guest bedroom, staring at the vines on the wallpaper until weariness overtook me and I drifted off to sleep.

Dreams assailed me, my own mind betraying me as it brought me visions of Irvine's face, his naked body wrapped around mine, of the surging in my chest whenever I was with him. I reached out to him, my whole body begging to touch him, to rejuvenate the bond.

Willow, you dinnae believe I'm evil, do you?

My fingers grazed his face, and the connection surged through my veins, dragging me from sleep. My eyes fluttered open to a soft feeling between my legs. The wallpaper blurred, and a wave of pleasure coursed through my body. Something shifted between my legs, and the warm feeling spread deeper into my core.

Curious, I reached down, my fingers grazing the top of someone's head. *Someone is between my legs, their tongue licking the entire length of me.* I knew I should be scared, but I was so close, right on the edge of orgasm. Part of me wasn't sure if it was still part of a wonderful dream.

I lifted the corner of the sheet up, just as the mysterious benefactor sucked my clit right into his mouth, and an orgasm tore through me.

From under the blanket, Irvine's eyes stared up at me, a wicked grin spread across his face as the pleasure rocked through my body. My blood grew cold, and as soon as my arms worked again, I scrambled up.

"Shit!" I slammed my stump against the mattress in my

frantic struggle to get away from him. Pain shot through my nerves. "What are you doing here?"

"I came to see you, of course. You didnae show up at the cabin, and I couldnae reach your mobile, so I thought I'd surprise you." He frowned. "Why are you looking at me like that?"

"Is that all you have to say to me?" I growled, trying to drive my heart rate back to normal. I dared a glance to the door. There was no way I'd be able to move fast enough to get around him. *Keep him talking. Find a way to call for help.*

"Nae. I want to talk about the stalker. We have some new information, and—" He frowned. "Are you okay? You look peeved."

"I *am* peeved. You know what? I'm sick of talking about the stalker. I'm sick of *thinking* about him. I want to discuss something else, like how you're working with the Lowe pack to dig up some ancient magical ring that you're going to use to brainwash the human race into accepting shifters."

Irvine's face darkened. He sat up, flinging the blanket off his thick shoulders. "How do you ken?"

"Why does it matter? Are you going to *eat* the person who told me? Are you going to tear them to pieces and leave them a cripple?" Tears burned in the corners of my eyes. "You know how I felt about shifters being public, but you don't care. My life will be over, but it's all the same to you. I thought you were different, but you're just the same as my father. You storm through the world, tearing flesh and bone and heart, and you don't care who you hurt."

"I care," he whispered. "I care very much, Willow Summers."

"Don't say that name! You don't care. If you cared, you never would even consider going through with this plan, bringing shifters into the world to terrorise innocent people. More people are going to end up like me—" I choked as tears poured from my eyes.

"Willow, no. You dinnae ken. It's the exact opposite. Most humans die because shifters have to protect their secret. So many horrible, senseless deaths—" He voice choked on the words. "Caleb has no evil intent. He just wants to do right by our species."

"What about doing right by *me*? What about not giving rights to the person who took my leg? What about allowing me to keep the only good things that ever happened to me?"

"What about it? I don't understand what you're problem with this is, because you won't tell me. You're keeping secrets, and I can't protect you if I can't understand. Your father escaped without being punished for his crimes because we have no ability to administer justice." Irvine's face darkened. "So many injustices are committed because shifters must remain secret. There are no options for our children – they have little choice but to become criminals to survive. Caleb wants to change that, and so do I. It was the most important thing to me in the world, until I met you."

"What do you mean by that?"

"I thought it was obvious. I mean that I love you, Willow Summers—"

"Don't say that name!"

"—I ken we have nae known each other long, and that we have secrets between us. But I donnae want it to be like this anymore. I want us to make a new arrangement. I want more of you, and to give you all of myself in return."

"You want more of me?" I picked up my prosthesis from the floor beside the bed and hurled it at him. "You're already taking everything from me! Willow Summers won't exist any more. She'll be gone, because of you!"

Irvine flung his hands up as the prosthesis hurtled toward

him. It clipped the side of his face, and he winced. "Willow, please. I want to make this right—"

"If you want to make it right, then you'll call off this stupid plan!" I screamed.

"Please, Willow. if you only ken why—" Irvine's face crumpled with pain. He held out a hand to me, but I slapped it away.

"*Don't* use that name—"

"Irvine, are you here?" Caleb's voice rang up the stairs. "We need to talk."

My whole body turned to ice. *Caleb.* The wolf behind this whole terrifying plan was inside the house *right now*.

31

IRVINE

*W*illow froze. The anger on her face crumpled into terror. "Caleb," she whispered.

"Yeah." He must want to discuss what we'd decided in the forest. Shit, he couldn't have chosen a worse time. Willow's face was turning white. She was scared out of her mind.

"Dinnae worry." I stood and took a step toward her. "I'm here. You're safe."

"He can't see me here." She scrambled off the bed and sunk onto the floor, grabbing her clothes from the pile beside the bed.

"What are you doing?" I hissed as she got on her hands and knees. "Are you going to pretend to be the maid, because if Caleb sees you scrubbing the floor without your clothes on, he's going to want to hire you."

"What do you think I'm doing? I'm hiding under the bed." Willow rolled her tiny body into the gap under the bed, dragging her clothes in after her. "Pull that corner down for me, and try and stop him from coming in here."

I did as she asked, not bothering to tell her that Caleb would probably be able to smell her if he entered the room, then went out into the upstairs landing and leaned over the balustrade.

Caleb stood in the entrance hall, his face stony. "What's taking you so long?" Caleb growled as he started up the stairs toward me.

"Sorry, I've been running errands. There's a lot to prepare."

"Where's Willow?"

"She's running some wedding errands for Alex."

"You have a train to catch in ..." Caleb glanced at his watch. "An hour and forty-five minutes. You've got the first meeting with the Lowell pack this afternoon, so you can't miss it." He jogged up the stairs and frowned as he noticed I was shirtless. "Look at you. You aren't even dressed yet. Have you even packed?"

I grabbed my crumpled shirt off the floor outside Willow's room and pulled it over my head. "I was just saying goodbye to Willow. It'll only take me a couple of minutes to grab my stuff. Relax, I'm nae going to let you down."

"You'd better not, not again. We've got a lot riding on this alliance." Caleb's eyes burned into mine. "You could be a little more grateful, man. It wasn't easy organising this at the last minute, and after the way you've been acting and all the trouble you've brought down on my pack, I could have just as easily left you to fend for yourself."

"I ken that. I'm just a bit distracted at the moment."

"Don't be distracted, Irvine. Just get this done. And I think it's best if you avoid Willow from now on."

"Aye?" I took a step to the right, placing my body between Caleb and the bed, hoping he wouldn't see Willow under the bed.

"I've found out something about Willow that you need to know. While I was away, I asked Rosa to have a look into Willow's background, see if she could find something that might explain this stalker. She was thinking it was connected to Willow's career, so she plugged Willow's name into a search engine, just to see some of the other weddings she'd done in London. And do you know what she found?"

I shook my head, my stomach tightening.

"Nothing. Because Willow Summers is not her real name. There's no record of her business in London, or any online presence at all before she set up a new website a month ago."

"That cannae be true." How would Willow run her company without a website?

Caleb shook his head. "And that's not all. Rosa found an article about another London wedding planner, Carol Winters. Apparently, this wedding planner is blonde, but she has an uncanny resemblance to Willow *and* a prosthetic leg – one that she's used along with an interesting story to get PR for her business. She was attacked by a werewolf when she was a girl, you see. She's in the tabloids and on YouTube videos all over the internet talking about how evil werewolves are and how much she wanted them all killed." Caleb frowned. "Irvine, Willow is the daughter of Helen Winters."

What?

That was insane. That didn't make sense. Helen Winters was the publisher behind the *Werewolf Watch* website, which attempted to reveal the crimes of shifters and other supernatural coverups. There wasn't a shifter alive who hadn't seen Helen Winters' ridiculous so-called news stories. Sometimes, her guesses about national news stories were spot on. Just last year, she correctly guessed that a scuffle with a wolf at a Ryan Raynard exhibition opening was actually a shifter attack and not the performance art the media claimed. Luckily, the site also included articles about other conspiracy theories, like the fake moon landing and the earth being hollow and filled with Nazis, so a lot of the truth got lost in the noise.

Helen Winters was a nutcase, and she *hated* shifters. Willow couldn't possibly be her daughter, could she?

From beneath the bed, Willow gasped. Caleb didn't seem to notice.

"That dinnae make sense," I said, even as the pieces of Willow's story started to fall into place. She'd spoken about her overbearing mother, and I ken she was hiding her past from me, but I thought it was an abusive stepfather or just extreme loneliness. Never could I have imagined *this*.

"I've seen the footage, Irvine. She's a blonde in the pictures, but there's no mistaking Willow's face. Her story is all over her mother's site. Don't you see what this means? It can't be a coincidence that she's here, trying to get everyone in our pack to hire her for their weddings right when we're planning the big reveal."

I reeled at his words. "Say what you mean, Caleb."

"Willow Summers, or Carol Winters, is here to expose our secrets. She's feeding information back to her mother. There are articles on Helen Winters' site that contain bits of information about us, about a plan that's afoot, about Robbie's appearance at the party. Where do you think she's getting this information?"

"It cannae be from Willow. I havenae told her anything."

"Don't be so sure. You might've said things in the heat of the moment that you don't even remember—" Caleb's eyes fell on the prosthetic limb at the end of the bed. *Fuck.* I couldn't believe Willow had forgotten it. He looked up at me and raised an eyebrow. I averted my eyes.

When Caleb spoke again, his voice was hard. "Tell Willow when you *see* her next, that the Lowe clan doesn't take kindly to infiltrators, and that no one else will be hiring her for their weddings." Before I could reply, he pushed passed me and thundered down the stairs.

Caleb slammed the front door behind him, leaving me alone with the woman who'd done nothing but lie to me.

32

WILLOW

*T*he front door slammed. Caleb had gone, but not before he'd shattered my entire life. My heart hammered in my chest. I crawled out from under the bed as quickly as I could, grabbing my prosthesis and attaching the vacuum. *I need to get out of here before Irvine—*

Too late. Irvine stood in the door, blocking my escape. His eyes blazed.

"Do you want to explain?" he growled, his arms folded across his chest.

"I could ask you the same question," I threw back. "We're talking about the secret project you've been working on, revealing the existence of shifters to the world?"

"Don't act like you didn't know, *Carol*," he retorted. "That's why you're here, isn't it? You're trying to expose everything we're doing so that we're hunted down and killed."

"I'm not working for my mother. I *left* my mother. She doesn't even know where I am or that I changed my name. She's the reason I can't stay here if shifters are exposed. If Helen Winters becomes an authority on shifters, then I'll never be able to be free again. I swear, I didn't lie to you, Irvine."

He snorted. "This whole relationship has been nothing but lies."

His words cut me, so I shot back. "What relationship? We don't have a relationship. This was about sex, nothing more."

Irvine sneered. "Lying to me is one thing, but how long will ye keep deluding yourself that this didnae mean anything to you?"

The side of my neck throbbed from where he'd bitten me. Even in the heat of our fight, the air around us sizzled. Seeing the pain and rage on his face now, my whole body ached to collapse against him and kiss that pain away.

But now I saw what I'd been trying so hard to ignore, that I'd hoped in my heart wasn't true because Irvine was the only man who'd ever cared who I was inside. We could never be together. We'd never be equal, because we were fighting for different sides.

A human and a werewolf – what had I been thinking?

"I don't owe you anything, Irvine Baird." I hated the way my voice wavered, the way the tears streaking my face showed just how false my words were. "Move out of the way. I'm leaving."

"No." He picked up the leather jacket he'd dropped on the floor. "*I'm* leaving. Goodbye, Willow Summers, or Carol Winters, whatever your name is. I hope you have a nice life. I hope all the shifters you've doomed to die make up for all the pain you've survived."

With a last, lingering look filled with pain and hatred, Irvine slammed the door behind him and stormed out of my life.

33

IRVINE

J was packed and ready to leave Crookshollow forever. I'd lost everything that was dear to me, and I was now a liability to the pack. What was the point in staying? Caleb was right. I'd be more useful in London, if I could pull my head out of my arse and start working on the reveal, like I was supposed to.

No more distraction. Willow is gone. She never even existed in the first place.

I had one final chore to do before I left for the train station. The whole pack were gathered at Clara's shop to witness the activation of the Benedict Ring's power. Caleb had ordered me to be there, and I was already late.

I pulled my car to a stop on the high street, jumped out, and rushed Astarte. Clara had the CLOSED sign up on the door, but it was unlocked, so I barged through. She was standing behind the counter, shuffling tarot cards, and tsked as I entered.

"The rest of them are in the back," she said, as she shut and bolted the door behind me.

I entered the tiny storeroom. All the male members of the pack glared back at me. My stomach churned, but I stood tall, not wanting to show them how much pain I was in. So Caleb had told them everything.

"Hurry this up," I growled. "I have a train to catch."

"Now that we're all *finally* here. Come on, Caleb." Luke jabbed his cousin in the ribs. "Let's see it, then."

Caleb stood at the rear of the storage room, holding out a parcel of black velvet in his hand. He lifted up the edges of the cloth, revealing the ring. "It's beautiful," he breathed, holding out his hand so we could all see.

It wasn't. It was tarnished from age, and was impossibly large and gaudy. A large stone that Caleb had called a bloodstone was surrounded by coiled snakes. It looked like the kind of ring you could pick up in Camden. It didn't even glow with power or give off a strange vibe.

Because of that ring, I lost Willow. I'm not even sure if it was worth it.

"What do we do now?" Ryan asked.

"I guess I just put it on." Caleb reached for the ring.

"Hold on, Caleb." Clara pushed her way through our circle. She picked up the ring and held it close to her eye. "Hmmm."

"What?" Caleb grabbed for the ring, but Clara held the ring out of reach.

"Let me just check ..." Clara rifled around in her pockets, and pulled out a small stone on a leather cord. She held the stone over the ring, dragging it back and forth multiple times. Finally, she sighed, and tipped the ring back into Caleb's hand.

"This ring won't help you," she told him.

"Huh?"

"That ring contains no power. It's as useless as one of the cheap pewter ones I sell out front."

"But ..." Caleb spluttered. "But this is the Benedict Ring!"

"That may well be true, my dear. I do detect a small trace of residual power. At one time, this ring did house a great and powerful force. But not any longer. What power it contained has long since dissipated."

"But how?"

Clara shrugged. "Some mysteries of the universe are simply outside my scope to uncover."

Caleb turned to Robbie, his eyes flashing. "How did you not foresee this? It must've been in your research?"

Robbie paled.

"Hey now," Luke said, placing his hand on his cousin's shoulder. "We shouldn't start yelling at each other. It's not Robbie's fault a centuries' old ring isn't what we expected."

Caleb dropped the ring on the ground, where it bounced two times and rolled against the side of my boot. He slumped down against the wall. "What are we going to do? We've got packs all over the world waiting on us to make the first move, but without the ring, how am I going to get Parliament on our side?"

"Do we need the ring?" I asked.

"Huh?" Caleb's voice was sharp as his gaze swung to me.

"Do we need it? Our cause is good and right and just, and other shifters see that. We pollute it by using magical persuasion to get our point across. I've nae felt good about using that ring – it's nae something we can easily control or understand. Maybe we dinnae need to bring ancient rings into our fight at all. If you want Parliament on your side, maybe you just need to go down there with as many shifters as you can and demand they grant us our rights."

"Irvine, don't be stupid. Without the ring, why would they listen to me?"

"Shifters and humans are already listening to you. Rolf kens the current ring is fake. He told me so." Caleb's face paled, but I continued. "All the Wulfrics ken, but they still allied with us. Why? Because this *matters*. It's about the future of every shifter, and all the shifters of the future. And that's important enough."

Caleb's face remained stony. All the shifters started between us, waiting to see what would happen next. It was Robbie who broke the silence. "I think Irvine's right," he said, his voice shaking. "We dinnae need the ring. Everything we've achieved up until this point proves it."

Luke rubbed his head. "We're going to have to completely rethink the plan, but I think we can do it, too."

Caleb glared around the rest of the room. "Do you all agree, then? Do you all think we can still do this without the ring?"

Every shifter nodded their assent.

"Fine." Caleb rose to his feet. He picked up the ring and handed it to Clara. "Then we'll do it. Now get out of here, all of you – you've got work to do. And Irvine, you have a train to catch."

WILLOW

"*I*f you hang on a second, I'll get those samples for you." The salesgirl took my order sheet and flashed me a smile.

I grunted in reply. Usually I had nothing but patience for anyone in the wedding business. Dealing with bridezillas every day was bad enough without adding anal retentive wedding planners into the mix. But today I just couldn't plaster a smile on my face.

While I waited, I dragged my mobile out of my pocket and stared at the screen. Nothing. No missed calls, no texts. Nothing.

He stormed out and told you to have a nice life. What did you expect him to do?

After Irvine left me at Elinor's that day, Caleb and Elinor came back and told me that Irvine had left for London, and the stalker wouldn't bother me again, but that I wasn't to have any contact with him or the rest of the pack, apart from finishing Alex's wedding. Elinor looked shaken and upset, but Caleb's stony face told me there was no sense arguing. I hurried out of there, so they couldn't see my cry.

That was two weeks ago, and I hadn't heard from anyone in

the pack apart from Alex since, and even she was standoffish and businesslike. *So much for friends.*

Even though I hated Irvine, his words never left me. They burrowed into my every waking moment. I thought a lot about that fight, and then I thought about why I thought about it so much. I thought so much that my head ached, although that might've been from the copious amounts of wine I was consuming on my own every night.

I hated to admit it, but Irvine was right about one thing – there was nothing casual about what we shared. The sex was amazing – oh god was it *amazing* – but it wasn't why I came back to see him over and over.

I love you, Willow Summers.

I'd thought … if he really felt that way about me, he would try and find some way to be with me. I expected flowers, heartfelt apologies, grand gestures like the ones in romance films that would somehow make everything right between us.

No. He's a werewolf. You don't want him back. It was better this way. I'd become too attached to him and the pack and my life here. I should have known it could never last. I shoved the phone back in my jacket, and tried to focus on the display of personalised party favours in front of me. Irvine wasn't my boyfriend. He wasn't my fated mate. He was the guy I was sleeping with. People did that all the time, and they didn't go into a maudlin depression when they stopped.

"Here you go." The bouncy salesgirl returned, carrying an enormous cardboard box stuffed with sample decorations. "We're all out of the green fairy lights at the moment, but I've added two strings of pale pink just so you can see how they look—"

"Take them back," I snapped, shoving the box back into her arms.

"Excuse me?"

"The pink fairy lights. Take them back. This is not a pink bride I'm dealing with. If you don't have the green then I'll just get them somewhere else."

"But—"

"Look, I'll do it myself." I grabbed a string of lights from the top of the box, dropped it on the counter, and stormed out of the shop. My gut twisted at the thought of how rude I'd been, but who cares? She was a salesgirl. Her job was to deal with rude people.

I leaned the box against the side of the car, bending back at an awkward angle to insert my key in the door.

"I want to talk to you," a voice growled right by my ear.

I jumped back, and the box clattered onto the footpath. Glass fairy lights smashed against the concrete. I whirled my arms in the air as I scrambled to remain on my feet. I glanced up from the mess, and my eyes met the face of my stalker.

I froze. My throat closed in terror.

"What … what do you want?" I managed to choke out.

"Please, don't run away. I'll help you clean all that up, I promise. Just listen to me for a second. It's really important that I tell you about your boyfriend."

"Well, then you have nothing to say to me, because I don't have a boyfriend." He shifted forward, but I backed up, so I was leaning against the car. "This is a busy street. If you don't back away *right now*, I'm going to scream."

He took a step back, and raised his hands in a gesture of supplication. "I'm sorry. I really don't want to scare you."

"You've been watching me. That's pretty scary."

"Only because I was trying to get you alone, so I could tell you that you have to stay away from the Scottish werewolf. He's dangerous."

I didn't know what to say to that, so I stayed silent.

The man sucked in a deep breath. "My name is Lachlan

Ross, of the Stoneleigh Castle Hunting Lodge. Five years ago, your werewolf murdered my father."

I stared at him, unable to comprehend what he was saying. *Murder?* That didn't sound like Irvine, even Irvine the wolf.

Lachlan nodded vigorously. "He *did*. I saw it with my own eyes. We were out checking fox traps, when we turned toward the ridge and there was this wolf standing there, plain as day. A *wolf!* In Scotland! It bared its teeth and growled. I think Pa wasn't sure what to make of it. I think he thought it was a big, rabid dog, and he was worried it might attack. I dinnae ken, because I'll never get the chance to ask him."

"What happened?" I whispered.

"Pa shot it. We raced up the ridge to inspect it, to see if our eyes really didn't deceive us. Then, from out of nowhere, there was a second wolf. It leapt at my Pa and tore his throat out. Blood stained the snow pink. The wolf shook Pa's body and dropped it into the snow, then turned to me. I thought I was done for, but instead, the beast transformed into a man. Right in front of me! A naked man with evil grey eyes and my father's blood streaming down his face. He told me to run. I ran. I ran back to the lodge and reported what I'd seen. I gave his description to the police. They found Pa and did an autopsy, but they said a wild dog attacked Pa. They said I must've been mistaken about the man I saw. Pa's death was ruled an accident and that was it, we were just supposed to go on with our lives. There's no justice for me. Do you have any idea what that feels like?"

"Yes," I whispered. "I do."

Lachlan didn't seem to have heard me. "But I ken what I saw. I never forgot his face. I've been looking for him for years, and I finally saw him in a photograph on the *Werewolf Watch* website. He was in the background of a wedding photo where another werewolf had transformed. The press said it was a stunt, but I ken better. So I came here to Crookshollow, and I saw him with you, and I ken I had to warn you, before you lost something you love, too."

For the second time since I fled London and promised myself I'd pretend I was normal, I lifted up my pant leg and showed him my prosthetic.

"A werewolf did that to me," I said, surprised that my voice didn't shake at all. Lachlan's eyes widened as he took in the prosthesis, then lifted again to my face.

"I ken it ... I ken you looked familiar. You're the daughter of Helen Winters, aren't you? You were the one whose own father ripped off your leg. I saw you in her YouTube videos—"

"We're on the street," I said sharply, dropping my leg. "I don't go by that name anymore. Thanks for your concern about my safety, but Irvine has gone from my life now. I don't think he'll be back."

His shoulders slumped with relief. "I'm glad to hear it. I just wish there was something I could do to stop them, you ken? I dinnae want anyone else to get hurt."

An idea started to form in my mind. "Maybe there is something you *can* do. The werewolves are planning something big. I can't do anything to stop it, but I know more about it than probably any other human. I can't go back to London, but if you really want to help stop this evil, then you could go to my mother. I'll tell you everything I know about what the shifters are planning, and maybe you can help her stop them."

Lachlan's face brightened. For the first time, I noticed that he was quite handsome. "I'll do it. I'll do anything."

I gestured to the box of smashed lights sitting on the footpath in front of me. "I have some work to do now. Come to my place at 7 p.m. tonight. I assume you still know where I live. I'll give you all the information you need."

We shook hands, and he helped me pick up all the broken glass and throw it into a nearby rubbish bin. I slid the box of unbroken strings into the backseat. "Thank you for listening to me," he said as I pulled away. I nodded, numb to his bright smile.

My mind whirred as I headed out toward Raynard Hall to deliver the lights. My skin crawled.

Irvine murdered someone. All this time, I'd been sleeping with a murderer. Did the pack know? They must've known, because they'd sent Irvine away and said the stalker wouldn't bother me. They knew Lachlan was after him.

They were supposed to be my friends, but they betrayed me, too.

That's it. I'm done being the quiet amputee who let everyone walk all over me and make my decisions for me. I am going to take matters into my own hands.

Willow Summers wasn't just going to lie back and let her life be taken away. Shapeshifters would become public knowledge over my dead body.

35

IRVINE

I hate London.

The thought ground at my head with every waking moment. It drummed in my ears while I met with pack leaders in secret and took tea with politicians at the Savoy and shoved my way through hordes of tourists crowding the street outside Buckingham Palace.

I hated the crowds and the smog and the grey, drab buildings. I hated the tiny closet in a filthy squat that passed as my headquarters. Most of all, I hated the fact that I hadn't seen or touched Willow in a month.

I hadn't realised how much I'd come to rely on her presence, until I found myself sleeping under the stars in my wolf form, without her warm body beside me.

Caleb sent me to London under the protection of the Lowell pack, hoping to hide me from the boy's wrath and protect Caleb's secrets at the same time. It didn't seem to be doing much good – stories about his plans were leaking into the *Werewolf Watch*, and discontent among the London shifter community was growing. Some agreed with Caleb, some disagreed, but all wondered if he'd be able to pull off what he was trying to do.

Today, I sat on a graffiti-covered bench in Highgate Wood. I'd been given an ancient laptop by the Lowell pack to help me with my work. It rested on my knees, with my phone providing a wifi hotspot, while I searched for yet more articles on Carol Winters – the woman I had known as Willow, my mate. No matter how many times I saw them, I couldn't seem to turn away.

There she was, a blonde wedding planner lauded as the genius behind the most anticipated royal wedding of the decade. There she was again, speaking in an interview with the *Daily Post* about the harrowing attack that left her an amputee. My chest tightened every time her picture flashed up on the screen – that beautiful golden hair that perfectly framed her heart-shaped face.

Every word she wrote stung me, twisting the knife of her betrayal deeper. *Werewolves are evil. They cannot control the monster within. They must be stopped. The only thing that protects humans is the fact that they must live in the shadows.*

The words burrowed their way inside me, a constant mantra that haunted my dreams and followed me to every meeting.

They cannot control the monster within.

I'd dared to hope that with her as my mate, I had a chance at a normal life. That I would have been able to step out of the shadows and atone for my sins. My love for her burned bright and hot in my veins, but because of who she was, we could never have a future.

There could be no redemption for me.

A burst of anger seized me. It wasn't fair. If Willow couldn't accept me for what I was, then no one ever would.

I grabbed my mobile phone, and tossed it as hard as I could. It landed in a deep puddle on the other side of the path with a sickening *splash.*

36

IRVINE

I'm a fool.

Three nights later, I was back in Highgate Wood, hiding in the edge of the trees, staring out at the same pond where I'd drowned my mobile phone and with it, my link to Crookshollow. Previously, Caleb had been calling me every few days with updates. He was tired of waiting and plotting. He wanted to move. Caleb's agitation practically vibrated down the phone, mirroring my own.

Now, after three days of no word, no instructions, no updates on what was going on, my agitation was starting to slide over into a full-blown breakdown. That was why I was here, to get answers.

The moon shone cold light through the trees, reflecting off the smooth surface of the pond. Somewhere in the distance, a car alarm went off, reminding me that I wasn't in some remote forest, but in the middle of an enormous city that was hostile to my kind.

Willow. I have to find Willow. I have to know she's safe.

I hadn't contacted her since I arrived in London. I didn't want to speak to her, but my love for her still burned in my veins. At least when I'd been talking to Caleb, he'd been able to give me updates, because he was watching her and waiting to see her pass information to her mother's people. At least when I had my phone, I still had the possibility of contacting her at a moment's notice, but now, I had nothing, and it was driving me crazy.

I had no idea how I'd managed to survive for a month without breaking down and calling her. Every time I passed by a red phone booth, the urge to pick up the receiver and dial her number stopped me in my tracks. But I resisted.

I'm doing this for you, Willow, so that you can get your justice. Why cannae you see that?

Caleb's words echoed in my head. *Don't get distracted. Remember why you're doing this.*

I tried. I tried so hard. I no longer saw my father's dead eyes when I thought about the plan. Instead, Willow's face burned in my vision – stuck in the moment of one of her rare smiles. I thought of the tears that sprung in her eyes whenever she felt nervous, the way she called herself "broken" in that deadpan voice, as though she was reciting her shopping list. Because she believed it. Because the humans in her life had made her believe it.

If I could just show her what shifter freedom could mean for her life, then maybe she'd forgive me, maybe she'd understand.

Willow needed to bring her father to justice for what he'd done to her. It was the only way she'd be able to see herself as whole, as the beautiful, amazing creature that I loved with every fibre of my wolfish being. If she got that closure, then she'd be able to fade away into the background of the world. People would stop focusing on her, and she'd be free to live her life the way she wanted.

And that was why I was here in Hyde Park, about to visit someone I hadn't seen in a long, long time.

In the distance, Big Ben chimed. Midnight. Time to meet my contact. I slipped back, hiding myself in the foliage. Even though it would be unlikely anyone would enter the dark trees this late at night, I kept my body low, ducking and weaving to avoid the paths of the few drunken teenagers who were making out on the edges of the miniature wood.

It took me only a few moments to locate the tree. It looks identical to every other tree, only its smell gave it away. I sniffed around the base, searching for a hiding place, but could find none. *Where are you? We had an agreement—*

Hey, wolfie. Up here!

The high-pitched voice squeaked inside my head. Relieved, I glanced up. Sitting on a branch high above my head, a small squirrel stood with its tiny hands on its hips.

You're late.

Don't blame me, Chip. It took twenty bloody minutes to get across town, and then I had to find somewhere to stash my clothes. Why cannae we meet in a pub like normal people?

The squirrel shook its tiny head. *I don't do humans, and neither should you. They're a waste of perfectly good oxygen, if you ask me. If they didn't make such delicious roasted nuts, I wouldn't bother with them at all. Speaking of which, did you bring payment?*

I lifted my paw, shaking off the tiny leather pouch. It hit the ground and the drawstring popped open, spilling a huge handful of honey-roasted cashew nuts across the fallen leaves.

The squirrel leapt down and gathered up the nuts in his arms, dragging as many as he could hold back up the trunk again and stashing them in a hollow.

I accept your payment, he said, collapsing in the crook of a branch and nibbling on a cashew nut. *Now, what is it you want to know?*

There's a wolf. I dinnae ken his name, but he used to live in

London twenty years ago, and he was married to a lady named Helen Winters. He attacked his own daughter. Do you ken him?

That's not much to go on.

I ken. So can you help me?

The squirrel nodded. *Lucky for you, I remember the story well. You're talking about Richard Carson. He's a mutt.*

A mutt. That was news to me. Mutts were shifters who had some kind of genetic defect, usually from a human woman without the shifter genes giving birth to a shifter's baby. A mutt had poor control over their shift or instincts, so they were often unstable and had difficulty functioning in the real world. Ryan and his twin brother Marcus were both mutts, but for some reason Ryan didn't exhibit many of the common traits. Genetics were freaky like that.

If Willow's father was a mutt, then that might explain *everything*.

I bet that's him. What can you tell me about him?

Not much. His mother abandoned him when he was born, and I don't know anything about how he survived, but he wasn't a member of any of the known London packs. He married this Helen woman – I think they were even fated mates – but it wasn't a happy relationship. They were both deep into a bad scene. Richard was a low-level street dealer, and they were high as a kite most of the time, even with that kid in tow. As far as I know from the stories I've heard, he was so fucked on the drugs that he didn't realise it was the full moon, and he was still inside when the change came over him. The daughter was the first thing he saw.

Shite. It really was as Willow had said. This guy was a complete lowlife. *His ex-wife owns the* Werewolf Watch *website.*

The squirrel tossed the macadamia shell away, and started on a peanut. *I don't do websites. All I know is that the last time he was heard of, he was living in the London sewers with the other mutts. He's probably dead in a pile of his own filth by now.*

Mutts live in the sewers?

Of course. The squirrel glared at me as he selected another cashew. *They've got to go somewhere. At least they're down in the shit, where they should be.*

How do I get down there?

There's a manhole at the edge of the trees, where the park meets Lanchester Road. You can get there without even needing to shift back, if you're careful.

And what do I—

The squirrel waved a paw in the air, cutting me off. *That's all the answers you'll get out of me until you bring more nuts.*

I glared at him. *For a squirrel, you're a real capitalist.*

He stuffed two nuts into his cheeks, and poked his tongue out at me.

I turned and headed in the direction he indicated, keeping as far from the edge of the wood as I dared. On Lanchester Road, I found the manhole Chip had described. Even better, a crew from the council were there doing some work while the traffic was low, and they had the cover open. I waited in the trees for them to stop for a break, then bolted from the trees and leapt over the barrier.

This is for you, Willow, I thought, as I aimed my body at the hole and fell down into oblivion.

37

IRVINE

*M*y paws splashed through dark water as I made my way along the tunnel. Even with my superior wolf vision, the place was pitch black. Which was just as well – I didn't want to look down at what I was standing in.

I was going to smell absolutely delightful.

Luckily, after fifty metres of so, I ken for a fact I was in the right place. Wolf scent clung to the walls, painting a picture as clear as a neon sign. Several wolves moved through these tunnels on a regular basis, and often branched off into other junctions. I followed the main scent path, winding through a maze of tunnels and junctions so confusing I'd never hope to find my way back.

I had no idea how much time passed before I heard the splash of other footsteps in the dank water. I stopped and listened. The footsteps came closer, and a powerful wolf scent wafted down the tunnel toward me.

I flattened myself against a wall as two wolves rounded the corner. But of course it did no good. They sniffed the air, and called out inside my head.

We can smell you, intruder. Show yourself now, and we may decide to spare your life.

I stepped out into the tunnel, lowering my front paws so I was crouching in the water. Rancid stench invaded my nostrils, but I didn't dare stand up. I needed to show them this honour, or I'd have no chance of leaving here alive.

Identify yourself, the first wolf said. He carried a small, pale light around his neck. I squinted into it, momentarily blinded. But after a few moments, my eyes adjusted and their features came into focus. The larger of the two wolves had a beautiful grey coat, while the other was mottled grey and brown, and stood back a foot, indicating the dominance of the larger one.

My name is Irvine Baird, I said. *I have come to speak to Richard Carson. Is he part of your pack?*

Our pack? The larger wolf gave a barking laugh. *We don't subscribe to your archaic pack system down here. We have no hierarchy.*

Interesting. I glanced again at the second wolf. He shuffled up to stand beside the larger one. They were right – this wasn't a hierarchy the way I understood it.

But it didn't matter either way. *I dinnae care about your political structure. Bring me to Richard, now.*

You're in no position to make demands, Baird-wolf, the second wolf snarled. *What business do you have with Richard?*

I have a message from his daughter.

The larger wolf stiffened, his whole body rigid. His eyes flashed with anger and ... something else. I tensed, ready to attack if he made a move. Instead, he too lowered himself into the muck.

From ... Carol? His eyes widened. I realised they were the same dark brown as Willow's eyes. This was him. I'm standing in front of her father, the man who'd attacked her and took her leg.

Dinnae say her name like that, as though you have a right to it.

Where is she? Is she okay?

You mean, is she okay being an amputee thanks to a despicable wolf who maimed her and then left her for dead?

The wolf flinched as though I'd hurt him. *You don't know what you're talking about,* he growled. *What is your message?*

I've come to tell you that justice is coming. What you did to her is abhorrent, and you got away with it because shifters have no system with which to punish criminals. But that's about to change very, very soon. When it does, I'll be coming back for you, and there's nae a place on God's green earth you can hide from me.

Take me now.

What did he just say? *Aye?*

The wolf's eyes widened further, and the sides of his mouth downturned. He lowered himself even further into the water. He wasn't commanding me, I realised. He was begging me. *Take me to her right now. I'll submit to whatever justice she wants.*

I dinnae understand.

The other wolf rested a paw on his shoulder. He glared at me with steel-grey eyes. *We need to show you something.*

Richard nodded. *Please, come with us. I promise that when you've seen this, I will come with you.*

Something in his voice, so full of pain and sincerity, made me believe him. Curious now, I followed the two wolves down the tunnel, my paws splashing through the fetid water. After fifty metres or so, the wolves ascended a short ladder into another tunnel.

This is an abandoned underground branch line, the other wolf explained. *No one comes here except for the occasional urban explorer.*

I walked along a wide tunnel, large enough for the tube to pass through, although there was no track bed and the walls were rough rock. We passed groups huddled in small circles or reclining on dirty mattresses. There weren't just wolves here, but other shifter species. They mingled in their human and animal forms. Many bore wounds or amputations of their own.

What is this place?

The tunnel opened out into a wide area. It was clearly going to become a tube station at one point, but it had never been completed. A half-finished platform lined the cutting for the track. Only half the floor bore the familiar grey tiles of London stations. The rest was bare concrete. A flickering fire in the middle of the platform punched light through the space, barely stretching to the far corners.

Tents and makeshift shelters lined the back wall of the platform. Behind them, I could see the passenger entrance cut away, but it went nowhere. There was no obvious entry point for the surface, nor escalators installed. An enormous stack of firewood lined the far end of the platform, presumably to keep the blazing fire in the centre alight. I was surprised the whole tunnel wasn't filled with poisonous smoke, until I noticed tendrils of smoke curling up toward a vent directly above the blaze. More animals and humans huddled around it, the humans talking in hushed voices while they shoved pots into the flames.

What is this place?

We call it The Mouth of Hell. All the shifters who come here have committed some kind of crime against our people.

I studied the sad faces, the filthy conditions, the wasting, weak bodies, malnourished and starved of light and space. *I don't understand.*

You say there is no justice in the shifter world? Richard frowned. *We agree. We have tried to make our own justice. Some come here because they have been ostracised from their packs, and have nowhere else to go. Others come because they do not trust themselves to live along among humans without causing pain. Many are here because their guilt eats them alive. We hide here so we do not hurt our loved ones. We may not have much, but we do have honour.*

His words left me speechless. I'd had no idea such a place even existed.

Richard led me over to the fire, where he shoved his way through the animals. *We have a guest*, he told a fox who stood beside a small chilli bin. *Do we have food for him?*

The fox grunted in reply. He used his muzzle to lift the lid of the chilli bin, and drew out a raw steak. He dumped the steak on the ground at my feet and backed away. The scent of blood and raw meat invaded my nostrils – the one delicious smell in this cesspool of filth. I bent down and took a huge bite.

I never meant to hurt Carol, Richard said. *She was a shining star in my life, which up until her birth had been a giant turd pile. I was trying to get off the drugs, so I could be a better father to her, but that meant stopping dealing, which was our only source of income. Helen wasn't exactly supportive. With my genetics ... it wasn't easy, and the withdrawal meant I had even less control than normal. But even then I never imagined that I ...*

His voice inside my head trailed off. I looked at his face and was shocked by the pain there. If wolves could cry, I ken that tears would've been streaming over his fur.

What happened that night? I asked, more gently than I'd ever imagined talking to Willow's father.

I was home with Carol while Helen was out scoring. I was so out of it from withdrawal I didn't realise how full the moon was. I shifted while Carol and I were playing on the floor, and I didn't see my daughter anymore. I saw food. I saw a way to release all that rage and pain and agitation that sizzled in my veins. As soon as she screamed, I realised what I'd done, and backed away. But by then it was too late. I couldn't even ring an ambulance. Luckily, our neighbour heard Carol crying and called one, which saved her life. But not her leg.

He hung his head. *I was so horrified with what I'd done, I ran*

*into the woods, and I never returned. I knew they'd be better off
without me.*

I finished the steak in three bites, not sure what I should say.
Richard broke the silence between us.

How do you know my daughter?

I tried to push the images of Willow's naked body out of my
mind. That wasn't something he needed to see. *She's my mate.*

He bristled. *Wow, my little girl is all grown up.*

He sounded so despondent. This wasn't what I'd expected
when I'd decided to find Willow's father.

*So my Carol is part of the Baird pack? I've heard that in recent
years you've cleaned up your act. You're no longer in the drug trade?*

I shook my head. *Like you, I wanted to get out and make a better
life for us. I took over as alpha after my father was killed, and we've
been extracting ourselves ever since,* I replied. *Of course, there still
arenae many options open to shifters, but we've managed to make our
way with mostly legal commerce. I'm currently working with the
Lowe pack—*

At the mention of the Lowes, Richard growled. *My Carol isn't
part of their scheme, is she?*

What scheme do you mean?

Don't fake innocence, Richard snarled. *The rumours have
reached us even here. The Lowes have an ancient relic filled with
power. They want to reveal the existence of shifters and control the
entire shifter population.*

*That's not entirely true. Yes, the Lowes have this ring, but Caleb
only intends to use it to legitimise his power. He's doing this for the
good of shifters. We already have many allies who see this.*

*That may be so, but you'd better be careful. While your intentions
might be honourable, there are plenty of shifters who like their
anonymity.* He cast his paw around the blazing fire. *And with that
wolf changing at that wedding, and then the animal attack on a shop
in Crookshollow, shifters are saying the Lowes are deliberately*

flouting all our unspoken rules because they have this powerful object to protect them. There are talks of stopping the Lowe pack before they can do any more harm.

I pushed back the scene from Clara's shop where we'd discovered the ring wasn't powerful at all. It would do no good if Richard heard that. *How do you know both of those events are connected to the Lowes?*

Because the Lowes control Crookshollow Forest, and ... Richard looked sheepish. *I saw them on Werewolf Watch.*

You read Helen's site?

It's the only way I'd been able to see how Carol was doing, he said gruffly.

My mind whirred with possibilities. Nothing was as black-and-white as it had seemed. A plan of my own was starting to form in my mind. It was crazier even than Caleb's, but it might just work.

I placed a paw on Richard's shoulder. *What would you do to have your daughter in your life again?*

His wide brown eyes looked up at me like I was his saviour. There was so much of Willow in him. *It would be a miracle, and would make every miserable year I've spent in this place worthwhile. But she'll never speak to me again, and I don't blame her. I don't deserve her forgiveness.*

Your daughter is the most amazing, forgiving person I've ever met, I said. *I think I might be able to help you, but you'll have to come back to Crookshollow, and do exactly as I say.*

38

WILLOW

I stumbled across my tiny apartment, my arms laden with yet more fabric napkin swatches and chair covers from the linen company. My phone buzzed in my pocket, probably Alex, demanding to know why I was late again. Ever since my secret had been revealed, Alex had become a real bridezilla. It was too late for her to find a new wedding planner, so she was stuck with me, but that didn't mean she couldn't find other ways to make my life even more of a complete misery.

Or maybe it was Lachlan, letting me know about the latest updates in our campaign against the shifters. He'd been working with Mum for a couple of weeks now, and with all the new information I'd provided, the *Werewolf Watch* website exploded with hits. According to Lachlan, Mum was assembling a horde of her most zealous followers – a motley army ready to jump in and oppose shifters wherever they popped up.

I longed to talk to Mum myself. She and I had been through a lot together over the years, and she was the only other person I knew who'd had her heart broken by a werewolf. But I couldn't talk to her about any of it. I was still trying to figure out how I could continue to be Willow after the big reveal, and that meant keeping my distance. If she knew I'd received the information through sleeping with a werewolf, she'd do something drastic. I just wanted to forget the whole thing.

I'd managed to avoid seeing Caleb or Luke or any of the other shifters since Irvine left, with the exception of Bianca's second (and this time very real) wedding to Robbie three weeks ago. Bianca had insisted I do the planning for her for free, to make up for the hurt I'd caused within the group. I'd had to drop all my other projects in order to pull the thing off in the tight timeframe. Luckily, since it was basically a repeat of her previous wedding and I still had a ton of the decorations in boxes in my flat, there wasn't too much to do. The wedding had gone perfectly, but I'd spent most of my night locked in the bathroom, trying to avoid any contact with *them*.

Thankfully, Irvine didn't show up. According to a frosty conversation I had with Elinor, he was too busy with arrangements down in London. She kept trying to drill me for information about the two of us and why we weren't talking, but I didn't give her anything. Although, he did have time to make a trip up to Aberdeen to bring Robbie's mother down for the wedding.

And now, because of Bianca, I was well behind on Alex's wedding plans, and she was grilling me about it big time. I needed to get these samples over there and—

"Willow."

"Argh!" My foot caught the corner of a box, and I toppled across the bed, scattering swatches everywhere.

"You're already falling on the bed for me. Way to stroke a broken man's ego."

That deep voice drove a stake through my chest. I whipped my head up. Irvine leaned against the doorframe. His face was tight with pain. His cold grey eyes met mine, and my stomach sank to my knees. The connection hummed between us, my own body betraying me as it longed to press against his.

You hate him, remember. He's a murderer who intends to make the whole world subservient to his species. He's dangerous.

I blinked, struggling to make my face even. If I showed him the simmering anger, he might go feral. "So you're back," I said flatly. I scrambled to my feet, hoping he wouldn't see just how much I was shaking.

"I am. I missed you."

"Huh. Fancy that."

"I'm sorry I didnae call."

"I didn't expect you to. Especially since I have no desire to ever hear from you again."

"Things got pretty crazy in London. I have so much to tell you, but first—" Irvine crossed the room in two strides. He stood close, his scent reaching up and teasing me, igniting all those parts of me that I'd tried to make forget him. He reached down and clasped my hand in his.

"Get your hands off me," I hissed.

Irvine squeezed my fingers, and his face twisted into an expression of such exquisite pain. "Forgive me, Willow Summers."

"What?"

He leaned in. Closer, closer. I was drowning in his eyes. "Forgive me for all the hurt I caused."

I opened my mouth to speak, to tell him to go away and never come back. Instead, my lips fell against his, and my pain was swallowed in the kiss.

All the pent-up frustration of missing and hating and wanting him hit my body with full force, making my hunger for him all the worse. His wolfish scent invaded my nostrils, and the room swirled. His hands seemed to be everywhere at once – cupping the back of my head, wrapped around my neck, stroking my thighs, clasping the curve of my back.

What am I doing?

I tore my body away from him, toppling over the edge of the bed again. My prosthesis slammed against the wood floor, sending a shudder of pain straight up through my thigh. I grunted and rolled over.

"Let me help you—" Irvine reached to help me.

"I can do it. Just get away from me." Irvine stepped back, his face stricken. I grabbed the edge of the bed and rolled over, using my good leg to lever myself up. I stood straight up and folded my arms across my chest.

"Do not ever touch me again. I want you to leave."

"I dinnae want to leave you, Willow. I want to keep you safe. Everything is changing, and I think if you gave me a chance you could see just how wonderful it would be. But right now it's nae safe. Your own mother's got information about us—"

"Of course. I told her everything."

"You did?"

I nodded. "The world needs to know what the Lowe family is planning. My mother has copies of Robbie's research, too. With any luck, one of her team will steal that cursed ring from Caleb, and stop this plan of yours even getting off the ground."

"I convinced Caleb to nae use the ring. You were right about that. But I explained to you how important this was for the whole world—"

"No, Irvine. You explained why it's important for *shifters*. I don't care about murderers and maimers. I care about the fact that as soon as you go public, my life and all my freedom is forfeit. The press will dig up all the old stories on me, and they'll come after me here, and I'll go back to being the peg-leg freak. I'll never be able to choose who knows my secrets and I can't ... I can't—"

I hated how selfish I sounded. But after everything I'd been through, didn't I deserve to think of myself for once? The idea of going back to being Carol – of seeing the whole world give me that horrible, pitying stare – turned my stomach.

Irvine's face twisted. "You won't forgive me? You won't give me a chance to explain?"

"I'm not in the habit of forgiving murderers."

Irvine's whole body stiffened. "You spoke to the boy," he whispered.

"His name is Lachlan, and he told me everything – how you tore out his father's throat right in front of him. It's true, isn't it? You're not denying it."

"Aye." His head hung down. Even though he towered over me, he suddenly seemed terribly small. "It's true. I lost control. I did a terrible thing."

"Then we have nothing more to say to each other. I thought you were different, but all along, you were the biggest monster of them all."

Irvine spun on his heel, heading for the door. His hand grabbed the frame, and he looked back over his shoulder, his eyes flashing. "Before I go, can you answer one last question? If I were to give you the one thing you thought you could never have – a father who loved and cared for you – would you give me a chance then?"

"No." I turned away, so he wouldn't see the tears running down my cheeks. "Now go."

After a few moments of tense silence, the door to my flat slammed shut, and footsteps sounded on the stairs. I collapsed onto the bed, my whole body shaking as my tears stained the expensive samples.

39

IRVINE

*S*hite.

I sat on a bench in Fauntelroy Park, staring at a picturesque pond surrounded by ancient oaks and flowering bushes and filled with paddling ducks. I hated everything about it.

My chest tightened. I'd really lost Willow. All that hope I'd had when I was back in London disappeared in a cloud of resignation. The one woman in all of the world who got me, and I'd lost her. And it was my own fault.

I was a fool for not understanding before. Willow lied, but not because she was working for her mother. It was because she was scared. She didn't want to go back to being the victim. She wanted to keep her new life, and that life could have included me if I hadn't been so desperate to believe the worst of her. If I hadn't kept my own secrets.

I should have told her about the guilt swallowing me up. She *might* have understood why it was so important that shifters be out in the open. But either way, I'd owed it to her to lay it out, and I didn't, and now it was too late.

I didn't think anything could salvage our relationship now,

and I didn't even want to. Even though my body burned for hers with a fire so fierce it scorched my skin, I ken that I was no good for her. All I did was hurt her. I had one thing left that could give her happiness, and I would make sure it happened, and then I would leave her alone forever.

Caleb could have his victory, his empire of shifters. I would leave my pack in his capable hands, and walk deep into the forest and never come back. If I found a place far away from humans, I could never again risk causing all this hurt.

My phone rang. I ignored it, continuing to stare out at the ducks. The ring stopped, and immediately started again.

"Your phone's ringing, man," a father called out to me as he ran past after his daughter.

"Aye," I muttered. I noticed Richard coming down the path toward me, dressed in a new set of jeans and a shirt I'd lent him. In his human form, I could see the family resemblance. Willow had inherited his soulful eyes and expressive features, but his hair was brown, and I now ken that her's was not. Richard sat down beside me.

The phone continued to buzz in my pocket. Sighing, I pulled it out. Caleb's face flashed on the screen. I turned the phone off and slid it back into my pocket.

"I hope that Lowe of yours knows what he's doing," Richard said.

"Caleb is a good man. I have faith in his judgement."

"Do you? He may be the most righteous man on earth, but what about those around him? What about the allies he's made, and continues to make? What about the shifters that will scurry to him in order to claw their way to the top? That kind of power will attract many people who are not trustworthy."

I hadn't told Richard that the ring was fake. "We'll have to take our chances. Caleb needs the ring in order to seize power and make the government listen to him."

"And you expect him to just put it down after he's subdued the government?"

"I do." Especially considering it doesn't wield any power. "I dinnae want to talk about it anymore. What are you here for? I told you to stay at the cabin." I'd got another of Margaret's cabins for Richard, so that I could keep an eye on him and make sure that Willow didn't see him before she was ready.

Thinking back to how cold she was back at her flat, I wasn't certain she'd ever be ready.

"I couldn't stay there. The walls were closing in on me. I'm used to having an entire subway and sewer network to explore."

"Then go run in the forest, or roll around in a pile of shit. I dinnae care. She's really upset, and if she sees you with me and figures out who you are—"

"Did you talk to her?" Richard's whole face lit up. "What did she say?"

I looked away. "That she nae wants to see me again."

"I thought you said you were her friend."

"I was. But now I'm not," I growled.

Richard rubbed his balding head. "And you're just giving up?"

"What choice do I have? She doesnae want me. And I cannae blame her." I buried my face in my hands. The two men who had hurt Willow the most sat together in the park, wallowing in their own guilt and regret.

40

WILLOW

"*H*i." I waved at Simon as I grabbed stacks of samples from the car boot. "I know, I know, I'm ridiculously late. Something happened—"

A murdering werewolf broke into my house and I kissed him, to be precise.

"Miss Summers, Miss Kline has been trying to contact you." Simon stood across the doorway, his wiry body blocking my entry. "She wanted to cancel today's meeting."

"She does? But there's so much that has to be done." The wedding was only a couple of weeks away, and we had to choose the napkins, and finalise the floral arrangements, and figure out the layout for the band. "Is something wrong?"

Simon's face remained stony. "Miss Kline is feeling poorly. She'd like you to come back another day."

Great. I knew what this was about. Irvine had got here first and told Alex I rejected him and now she hates me even more than she already did. I dropped a pile of samples on the steps in front of him, tossed my hair over my shoulder, and fixed him with what I hoped was an authoritative stare. "Fine. She doesn't want to see me. That's fine. Help me pick these up, won't you?"

Simon hesitated, then crouched down and started carefully stacking napkins. "You really should be more careful—"

I whipped past him and dashed into the house, hobbling as fast as my prosthesis would carry me. Simon yelled behind me, but I disappeared down a hallway, and I knew that with my head start, he'd never be able to find me in that maze of a grand home.

Now all I had to do is figure out where the hell Alex was—

I heard a crash, and Alex screaming with rage. *Ah, well at least she'll be easy to find.* I followed the sounds of stuff being thrown and smashed, until I reached a short hall I'd never seen before. I cringed as another heavy object crashed against a wall. Alex was *really* pissed.

Fear fluttered in my chest as I pushed open the door and stepped into an enormous space. My shoes clacked across a polished marble floor. I looked up, and up, and up, taking in the gilded carvings on the ceiling and paint-splattered marble columns. Natural light spilled into the room – if you could call it a room, "cavern" was certainly more accurate – from mullioned windows along either side, and a tall grand piano stood in the centre. It was also splattered with paint and covered with half-coloured canvases.

This is Alex and Ryan's studio, I realised. I stepped back, feeling as though I'd intruded upon something private.

But all thoughts of retreating fled when I saw Alex. She stood behind the piano, hurling canvases and pots of paint and even a giant easel at the wall. A pile of smashed items had gathered around her feet. As I watched in horror, she picked up a wood knife from on top of the piano, and stabbed it into a half-finished canvas hanging from the nearest easel.

"Alex!" I raced across the room as fast as I could, and clasped my hands over hers. Alex turned to me, fury in her eyes. She screeched, and tried to yank the knife away. It took all of my strength to pry her fingers off the handle. Finally, I freed three of her fingers, and the knife clattered to the floor.

Losing the knife seemed to deflate Alex. Her body sagged, and the rage fell away, replaced by a look of desperation. "I can't —" she started, but her words dissolved into tears.

"Hey, hey, don't worry." I placed my arm under her shoulder, and led her to a bench under the window. Three canvases were set up nearby, with trays of paint still wet beneath them. Unlike Alex's usual work, which was bright and carefree, these pieces were dark and abstract, with angry red and black slashes and blobs on stark white backgrounds. One of the canvases had also been slashed up. "Sit down. Tell me, what's wrong? Is it … is it about me? Are you angry at me because I lied about who I was?"

Alex shook her head. "I don't care," she whispered.

You could've fooled me. "Then is it … about your baby?"

Alex howled. Tears splashed against my cardigan. Okay, so I'd hit the jackpot. She must've had her period again.

"It's okay," I said, patting her shoulder in a way I hoped was comforting. This was so far out of my realm of experience. I'd love to be a mother, but I was never going to find someone who wanted to have kids. The only person who I might've considered just turned out to be a murderer. "It will happen for you guys. You're so young, I know it doesn't seem like it, but you've got plenty of time. Maybe it's just too much for you right now. You can pick things up again after the wedding—"

"Don't even talk to me about the wedding," Alex growled, her hands balled into fists.

"What's happened? Is something to do with Ryan? Has he hurt you?" An image of Robbie shifting at Bianca's wedding went through my head, followed by Irvine's face twisted in rage as he looked over the body of Lachlan's father. Fear clutched at my stomach. This is why you shouldn't be involved with shifters.

Sometimes they couldn't control themselves. They could really hurt someone, even if they claimed to love them.

Alex laughed bitterly. "Ryan? Hurt me? I'd like to see him try."

"Alex, I know that Ryan's a shifter." Alex stiffened. I pressed on. If he's hurt her, then he'll pay. I'll make sure he pays. "I know that sometimes they can't control themselves and—"

"Willow, stop. I know you think you know about shifters because of what your mother taught you, but you've got it all wrong."

"So he's not a shifter?"

"Ryan's a shifter, all right. But he's not a danger to me. He's trying to keep me safe and do what's right for shifters everywhere." Alex sniffed. "Shifters live in secret, which means that they don't have access to a lot of benefits us humans have. There's no healthcare to deal with shifter problems. There aren't many jobs that will allow them to take leave every full moon. A few lucky guys like Ryan find a way to make their own fortunes, but a lot of shifters turn to crime to survive. You know that if you've been seeing Irvine."

"I don't want to hear about the plan—"

"No." Alex gripped my hand, her wide eyes imploring me. "Please, just listen. It's getting worse and worse. One of our friends married a vampire, and their community has even greater problems, because of their extreme age. Ryan wants to change that. The whole pack does, especially now that they're starting to have kids—" Her throat caught on the word *kids*. "There's only one way to make things better for the next generation of shifters, and that's to stop hiding in the shadows. It's the right thing to do. It's going to upset the world for a while, but in the end, it will make everyone's lives better. If Ryan and I manage to have a cub, I want them to have every option in life—"

"If you agree, then what's the problem? What could possibly have you so upset?"

Alex's face screwed up again. Ugly, fat tears rolled down her cheeks.

"They want to do it at our wedding! They're planning to reveal themselves as shifters in front of all the cameras and journalists who show up for the reception. Ryan told me today. He's so excited. He loves the fact that he's able to be a part of making this happen. But why did it have to be on my wedding day?"

My heart thudded. This was a nightmare. My worst nightmare come true. "That's awful."

Alex balled her hands into fists. "I mean, it's not as if he spends the rest of his time risking his neck for them. Just the other month, he had to save Bianca from that knife-wielding maniac. Then there was that wedding where he rescued Belinda, and not to mention all the times he protected me. He spends all his time thinking about the future of shifters, of the good of the pack. But what about me? What about *our* future? Why couldn't I have this one day where it just got to be about me and Ryan and not the damn pack?"

I stood up. "You're damn right. You deserve your wedding day, and I'm going to make sure you have it."

Alex blinked. "Why you?"

"I am your wedding planner, and it's my job to make sure you have the wedding of your dreams. That means, no stains are going to mar your perfect dress, no photographer is going to shoot a bad angle, and no wolves are crashing the reception."

"But how—"

"Don't worry," I growled, folding my arms across my chest. "I'll find a way to sort this. Willow Summers will not take this lying down."

41

IRVINE

"*I*rvine, open up!"

Willow? I glanced up from the kitchen, where I was busy preparing a meal. Richard sat in the chair in front of my tiny stove, moving the logs around with the poker but not doing anything to actually make the fire burn better. I glared at him and gestured to the bed. He dived under the mattress, dragging his thick legs in after him.

How is she here? Why would she possibly come back? Does she want to forgive me? Could we really have a fresh start? A real future?

My heart surged. I pulled the door open and threw my arms wide. "You dinnae ken how much I prayed for this—"

Instead of falling to my arms, Willow shoved past me and slammed her purse down on the table. "Did you plan the grand reveal of shifters on Alex's wedding day?"

"How do you ken about that?"

Willow's eyes blazed. A vein in the side of her neck throbbed. I'd never seen her so angry before, not even earlier today, when she was tearing out my heart. She was usually so timid. Those fierce eyes were actually kind of hot. "Alex told me. I just came from Raynard Hall where she's crying her eyes out because you bastards have ruined her wedding."

"We haven't ruined it at all. Ryan said it was fine. He said he's talked to Alex and she's happy with it."

Willow's eyes flashed. "I don't care what Ryan said. He clearly doesn't know his wife very well, if he thought she'd be happy having her wedding day turned into some kind of shifter political rally."

I took the pasta off the stove. "It's Ryan's wedding, too."

That was the wrong thing to say. Willow let out a strangled cry. "I can't believe you support this, that you spearheaded this."

"You can, too. You ken what I had to do to keep the shifter secret from the world. You want to ken why I am capable of murdering someone? You want to ken how I can even begin to live with the guilt of the terrible thing I've done? It's because I had nae choice. If I didnae kill that guy, he would've told our secret, and maybe he wouldnae be believed, but what if he was? I had to protect my pack, protect my family ..." I balled my hands into fists. "I should have killed the boy, too, but I couldnae do it. He was so young, barely a teenager, and I thought if I spared him, no one would believe him. This is what the secrecy reduces us to – it makes murderers and criminals of men who only want to protect their families."

"Irvine—" Willow's voice cut in, but I pressed on.

"If I can save another generation of shifters from carrying this guilt, then I'm going to do whatever it takes to make that happen. I hate that doing it causes you pain, I hate it so much, but I cannae put one person before my entire race, even if I care more about that person than anyone else in the world."

"But you—"

"Ryan believes the same thing, and he ken we needed a big event with lots of reporters, so he volunteered the wedding. It makes perfect sense. Ryan's a beloved public figure, which means when he reveals what he is, people will trust him."

"I can't believe you're saying this, to *me*."

"I donnae see why you're so upset. Dinnae think these are your friends that you speak of. You betrayed us all by keeping your own secrets, *Carol*. We havenae ruined anything. They'll have their beautiful ceremony, and the reception with the speeches and first dance and everything. We've let them have all that guff—"

"Guff is it? You've *let* them have it, have you? God forbid a person might want to actually *enjoy* their wedding day without a bunch of wolves stampeding everywhere, causing mass panic and injuring their guests—"

I held up my hands. "Whoa. Hold on a minute there, lass. No one's getting injured. All we're doing is transforming into our animals, and then transforming back. Yes, we expect a bit of panic, but Ryan's made arrangements to deal with that, and—"

"What do you call this if not an injury!" Willow yelled, kicked out her prosthesis. Her leg sailed across the room and slammed into the wall. She planted both her hands on the table to keep herself upright. Tears streamed down her red, blotchy face. "Don't you *dare* tell me you care about me, and then take away everything good in my life. Don't try to tell me you can control yourself, because I know better than that. If my father can hurt his own daughter, then what are you lot going to do at a party full of strangers?"

"I didn't mean to hurt you, Carol."

Shit. Richard, no, no.

Willow froze. I turned around slowly, kenning exactly what I would see and dreading it. Richard had poked his head out from beneath the bed.

"Irvine … there's a man under your bed." Willow's voice was breathy.

"Um ... yes, there is." I bent down and dragged Richard out. "Willow, I didn't want it to be like this, but this is your father, Richard."

Willow's face paled. Her hand started to slip over the edge of the table. "What are you talking about?"

"Maybe you should sit down." I pulled out the chair next to her, but she didn't move. Her eyes remained glued on Richard. I wondered if she was noticing the familiarity of his features.

"I know this is a big shock," Richard said, taking a step across the tiny room. "I've been living under the sewers of London. Many shifters live there with me, who have committed crimes that go unpunished. We punish ourselves instead. Irvine brought me here because he thought I might be able to help you understand—"

"I understand that you're a monster!" Willow lifted her right hip, waving the stump of her residual limb at his face. "What kind of a person does this to their *own daughter*?"

Richard's entire face crumpled, his whole body slumping. "I ... I ... am so sorry," he said.

"I can't—" Willow was shaking uncontrollably. Her hands slid forward, grasping in the air for something to steady herself. "I have to—"

I rushed forward to grab her, as her whole body crumpled, and the light in her eyes went dim. "Stay inside," I growled at Richard, as I hefted Willow's body into my arms and carried her limp body out of the cabin.

42

WILLOW

I woke up in my own bed at my flat. All the samples had been cleared off and stacked neatly in the corner of the room. I was wearing a pair of fluffy pyjamas, and I wasn't wearing my prosthesis. My head throbbed like I'd been hit with some comically huge mallet.

Alex and Elinor sat on the end of my bed, staring down at me with worried expressions. "You're awake!" Alex grinned, stroking my hand.

"In a manner of speaking," I replied. Talking made my head pound harder.

"Do you remember what happened?" Elinor asked, holding out a glass of water for me.

"No. I—" And then it all flooded back to me. Alex's wedding. Irvine's cabin. My father crawling out from under the bed.

My father.

That was my father.

Irvine brought my father to Crookshollow.

"Irvine told us what happened," Alex said, continuing to stroke my hand. "You hit your head when you fainted. You might have a concussion, but we'll get the doctor back later to check. Oh, Willow, I'm so sorry. We've been so mean to you."

"S'okay," I said, wincing as I tried to sip the water.

"It's not okay," Elinor said, pushing her glasses up her nose. "You're our friend. And friends don't desert each other just because they disagree with their choices. You were wrong not to think you could trust us, but we shouldn't have acted the way we did, so consider us even." She gave me that brilliant smile. I tried to smile back, but something sharp stabbed into my skull, and I flinched instead.

"I wasn't here to spy for my mum," I managed to choke out.

"We know," Alex said firmly. "And the others would've known too, once they stopped to think about it."

"Irvine also told us about what your mother did to you, and we understand now why you lied about who you were," Elinor added. "You just wanted to start over. I totally get that. And that's why you're so afraid of the reveal, because of what it means for you."

"That wasn't what Irvine said," I said, but I thought back to some of his words in his cabin. *I cannae put one person before my entire race, even if I care more about that person than anyone else in the world.*

"Irvine was just upset. You did break his heart."

And he'd repaid me in kind, and then dug up my father to rub salt into the wound. "Yeah, well—"

"We're not talking about Irvine," Elinor said brightly. "We're here to help Willow get back on her feet, so she can finish preparations for your wedding."

"Do you want to be called Willow?" Alex asked. "Or do you prefer Carol?"

"Willow," I said instantly. It fit. I'd left Carol behind when I left London. I couldn't go back, even if the world forced me to.

"And trust me, this wedding is going to be perfect. I'll make sure of it."

"Of course it is, because we're going to help." Elinor glanced around the flat. "Now, you're not moving from this bed for a few days. So just tell us what needs doing."

Despite the pain assaulting my temples, I managed a small grin. My heart soared in my chest. I may have lost Irvine, and he may have sided with my father, but at least I had real, honest-to-goodness friends. I pointed a shaking finger across the room to my suitcase. "Grab that organiser from on top there. You have lots of calls to make."

43

WILLOW

"*W*here's the wedding planner?" a delivery man yelled as he entered the garden, dragging a trolley of glassware behind him.

"Coming." I dropped the box of napkins I was setting out and rushed over to direct the man toward the bar.

It was 7:02 a.m., and my crew was putting together the finishing touches on the marquee. The tables and chairs had been set up the night before, and I'd been here since 5 a.m., laying out the place settings for the four-hundred guests and checking everything against the seating chart. Now I laid out the napkins – each one printed with a different image from Ryan or Alex's paintings – and the florist bustled around me, fussing with the towering arrangements that rose nearly to the ceiling.

As soon as I finished, I hightailed it over to the Hall's kitchen. Belinda had taken it over, and her partner Cole and friend Alice helped her lift huge trays of *hors' d'oeuvres* into the industrial oven. Alex and Elinor had gone around all the girls in the pack, and got them all to start talking to me again. Even though there was still a huge hole in my heart, and none of the shifters were likely to ever speak to me again after all the information I shared with Mum, at least my life Crookshollow was looking brighter.

I hadn't seen Irvine since I fainted at his place, nor that man he said was my father. It probably helped that I barely left my flat, except for errands for the wedding or to Elinor's house for wine. Mum would laugh if she saw me now, free to do whatever I wanted but still too afraid to go outside, lest I be attacked by a werewolf.

"Everything okay in here?" I bellowed, as a plume of black smoke rose from the oven. "That's not the cake burning, is it?"

Without looking up for the chopping board, Belinda jabbed her finger at an enormous box in the corner. "No, the cake's fine. Cole, get the oven."

I lifted the flap on the box just enough for a thin shaft of light to fall over the beautiful cake – white fondant laced with thin strips of chocolate placed to look like gnarled branches. On top, two foxes frolicked together. It was a work of art.

"It's amazing," I beamed. I wrapped my arms around her middle and gave her a squeeze.

"Hey, no hugging the chef while she's got a knife," Belinda replied, but she grinned back at me. "Glad you approve."

"I hope you're ready to make many more cakes, because I didn't have a baker even half as good as you in London. I'm going to send you so many clients—"

"Willow."

Irvine. That gravelly Scottish brogue sent a shiver right through my body. I didn't turn around, not wanting to acknowledge him. I closed the lid on the box and stared at the wall, red welts appearing in front of my eyes. "You were told that you weren't welcome here."

"The couple wants me here."

"Ryan might, but only because you're part of his disgusting plan. Alex made it clear that you weren't to show your face before the reception. She's *my* friend and you've turned her wedding day into a sideshow. You can't just turn up like a normal guest. Do you have any idea what she's going through right now?"

"And I told you that this was our only shot," Irvine said. I didn't look back. I couldn't bear the thought of seeing him lean against the doorframe, his muscled body perfectly filling out a tailored tuxedo. "So many people have sacrificed so we can have this chance. If one stupid wedding has to be disrupted so we can get a shot at winning over the public and potentially saving hundreds of shifters from turning to crime, then it's worth it."

"One *stupid* wedding?" My voice hit a pitch that made the windows shudder. "This isn't stupid to Alex. This is the dedication of her love, and you're taking it away from her."

"And what about everything that's been taken from *me*? What about what's been taken from the other shifters, and the humans who they hurt because they had no choice?" Irvine shot back.

I balled my hands into fists. "I don't care."

Irvine kept going, his voice rising to the same angry pitch as mine. "That's right. You only care about yourself, and what *you* lose."

His words cut deep. I staggered back, as though he'd slapped me. Irvine's face twisted with pain, but he kept going.

"What about Ryan's right to be able to stand as a shifter and declare his love as he truly is? He is a good man and yet he's forced to live with secrets and lies and—"

"Hey, Willow, is something wrong here?" Belinda bustled over, a huge bowl of salad in her tiny hands. She placed a hand on my shoulder and glared behind her at Irvine.

"You're damn right, something's wrong," I snapped, trying to force up my anger to cover up the shame I felt. "You saw how upset Alex was this morning? Well, it's all this guy's fault. She doesn't want him here and yet, here he is."

Belinda's eyes flicked between us. "Irvine, maybe you should come out into the hall."

"No, I shouldn't, because this isn't about Alex at all." Irvine's cold eyes flashed. "This is about Willow and me."

"This has *nothing* to do with me. It has to do with the fact I have a sobbing bride upstairs—"

"Admit it, it has everything to do with you," Irvine growled. "You don't want shifters to become known. You want us to stay in the shadows. Because if I stay hidden, then you can keep hiding, too. You can keep everyone who cares about you at arm's length. You can keep pretending I'm nothing but a shag to you."

My face stung as though he'd slapped me. Belinda flinched and slunk away.

"You really believe that we were ever anything but?" I shot back, still refusing to face him. The connection tugged at my body, begging me to turn around and fall into his arms. I dug my fingernails into my palms. *Stay strong.* If I saw him, with all that rage and pain in his voice, I'd break. I knew I'd break.

"You're nae seriously going to deny it?" Irvine's voice dropped low. He'd moved closer, and his words slid over my ears like a caress. "You and I are mates, Willow. We're fated to be together. I ken you can feel the bond that draws us to each other. It's what kept you returning to my bed, even though you hated what I am."

"You're scaring my kitchen staff. You have to leave." Belinda pushed Irvine toward the door, but he must've been resisting, because I heard a scuffle, and then he was shouting at me from the hall.

"I love you, Willow Summers!"

Tears brimmed in the corners of my eyes. Furiously, I wiped them away. *Damn him.* I had to forget it. I had work to do.

"—I now pronounce you husband and wife," Ryan's mother, Clara intoned. "Go now, with the blessings of your family and friends, and seal your union with a kiss."

Ryan's face lit up into a grin. He leaned down and lifted the lace veil over Alex's hair, revealing her matching radiant smile. They pressed their lips together, and the heat radiating from their kiss torched my soul even from my spot right in the back row.

At least the wolves gave her this moment, I thought, the rage growing inside me. How could they possibly believe a wedding was the appropriate time for what they had planned?

The Ghost Symphony song *Carmilla* struck up, and the wedding party danced down the woodland aisle and out into the enchanted garden. Guests filed out through the enchanted garden, and I checked that the serving staff were waiting with flutes of champagne and Belinda's delicious nibbles.

The guests lined up to congratulate Alex and Ryan. I tried to fight my way to the front to say something to her, to plead with Ryan to call off the pack's plan. But at the last minute, Elinor called me over because some of the guests wanted the shade cloths unrolled to keep them out of the sun. Sighing, I went off to sort out some shade.

For all I know, they could all be vampires. I almost laughed at the absurdity of it all, but then I remembered it was about to get very, very serious.

Elinor and Alex were off taking wedding party photographs, and Bianca and Robbie were talking to Caleb, who I had no desire to see right then. Luckily, I had so much to attend to, it didn't matter that I had not a single friend to talk to. Thankfully, I didn't see Irvine again, and if he saw me, he knew to stay away.

Before I knew it, the mingling portion of the evening was

over, and we were being called into the marquee for the reception. My stomach churned. So far, the wedding was perfect, but I knew what was coming.

The werewolves are about to ruin it all, just like they've ruined the rest of my life.

I'd arranged the tables so that I wasn't anywhere near the pack. Instead, I'd talked my way onto a table of rich art collectors right down the back. I'd even angled my chair away from the head table, so I wouldn't have to face any of them.

My stomach was tight with knots as the bridal party entered and sat down, and Alex and Ryan gave their thank-you speeches. The first course was served, but I was too anxious to eat a bite.

After the plates were cleared, Caleb and Irvine stood up. "As a close friend of Ryan and Alex," Caleb began, his voice loud and clear, "I'd like to say a few words on this most auspicious of days." He launched into a short series of funny stories about Ryan, and then passed the mike to Irvine.

This time, I couldn't help but look at him. I was right, that tux did look amazing on him. My heart thundered against my chest.

"Caleb and I came to Crookshollow as outcasts," Irvine said. "Our families have lived in secret for many years, far away from others. We lived with shame and fear. Ryan has lived with his fair share of this same shame and fear. He spent many years as a recluse, afraid to leave the walls of his mansion for fear of how the world might judge him. Now, with Alex by his side, he has emerged into the light, and you all welcomed him with open hearts."

"I now ask you to open your hearts for Caleb and me, and for our families, and for all the others who've been forced into the shadows."

Most of the crowd barely seemed to be listening to the speech. Their faces were glazed from the free-flowing alcohol. A few people had confused looks on their faces. The dealers at my table were too busy arguing over the merits of the grape vintage to even listen. I guess people didn't expect wedding speeches to take such a weird turn.

They sure did look up when Irvine's face started to change. As soon as it started, I couldn't turn away. I watched, stricken with horror, as his features contorted, and the Irvine I knew fell away as his face sank and twisted and melted into something completely foreign. Dark grey fur sprung from his skin, and his ears shifted back on his head and grew sharp points. He dropped the mic and pitched forward, knocking several glasses from the table as his paws slammed against it. He threw his head back, and let out a mighty howl.

He promised he'd never shift in front of me. Yet here he is, breaking another promise.

"This is not a trick," Caleb said, his voice forceful as he grabbed the mic from where Irvine had dropped it. "My friend Irvine really did just turn into a wolf. He is a werewolf, as it happens. Several of us in this room tonight are werewolves."

Irvine walked along the front of the head table, his head held high, letting everyone in the room get a good glimpse of his body, leaving us in no doubt of what he was.

The panic started as a low ripple, spreading out from the centre of the room and capturing every guest in its grasp. People shoved back their chairs and scrambled toward the rear exit. Robbie stepped out from behind a pillar, his own body changing and transforming. The guests skidded to a halt as a grey wolf now blocked their only way out. People started screaming.

"What are you going to do to us?" a woman cried.

"Nothing," Caleb said, his voice completely calm. "We're not here to hurt you. All we want to do is show you we exist, and that we don't mean any harm."

"Let us go!" a man roared as he used his body as a human shield between Robbie and his family.

"We're going to do just that," Caleb said. "But we just need to explain a few things first—"

"Please, don't eat us." the dealer next to me begged, dropping to his knees. His foot kicked out and hit my leg, and he winced as he connected with my prosthetic.

All around me, chaos raged as the guests frantically tried to escape, only to find every exit blocked by a wolf or fox or stag or bear shifter. The bear was a terrible idea – people were falling over themselves in panic, and it hadn't done anything except sit there and look dopey.

Meanwhile, Caleb was up front, intoning his speech like he was giving a science lesson to a bunch of kids. "We don't eat humans. We're not monsters. We are men and women, just like you. The only difference is that inside of us is another skin, another body, and we can change between the two. When we're in our wolf form, we see and hear and feel as a wolf, but we still have our conscious minds – we remember our loved ones, we understand when you speak to us, we feel pain and love and guilt and joy."

"What do you want from us?" someone yelled over the din.

"We need to you tell every reporter and every official and every person that you meet what you saw here tonight. I hope some of you will stay and speak to us, ask us about our lives and what we're trying to achieve here. But I know it's scary, and we want to give you time to process it. So we're going to let you leave now. Please, be kind to each other, and drive safe." Caleb set down the mic, a broad smile across his face.

Drive safe? *Drive safe?* Who the fuck was he *kidding?*

All the shifters at the exits stepped aside, and the guests flooded toward the doors. I grabbed my purse and charged into the crowd, pushing my way through the stampede toward the front of the room.

I ran down the length of the head table, passing Irvine as he sat calmly on the end, beside the beautiful cake that would never get cut. His eyes met mine, and a mess of emotions assailed me. I pushed them all down.

"Goodbye, Irvine," I growled, breaking into a jog as I dashed past him and out into the cool moonlight.

Irvine and the pack had done it. And now, I could never come back to Crookshollow. I would never be able to live or work in peace. Nothing would ever be right again.

44

IRVINE

*I*rvine, where are you going? Caleb's voice rang inside my head. *You're supposed to stay with me.*

Ignoring him, I surged across the marquee, trying to catch Willow before she got out onto the lawn and I lost her in the crowd. As I moved around the tables, the guests leapt out of my way, giving me a clear path.

Why aren't you in position— Robbie's protests cut off as I shoved my way past him and emerged into the "enchanted forest" courtyard outside. The whole place was chaos. Everywhere, people held up cameras and phones, snapping pictures of the shifters and filming every movement, while others screamed in terror as they sprinted over the lawn or crashed through the forest.

I sniffed the air, searching the muddle of scents for Willow's unique marker. I caught it immediately and headed left. Most of the guests were scrambling up the hill toward the house and their cars, but Willow had gone the other way, toward the forest.

Her scent grew stronger. I was getting closer. My paws pounded against the soft ground. *I have to find her.*

She was right up ahead, crashing through the trees toward a

narrow service road that led to one of the side entrances. Her car was the only one parked under the trees. *She must've planned this in advance, to make sure she could get away quickly.*

Willow grabbed the door handle. I let out a howl, frantically trying to stall her. Willow whirled around, her face flashing with anger so intense, it stopped me before I'd even started to shift.

"Don't follow me," she yelled, her voice dripping with hatred. She was not crying or hysterical. Her face was rigid with hatred. She had never looked more fierce or more beautiful. The fact that all of that anger was directed at me made me sick to my stomach.

"Don't ever look for me again," she said, as she opened the door and climbed into her car. "You and I are over."

45

WILLOW

"Oh, Carol," Mum sobbed into the phone. "I'm so glad to hear your voice, sweetie. It's all over the telly. The wolves ... they're at a wedding, and they've revealed themselves. It's for real this time. They're—"

"Yeah, I know." Now that I was in the car and the full horror of what I'd just witnessed rolled over me, the tears spilled over my cheeks, and I sniffed. "I was there."

"Oh god, *Carol*—" Mum sounded like she was having trouble breathing.

"They were my clients, and then all those wolves appeared. Mum ... I'm scared. I don't think I'm safe here any longer."

"You have to come home. I'll look after you, just like I always did."

Home. The place I'd fled because of her stifling love, because she wanted to lock me away from the world's cruelty, and ended up depriving me of all its joy, as well.

Irvine never wanted to lock me away. His strength made me stronger. He believed in me when no one else did. He saw me, truly *saw me. But did I ever truly see him?*

Just the thought of going back to Mum's house made my

stomach turn. I was a failure. A sassy new name and a different haircut couldn't change the fact that I wasn't able to cut it in the real world. Now, I had to go back, because I couldn't run away from who I was – the broken girl with the peg-leg who needed to be kept away from the cruelty of others.

Mum had been right all along.

"I know you'll look after me." The tears rolled down my cheeks and splashed onto my lap, no doubt ruining the expensive fabric of the floor-length gown I'd worn for the wedding. "I'm on the M1. I'll be at your place in a couple of hours."

"Be careful, honey. I love you."

"Yeah, love you, too." I hung up the phone, choking on the sobs that tore through my body.

The radio blared news reports from the wedding. Panic gave the announcer a high-pitched squeal. I jammed my mobile into the jack and turned the volume up on my loudest, angriest playlist. The drive sped by in a blur of ugly, angry tears and rage against the world. I must've run a hundred red lights and drifted over the line several times. It was a miracle I made it at all.

By some stroke of luck, there was a street park available right outside Mum's semi-detached Chiswick residence. I parked up, grabbed my suitcase from the backseat, and rushed up the path.

Mum was outside before I'd even opened the car door. "Come on, come on," she yelled, dragging me toward the house. "It's not safe outside. They could be anywhere."

I highly doubted that even in wake of what happened, any shifters were staking out Helen Winters' house. But there was no use trying to convince Mum of that. Instead, I hobbled after her, dragging my heavy case up the steps.

The house was exactly as I remembered it. Piles of old newspapers filled the hall and lined one wall of the stairwell. Each one had huge sections torn out, articles circled and notes scribbled everywhere in loopy handwriting. A mountain of takeout containers floated in dirty water in the kitchen sink. Dark blankets were nailed over all the windows, and stacks of old recording equipment, occult books, and other junk cluttered the living room. The whole place smelled faintly of mouldy cheese.

Unusually, the cramped living room teamed with people – Mum's fellow werewolf hunters, all of whom had seen the wedding on the telly and were jostling for action. They were loudly discussing how to proceed. One guy was even stroking the barrel of a rifle. I followed Mum into the kitchen, eager to get away from them.

Mum bustled around me, putting the kettle on and preparing tea for both of us. It was the English way – existence of shapeshifters confirmed on national TV, time to make a cup of tea and figure out what to do next.

Finally, she set down a cup in front of me. "Your new hair looks nice."

"Thanks. I changed my name, too."

"I figured that." She sipped her tea. I blew on the top of mine. "What to?"

"Willow Summers. I kind of like it. I think I might keep it."

Mum flinched, but she didn't say anything else. In the other room, someone yelled for revolution, and twenty people started chanting something in Latin.

"You told me you weren't in that village," Mum said. Her tone wasn't accusatory. She just sounded ... sad.

"I didn't want you to worry. I thought I had everything under control." I laughed bitterly as I raised the cup to my lips. *Too hot.*

"I'm your mother, I'll always worry about you." She stared at me with huge eyes, and wiped a strand of dirty blonde hair out of her face. I noticed then that her usually pristine face was devoid of makeup, her features drawn and the skin under her eyes were sagging from lack of sleep. She looked older than when I'd left. "I wish you'd been able to trust me with your location, but I understand now ... that you couldn't. I've done wrong by you, my beautiful daughter. I've kept you locked up because of my own fear, and all I succeeded in doing was driving you straight into the hornet's nest."

"I was the one feeding Lachlan all that information," I said. "I'm so sorry. I should have trusted you then, but I—" The words failed me. I sipped my tea. *Better.*

"Oh, honey, what happened?"

"I ..." I screwed up my face, forcing out the words. "I fell in love with a werewolf."

I expected her to scream, to curse, to wring her hands and beat me over the head. Instead, Mum's face warmed. She reached across and wrapped her hand around mine. My heart skipped. "Are you mated?"

"Yes ... um, I think so ... he gave me the bite ... he said we were fated to be together ..."

Mum lifted her hand from mine, and placed it on the neck of her jumper. She tugged down the collar, revealing a semi-circular scar on her shoulder. It was a scar I knew well, for I'd seen it there for my entire life, and because she bore it in pictures for every article and YouTube video she did. It was a bite mark from my father, one that she'd earned when she was trying to tear him off me.

"Like mother, like daughter," she said.

Her words sank in. "You mean ... you and Dad were ..."

Mum laughed woodenly. "Yes, I lied to the press because I was so angry about what happened to you. Your father was the after-hours cleaner at the office where I was doing temp work. I would often stay late at night to try and get extra work done to impress my boss. Richard would bring in his dinner and share it with me. I felt this ... tingling under my skin every time we touched.

"I ran away to be with him. It was all so exciting at first, but we were young and foolish and we were into drugs ... and then, you were born, and I got scared. Richard was talking about going clean, but that meant he'd give up the street dealing he was doing, and how was I going to be able to look after you on a janitor's wage?" Her eyes grew sad. "I saw no future for us, so I decided to take you and leave him. I would go and hide. But he was looking after you one night, and he found the bus tickets I'd booked, and he panicked. He always had this problem ... if he got agitated, he'd shift and go all beastly. It was even worse either side of the full moon. Richard said it wasn't normal for shifters, but he had some defective genes. Anyway, he realised I was leaving, and he got agitated, and so he shifted and latched onto the first thing he saw, which happened to be you, my precious girl."

"Mum—" I couldn't believe this. Why had she kept this secret from me?

Tears glistened in Mum's eyes. "I don't think Richard meant to hurt you, truly I don't. He couldn't control himself. But as soon as he realised what he'd done, he dropped you, and he fled. The neighbour heard you screaming and called the ambulance and found me on the street corner trying to score crack ... there was so much blood and you weren't screaming. You'd gone so quiet, so still ..." Her breath came out in a short, ragged gasp. "They got there in time to save your life, but not your leg."

"Oh, mum."

She wiped her eye. "I never knew what having your heart broken felt like, but that night, my chest was torn open and someone ground their heel right into mine. I watched them take you into surgery, and when you came back ..."

... and when I came back, I didn't have a leg anymore.

"Why did you lie to me? Why?" Tears burned my own eyes. "You made me do all those videos, and appear in all those interviews where I told people that my father was evil. You made me into the laughingstock of London, all to rail after werewolves when it was all just a horrible accident. He had a *disability,* just like me. You robbed me of the chance to get to know him. Even if you couldn't forgive him, I should've been given the choice. It's *my* leg. It's *my* life."

Mum's face paled. I'd never spoken to her like that. "Do you hate me?" she asked in a small voice.

I looked up at her then, and on her face I saw the pain she'd felt that night, watching me go into that surgery with a leg and coming out without one, knowing that she was the one who'd put me in that position. I saw the guilt that ate away at her from the inside, every day of her life that she had to look at me. How could I hate her? She'd done what she thought was right.

The same way you tried to. The same way Irvine has done.

I shook my head. "I don't hate you."

Her tears flowed freely now. "I just wanted to protect you. Because I knew that you had the genes that would make you desirable to them, that one day would attract you to one of their kind, maybe even have a child of your own with one. I thought … maybe if you hated them enough, you wouldn't have to go through what I'd been through with you." She reached across the table and squeezed my hands. "I'm so sorry. So, so sorry. I was afraid to love again, and so I channelled that fear into anger, and I channelled that anger into you."

My mind reeled. Everything I'd been told about my life was wrong. My father … he wasn't this terrible beastly werewolf with a taste for my blood. He loved Mum. He *loved* me. He left me because he loved me. He'd tried to do the right thing, too.

"Irvine found him," I whispered.

"Who?"

"Richard, my father. Irvine – that's the wolf – found him and brought him to London. He was living in a sewer under London.

He cast himself off from the world because of all the guilt ..." I brushed the tears from my eyes.

"Richard?" Mum's eyes widened. "You saw Richard?"

I nodded. "He tried to speak with me, but I ... I didn't want to hear it."

"Can you find him again?" She leaned forward, her eyes sparkling, even through her tears.

She still feels something for him, I realised. *Even after all these years. Even after all her work trying to destroy shifters, she still cares for my father.*

I buried my face in my hands. It was all messed up. Everything was completely messed up.

46

IRVINE

*T*he world turned upside down. Overnight, the Lowe pack went from being a bunch of guys living on the edge of the forest to superstars of the most notorious variety.

I was right. They didn't need the ring. The unquestionable evidence of the footage from the wedding and the sheer force of Caleb's personality carried the day. I didn't quite fathom it until shifters started to arrive in Crookshollow. First a few dozen, and then a few hundred, and then the forest was teeming with every species under the sun, all talking and yapping and howling and mewling and chittering and squawking at once.

As one force, we marched to London, picking stragglers up from every small village and woodland reserve on the way. Rolf and the Wulfrics were already in place with their security uniform, keeping the peace in our enormous mob. Many of the shifters marching were in packs with long-held rivalries, and a few fights broke out. But now united under the Lowe crest, we held our ranks with a single purpose – equality for shifters.

Groups of humans approached our convoy, tentatively at first, waving placards bearing the Lowe crest. Then they came in greater numbers, swelling our ranks with their voice of companionship, a voice begging for peace.

For three days, we camped outside Westminster, yelling our demands up to the frightened politicians above. The army came in, putting up cordons and providing a show of arms. They could not attack us until we made the first show of violence, and we didn't give them the pleasure. With shifter groups all over the world rising up and following suit, they knew that any show of human force would result in chaos.

Every day, more shifters poured into the city to fuel the rally, and more humans joined our cause.

Parliament convened a special sitting. Representatives from all the major packs attended. I sent my nephew in my place. He'd done an excellent job of leading the Bairds in my absence. I wanted him to have his glory in shaping the new world.

Caleb and Luke were also in attendance. They entered Westminster unsure if they'd ever see the outside world again. They emerged sixteen hours later, triumphantly holding aloft the first ever piece of legislation granting shifters rights within the human world. The Shifter Act 2017 would become the precedent from which other countries modelled their own agreements and laws.

It was tremendous. It was the greatest achievement of my life, and yet, without Willow by my side, our victory felt hollow, meaningless. I'd fought for so long to be recognised as a person, and to give justice to people like her who'd been wronged. She had so much to gain from this – she should have been here to enjoy it with me.

Only Richard noticed my pain. "You miss her. I understand. But perhaps it's just not meant to be. Perhaps the divide between you and she is just too great." He had a faraway look in his eyes, and I wasn't sure if he was referring to me, or to himself.

Now that her crackpot theories had been vindicated at last,

Helen Winters was in her element, appearing on all kinds of talk shows and in the tabloids as some kind of shapeshifter expert. There was a rumour she'd even been on a special government working group. I picked up every article with her face on it, hoping for some mention or image of Willow. But apart from telling the story of Willow's amputation again and again and again, I learned nothing about where she was now or how she was faring. It seemed as though Helen Winters was deliberately leaving her daughter out of the press.

As I was walking to the store, one particular headline caught my eye. HELEN WINTERS' SECRET WEREWOLF LOVE. I dug £1 out of my jeans for the paper and practically tore it open as I scanned the article. It was another interview with Helen, except this time, the interviewer was asking her questions about Willow's father.

This time, the story she told was very different – she spoke frankly about her drug problems, about her great love for Richard, about his disability and how his attack on Willow had been a horrible accident. She admitted that it was her own guilt for her part in her daughter's amputation that had fuelled her vengeful crusade.

"Do you still have feelings for him?" the interviewer asked.

"I do," her answer read. "I know it's too late for the two of us, after everything I've done. I've deprived him of knowing his daughter, who grew up to become a bright, beautiful, kind, and profoundly strong young lady. There's no forgiving that. I only hope that in this new world his kind have created, he can find a new life for himself, and receive the peace and love that I have deprived him of."

I read the passage again and again. I ken what I had to do. Even if there was no hope left for me, at least I could give it to someone else.

I raced back to the hotel. "Richard," I cried, thrusting the paper in his face. "You've got tae see this!"

"THIS ISN'T GOING TO WORK." Richard tugged on his tie. "It's been eighteen years, and she's spent all of those years running a werewolf hate campaign. She was probably just playing up that story for the press."

"Nonsense." I slapped his hand down. "Stop fiddling with that. Now, knock."

I'd managed to get an appointment with Helen by pretending to be a reporter from the *London Underground*. It was some kind of blogging site about stuff happening in London. I only knew about it because the reporter who attacked Bianca worked there, so it seemed as good a lie as any. I just hoped Helen wouldn't ask too many questions about blogging or London, but I figured that if what she said in her article was true, she'd be too preoccupied with Richard to care.

I *hoped*. Someone deserved some happiness from this mess.

"I can't do this," Richard moaned, his fist paused an inch in front of the wood.

"You can." I rapped on the door. "There. Easy."

The door opened. Richard yelped and leapt behind me. Great, so I was on my own then. Helen Winters stood on the doorstep, all made up and ready for an interview. I'd seen her picture in the paper a hundred times, but nothing prepared me for being in front of her in real life. If Richard had gifted Willow with his soulful eyes, then Helen's gift had been her knockout body and flowing blonde waves. *Damn, those were some good genes.*

"Helen Winters?" I reached out my hand. "We're, ah, here for the interview."

"I know you." Helen narrowed her eyes at me. "I recognise you from somewhere. You're not a reporter, are you. You're one of *them*. You're one of the wolves who first transformed at that wedding."

Gosh, and she was fast.

"Um, that might be true, but—"

"Hang on a sec." She leaned against the doorframe and placed her hand on her temple. "I'm getting a psychic revelation ... you're the shifter my daughter was seeing. You're her mate."

"Um ... that's true enough." I didn't know what else to say.

"She doesn't want to see you again," she said.

"I ken, and I aim to respect that. Truthfully, I'm nae here to see Willow. I'm here to talk you. Or rather, someone else is."

"Who?"

I stepped aside, leaving Richard trembling on the steps in his shabby secondhand suit.

"Helen," he said, his face a picture of terror. "H-h-hello."

"Richard!" Helen leapt back, her hand on her chest.

"Yeah, it's me. I wanted to ... that is ... I wondered if we could talk ..."

Helen backed up, her hands in front of her in a strange sign like she was fending off a demon. "Get that creature away from me!"

"He's nae evil," I said. "He made a terrible, horrible mistake. And he wants to try to make it right."

She wavered, her eyes darting to Richard's face again. "It's ... it's really you?"

He dared a tentative step forward. "It's really me. It's been so many years, but you're still as beautiful as ever."

"You can't come in my house." She folded her arms, but she stopped backing away. I could see the corners of her mouth crinkling up. *She's pleased to see him.*

I elbowed Richard in the ribs, urging him into the speech we practiced.

"Helen, I know it means nothing after all these years, but I'm so sorry for what happened to Willow. Words can't express my grief and guilt over what happened, what I did. You were right – I was never going to be a good dad, because of my disability. I guess the good news is, now that shifters are no longer secret, they're going to be working on some drugs to help regulate my shifting. I won't be a risk to anyone else." He gave her a wobbly smile. "I ... I've missed you. I'd really like to talk some more. I wondered if you could show me some photos of Carol when she was a girl?"

Helen opened her mouth to speak, but no words came out. She tried a couple more times, and finally managed to get some sound out.

"C-c-come in."

I hovered in the doorway of the kitchen while Richard sat at the table. Helen darted around, boiling the kettle and preparing the tea. Richard talked nervously, trying to fill the silence with apologies. Helen handed us our tea, then excused herself for a moment. I half expected her to come back with a gun, but instead, she was holding a photo album.

"Here." She shoved it into his arms.

Richard laid out the album on the table, and flicked through the pages. The entire thing was filled with photographs of Willow – Willow sitting in hospital with a gap-toothed smile and a tiny prosthetic leg, Willow with bouncing blonde pigtails sitting with a porcelain doll, Willow eating a hot dog with all the mustard and sauce leaking out the end.

He turned another page. Willow as a gangly, awkward teenage, her eyes betraying her loneliness as she smiled over a miniature birthday cake. Willow at her college graduation, beaming as she accepted the cup for Dux of her school. Willow waving goodbye from the gate of the University College of London.

My heart ached for Willow. I longed to take her into my arms and kiss her pain away. I wanted to see that smile play across her lips again, a smile that was reserved for me. I wanted to make her scream with ecstasy and laugh until she couldn't breathe.

I wanted her, but I couldn't have her, because of what I'd done. I didn't ken how long I could live with the pain of it.

So I didn't break down in front of Helen, I focused on Richard. He was *enraptured,* with the album and with Helen. Helen pointed to photos and told the stories behind them, and with every story, his whole face brightened. By the time he reached the final page and closed the album, he and Helen were staring into each other's eyes and talking in soft voices as though they were the only two people in the room.

I wanted to leave, before things took a turn for the primal. But we had one more matter to discuss first. "Richard," I prodded. "Why don't you tell Helen about the job we have for her?"

He jumped at my voice, as though he'd completely forgotten I was there. "The job? ... Oh, yes!" He reached over and patted Helen's hand. "Irvine and I talked to some of the new shifter representatives in Parliament about you. We think you'd be an excellent advocate for shifters. You already have the audience and the knowledge, and I think you'd just be wonderful at it."

"Most importantly," I added, "you have a story, and a connection to both the human and shifter worlds. You can help show people that by accepting shifters into society, we can work together to make the world a better place for everybody."

"Me? I don't want to do anything for shifters." But her voice lacked her usual vehemence. She glanced at Richard.

"Like it or not," I continued, "you're going to have to deal with shifters in your everyday life from now on. You no longer have to fight for every scrap of information about them. You were right all along. You won. But what are you going to do now?"

"I—I haven't really thought about that—"

"Exactly. Shifter society has a lot of problems. High crime, low education, lack of representation in local and national government, poor resources, lack of study of shifter-specific diseases. You could help change these things, and be a real part of making sure an accident like Willow's will never happen again."

"Why would I want to help *you?*" She turned her gaze to me. "You hurt my daughter, and her name is *Carol.*"

"I ken," I said. "And I curse myself every day for the decisions I've made. But Helen, Wi— I mean, Carol is all grown up now. I've come to ken her over the last few months, and she's *amazing.* She's a bright star in the night sky. But she has a lot of bitterness in her heart. Some of it was put there by me, but some of it ..." I trailed off. Helen gave a tiny nod. She ken what I was saying.

"If she could see you forgiving, moving on, finding your own place in this new world, then she'll be able to find her own place, too."

Helen's eyes narrowed. "You mean, her place with you?"

"I didnae mean—"

"I'm not a fool, young man. I know you're still carrying a flame for her. I can read it all over your face." She glanced over at Richard, and tentatively patted his hand. "I can read you both better than you can read yourselves."

I blushed. "Yes, I still love her dearly, but there have been too many lies between us, too much that cannot be forgiven. She couldnae share my vision for the future, and I didnae understand why at first, but I do now. I won my freedom, and she believes she will lose hers. With all due respect and deference to your daughter, I think she's wrong."

"She doesn't think so. And for Carol, she's been unusually

stubborn about it." She dared a small smile at me. "Your influence, I presume."

"Might be."

Richard squeezed Helen's hand. "Do you have any idea how you're going to get my daughter back?" she asked.

I thought for a moment. Willow's face floated in my mind – not the cold glare she gave me after the wedding, but the warmth and uncertainty of our early days together. I froze her memory at the first quiet smile she ever gave me – a gift that shone brighter than any diamond.

There must be a way to give her the freedom she earned, the anonymity she deserved. There *must* be a way to show her that there was a place for her in this new world.

It came to me in a flash, and I leapt forward, consumed by the sheer joy of it.

"Yes." I threw my arms around Helen. "I do have a plan. It's shocking and audacious, and it's probably nae going to work. But Willow ... that is, *Carol* ... is worth any attempt. But we're going to need your help."

47

WILLOW

*J*tried to settle back into my old London life. As soon as word got around that I was back in the city, my phone started to ring with requests from past clients. Apparently, the shifter reveal has made many humans decide to seize the day and get married, and when people heard that Alex and Ryan's wedding was one of mine, I suddenly became the most in-demand wedding planner in the city.

It was weird hearing people call me "Carol" again. It didn't fit me anymore. But I didn't correct them. Obviously, they knew me better than I knew myself. Willow Summers was a failure. I was where I was supposed to be.

I threw myself into the work, going to all the meetings, sorting the samples, calling the vendors, smoothing the ruffled feathers of society brides ... but the job had lost all its magic. Every veil disaster made me angry that I'd never be able to wear one of my own. Every corny love song made me remember that I had something special and I'd thrown it away. And every time I left the house, the stories of shifters followed me, taunting me with Irvine's success.

He was right about everything. And I screwed it all up.

I couldn't escape shifters at home, either. I was still sleeping in my own bedroom at Mum's house, which meant every day I had to deal with an onslaught of her mad friends. She had a long talk with me about why I ran away, and she'd done her best to keep me out of the press and to correct the story she had told about my amputation. Reporters still called me every day, but I found it easier to tell them that I wasn't interested. And now that the story wasn't as dramatic as it had once being, the calls were becoming less and less frequent.

It wasn't as bad as I'd feared. But without Irvine, it was a thousand times worse.

With her new appointment as the head of the shifter rights working committee, Mum's website pageviews skyrocketed, and she'd even signed a book deal to tell the story of her and my father.

Speaking of my father, he was back in our lives. He and Mum had made up, and they were acting like two teenagers, canoodling on the couch and giggling to themselves. I'd had a couple of really good talks with Richard, and I was starting to warm to him. It helped that he had such kind eyes.

I knew I should be happy for them, but their constant displays of affection grated on my already frayed soul.

Mum's new job kept her pretty busy with what she called "secret government stuff." She spent a lot of time dashing out of the room whenever the phone rang and hiding her mobile phone screen from me while she tapped frantically.

One day, she came home, all harried, her phone clutched in her hand. "The shifters are at Westminster again, but this time it's bad. A huge fight has broken out."

I leapt up from the couch, a finger of fear stroking my heart. *Irvine* ... "What happened? Who's involved? Is everything okay?"

"Oh, Carol, it's terrible. Everything's backfired. There are shifters dead everywhere."

No, no, no. This can't be real. It can't be happening. "What can we do?"

"Richard's outside. He's put a couple of boxes of medical supplies in the car. We're going to try to get as close as we can, and see if there's anything we can do to help."

I grabbed my coat. "Let's go."

I was bustled into a car, and shoved between two of Mum's *Werewolf Watch* buddies who were now members of her working group. Richard was at the wheel. He drove erratically through the streets, swinging in a wide arc around Westminster. I expected to see traffic jams, people running from the scenes, and police and riot control trying to keep order. But everything looked perfectly normal.

We passed Portcullis House and turned off into a wide street. We were now heading away from Westminster. "Mum, where are you taking me?"

"My people have just texted me a safe location," Mum called back, waving her phone in the air. "We're heading there now."

I sat back on my hands, trying to stop my heart from pounding. If only I could communicate telepathically, the way Irvine could with other wolves. I could just find him in my mind and see if he was okay.

Caleb ... Luke ... Ryan ... if any of them were dead ... I thought of Alex, how she'd glowed with happiness at the altar. I thought of all my friends back in Crookshollow and how kind they'd all been, how much fun I'd had with them at the pub. *Please, let them all be okay.*

But Irvine ... if he had died, a light would have gone out in the world. How could I keep going, knowing that I hadn't supported him when I should have? I'd been selfish because I was scared, and instead of drawing strength from his love, I pushed him away.

The "safe location" turned out to be a grand old Victorian

home that I frequently booked for client weddings. Richard helped me out of the car, and I gazed up at the stately façade, confused. If this was the safe house, then why were there no lights on in the windows? Why did it look completely deserted?

Richard held the door open, and we all bustled into the grand entrance hall, our shoes clapping loudly against the marble floor. All the lights were off. I heard nothing that indicated this was being used as a field hospital. No voices, no crying. No shuffling of feet or beeping of medical equipment.

"Come quickly, quickly now!" My mother dragged me down the darkened hall, stopping in front of the double doors leading to the main ballroom. She pushed one of the doors open, revealing only a sliver of even deeper darkness.

"Mum, this doesn't make any sense—"

"Of course it doesn't." She shoved me toward the door. "Now get inside."

Terrified of what I might find, I pushed the door open wider and stepped into the darkness.

48

WILLOW

"*S*urprise!"

The lights went up, momentarily blinding me. A wave of shouting and cheering rolled over me, like a great tsunami swallowing me up.

What the—

My vision adjusted. A hundred faces grinned back at me. They were all here – Ryan and Alex, Bianca and Robbie, Elinor and Eric ... everyone I'd met in Crookshollow stood around the room, dressed in glittering dresses and handsome tuxedos. Past clients, vendors I'd worked with over the years, my mother's crazy *Werewolf Watch* friends all grinned maniacally as they hooted and applauded. Even Ryan's mother Clara was there, grinning like a cheshire cat and clapping like mad, her signature black hair swept into an elegant do. Behind them, several tables were set for an elegant meal, and beautiful arrangements of calla lilies cascaded from the ceiling, framing the space in tall, majestic floral arches.

"What is this?" I breathed.

"Isn't it obvious?" a deep voice asked from behind me.

I whirled around. There stood Irvine, resplendent in his

clan's kilt and dress shirt, complete with his leather sporran and ceremonial sword hanging from his belt. Those ice blue eyes met mine, and he dared a smile. My heart fluttered.

"This is your wedding, Willow." His deep voice coursed through me like hot chocolate in my veins. "I made it for you."

"But—but I'm not getting married."

"I can change that." Irvine took a step forward. His scent swirled around me, and I lost myself in it, letting it take me back to that cabin in Crookshollow Forest, where he'd given me every part of himself.

I gasped as he dropped down on one knee. My heart pounded. Irvine fished around in his sporran and produced a small box. He opened it wide and held it out to me.

From the velvet box, a beautiful diamond glittered up at me. My breath caught in my throat. My head swam. *This isn't real. I'm dreaming and any moment now I'm going to wake up and I'll be all alone again—*

Irvine dared a slightly larger grin. The love in his eyes shone radiant, like the sun, and I ken. I ken this was real. He was asking me to marry him.

"I—I—I—"

"Before you say no and hit me in the face," Irvine said, "just hear me out. I am so incredibly sorry that I hurt you, Willow Summers. I should have told you everything right from the beginning, including what I did to that poor man. I was stupid. I was so amazed that such a wonderful person came into my life, and that she wanted to be with me, that I didnae want to ruin it. I was afraid, and selfish, and that wasnae fair."

Tears pooled in the corners of my eyes. I started to speak, but Irvine held his finger to his lips. "Hold your tongue, Willow Summers. There's more to come. I am also sorry that all of the things you thought of me turned out to be true. I showed myself to be the monster that you feared. I jumped to conclusions about you, when I was the one who saw deepest into your heart. I should have seen your fear and helped you through it, but instead, I broke your trust. I nae deserve someone as bright and bold and beautiful as you, but if you accept me, I promise I'll spend the rest of my life showing that I'm worthy of your love. Starting with this."

Irvine pointed behind him. Lachlan stepped out of the crowd, and gave me a small wave before merging with the pack once again.

"I cannae give him back what I took from him, but I have asked Lachlan what punishment would fit the crime. He has decided that I will pay him a sum of money, which he will use to set up a scholarship fund in his father's name for students in Aberdeen, and that I will dedicate the rest of my life to the task of helping wolves integrate into society and get out of the criminal world, so that such a crime never happens again. I have agreed to this." He smiled. "It feels right. It feels true. It feels like something I should've done a long time ago. It took being with you to make me see that. Because you make me a better person, Willow Summers. And I ken you have a different name, but you'll always be bright and warm like summertime to me."

I reached down and squeezed his hand. The connection surged through my body, drawing me deeper into his eyes. The tears fell thick and fast now, dribbling down my face and splashing on the marble floor. "I think this is the most words you've ever said to me at once," I said, laughing through my tears.

"Aye, and it's not over yet." Irvine took another breath, and I noticed a tear sliding down his cheek. "I should have talked to you before I went to find your Pa. Sometimes, I think I'm doing something useful, but I'm really just being a cock. I didnae respect your decision. I thought that a grand gesture would show you how I felt about you, but it totally backfired." He glanced up then, looking around the room at all of the people gathered around us, all of the friends and colleagues he'd rounded up for me. He laughed nervously. "I guess I havenae really learned my lesson after all."

I laughed, tear streaming down my cheeks.

"What I'm saying is, I'm a fool, but I'm a fool who loves you, Willow Summers. I'm absolutely crazy about you. I want to be by your side for the rest of our lives. I want to make a million more apologies to you ... no, wait, that didn't come out right ..." He scratched his head. "I'm nae good at these kind of things. ..."

"You're doing pretty good," I choked out. "And my answer is yes. A thousand times yes."

Irvine's whole face erupted with a delicious, mischievous grin. He stood and swept me up into his arms, his lips pressing against mine as the warmth of him enveloped me. The joy in my heart burst forth, sweeping through my whole body.

Irvine broke our kiss to slide the ring on my finger. It fit perfectly. I held it up and watched the facets glitter in the light.

This is real. This is really happening. I'm getting married to the perfect guy. The perfect werewolf.

Irvine leaned in, and our lips met again. Around us, I was vaguely aware of people cheering and hooting, but all that existed for me was Irvine – his kiss, his touch, his wild, beautiful heart.

Irvine broke the kiss, a wide grin spreading over his face. "The first time I saw you, you were kissing Bianca, and I was so jealous." He pointed her out in the crowd. "Do you think she's jealous of us now?"

"I doubt it." Bianca was pressed up against Robbie in a slinky black dress and combat boots, and he looked like he'd won every lottery in the entire history of the universe.

Irvine grabbed my hand and led me across the room. "Come on," he said. "Let's get you looking like a bride."

He led me down a short hall and into a tiny bedroom, with a bed covered in clothing. Makeup bags cluttered the top of the dresser. Alex and Elinor squeezed in after me, grinning from ear to ear as they took my old coat and smothered me with hugs and kisses.

"Did you guys have something to do with this?"

"Maybe." Elinor grinned, tossing her hair over her shoulder. I noticed they were both wearing matching pale blue dresses, with flower crowns circling their heads. They looked a little like ... bridesmaids.

My bridesmaids.

"I'll leave you in their capable hands." Irvine gave me one last, lingering kiss, before ducking back out into the hallway.

"You both look amazing." I embraced Alex.

"Of course we do, we've had all day to prepare," Alex said, sitting me down at the dressing table.

"Sorry for the presumption of not waiting for you to ask us to be bridesmaids," Elinor said, as she cracked open a makeup box. "You spend so much time sorting out other people's weddings, we figured the best gift was not having to plan your own. Irvine was just going to forgo the wedding party completely, but we figured, given the circumstances, you'd want your friends by your side."

Friends. I beamed, fresh tears welling up and spilling down my cheeks. I'd never had real friends before. At least, I'd never believed I had friends. But that whole crowd of people out in the ballroom suggested otherwise. I swiped at my tears. *Pull yourself together.*

"Hey, quit that crying." Alex dabbed at my eyes with a tissue. "It's time to make you look like a bride."

Bride. Such a magical, beautiful word. I'd never in my wildest dreams imagined it would apply to *me*.

"But I don't have anything with me. I don't have a dress, or shoes, and ... oh god, my underwear ..." I was wearing a sports bra and a pair of cotton granny panties. Why hadn't I put on my nice cream lace bra?

Because when I got up this morning, I had no idea I'd be getting married. This was going to be one interesting wedding night.

"Oh, you look so panicked." Elinor giggled.

"We've got you covered, and I mean that literally." Alex reached into a wardrobe and tossed me a box. I lifted the lid. Inside, nestled in a bed of powder pink tissue paper, was a beautiful set of ivory silk lingerie, edged with delicate lace.

I ran my fingers over the delicate fabric, touching the edges. "This is beautiful."

"I know it is." Alex grinned. "I picked it out."

"I'm so sorry," I said to Alex, as I shrugged off my sweater and shirt and clasped the bra around my chest. It fit perfectly. "I get to have this amazing wedding, and yours turned into a political coup."

"It's okay, Willow, really it is." Alex beamed. "I'm fine with it now. My wedding will go down in history, which is pretty rock-'n'roll. I got to have my dream ceremony to my perfect guy, and Ryan says we're going to have a big party as soon as everything calms down, so I'll get the perfect reception, too. And it turns out, it wasn't the wedding that was upsetting me so much, but my hormones going crazy."

It took me a few moments to figure out what she was talking about. "You mean ...?"

"I'm pregnant!" She leapt into my arms. "For real this time."

"That's amazing, Alex. Congratulations."

"Thank you." Alex's radiant smile lit up her whole face. "But tonight is not about me. Tonight is about you marrying the man of your dreams ... in this!"

She grabbed a hanger from behind the door and thrust it in front of me. My eyes bugged out of my head.

It was *the* dress. The Marsha Babcock dress.

My heart leapt into my throat. I reached out and ran my fingers over the scalloped neckline. *They found it. I can't believe they did this for me.*

I hugged the dress to me, admiring it in the mirror. The ivory colour perfectly matched my skin. The sweetheart neckline elongated my neck and made light of my lack of cleavage. The fishtail skirt swirled around my legs.

"Go on," Alex urged. "Try it on. Your groom is waiting."

I glanced around the room, but couldn't see a bathroom door anywhere. That familiar lump of fear rose in my throat. With shaking fingers, I undid the buttons on my fly.

Alex and Elinor watched me as I pushed my trousers over my thighs and sat down, bending my knee so I could pull them over my prosthesis.

Alex's eyes widened as it came into view. But neither of them looked away in disgust. "Stand up," Elinor commanded me. I did as I was told, slipping into the matching ivory panties. Alex took the dress from the hanger and pulled it over my head, yanking the stiff bodice over my shoulders and arranging it perfectly.

"Look at you," Elinor breathed. Her eyes glistened with tears, too. "Don't make me cry, Willow, or we'll all be in here all night adjusting our makeup."

Alex finished fussing with the dress, then pulled my head back into a high bun, leaving a few curls loose around my face. "The final touch," she said, holding out a short veil with an unusual clasp. It was a comb that inserted into my hair, and the edge of the comb was decorated with a row of tiny, glittering crystals wrapped with silver wire.

"Do you like it?" Alex asked, positioning her handiwork and showing it to me in the hand mirror.

"I love it," I said, grinning.

"Good, because I've got a matching necklace and earrings for you."

After some quick makeup, we were ready for showtime. Alex disappeared for a moment to cue the music, then returned with a big grin on her face. "You ready for this?"

I checked my reflection one last time. I looked amazing. The dress hugged every curve and flared out around my legs, shimmering with every movement. I looked like a mermaid.

I slipped on the flat shoes Elinor had found for me, and realised that whenever I moved, the guests would be able to see the ankle of my prosthesis. I stood up, and checked in the mirror again. Yes, they would definitely see it.

I smiled to myself. Good. Let them see it. Willow Summers wasn't hiding from the world anymore.

"I was born ready." I grinned at my bridesmaids. "Let's get me married to the wolf of my dreams."

49

IRVINE

I stood at the end of the ballroom, flanked by my two groomsmen, Ryan and Caleb. Behind us, Eric's band kept up a steady stream of sweeping neo-classical music. They were dressed in tails and top hats and would be playing acoustic versions of their famous songs. I'd been waiting forty-five minutes for Willow to emerge from the dressing room. The rest of the guests were enjoying the free-flowing bar, but I couldn't drink. I was too nervous.

Ryan's mother Clara stood beside me, her hand on my arm. "Give her a moment," she said in a soothing voice that did very little to soothe me. "A lady always wants to look her best on her wedding day."

I grunted in reply, imagining Willow in one of the back rooms, trying to manoeuvre her prosthesis out of a window so she could escape. I pictured her running across London in her wedding dress, arms flailing, ready to tell the world about the crazy wolf who'd tried to coerce her into marrying him—

"We're ready!"

Alex made the call from the doorway. The room fell silent and the guests stood on either side of the arched aisle as Ghost

Symphony broke into a slightly gothic version of the classic wedding march.

Everyone oohed and aahed as Elinor and Alex swept into the room, their flowing dresses sweeping around them. They came to stand opposite me and my two groomsmen. Alex grinned and waved at me.

Willow appeared in the entrance, her mother on her arm.

My heart rose to my throat. She had never been more beautiful than at that moment. A rush of emotion hit me in the chest, and I stepped back as though I'd been punched. My eyes stung as tears pricked in the corners. I'd never cried before in my life, but right now, it seemed the only response to the beauty before me.

Their walk up the aisle was agonisingly slow. The whole time my eyes remained locked with Willow's. The love I saw there reflected my own.

Finally, they reached the end of the aisle, and I stepped forward, wrapping my arms around Helen, and kissing her cheeks. "Welcome to our family," she said. "I hope that this marriage is going to be the start of mending the mistrust between our species."

"I couldn't agree more," I said, kissing her cheek again.

"Look after my daughter." She squeezed my arm while tears poured down her face.

"I will always love and protect her. Thank you, Helen, for everything. This wouldnae have happened without you."

"Oh, my son-in-law." Helen clapped my shoulder. "You have the rest of your life to make it up to me. I'm already making a list."

I laughed. She left us then, and I turned to my wife. My beautiful wife. Willow extended her arm, looping it through mine, and I led her back to stand in front of Clara.

"Hey," Willow said, her smile piercing my heart.

"Hey, yourself."

I tried to concentrate on Clara's words, as she spoke about the meaning of marriage and the significance of our commitment. But they all fell in one ear and out of the other. All I could focus on was Willow. I couldn't believe my luck – this incredible woman was not only willing to forgive my horrific stupidity, but she was going to become my wife and love me and be with me for the rest of my life.

"The couple will now exchange rings," Clara intoned. My fingers clasped Willow's, and I kept my gaze on her as I repeated the words. "With this ring, I make you my wife. I promise that I'll protect you, honour you, and do everything in my power to make you happy, for the rest of my days." Willow beamed. Another tear escaped my eye as I slid the ring onto her finger.

Willow clasped my hand in hers, and tears streamed down her face as she made her own vow. "With this ring, I make you my husband. I promise that I'll protect you, honour you, and do everything in my power to make you happy, for the rest of my days."

No words had ever sounded so good to me before.

"Before your family and friends, I have the honour of pronouncing your husband and wife." Clara stepped back and raised her hands. "You may now kiss the bride!"

Damn right. I wrapped my arms around Willow, and devoured her with my lips. Her tongue slipped against mine, and we lost ourselves in the power of our bond. The roar of our friends clapping and cheering and howling for our joy brought us up for air. We linked arms and danced down the aisle while streamers and confetti swirled in the air around us.

My wife. My amazing wife.

Willow gazed up at me, her bright eyes dancing. I felt like a majestic medieval knight who'd just slayed a dragon. She knitted her fingers into mine. "What now, wolf?"

"Now, we party."

~

WE PARTIED long into the night, drinking amazing cocktails and eating great food and tearing up the dance floor. It was amazing, but at the same time, I wanted everyone to go away so I could have some quality time with my wife. Ever since our kiss, my cock was stiff, ready to enjoy our wedding night.

Willow didn't seem to have got the hint. Every time I tried to drag her off the dance floor, she pulled me back for one more song. My shy wife who never wanted to do anything to attract attention to her leg was starting conga lines and hopping around like an Energiser bunny. I would have found it completely adorable if I wasn't so desperate to tear that gorgeous dress off her.

Finally, Big Ben struck midnight. One by one, our guests started to wander away, heading back to their own hotel rooms, or to the Mouth of Hell. Helen and Richard were the last to say goodnight, and they left arm in arm, Helen blowing kisses to us over her shoulder.

I hailed us a taxi back to the hotel I'd booked, wrapped Willow in my arms, and carried her over the threshold, slamming the door shut behind with my foot. Finally, Willow and I were completely alone.

"I'm so tired," she said, as I laid her down on her bed. Her eyelids fell heavy, her gaze studying my face. The bond swirled around us, uniting us as one.

"Hey." She ran her fingers over my cheek. "I love you."

"I love you, too."

"You know, we never did the garter toss."

I grinned. "I'm surprised you go in for such silly traditions."

"I'm the wedding planner. Silly traditions are what I'm all

about." Willow scooted up the bed and rolled up the hem of her dress. Wrapped around her lower thigh, just above socket of her prosthesis, was a pale pink garter festooned with a tiny ribbon rose.

"Willow Summers, you *are* bold." I knelt down in front of her and grabbed the garter with my teeth, sliding it slowly down her leg. My hands roamed over her soft skin, teasing her with what was to come.

As I lifted the garter free, I helped her remove the prosthesis. Then, our desire took over. We tore at each other, drunk on the fire of our connection and the joy of our perfect future stretching out before us.

"Show me a different position, husband," Willow begged, biting her lip in what I suspected was a purposeful gesture. Who could say no to that face? I spun her around, grabbed her hips and thrust her back onto my cock, doggie style. She gripped the frame of the painting above the bed to brace herself, and I moved a pillow over so she could support her right knee. I slid deep inside her, using my hands to tease her nipples and stroke her clit. She yelped with pleasure until her lack of traction meant she toppled over.

A few months ago, that would have made her burst out crying, but now my wife just pulled me to her. I dropped down behind her on the bed, wrapping her body in mine, and entered her from the side. She lifted her leg to allow me better access, her warmth drawing me deeper. I kissed down the side of her neck, relishing her shudders of delight.

Her body yielded to me, and our connection drove the urgency of her touch. She folded against me, a perfect fit. The bond wrapped around us, binding our bodies as one.

As soon as we finished, Willow settled back against my shoulder. Her eyelids fluttered with bliss. Soon, she'd be asleep.

"Irvine," she murmured against my chest.

"Mmmhmm?" I stroked her hair, unable to believe that she was mine.

"I'm not broken anymore."

"You nae were, Willow Summers." I kissed her, my lips lingering against her soft skin. "If anyone was broken before, it was me. But as long as we're together, we'll nae have to feel that way again."

"Amen," she agreed, her eyelids closing. In a few moments, she was asleep.

THE END

50

EPILOGUE

SIX MONTHS LATER

"*Y*ou may now kiss the bride!"

A heavy guitar riff roared to life as Eric's band struck up a thundering metal anthem. Eric himself wasn't in front-of-stage – as he usually was, long hair streaming behind him as he furiously bowed his violin. Instead, he stood in front of the grand altar, holding his new wife Elinor in his arms. Their lips pressed together in a long sensuous kiss.

"Yay, Elinor!" I raised my hands and clapped furiously. My heart soared for my friend. We'd been working non-stop for the last few months to create the perfect gothic wedding, all while Eric was away on a European tour. As I glanced around the garden of Marshell House – transformed into a gothic wonderland in red, black and purple – I couldn't help but feel a surge of pride that we'd pulled it off. And judging by the excited "oohs!" from the guests and the frantic *click click click* of the cameras as they took in all the details for the wedding magazines, everyone else thought so, too.

Elinor and Eric came up for air. They linked arms and danced back down the aisle (lined with skulls and purple garlands, of course). Elinor had never looked more radiant. She laughed as she gathered up the cathedral train of her blood-red dress so she could maneuver through the throng. I clapped and cheered louder than anyone.

"Careful, Willow Baird," a husky voice growled in my ear. "No straining yourself. You wouldn't want to do the wee one any damage now."

I turned around to face my husband. Today, Irvine looked even more handsome than usual, standing proud in his family tartan. The long sword of his pack dangled at his side. I wrapped my arms around his neck, and leaned up to kiss him.

My mind flashed back to the first time we met. It had also been at a wedding, albeit a fake one. Irvine wore the exact same outfit, complete with that kind smile and those penetrating eyes. So much had changed since then, and yet, so much was exactly the same. The members of the pack had new roles within the various government working groups or delegations, and they had already won so many rights for shifters. Irvine was working with Lachlan's non-profit to help young shifters transition from criminal activities into active roles in the community. Now, when the press contacted us, it was usually to speak to Irvine about his charity work. No one cared about me or my leg anymore.

I didn't have time to care either, I was too busy finishing assignments for university (I'd enrolled part time to finish my history degree) sourcing the perfect wedding dresses for my clients, and preparing for our new arrival.

"You worry too much, husband. I'm perfectly fine. And I'm not stressed at all, see?" I gave him my most radiant smile.

Irvine rubbed my stomach, which was just beginning to protrude noticeably with the growth of our baby. My heart swelled again as I sensed the love he already felt for our child. The connection that drew us together pulsed stronger than ever.

"I dinnae believe it. This is the first wedding you've ever delegated to someone else. You're supposed to be relaxing and enjoying your friend's happiness. Already today I've caught you straightening the garlands and trying to brief the MC." Irvine wagged a finger at me. "Donnae think you can hide it from me. You cannae help getting involved."

He was right. When we first found out I was pregnant, Irvine put his foot down about the stress level in my business. Ever since word got around that I was the planner behind the infamous Raynard wedding, prominent shifter couples up and down the country were clamouring to book me for their big day. I'd been working non-stop since The Big Reveal, and Irvine had been on at me to hire an assistant. Finally, after Elinor threatened to fire me if I didn't take better care of myself, I relented.

My assistant, Lacey, was racing around like a mad thing, making sure all the details were perfect. I cast my eye around and noticed her over by the sound desk, gesturing madly at the technician and looking utterly furious. I stepped out into the aisle. "Maybe I should—"

Irvine grabbed my arm. "None of that, lass. Lacey's got a handle on it."

"But—"

"I see Alex and Ryan," Irvine yanked me through the mass of people crowding the aisle, heading away from the sound desk and whatever problem Lacey was trying to straighten out. We followed a line of guests out onto the manicured lawn, where Elinor's train swept elegantly over the grass. She looked absolutely magnificent in her corset studded with glittering black beads. Her brown hair was swept up in one of Alex's crystal and wire tiaras, and her skin glowed with the happiness of a new bride. Eric didn't look so bad himself, in his tailored damask frock coat, his long dark hair streaming down his back.

Ryan had already snagged us a table, and was pulling out a chair for a heavily pregnant Alex. "Ooh," she moaned as she collapsed into it, stretching her feet out under the table. "I wish this baby would hurry up and pop. Just standing after that kiss has killed my back. And my feet. And I need to pee *again*."

"You're just a one-stop pee machine," Ryan kissed her cheek. "I'll get us all some drinks."

"No! No more drinks! This is just one of the things you have to look forward to, Willow." Alex patted my hand. "Endless trips to the loo. I never appreciated my bladder before, until it was being permanently kicked by some ratbag that's taken up residence in my belly."

I grinned at her. *I can't wait.*

We chatted about the ceremony while Ryan braved the crowd around the bar. He returned ten minutes later with an armload of drinks. As I sipped my Lemon, Lime, and Bitters, I gazed across the lawn at the unfolding scene. Now that shifters weren't a secret any longer, seeing wild animals in odd locations was a pretty common occurrence. An entire pack of foxes sat grooming themselves on the edge of the marquee, and two stags had their heads in a water trough at the back of the garden. Rolf and two of his Wulfric chums stood in their human forms at the entrance to the garden, arms folded and sunglasses pulled over their eyes. They were keeping back a horde of obsessive Ghost Symphony fans who'd shown up in the hopes of glimpsing the newlyweds.

It was still completely surreal. Yet, at the same time, it felt totally normal. I no longer saw enemies and beasts who might hurt me. I just saw families and friends, people of all shapes and sizes and colours and races and species, laughing and joking and getting on together. It truly was a new world.

"—and Ryan and I have been offered the chance to do a joint

exhibit at the Tate Modern," Alex was saying to Irvine. "It's such an amazing opportunity, but I have no idea how I'm going to find the time to paint with this little guy needing my attention all night and day. We talked about hiring a nanny, but it just seems so *impersonal.* I'm always worried we'll end up with someone who'll sell stories about us to the media."

"Actually," I grinned, squeezing Irvine's hand. "We had an idea that might help with that."

Alex leaned forward. "I'm all ears."

"My wedding business is doing so well that I don't really want to take so much time off right now, and apart from advising Lachlan, Irvine isn't doing much at the moment, so we've decided that he's going to be a stay-at-home wolf."

"That's so cool!" Alex beamed.

"It is. I can work from home most of the time, so I'll be able to be there for feedings and to watch every breath this little guy takes," I patted my stomach. "But Irvine thought that since he was looking after one baby, he could help anyone else out if they needed it."

"You mean, our own drop-in shifter-friendly playcentre?" Alex's eyes gleamed. "I love it. Count me in."

"I've got two more customers for you!" Belinda piped up, her hand touching her own stomach. She and Cole had just announced they were having twins, and I knew she was worried about how they were going to manage the demands of her popular bakery around the kids.

"I just hope I can cope with all the wee ones," Irvine said, a note of worry creeping into his voice.

"I think you'll be great," Belinda leaned across the table and squeezed his hand. "You're so patient."

"Feel free to come around to our place any time you want some practice," Robbie grinned, as he and Bianca wandered over to our table. Even behind her makeup, I could see Bianca's eyes were ringed with dark circles from lack of sleep. Robbie looked worse, but he couldn't keep the pride out of his voice as he spoke about their daughter. "I think you might change your mind about looking after more than one of the wee terrors at once."

"Your Silvie is a wee darling," Irvine told him.

"She's the devil's child," Robbie shot back, but his eyes were full of love. Bianca had given birth to their daughter a few months ago. From what I'd heard, she'd never once slept for more than an hour at a time, and she had a pair of lungs on her that seemed impossibly large for such a tiny girl. She was definitely Bianca's child.

All baby talk ceased as Elinor and Eric passed by our table, and we rushed to congratulate them. "Come on you lot," Elinor waved her arms around. "It's time for the group photo."

"But we just found the booze," Caleb complained, holding up his beer.

"My feet!" Alex wailed.

"Tough. Getting drunk can wait until after you've looked pretty for us."

"I never look pretty," Caleb grinned, as he drowned half his pint in a single gulp.

"I'm the bride, I get some say in what happens at my own wedding. Now up, up, the lot of you!"

With Irvine's arm for support, I lurched to my feet again, and Alex and I waddled across the lawn toward the photographer. In true Elinor and Eric fashion, the photographs were being taken in front of the crumbling stone mausoleum at the back of the garden. We arranged ourselves in a haphazard semi-circle around the bride and groom, our arms around each other.

As the photographer fiddled with his camera, I looked around at the faces that surrounded me. Elinor and Eric stood in the middle, flanked by Alex, Ryan, Kylie, Marcus, and Belinda and Cole. The taller wolves – Caleb, Luke, Robbie and Irvine, stood in the back, and Anna, Rosa, Bianca and I stood along the sides. Irvine swapped places with Robbie so he could stand behind me, and he wrapped his arms around me, pressing his warm palms against my stomach, his chin nuzzling into my neck.

It was hard to believe that less than a year ago I'd come to Crookshollow with a new name to escape my mother. I'd spend my entire life running away from werewolves, and now, thanks to the pack, I'd found everything I'd ever wanted – family, love, friendship, people who saw me for who I was, not what I looked like. My parents were back together, and they were talking about moving to Crookshollow to be closer to their grandchild. And now, a tiny cub was growing inside me. I couldn't believe how lucky I was.

"Okay guys, you're all in position. On the count of three, say ..." the photographer squinted at the paper in his hands. "Um ... dead brilliant?"

"Dead *pure* brilliant," Robbie called out, and everyone laughed.

"Right, say that." The photographer looked into his camera. "One ... two ... three ..."

"Dead pure brilliant!" We all yelled. Elinor and Eric kissed again. Irvine touched his lips to my neck, and I grinned so hard my face hurt.

This was family. This was love. This was my life. This was Crookshollow.

THE END

It's wedding bells in Crookshollow, but what's next for the pack? Find out what Willow and Irvine get up to in a FREE BONUS SHORT STORY. Sign up to Steffanie Holmes' VIP Readers Club to read it, as well as free books, exclusive giveaways, and other fun stuff.

ALSO FROM THE WORLD OF CROOKSHOLLOW …

Love so fierce it transcends even death.

When Elinor Baxter arrives at the dilapidated Marshell House to settle the estate of her law firm's oldest client, she can't help but feel a little spooked. The creaking gothic mansion is a far cry from her life as an adventurous party girl back in London.

Then she meets Eric Marshell, a man dressed entirely in black with a wicked smile and the ability to float through walls. Eric was the violinist in popular rock band Ghost Symphony until a hit-and-run accident claimed his life. Now he's trapped inside his mother's house for all eternity, and the only one who can see or hear him is Elinor.

Eric and Elinor fight their attraction for each other as they dig into the mystery of Eric's death. But when they uncover a dark and sinister plot that threatens Elinor's life, their bond draws them into a world neither of them understands. Can their love transcend the boundary between life and death?

The Man in Black is a steamy gothic romance by USA Today bestselling author Steffanie Holmes, Set in the English village of Crookshollow, it's a standalone novel of love, redemption, and second chances. If you love clever BBW heroines, crumbling gothic mansions, and brooding rockstars who know what they want, then this book will have you shivering all over.

READ NOW: The Man in Black

THE MAN IN BLACK

AN EXCERPT

Elinor moved her hand, so her palm lay flat against mine. It was so odd to see her fingers nestled right inside my body, and even odder to *feel* them there, not as fingers usually feel, but as a hot ball of energy, emanating heat to a steady rhythm.

It took me a few moments to realise the rhythm was Elinor's heartbeat.

I stepped forward, my hand shifting against hers, her fingers dancing inside mine. I pressed my other hand against her back, my palm sinking into her flesh. If I were alive at this moment, I would push Elinor against my body, and relish the warmth of her, the shape of her, against me. But I couldn't do that, so instead I folded myself in closer to her. The front of my jacket brushed against her chest, sending waves of pulsing heat through my whole torso.

"This is amazing," Elinor breathed, her bow-shaped lips parting slightly. I didn't trust myself to reply, so I smiled back at her. I started to sway, pushing my right hip forward, moving the warmth through her leg. Elinor sensed the movement through her skin, and she moved backward, turning her body with me. I stepped again, and again we slid across the floor, our bodies sweeping and dipping with the music.

With my next step, I pushed myself closer, bowing my head slightly, so that my face hovered inches above hers. My eyes locked on those bow lips, ripe and delicious like the first berries of spring. I could feel my spectral cock straining against my boxers, ready for action. *God, I want this woman—*

"I like the music," Elinor said. Her voice wavered. She sounded nervous. I wondered if she was speaking because she sensed what I wanted to do, and she was trying to fill the space between us, to stop me from doing something I couldn't take back.

"Mmmm ..." I shifted my fingers in her hand. The heat flickered, thrumming through my body with a quickened pace. She *was* nervous. *Interesting.*

"I love the ... distortion. The way it crackles right through my whole body," Elinor breathed. "It's almost as if the music is mirroring the sensation when we touch."

"This piece is originally written by the composer Niccolò Paganini, a Greek violinist in the early nineteenth century," I murmured. If she wanted to talk, I could at least impress her. "He was known for making liberal use of the *diabolus in musica,* the devil's tritone, which creates that haunting dissonance you hear in the piece. Of course, Paganini's composition has been sped up and updated, and accompanied by the electric guitar, bass guitar, double bass, and drums, it's quite the feat of modern gothic rock."

"Who is playing the violin in this piece?" Elinor asked, her lips barely moving, struggling to form the words.

"I am, on Isolde. Ghost Symphony is my band."

"Eric ..." Elinor's face turned up to me.

I leaned closer, I could practically taste the sweetness of those berry-red lips, feel the warmth of her mouth against mine.

The air between us crackled with electricity. Elinor shifted her weight against mine, falling into me as she leaned forward, her lips pursed, waiting.

I brushed my lips against hers. It was like no other kiss I'd ever experienced before. The heat leapt through my body, twisting from my mouth right through my core. I felt as though I'd swallowed a hot coal, and though it burned me deeply, it was the most delicious thing I'd ever tasted. I leaned forward, my weightless body pressed against hers, my lips parting to devour her heat as our bodies hummed with pulsing energy.

READ NOW: The Man in Black

OTHER BOOKS BY STEFFANIE HOLMES

This list is in recommended reading order, although each couple's story can be enjoyed as a standalone.

Nevermore Bookshop Mysteries

A Dead and Stormy Night

Of Mice and Murder

Pride and Premeditation

Memoirs of a Garroter (available May 2019)

Briarwood Witches series

The Castle of Earth and Embers

The Castle of Fire and Fable

The Castle of Water and Woe

The Castle of Wind and Whispers

The Castle of Spirit and Sorrow

Crookshollow Gothic Romance series

Art of Cunning (Alex & Ryan) - READ NOW FOR FREE

Art of the Hunt (Alex & Ryan)

Art of Temptation (Alex & Ryan)

The Man in Black (Elinor & Eric)

Watcher (Belinda & Cole)

Reaper (Belinda & Cole)

Wolves of Crookshollow series

Digging the Wolf (Anna & Luke)

Writing the Wolf (Rosa & Caleb)

Inking the Wolf (Bianca & Robbie)

Wedding the Wolf (Willow & Irvine)

Fallen Sorcery Fae (shared world)

Hollow

Witches of the Woods

Witch Hunter

Coven

The Curse (coming in 2018)

ABOUT THE AUTHOR

Steffanie Holmes is the award-winning author of steamy historical and paranormal romance. Her books feature clever, witty heroines, wild shifters, cunning witches and alpha males who *always* get what they want.

Before becoming a writer, Steffanie worked as an archaeologist and museum curator. She loves to explore historical settings and ancient conceptions of love. From Dark Age Europe to crumbling gothic estates, Steffanie is fascinated with how love can blossom between the most unlikely characters. She also writes dark fantasy / science fiction under S. C. Green.

Steffanie lives in New Zealand with her husband and a horde of cantankerous cats.

Steffanie Holmes Mailing List

Want to be informed when the next Steffanie Holmes paranormal romance story goes live? Sign up for the mailing list!

Come hang with Steffanie
www.steffanieholmes.com
hello@steffanieholmes.com

www.ingramcontent.com/pod-product-compliance
Lightning Source LLC
Chambersburg PA
CBHW030656120726
47905CB00001B/233